Adam

A bonafide pop diva, all sass and scandal, Cristy Valor commands headlines wherever she goes. The tabloids love her—and love to hate her. From the first time her sexy alto voice rolls over me, she has all my attention. When she joins Balefire on our latest tour, she sashays across the stage in her wild-ass costumes and parties hard enough to keep up with my boys and me. She drives me batshit crazy—and I love every second of it.

Sex on stilettos.

Pure trouble.

Our sizzling chemistry could shoot a rocket into space, and it's not long before I crave her. For the first time in my life, I want to share everything with a woman. But Cristy is hiding something, something that holds her back from giving me all of herself. She's about to find out that I'm a patient man—and I always get what I want.

Cristy

Adam Tron is the poster boy for tall, dark, and sexy. His bass rhythms are enough to make me cream my panties every time I hear them. Flirting with him during our live shows is a rush but nothing compared to what happens when I finally give in to my lust and share his bed. The problem is, sex isn't all he wants.

For my entire career, I've set the narrative, teased the tabloids with scandals that kept them too busy to look into my past, too busy to discover the secret that could end the party for good. Adam Tron could wreck me, steal my heart—and my music. I can't let him in. I can't let him discover the secret behind the nightmares I have nearly every night. He thinks he can slay all my monsters, and it would be so easy to let him. But if he finds out the truth, will he still be hot for me?

Other Books by Tam DeRudder Jackson

The Talisman Series
Talisman
Warrior
Prophetess
(novella)
Bard
Druid

The Balefire Series
Play For Me
Sing For Me
Wild For Me
Hot For Me

HOT FOR ME

TAM DERUDDER JACKSON

Editor: Nikki Busch Editing
Cover Design: Steamy Designs
Formatting: Damonza
Distribution and POD: IngramSpark

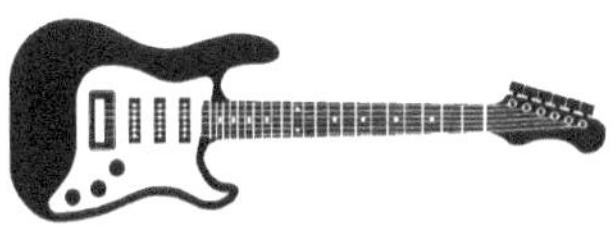

CHAPTER ONE

Adam

MY BLOOD SIZZLED at the thought of all the glitz and glamour waiting for the boys and me to dirty it up with our kick-ass show. Our music absolutely begged the ladies to lose their minds—and their lacy panties and pretty bras, which they were only too happy to toss at us when we played. Every. Single. Show. Damn, the fans' response to us never got old. Kicking off our West Coast tour in LA only pumped me up more as I looked around the interior of our jet at my bandmates—my brothers.

After ten years on the road, I still anticipated a tour like other people looked forward to vacations. One additional variable popped into my head—*Cristy Valor.*

This tour promised to be epic.

"What put that smirk on your face, Tron?" Blu asked from his comfy seat on one of our jet's three couches.

"Just thinking about the tour. Damn, I do love playing to a sold-out Coliseum. Makes this rock 'n' roll circus of ours too fucking fun."

Blu grinned. "I know what you mean, brother. Next to being

with my girl here"—he gave his fiancée Ashleigh's thigh an affectionate squeeze—"playing the big venues is the greatest rush in the world."

"Adding in that wild thing named Cristy Valor is definitely going to make this tour a circus," Garrett groused from his captain's chair beside me.

"Are you pissy because it wasn't your idea or because we all agreed to the experiment?" Dakota asked.

Huh. I thought Dakota was sleeping off his early morning after squeaking out a tie in his newest race-to-the-airport competition with Jack.

Instead of answering, Garrett tried to use his eyes to burn a hole through Annabelle Stewart's sleeping head resting on Dakota's shoulder. Without another word, he turned away with a look of disgust.

I'd joined him in a little day drinking during the flight, but apparently my brand of beer had a more mellowing effect than his. Either that or he thought he'd been shown up by Annabelle, the band's intern. Whatever his problem, he needed to get over it.

"Lighten up, Garrett. The whole point of this gig is the fun factor. Have another beer," I said as I popped the top off a bottle of Fort Collins's finest microbrew, the good stuff we always kept stocked on the jet, and handed it to him. I didn't know who or what put a bee up his ass, but our manager had radiated attitude almost since he boarded the plane.

"I'll have one of those too since you're buying," Dakota said.

"Count me in," Blu added.

"Jack? Ladies?" I asked Ashleigh and Jack's wife Clio as I uncapped beers for my friends.

"I'm good." Jack's response surprised no one as he played with his daughter on his lap.

"Really, Jack? Are you still pissy 'cause Annie and I almost beat you and Clio to the airport this morning?" Dakota taunted.

"Think you guys already established the consequence when

either of you loses your game, Dakota. Drink a beer and give it a rest," I said as I handed him an opened bottle.

Jack made a face, but he aimed it at Angel. "It's your mom's turn for this one, little girl."

"How is it you always get the easy ones?" Clio demanded.

"Timing, Clio." Jack grinned. "Remember what I do for a living? Drummers are not only good with rhythm, but we also have excellent timing." He waggled his eyebrows at her.

Rolling her eyes, Clio smiled and took their daughter from Jack.

"I'll help you," Ashleigh volunteered.

"Guess that means you ladies don't need a brew right now." I stated the obvious just to be a pain.

"Not unless you'd like to take over?" Clio pretended to hand Angel to me.

Waving a hand in front of my nose, I said, "I'll pass. Angel's adorable, my all-time favorite kid, but diapers give me hives."

"One day some woman is going to call you out on that, Tron," Blu said with a smirk as I handed him his beer.

"Fat chance of that. As part of the last half of the band still standing"—I saluted Dakota with my beer—"I think it's incumbent upon me to uphold the reputation of Balefire. Music, girls, and booze." I grinned and downed half my beer to punctuate the point.

"Incumbent? Are you for fucking real?" Blu asked, laughing.

"Hey, if that online college you got your degree from didn't teach you any vocabulary, you should probably demand your money back," I shot back.

"Jack, I think we need to give this guy more to do when we write in his parts. Obviously, he has way too much time to think."

Jack smiled at Blu. "Or he can write more songs himself. Slacker." The last part Jack directed at me.

I flipped him the bird and looked over at Dakota who hadn't chimed in with his usual off-the-wall shit. He'd pulled the bill of his hat down to pretend to sleep, but he brought his beer to his mouth and took a pull. Which in and of itself didn't mean much. His other hand, however, tracing patterns on Annabelle's knee where she sat beside him on the couch definitely warranted my attention.

Raising my eyebrows at Jack and Blu, I drew their attention to the tableaux on the third couch, and both raised their brows in question. I couldn't help but notice Dakota's interest in our new intern at Jack and Clio's wedding during our summer hiatus. The developments on the couch warranted further investigation—or torture. Whatever.

"It's not enough at least two of you are whipped," Garrett said, shooting a venomous glance in Annabelle's direction. "But we have to bring a kid along on tour these days too. Are we a rock 'n' roll show or the goddamn Brady Bunch?"

"Jesus, man. Relax. Have another beer," I said, uncapping a bottle and handing it to him.

"Don't know what's up your ass, Garrett, but get over it. You booked us on a sold-out tour. We're going to blow the minds of every fan in attendance, the press is going to love us, and the party starting in LA isn't stopping until we hit Houston after Thanksgiving." Blu downed the rest of his beer for emphasis, I think. "Hit me with another, Tron. Since you're up."

"Since when did I become the freakin' bartender on this ride?"

"Since you're the only band member not shackin' up with some woman," Garrett mumbled, turning his back on the rest of the cabin.

As I pulled another beer from the fridge, I shot Blu a look and caught him glaring at Garrett's back. Right when I thought I might be stepping in to clean up the mess before he made it, Blu stuck out his tongue and blew a raspberry at Garrett. One second it felt like the cabin pressure might blow out our eardrums: the next, the whole place filled with air and morphed into peals of laughter.

Cristy

"Balefire wants you to tour with them."

When Gretchen Hoff, my manager and oldest friend, first approached me with a request from someone associated with Balefire, I thought she was joking.

"You know, Gretch, the hottest band in the universe doesn't need anyone to help amp up their popularity—or their sound. Neither do I. I've played sold-out shows in major stadiums all over the world." I raised a brow. "Shows you've booked and organized."

"You've made a name for yourself, especially these last four years, Cristy-girl. For sure." Gretchen kicked back in a lounge chair and slugged back some of her favorite vodka cocktail. "But this is a hell of an opportunity to showcase your range, launch you beyond pop diva and into the realm of megastar."

Lying now on the massage table in my hotel suite, I remembered our conversation from a few months back. The idea of being a megastar, whatever that was, wasn't one of my biggest goals. Yet, the more I'd thought about it, the more the idea of playing some shows with the Balefire boys intrigued me. The bad boys of rock 'n' roll teaming up with the naughty girl of pop presented all sorts of possibilities for fun.

The kind of fun that would mortify my parents. Geez, I hated it when they invaded my head whenever I thought about cutting loose. Though I'd traded my long brunette locks for a bottle-blond pixie cut, sometimes I could still feel the tightness of the severe bun my mother insisted on. These days I wore tops with plunging necklines and tight miniskirts. But every now and then, I could still feel the collar and top button of my thick, formless shirt chafing my neck, the constriction of maxi skirts falling to my ankles. The censure in their voices as they bombarded me with cherry-picked Bible verses chastising me on my behavior, my dress, my songs echoing in the corners of my mind. Because of course, everything about me had always been wrong. My growl of frustration at myself resulted in the extra pressure the masseur exerted on my shoulders.

Sighing, I turned my thoughts to the other consideration involved in going on this tour—one-upping my former BFF. Picturing Mali Tatum's claws scratching ineffectually at the news of me touring with Balefire, I purred with self-satisfaction. She'd been doing a number on me in the tabloids for weeks. Rumor had it, she'd also started working on a song—or maybe an entire album—documenting all the ways I'd "wronged" her. Except for the real reason—the part where I had more number one songs than she did on every outlet from Spotify to iTunes to the good old *Billboard* Hot One Hundred. A no-holds-barred war in the tabs loomed when she found out about me joining Balefire's most recent tour. If *she* weren't such a diva, the two of us could have rivaled Balefire with a tour of our own. Now she could sit her jealous rump on the sidelines and try to disguise her whining in her pathetic little songs.

No doubt the grin spreading over my features looked feline as I stretched lazily and rolled over onto my back. Not that I cared. The masseur repositioned the drape and went to work on my legs, his strong, warm hands relaxing and energizing me at the same time. Obviously, he'd taken Gretchen's instructions well since he hadn't said one word to me. Exactly the way I liked it—a man keeping his mouth shut while he took care of me.

"Sorry to interrupt," Gretchen said, not sounding the least bit sorry as she breezed into the outer suite of my hotel room. "The team wants to know if you're planning to glam it up tonight to watch the show or if you'd rather stay on the down low."

My entourage had taken up residence with me in the hotel the night before my debut concert with Balefire. Even though we all lived in LA, I wanted us together for my shows. Gretchen and my makeup, hair, and costume team took up most of a floor in the Hotel Bel Air near the Coliseum.

"Tell them to dress me like a casual fan. Oh, and I'll need a wig. Something long and dark."

Gretchen ticked off something on her iPad. "Annabelle Stewart, the intern I've been working with, said all the people at last night's and tonight's shows are wearing Balefire T-shirts. Something about photos for the cover of the band's new album." She glanced up from her tablet. "Shall I get one for you?"

"Yes, absolutely. And I want to be in some of those pics."

Her eyebrow arched. "Hard to do from a private VIP box."

"I'm sure you'll figure out something, Gretch. You always do." Resettling on the table, I focused on the masseur's talented hands working over my legs.

I hadn't mentioned to anyone in Balefire I'd be attending their second LA concert. I wanted the pure experience of seeing one of their shows live before I performed with them. As part of the contract for joining their tour, I'd asked the guys to record instrumental versions of my songs that I planned to sing with them so I could practice in my studio. Balefire's versions of my pop music gave it a rock edge, which I liked. It remained to be seen how our little experiment would play with the fans. Thinking about the band backing up my songs put a genuine smile on my face. My masseur lifted a brow when he caught me smiling, so I closed my eyes.

♪

Gretchen and I arrived at the Coliseum incognito. One of the roadies for Balefire met us at the VIP gate and led us to an unused locker room backstage. Garrett Phillips, Balefire's manager, awaited us there.

"Miss Valor. A pleasure," he said, gripping my hand about ten long seconds too long.

"Mr. Phillips. I believe you already know my assistant, Gretchen Hoff."

He inclined his head at Gretchen, but I noticed he looked her over from her five-inch Jimmy Choos, up her fishnet stocking-clad calf, and all along her tight black pencil skirt. He lingered on her hips then continued his perusal of her Balefire T-shirt straining to cover her girls before giving her face a cursory glance.

I growled my impatience with the man. "Don't get your hopes up, Mr. Phillips. Gretchen already has a girlfriend."

To her credit Gretchen tortured the man, resting one bloodred manicured hand on her cocked hip and subtly lifting her chest while she pulled out and played with the emerald pendant nestled in her cleavage. "You were able to meet Cristy's request to be photographed with the other fans during the show." The command in her voice required only one response.

Apparently, Garrett wanted to send his own message.

Jerking his attention to me, he replied, "It's going to be tricky, but I think we have a way of including you in the photos for the album cover. That wig is going to waste the effort though."

"Not if you alert the photographer to who's under this wig." Licking my lips, I twirled a lock of long chocolate-colored hair around my finger and rocked on my six-inch boots. Flirting like a sixteen-year-old seemed to work with this guy. How again was he the management genius behind the biggest act in the world?

"At my direction, my intern stationed a photographer at the top of the stairs leading to the VIP boxes. I'll see to it he knows to look for your wig. Are you sure you don't want to join us at the party after the show? We could solidify your plans for tomorrow night."

He took a step toward me, a smarmy smirk on his lips. No doubt he thought he looked and sounded sexy, but the man made my skin crawl.

"I think that's what tomorrow afternoon's rehearsal is for."

Softening the rejection with a sexy wink, I turned and headed out of the locker room, giving my tight fuchsia miniskirt a little extra sashay. Knowing she always had my back, I didn't wait for Gretchen to catch up as I strode down the hall to meet the roadie guiding us to my box.

"Is that guy for real?" she hissed as she caught up with me. "I know he manages a monster rock band, but you aren't just any woman. Certainly not a groupie he can impress into a hookup." Attitude rolled off her in waves. "And what the *fuck* is up with his outfit? A leather vest over a cut-off band T-shirt paired with five-hundred-dollar dress pants and Italian leather shoes? Does he even know what effect he's going for?"

I grinned at Gretchen's indignation at Garrett's not-so-subtle come-on. Her description of his terrible fashion sense made me giggle, which of course infected her.

"What a self-important asshat. 'At my direction, my intern,'" she mimicked him perfectly. "Could he sound any more pretentious?"

When we reached the stairs leading to our box, we were nearly in hysterics. That's when the flash lit up our faces.

"Wow! It really is you," the photographer gushed as he continued snapping photos.

I struck a pose, tossing my flowing locks over one shoulder before I pulled my oldest and most loyal friend into the frame with me.

"On three," I whispered. "One, two, three."

Together, we crossed our eyes and stuck out our tongues, just touching the tips to each other while making sure our chests with the Balefire logo faced forward. The photographer nearly lost his balance on the step as he leaned down for a closer angle.

"Have a nice night," I said as I stepped past him, Gretchen in tow.

"You know that shot's going to be all over the tabloids in the morning," Gretchen said as we found our way to the minibar in our box. "People are going to speculate like crazy. Again."

"Let 'em speculate. At least this way I get to set the narrative." She slanted me a look.

"Gretch," I began, "Kelsey knows the truth."

"I'm not worried about Kelsey. She and I are solid." Gretchen fingered the monster emerald dangling from her neck. "You, however, need to look around for someone who's going to snag the fans' attention, someone they think they know. That's the only way to solve your little problem."

Blowing out a breath, I stared at my best friend. "You're right. As always. Have a drink." I handed her a glass of champagne. "The tour dates with Balefire offer all kinds of opportunities for solving that, beginning tomorrow night." I flipped back a long curl on my wig. "So how 'bout we let our hair down and have some fun tonight?"

We mingled our way to the front of the box where we found to my delight most of the members of Metallica in attendance along with Gwen Stefani and Rihanna. Since I'd opened for Gwen early in my career, she held a sacred place in my heart. As for Metallica and Rihanna, I was just another big fan. However, everyone in the VIP box buzzed about Balefire. Gretchen and I exchanged a secret smile at how people were going to react to my part at their next show.

The lights dropped down in every part of the stadium. Somewhere beyond the roar of ninety thousand frenzied fans, the unmistakable rhythms of Jack Whitehorse's drums rumbled to life. Gold and silver lights sprayed across the stage as he rose from beneath it, a wizard commanding the heartbeat of the crowd. His drums crescendoed, his hands and sticks a blur as he tom-tomed in synch with the flashing red lights signaling the arrival of Dakota Perri. The wail of Dakota's electric guitar intensified as he made his deliberate way into the light from stage right.

The tension in the Coliseum ratcheted up like a too-tightly wound guitar string when the lights turned green and a throbbing bass rhythm signaled the arrival of Adam Tron. As if by magic, he appeared at the base of Jack's platform. When the lights changed to electric blue, the crowd went bananas. Lingerie of every style, color, and fabric rained down on the stage as Blu Connelly belted out the opening verse to "Helluva Ride" from his place at stage left.

Flash pots burst flames from the sides and back of the stage. A massive shower of fireworks lit up the night sky above the crowd. The gravitational pull of Balefire's sound coupled with their crazy-good pyrotechnics and mesmerizing light show sucked me right into their rock 'n' roll universe. When they finished playing their opening song, I was both elated and wrung out. And they'd only started the show.

Judging from the shouts, high fives, wide-open grins, and the general need to fill our lungs with air, everyone else in the box experienced the same thing I did.

Holy buckets! These boys came to *play*.

"That was some opening," Gretchen shouted in my ear.

"They definitely blew the doors off this place." No doubt everyone in the box could hear the awe in my voice.

That was all the time Balefire gave us before they launched into their next song. For a solid hour, the band didn't give the crowd a rest. Sweat poured down my back from beneath the heavy hair of my wig because I couldn't stay still. It wouldn't have surprised me if we cracked the cement floor of our VIP box with the way we all danced together to Balefire's kick-butt music.

Then the band took it up a notch. All the lights dimmed except for one spot on Dakota Perri. His guitar solo wowed the whole house—before he started slowly rising into the air. When he stopped about fifteen feet above the stage, someone slingshotted a lacy red thong, landing it perfectly to dangle from the neck of his guitar.

Dakota burst out laughing. "Fucking beautiful shot, babe. Makes a guy wonder what else you do well," he said into his head mic.

The screams from the adoring female fans in the audience drowned out whatever else he said. The rest of the band showed back up onstage to play a new song off the album they were touring. Watching Dakota play from his perch high above the stage, I knew exactly how I wanted to make my entrance at tomorrow night's concert.

Throughout the show, though, I kept homing in on Adam Tron.

Like the rest of Balefire, he had his fans, and he wandered out to the edge of the stage often to give them a show. But there was something steady about him, something not so rock star show-off that drew me to him. Even when he melted back to stand near Jack's platform, I couldn't help but watch him. He was easily the tallest man on the stage, but it wasn't his size, black hair and dark brown eyes, nor the muscles rippling down his arms exposed by the tank top he wore to show off his ink that drew me. No, there was something in his expression that reached inside me and told me to relax. Everything was under control. Everything was fine.

By this point in the show, Blu, Dakota, and Jack had soloed already, which was regular for a rock band. Usually, the bassist stood back and drove the beat—except, apparently, for Adam Tron. He stepped to center stage and launched into a solo with his four-string bass, rivaling Dakota's prowess with his six-string lead guitar. Adam mesmerized me as he pulsed, throbbed, and thumped his way into my blood. It took me nearly to the end of the song after the other guys rejoined him to discover I'd locked my legs together as an orgasm rolled through me.

I sucked in air. He did that with his bass? Adam Tron had never met me in his life, and he gave me an orgasm that left me reeling.

"Hey, you okay?" Gretchen asked. She waved her hands in front of my face. "You look a little flushed."

"It's the wig. There's a reason I wear my hair so short."

"Uh-huh. Wouldn't have anything at all to do with tall, dark, and steady out there, would it?"

Her left eyebrow arched in a look that said she knew everything. Good thing for me, Adam Tron didn't have a clue.

Chapter Two

Adam

THE KICK-ASS REVIEWS for our first two shows blew up every form of media from Instagram and Twitter to the *LA Times* to *Entertainment Tonight*.

Those two shows rocked the universe. With the pyrotechnics, the rainbows of lasers and strobes, and the wild music videos featuring each band member individually and collectively playing behind us on a massive screen, we blew the audience's ever-lovin' minds. It went without saying that our sound, always so tight, always so melodic with our screaming guitars and pounding drums, stunned the fans, not to mention the reviewers.

All of which meant we'd been partying almost nonstop after we stepped off the stage the first night. Since we'd been on hiatus from touring for four months, none of us was back in party shape yet. Read that, we were hungover as fuck for our first rehearsal with Cristy Valor—who mercifully seemed to be running late.

Standing beside Blu on the side of the stage, I sipped the special green smoothie hangover cure our head road engineer Bailey Saunders concocted for us and watched the man in question.

"I didn't think that hydraulic lift would be so badass."

I raised a *what-the-fuck* brow at Blu's comment. "Really?" I asked, drily. "Do you not pay attention when we raise Jack from the bowels of the stage to start every show?"

"Well, yeah. But that's different."

"How?"

"Jack's behind that massive drum kit. The whole damn thing lifts up above the stage. Not just Jack himself."

We were taking a break from sound checks to watch Bailey as he practiced with the stand and harness contraption that raised Dakota high above the stage for his solo during the show. Though we'd practiced and practiced with the device at home in our Quonset-hut-turned-studio, even I had to admit when Dakota lifted into space during the first show of the tour, the audience's reaction might have broken the sound barrier. Having that kind of adulation would tempt a saint to sin.

Blu was no saint.

"Is he whining about the hydraulic lift again?" Dakota asked as he joined Blu and me.

"Nah. He's hungover from last night's crazy-as-fuck party with all the movie stars who came to our show."

"I don't think it'd hurt to share. Maybe one night you solo from the lift, the next night I sing from it," Blu suggested with a hopeful half grin.

"You trying to compensate for something, Blu? You lacking somewhere?" Dakota teased.

"Fuck you, Dakota."

Jack strolled up and added his two cents to the conversation. "I think you might be onto something, Dakota."

"If that's what you're implying, dumbasses, what does that say about the two of you?" Blu fired back.

In a rare show of being on the same team rather than in their usual competition, Jack bumped his fist with Dakota's. "My lady isn't complaining about my hydraulics." His eyes danced over the rim of his smoothie as he took a pull from it.

"Judging from the way she responds to me every night, Annabelle's got no complaints about mine," Dakota said with a not-so-discreet crotch adjustment.

"Jesus, you guys. Give it a rest." I laughed. "Judging from all the satisfied smiles of the ladies leaving our hotel suites over the years, I'd say none of us has to worry about our hydraulics."

"Hello, boys."

Talk about hydraulics. Since I'd spent our summer hiatus listening to her recent album, I'd know that sexy alto anywhere. Didn't matter if she sang a party tune, a ballad, or a soaring rock anthem, her voice reminded me of white-hot sex. Listening to her sing always left me half hard. With two words, she had me paying all kinds of attention.

Cristy Valor had arrived.

When she walked around an amp to join us on the stage, my eyes took a little tour. Thigh-high black leather boots with six-inch stilettos hugged her long legs to the pretty space between her thighs. The black miniskirt masquerading as a second skin left inches of creamy skin bare above those boots, making her legs go on forever. The skirt hugged her hips in a way that had my hands grasping air at my sides. Then I caught a glimpse of smooth belly and deep cleavage revealed by the bright red crop top she wore under a bulky black-and-white faux fur coat. So fucking hot. With her bleached blond hair cut in a close cap over her head and covered by a jaunty little red hat, she reminded me of a pixie. But Cristy Valor was no pixie.

She might have stood five foot three in her bare feet, but even barefoot, I bet she commanded a room. In that outfit, she owned it. Discreetly, I adjusted myself as I stood a little to the side of Dakota and Jack.

Her gaze took a slow wander around our group, and my dick hardened even more uncomfortably in my jeans as I admired her high cheekbones and the pout of her bright red lips. I wanted to finger the silk of the skin covering those bones, test the plushness of those lips with my own. When her eyes landed on me, their color and sparkle rivaled the big-ass sapphire nestled on a gold chain in the hollow of her throat. My mind blurred with visions of her wearing nothing but those boots and that necklace, her sparkling eyes on me as I drove into her.

She gifted me a secret wink, like she knew exactly what thoughts swirled in my head, before she shifted her gaze to Blu.

After she finished her thorough perusal of the band, she smiled. "If they knew where I was right now, and with whom, the whole female population of America under the age of fifty would be tearing up their best pair of panties in jealousy."

The purr of that voice left me rock hard, something I needed to remedy right away if I had a chance in hell of being professional for the next two hours. Like she knew exactly what kind of effect she had on us, she let out a throaty laugh at herself and at us, and I swear even the very married Jack Whitehorse and the very engaged Blu Connelly fell a little in lust with her. Never mind the way Dakota blinked at her, for once completely speechless.

Everything about Cristy Valor, from her take-no-prisoners outfit to her sexy voice to her obvious sense of humor appealed, leaving no man in the room unaffected.

Naughtiness personified.

Sex in a human suit.

Pure tempting trouble.

I couldn't look away.

When the entire band remained speechless, Cristy stepped right up and blew us away. "I caught your show last night."

Her little bombshell blasted us out of our Cristy-induced stupor.

"What?"

"You did?"

"Fuckin' A!"

"How did we not know this?"

Like we were of one mind, the boys and I gathered around her, dwarfing her in our midst.

"I asked to remain on the down low. Since I've never seen one of your shows live, I wanted to have the fan experience, you know? Feel what it's like."

Though she didn't shrink away from us, she rolled her shoulders, and I had the impression we made her a little nervous. Good. She made me a lot nervous.

"What did you think?" Dakota asked. "Did we kick some ass, or what?"

That's what we all loved about him. Dakota never passed up an opportunity to show off, which let the rest of us relax.

"You guys are the freakin' bomb. Last night's show was the best performance I've ever seen. You've set an incredibly high bar. Everyone in my box said that." She smiled.

"Who all was in your box?" Blu asked.

Dakota and Blu bounced on the balls of their feet like two little boys waiting for Santa Claus.

"Well," she drew out the word with a flirty grin.

That's it, darlin'. Make 'em suffer. But I had to admit, she had my curiosity too.

"There was James Hetfield and Lars Ulrich from Metallica."

"Oh, yeah. We had a drink or maybe five together at the afterparty last night," Blu said with a grimace.

I knew what he meant because I was still waiting for Bailey's special hangover cure smoothie to kick in too.

"There was also my queen, Gwen Stefani." She put her hands together in a reverent gesture. "Rihanna. Some other people enjoyed the show from that box as well, but by the time my friend Gretchen and I arrived, we barely had time for a drink with Gwen before you guys blew up the house with your first song." She laughed. "After that, we were busy hanging on for the ride."

Her smile lit up her features as she looked around at the four of us. "Now that I've watched your set, I think I'd like to join you— from Dakota's platform. Drop the lights, raise me up, and let the flash pots illuminate me when I sing the first couple bars of 'Wonder Woman' a cappella. What do you think? Can I make an entrance from your special stage, Dakota?"

She'd taken a step toward him, one hand lightly resting on his chest, then she traced it up to his shoulder to give him an encouraging squeeze. Until that moment, I didn't envy my friend his special stage. But if having it meant Cristy's undivided attention—and her hand on me—I wanted a hydraulic platform too.

"After all, I'll need something over the top for my entrance if I'm going to maintain the expectations you've already set for the fans," she coaxed.

Dakota shrugged. "What the hell? Sounds like a great idea to me."

"*What?*" Blu's eyes nearly bugged out of his head. "You'll share with someone we just met, but won't even *entertain* the idea of sharing with your oldest friend? What the fuck is up with that, Dakota?"

Dakota ignored him. "You come on in the last third of the show, yeah? After my solo?"

"Yes."

"Well, then. It seems only right to be polite to our guest. Let her make an entrance."

Blu gifted Dakota with a middle finger, and I busted out laughing. "That was a neat trick, Cristy. I think you're going to fit in fine."

"Whatthefuckever," Blu muttered.

"I was also thinking I should make a tour of the band after I'm lowered back down to the stage. Sort of a get-to-know-you kind of dance during my second song."

"What did you have in mind?" Jack asked.

"Why don't we try it and I'll show you?"

She smiled wickedly, her eyes on mine. For the briefest second, she dipped them to my crotch then turned away and headed over to Bailey where he stood beside Dakota's platform.

Clearing my throat, I walked with purpose to the guitar cart to grab my axe. At least with my bass in front of me, I could hide the telltale bulge taking up the front of my jeans. As I slid the strap over my head and settled it on my shoulder, I was grinning though. No doubt Cristy Valor was nothing but trouble, but it appeared I had her attention every bit as much as she held mine.

CHAPTER THREE

Cristy

AS I WAITED backstage for my cue to go on, nerves threatened to overwhelm me. In fact, for the first time in years, I'd be going on in front of thousands of fans stone-cold sober. Back in the green room, Gretchen tried to talk me into at least one drink to settle me down, but I was afraid whatever I drank would come right back out. Now as I listened to the crowd screaming and roaring their approval of Balefire's show, I wondered if maybe I should have done shots—starting five minutes after rehearsal ended this afternoon.

The last notes of "Missing You" faded into the crowd's cheering response. The lights dropped, cueing me to take my place on Dakota's platform. Sucking in a deep breath, I whispered thanks to Bailey Saunders who buckled me onto my stand. Then I was climbing into the air. When the noise of the crowd dropped in anticipation of Balefire's next song, I swallowed, shot the heavens a wink, and started singing the opening lyric of my signature song.

A gasp rolled through the audience then it erupted into raucous cheers and applause right on time with the flash pots lighting up the stage. Balefire's instruments joined in, and I knew I'd never be this high—in every way—ever again. From my perch above the stage, I sang the hell out of "Wonder Woman" and smiled in delight as the fans responded in a frenzy of cheers, applause, wolf whistles, flashing phone cameras, and another rainstorm of lingerie.

After I sang the first verse and chorus from the platform, I stepped neatly away from it when Bailey lowered me and unhooked my harness during the wildly embellished bridge the boys devised. During "Wilderness," I made my tour of the band, starting with Blu who played rhythm guitar and added harmonies as I danced beside him. Next, I hammed it up with Dakota, pretending to "help" him play through his improvisation following the second chorus. Jack added his wild tom-toms I loved so much as I skipped up the stairs on the side of his platform to sing and dance behind him. Knowing the camera crew projected a close-up of us on the screen behind the stage, I made sure to play up my impressed response to his prowess before I made my way back down to the stage floor.

Finally, I reached my destination—Adam Tron. He didn't miss a beat as I changed up the order we'd practiced. Having witnessed— and enjoyed—his reaction to me when we met in person, I wanted to push. After all, he'd already made me cream my panties during his solo the previous night. It seemed only fair to give him some back. I undulated around him to the rhythm of his bass, sliding a finger lightly across his shoulders, skimming the warm skin on the back of his neck. Good thing I needed a breath in the verse right then because the tingling in my fingertips from touching him took me by surprise.

When I stepped in front of him, I blew him a kiss, satisfied as his deep brown eyes heated nearly to black. But his rhythm didn't falter. "Tall, dark, and steady" Gretchen had called him.

So far.

After we finished the song, Blu introduced me. "What do you think? Does Cristy Valor rock or what?"

The crowd responded with a deafening roar, and I could have stood there all night drinking it in. I sang three more of my biggest hits, with two quick costume changes during the applause like I did during my own shows, before I left the stage to the boys. They added two final numbers and joined me to take a little rest and down quarts of water before the encore. When all of us returned to the stage, I thought it likely the audience's screams could be heard in my hometown of Phoenix. Perversely, I hoped that was true because that was as close as I'd ever come to playing a show there.

To finish the concert, I sang harmonies with Blu on the three songs we'd rehearsed. Even with my ear pieces securely in place, the sounds of ninety thousand ecstatic fans echoed in my head as we exited the stage. Jack and Blu high-fived me. Dakota picked me up and spun me around. Adam, however, merely nodded and said, "You were something out there," a ghost of a smile playing over his full, sculpted lips.

"See you at the after-party, Cristy," Dakota called as the band half jogged down the hallway to their locker room.

I stared after them, laughing at their antics as they fist-bumped each other and danced. Jack jumped on Tron's back and Dakota jumped on Blu, the four of them laughing and cheering and congratulating themselves on the raucous start to their tour.

At a loss as to what to do with my emotions soaring so high after the show, but without bandmates to share them, I entered my dressing room. Gretchen, bless her, met me there.

"Cristy-go-to-church you fucking rocked that show. I've known you all my life, and I've never heard you sing like you sang out there tonight," she gushed as she wrapped me tight in her arms and hugged me hard.

"Yeah? That good, huh?"

"If the folks at home could see you now. You rose above all the bullshit people put us through because we were 'different' when we were kids. And I mean that on every level."

"I couldn't have done any of this without you. You, Gretchen Hoff, are a rock star." I hugged her close again, nearly squishing her in my need to connect with another human being, my need to off-load some of the adrenaline coursing through me.

Her hundred-watt smile warmed me. "This could be the start of something really big for you, sister. How do you feel?"

"Like I own the world."

She nodded. "Uh-huh. That's it. There's the name for the live album. *Own the World.*"

"What?" I asked, confused. "I'm not doing a live album."

"About that. I had a feeling about this tour, so I brought in our sound guys. They recorded every song you sang, including the ones you collaborated on with Balefire."

Clapping a hand over my mouth, I stared at my best friend. "Oh, my freaking heck."

Gretchen was a genius, and I hugged the snot out of her again. "I can't believe you did that, but ohmigosh that's awesome. Freakin' spectacular." An unpleasant thought sucked all the air out of my post-concert balloon. "What if Balefire doesn't give permission for it? This is their show after all."

"All taken care of. I arranged it with their manager this afternoon while you all were rehearsing. He's a slimy dude"—she shuddered— "but a smart businessman. We could both hear the reason for doing a live album from the first time their instrumentals joined your voice. When the boys hear the tapes, they'll be all over a live album with you. You'll see." She winked.

Turning me, she gave me a not-so-subtle push toward the shower. "Enough shop talk. Shower and change so we can join the party. We need to celebrate, sweetheart."

She smacked me on the butt for emphasis. I shot her a crusty over my shoulder and caught her laughing at me.

Kelsey Myers, Gretchen's smoking-hot girlfriend who ran a successful LA temp agency, awaited us with drinks when we arrived at the after-party in the band's green room. I'd barely taken a sip of my delicious—read that perfectly chilled—vodka cranberry when two of the biggest "it" stars in Hollywood, Parker Malone and Jennifer Hartwell, materialized at my side.

"We were here for last night's show, which fucking played like a souped-up action movie on steroids. Or so we thought. 'Cause I gotta tell you, Cristy, adding you to the mix rocketed Balefire's brand into the stratosphere." The usually uber-cool Parker Malone gushed all over me, pulling me in for a hug.

"Parker is so right," Jennifer added, sliding her hand through the crook of his arm. "Maybe you could team up with Balefire and write the theme song to our new movie. Wouldn't that be epic, Parker?"

Slanting her a grimace, he said, "We're here to party, Jennifer." He turned to me and flashed his trademark smile. "We partied hard with the boys last night. In fact, it was all I could do to drag my ass out of bed to make the shoot on time today, but I think what you brought tonight merits shots."

Taking my hand, he pulled me along with him, Jennifer in our wake as we made our way to the bar. The bartender lined up shots of Jameson, and the party began. Before I knew it, Chad Kroeger of Nickleback and Blu and Dakota had joined us in some kind of drinking game I think Parker was making up on the fly. At some point when I came up for air, I saw Jennifer Lawrence cheering us on, and then I lost track of the night.

Except for the part where Adam Tron entered the party with a girl under each arm. During the whole night, I never saw him without at least one woman wrapped around him. Somewhere in my foggy drink state, I registered that Adam went through girls at the party like a revolving door while the other three guys stayed with the same girl all night. That must have meant something. Someone pressed two more shots of Jameson into my hands, and I stopped wondering who paired up with whom.

Chapter Four

Cristy

WAKING UP IN my hotel bed with no recollection of how I'd arrived there, I yawned, stretched, and recoiled into a tight ball as pain ricocheted through my head. After several deep breaths to calm the racket banging in my brain, I cracked open one eye and took stock. I still wore the neon purple sequined minidress from the party but not my boots, no one shared my bed, and blessed darkness and silence cocooned me in my suite. As I lay there, snatches of the previous night flashed behind my eyes. The euphoria the roar of the crowd gave me when the fans figured out who had joined the band, the wild lights, the sense of loneliness when I entered my locker room by myself after the concert.

Darn it. I didn't need that memory.

So many people at the after-party. A ride in a stretch limo with the boys to their hotel. They were laughing so much. At me? I don't remember. Shoot. Did I have any cool at all after those shots?

The shots. No wonder I had cotton mouth like I'd been born with it. Smacking my lips, I tried to generate some spit, do something about the fur that had grown on my teeth overnight. Geez, why did I do those shots? After everything that happened early in my career, I knew better.

My bladder pushed on me to end my pity party long enough to take care of things. Gingerly, I sat up. On the nightstand, a glass of water and a bottle of Advil awaited my return to consciousness. Bless Gretchen. She never failed to look out for me. I took three of the lovely tablets, downed the glass of water, and willed myself into the bathroom.

Without looking in the mirror, I dropped my dress and underwear on the floor, turned on the shower, and stepped inside. As much as I tried to pretend I couldn't hear them, my parents often managed to sneak into my head when I was weak. Hungover. Worried about what I'd see in the tabs when I forgot to set the narrative myself.

"Cristy, a lady does not mingle with young unmarried men without a chaperone. Remember yourself."

"Alcohol, Cristy? You drank alcohol? We raised you so much better than that."

"You are a disgrace. You should drop down to your knees and repent. Pray hard for forgiveness. We forgive you, but you have seriously angered the Lord."

The hot water worked its magic, relieving me of some anxiety over my party faux pas, drowning out the voices playing on a loop in my head. Maybe if I was super lucky, a hangover would be the only thing about last night I'd have to be sorry for.

Gretchen's arrival in my bathroom right as I'd started to relax stopped that happy train of thought in its tracks.

"Good thing you're not headed out on the next leg of the tour today, girlfriend."

I groaned. "I know."

"Seriously. It's two o'clock. That's p.m. in case you were wondering. And you look like death warmed over."

I turned my back on her, facing the spray of water and willing her to go away.

"Yeah, yeah. You're sending me vibes." Her tone bubbled on a grin. "I'm just not receptive today. After your debut last night, we have ground to cover to keep your part of the show at that level. So get your pretty ass moving faster, wouldja?"

"I could do that maybe if you stopped haranguing me and disappeared," I grumbled into the hot water flowing over my head like a benediction.

My evil friend laughed.

"Dang it, Gretch. Do you need to echo through the entire hotel?"

"Oh, Cristy-girl. I'd like to say that'll teach ya, but I know better," she said through her laughter. "Fortunately for you, the boys sent over a pitcher of some kind of green stuff they swear does wonders for a hangover. I gave it a go and it seems to be working."

"I'll try anything right now."

Needing the tension relief of hot water on my shoulders and back meant facing her, but since she clearly didn't plan on leaving, I sighed and turned around. When I opened my eyes, Gretchen stood outside the glass of the shower holding a huge plastic go-cup.

"This magic elixir will be waiting for you right here"—she placed the go-cup on the corner of the vanity farthest away from the shower—"for when you finally haul yourself out of the shower."

At last she walked away, leaving me in blessed privacy again. That hangover cure—if it actually worked—called to me like a siren, so close yet so far. Finally, I gave in, shut off the lovely hot water, stepped from the shower, and pulled a fluffy white bath sheet around myself. Carefully, I lifted the lid on the cup and sniffed. When my stomach didn't roil, I recapped the cup and took a pull through the straw sticking out of the top.

After the first sip, I did my best not to gag. "Ugh! What is this stuff? It tastes like something my mother would make from whatever leftover moldy salad bits she found in the fridge."

I shoved the cup of offensive green ick to the corner of the vanity far away from me.

Gretchen reappeared in the doorway of my bathroom. "Hold your nose and drink it fast. We need you in top form for the press conference you're doing in an hour."

"What press conference?"

In the mirrors framing me on two sides, a pissed-off hedgehog spiked the reflections. Gretchen couldn't mistake my attitude about her latest bombshell.

"Why do I employ you again? Why do I consider you my friend?"

"Because I've always looked out for you. Always."

Her eyes echoed in the mirrors, leaving me no room for escape, her meaning stentorian in its clarity.

Deliberately, I grabbed the go-cup, lifted the straw to my lips, pinched my nose with my other hand, and sucked down as much as I could on one breath. As a singer, my breath control, even when hungover, blew most people's minds. I finished half the smoothie in one giant gulp.

Setting the cup on the vanity, I tried not to gag on the aftertaste.

"Good girl. Once more ought to do it," she encouraged, her tone gentle.

"Gah!"

Yet I sucked in another deep breath and finished off the disgusting concoction.

"Give it a couple minutes, and you'll see how much better you feel." She rubbed my arm. "Now, I have your outfit laid out on your bed. Jilly is waiting for the all-clear to come in and make you up, and the town car is idling out front." Her change of demeanor from soothing to brisk challenged my legendary breath control. After twenty years of friendship—beginning on the first day of third grade—I should have been used to her abrupt mood changes. Yet, sometimes she caught me by surprise.

Her flipping the switch compelled me to move. Likely, there was a method to her moodiness.

Twenty minutes later, I looked and felt like I'd spent a week at a spa rather than the previous evening partying like it was my job. I hated to admit it, but Balefire's special hangover cure worked. As did my team. Jilly used a light touch with my makeup, the usual antidote to any nasty comment the press might make about my state of health after partying all night following a show.

My costumer—Steve Pullman—chose a tight, baby blue pencil skirt accented with layers of fringe that shimmered and shook when I walked. Paired with a sleeveless magenta silk blouse and sky-high magenta stiletto sandals, I looked ready for the next party. Gold and silver bangles on my wrists jingled merrily when I moved. Monster hoop earrings skimmed my shoulders over the top of a silk scarf swirling in the colors of my outfit. The brilliant green clutch I carried contained my phone, an extra lipstick, and my emergency credit card.

I knew that last one always bothered Gretchen, like I couldn't quite trust her to take care of me. Truth was, I never wanted to be anywhere without access to money. I'd experienced enough of that as a kid, and some fears never left.

We arrived at the studios of one of the LA television stations. Gretchen and several news assistants escorted me down the short hall to the press room, where I could hear the crescendoing and decrescendoing hum of voices. From the sound of it, a packed house awaited us.

Slipping in a side door gave me a chance to compose myself and psych up for the questions Gretchen prepped me for on the ride to the studio. *Be cool, Cristy. Be cool. Don't say everything going on in your head.*

Like she could read my thoughts, Gretchen discreetly squeezed my hand. Another deep breath, and it was showtime.

Without any fanfare, I mounted the platform and took my place behind a mountain of microphones.

"Can you all see me from here? 'Cause I'm having a little trouble seeing some of you." I punctuated my comment with a breathy little giggle.

The room momentarily dropped into silence before the crowd of reporters surged forward, cameras flashing like emergency beacons, everyone talking at once.

"What's it like to play with Balefire?"

"How did you get the gig to play with Balefire?"

"Are you making a statement about a change in your musical direction?"

"Are you and your assistant now an item?"

"Is it true you spent part of the night dancing on the bar to impress a certain member of Balefire?"

"Are you trying to break up the band?"

"Whoa! Whoa! Whoa! One at a time. Geez, you guys. I can't answer you all at once." I smiled and gave a flirty little wink. The flashes going off on three sides of me left me no doubt how onstage I was.

"It's a blast to play with the boys. No, they aren't breaking up. It was their idea to invite me to play with them. We had an awesome time rehearsing and playing, so you can expect me to join them for a few other shows on their current tour."

"What about you and your assistant?"

"She helped set up this whole collaboration. Genius, isn't she?"

"Are you hooking up with Dakota Perri? Or is it Adam Tron? Or maybe both? The band has a reputation for sharing everything," one cheeky reporter said. "Or do you have your sights set on Blu Connolly or Jack Whitehorse? The guys have a reputation for enjoying multiple ladies."

"Are you here to hear about the music or to start gossip and rumors?" I smiled ever-so-sweetly for the cameras and waited.

"Do you deny you have a reputation?"

"For breaking up bands? I categorically deny that. Do you have any questions about the music?"

"Your versions of 'Wonder Woman,' 'Wilderness,' 'Only the Brave,' and 'Heart' took on a decidedly hard rock sound. Can we expect more of that from you in the future?"

"The collaboration with Balefire on those tunes sounded totally hot, didn't it? Perhaps we should record a live album together. What do you think?" I replied, batting my eyes coyly. Gretchen made a discreet cut-it gesture with her hand at her throat, and I wondered how on board Balefire truly was with the whole live album idea.

That tiny teaser was exactly enough to send the crowd of reporters into a frenzy, peppering me with questions all at once again.

"Are you recording an album together?"

"When can the fans expect it?"

"Will there be new songs you've cowritten on the album?"

"Are you considering joining the band on a more permanent basis?"

"Wow! I always forget how relentless you all can be," I began before Gretchen strolled out onto the platform.

"That's all the time Cristy has for now. Thank you for coming out on short notice. Cristy always appreciates your interest."

In a heartbeat, Gretchen had me by the elbow, guiding me toward the side door. Reporters clamored behind us, the questions continuing to fire even after the door closed. When we stepped outside, an assistant showed us another door away from the hordes of reporters no doubt spilling out of the main room to intercept us in the lobby. The town car idled in the alleyway, the driver's hand on the door handle when we stepped outside.

"Well, that was fun."

"Uh-huh. You maybe could have dispelled some rumors rather than create additional ones," Gretchen grumped from the corner of the seat where she'd thrown herself when we slid into the limo.

Being deliberately obtuse, I said, "Ah, Gretch. You said yourself that you and Kelsey are solid."

She shot me the stink eye. "That's not what I meant."

"So the live album hasn't been approved. It hasn't even been run past the band yet, has it?"

"No, but Garrett thinks it's a super idea, and he insisted he can talk the band into it. After all, they agreed to bring you along on several dates of their tour, and they did record the instrumentals of your songs."

She gnawed on the inside of her cheek, her tell for when maybe she'd stretched the limits too far. Having grown up with her, I recognized the habit she'd had since we were kids.

Uh-oh.

I'd gotten off on the adulation of the Balefire fans, fans even more rabid than my own. The Balefire fans had accepted me. Even enjoyed my part of the show. That one concert had introduced me to a whole new audience, and I didn't want to lose it before I even had time to grow it.

I reached inside the minibar and pulled out a can of Monster. The situation probably called for shots, but my hangover, though cured, still loomed large in my mind. I popped the top, swallowed a big drink and asked, "Does Balefire read the tabloids? Do they even have time?"

"Let's hope not. At least until we meet back up with them in San Francisco. Good thing you made a stellar first impression on them."

"That show was an absolute scream. Heck, the rehearsal rocked." I smiled over my drink. "So, yeah, I think I made a good first impression."

"Not what I meant. When you threw down with them, matched the guys shot for shot last night, they loved the hell out of you. Especially Tron. He couldn't take his eyes off you all night long."

"Really?" I tried to rein in my excitement over that news, but Gretchen knew me too well.

"Yeah, really. When you danced on the bar, I think he forgot all about the woman imitating a vine wrapped around him. Face it, Cristy-girl. You have some *moves*." She smiled her first genuine smile of the day at me.

"Oh, heck, Gretch." I dropped back against the seat. "I don't remember the dancing on the bar part."

"Don't worry. You were hot, not sloppy. Garrett even asked if I thought you might dance like that for part of the encore songs at the next show."

Sighing, I threw my arm over my eyes and tried to melt into the deep leather seats in the car. "You're supposed to watch out for me, Gretchen. Stop me from going so far that I can't remember what I did. After what happened with Mali Tatum, I can't afford to alienate any more superstars."

A laugh escaped her. "Speaking of Mali, she's absolutely going to fucking explode when she finds out who you're touring with. Those are fireworks I'd pay to see."

"You're evil, Gretchen Hoff. Diabolically evil." Love and awe warred a little with pure terror at the unadulterated glee she clearly felt at Mali's jealous reaction. Despite the rather arctic nature of our current acquaintance, Mali Tatum was a woman and an artist I still admired.

"What's next? I do a show with Balefire in San Francisco in three nights, another in Seattle, and one in Vancouver after that. Then what?"

Gretchen tapped her finger to her lips. "I think you're going to do two shows with the band in San Francisco."

My brows shot up.

"They're playing the stadium shows in Levi's Stadium, but they've also scheduled an intimate gig at the Fillmore. How fun would it be to play with them at that little party? You'd wear one outfit, stay onstage, wow the fans up close and personal, make a case for the live album…"

I beamed at her. "You really are a genius, Gretch. I love it."

"We'd better pack up and hit the road then. 'Cause they're playing that show tomorrow night."

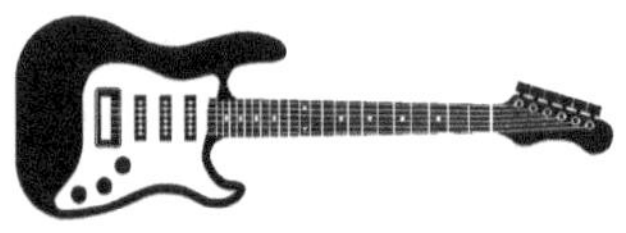

Chapter Five

Adam

OH, YEAH, CRISTY Valor was a wild card. I didn't realize how wild until she showed up for sound checks at the Fillmore in San Francisco, ready to join the band for an extra night. Not sure how that would work out with the contracts, but watching her strut her stuff in those painted-on ripped jeans and that camisole stretched tight over her generous rack left me brainless enough to go along with anything she wanted to do.

Guess the other guys agreed. They stared at her, not even Dakota interrupting, until she finished.

"What do you think? This one won't be like your usual shows anyway since the venue doesn't lend itself to massive pyrotechnics and lovely hydraulics." She winked at Dakota. "So that means you can try something different."

Seeming to come out of the trance Cristy wove around us, Jack said, "We're already doing that in nearly every town we play on this tour."

"What do you mean?" she asked. The innocent look she gave him reminded me of the way my sister Adele used to look at me right before she tried some stupid shit I'd eventually have to bail her out of.

Jack crossed his arms over his chest. "You're already playing our show at Levi's Stadium. Plus the one at Lumen Field in Seattle and the ones in Vancouver, Las Vegas, yada, yada, yada. I think we've got different covered."

"Yeah, but the fans will be expecting to see Cristy at those shows. This idea of hers is great," Dakota said. "Wouldn't it be a kick to surprise the fans again by having her join us tonight?" He grinned. "It would definitely keep the buzz up for our tour."

I had this idea Dakota had something going on with Annabelle Stewart, but maybe he was hedging his bets, wooing Cristy with his generosity. Oh, fuck that. She'd been on my radar since before she joined the tour. After the way she threw down with us following the last show in LA, along with the way she *performed* at the last show, I had plans for her. For us. Those plans didn't include sharing with my buddy.

"I like the plan. All of it. You singing harmonies and background vocals as well as some of your own tunes. In fact, I think you should introduce the show, sing the opening bars of 'Helluva Ride.' That would set the tone and blow the doors off this old girl," I said, touring the auditorium with my eyes.

"That's two. You haven't said anything yet, Blu. What do you think?" Cristy asked.

"I think the point of this whole rodeo is to have some fun. Let's play some music together and have some fun."

Jack relaxed. "I'm in too. My wife's a big fan of yours, Cristy. When she finds out about tonight, I'll probably get laid twice," he added with a grin.

"You're so whipped." Dakota snorted.

"Watch it, Dakota. Falling for someone tends to happen to the best of us," Jack said as he stared pointedly over Dakota's shoulder.

I turned to see what had his attention and watched as Annabelle and Garrett approached, Cristy's manager following close behind.

"What's the plan for tonight? Is Cristy joining you?" Garrett asked.

For some reason, he looked and sounded pissed. Whatever had him going even before the tour began still bugged him. He needed to figure it out—fast—because I was already over his attitude harshing our buzz.

"She is. We're gonna rock the shit out of this place," I said.

"Fine," he huffed. "We'd better start sound checks right away then."

Damn, he sounded more and more like a clingy chick every day of this tour.

♪

Sunshine. Pure fuckin' sunshine. That described Cristy Valor and her contribution to our set. By the time we finished our sound checks and impromptu rehearsal two hours later, the band, the sound team, the roadies—everyone had a grin on their face. Cristy brought the fun factor from the second she stepped on stage. Not to mention, she was a total professional. We sounded tight, even with the distraction of her sexy dance moves focusing everyone's eyes on her long legs and sweet ass. She didn't need the sequins and the short skirts to draw people's attention. All she had to do was move, and all eyes riveted on her. Sex on stilettoes. *Da-amn*. That woman might drive me right out of my head before the end of the tour.

As we put away our guitars and headed out of the auditorium for dinner before the show, Cristy fell in step beside me.

"I'm curious. What's your background?" she asked.

"What do you mean, what's my background?" Though I was pretty sure where she was headed, for some reason it pissed me off coming from her. After all, it wasn't like I hadn't been hearing it all my life.

"You're rock steady. Balefire's sound comes from the way Dakota's guitar complements Blu's voice, but it wouldn't be the same without your bass."

I blinked. That wasn't what I thought was going to come out of her mouth.

"Thanks. I appreciate the compliment."

I towered over her even in those sexy six-inch stiletto sandals she walked on like she'd been born in them, but she didn't seem the least intimidated.

"So, what's your story? The rest of the guys in the band seem to have girlfriends. Why not you?"

I grinned. "This life is one big party, Cristy. From the way you hung with us the other night, I had the idea it was that way for you too."

"Right." She paused. Then almost like she couldn't help herself, she whispered, "But you're so hot."

Now we're getting somewhere.

"I don't need to guess what you are."

"No?"

"No. From the second I laid eyes on you, I knew you were pure trouble."

"Yet you're still looking." She grinned impishly up at me.

"Yeah. I'm still looking."

With a nod toward the door of the auditorium, I invited her to where everyone else had already exited. Because I couldn't resist, I set my hand on the small of her back, escorting her off the stage. With a tiny exclamation, she hustled out to join the rest of the band. The wide smile on my face as I trailed behind her didn't reflect the way my hand tingled with the contact it made with her body.

♪

With the exceptions of the furtive glances Annabelle kept throwing Garrett's way and the stony stare on his face every time he looked up from his meal, the raucous affair otherwise known as dinner continued the good mood from rehearsal. I'd made sure to seat myself next to Cristy, which entailed lots of *accidental* brushes of my arm against hers as we tucked into our meal. A slide of my hand across the back of her chair as I ignored my manners to reach across the table in front of her for the salt. A casual slip of my hand along her thigh when I adjusted the napkin in my lap.

Every time, she rewarded me with a breathy laugh she pretended to direct at the conversation roaring around the table. Or a quick sip of air. Or a tiny wiggle adjustment in her seat. But she didn't retreat. If anything, she moved a little closer.

I get to you too, huh, sweetheart? Good to know.

When she changed the game, I nearly choked on my beer. She discreetly slipped her hand under the table to slide it down and up my thigh, giving me a squeeze damn close to my package. As she lifted her hand to slap me on the back, she ghosted the side of it against my junk, and my eyes nearly bugged out of my head.

"Whoa there, big guy. Maybe you shouldn't try to drink the whole bottle on the first swallow," she teased.

"Yeah, Tron. Slow your ass down. We don't need you making a scene." Dakota laughed.

"'Cause you've already got that covered," Garrett grumbled as he stared pointedly at Dakota's arm wrapped loosely across Annabelle's shoulders. The way Dakota held her to him, she nearly sat in his lap. Same as Blu with Ashleigh and Jack with Clio.

While I tried to drag myself under control, Blu said, "For fuck's sake, Garrett, lighten up. Everyone here is having a good time except you." Dismissing him, Blu turned to me. "At least you didn't spray the table, Tron. I think I speak for all of us that we're eternally grateful for that."

I grabbed my water and gulped some down and wiped my eyes with the back of my hand. Grinning, I said, "You're welcome. You've observed another of my hidden talents. Keeping my beer inside me." I inclined my head in a little bow.

A waiter made his timely appearance, so I ordered another round of drinks. When he reappeared a few minutes later with a dinner tray loaded with beers, I took advantage of everyone's attention on him to whisper into Cristy's ear, "Pure trouble."

An enigmatic smile accompanied the side-eye she shot me, and I added, "Let the games begin."

That got me a throaty laugh that left my jeans tight.

Turns out, she left me hanging until after the stadium show two nights later.

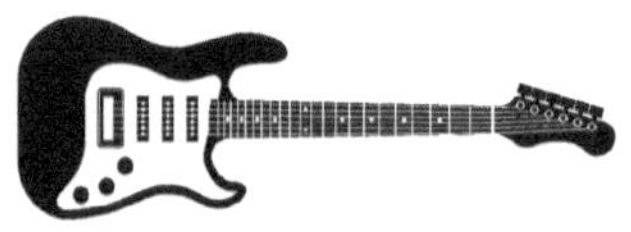

Chapter Six

Adam

CONSIDERING THE INTIMACY of the Fillmore, our show there should have been a shadow of the mind-blowing adventures of our stadium concerts. Instead, we attempted to set off the next San Francisco earthquake. After the way rehearsals went, we should have had a clue that the addition of Cristy Valor would rattle the foundations of the old house all the way back to the Grateful Dead, Led Zeppelin, and Cream.

Then there was our light and film show. In homage to the venue's original master lighting engineer Danny Williams, our lightshow fucking *mesmerized*. Of course, we had to give the fans something extra since we couldn't blow off our usual pyrotechnics in such a small indoor space.

Still, I don't think any of us could have predicted that concert would go like it did. After all, it wasn't like we'd never played the Fillmore before. We didn't rival The Dead for consistent dates there, but we'd played it several times in the past. Nothing like our show with Cristy though.

"That was freaking awesome!" she gushed as we ran offstage after the encore. "The best show I've ever been part of. You guys are the freaking best band on the planet."

"You, little girl, definitely do not suck. Strutting your stuff like you own the world," I said as I pulled her in for a one-armed hug.

A weird look crossed her face. Before I could decipher it or make a play for more contact, Dakota sneaked up on us. Grabbing Cristy around the waist from behind, he swung her around in a full circle, morphing her stiletto boots into lethal weapons. I jumped away in time for her to clear me before he set her down, spun her around, and jacked her up into the air with his hands on her waist. She laughed down at him, the sound echoing joyfully in the hallway. Finally, he set her back on her feet.

Before I could process why his attention to her set me off, Jack and Blu joined us, each of them taking a turn to grab Cristy in a bone-jarring hug. Turned out the only one not currently shackin' up with some chick was the only one who'd missed out on having Cristy's gorgeous rack pressed against his chest, even for a second. Guess I had a few things to learn.

"Holy shit, we fuckin' killed it tonight!" Blu shouted.

"Best fuckin' time I can remember." The grin splitting Jack's face mirrored the expressions of the whole band.

"If you don't count our kick-ass shows in LA." Dakota waggled his eyebrows and laughed.

"Damn good idea it was for you to join us, Cristy," I said. "How is it again that you're a pop singer? Your pipes were made for belting out rock anthems all night long."

She smiled up at me, her eyes shining with undisguised happiness. "Thanks, Tron. I think that's the nicest compliment I've ever had."

"Just telling the truth, sweetheart."

"This definitely calls for a celebration," Dakota declared. "I believe we have a fully stocked bar awaiting us in the green room. In fact, I might have mentioned to Garrett that we're especially fond of Jameson on this tour." He playfully bumped against Cristy's shoulder.

"Oh, hey, guys. Maybe we could take it easy on the shots tonight—"

"And miss the second half of the show? Oh, hell no," Dakota said.

"I gotta admit, Cristy, you're real fun to watch when you dance. Along with those incredible pipes in your throat, you know exactly how to move. Come on. The party awaits." I didn't give her another chance to protest. Instead, I grabbed her hand and pulled her along behind me, the two of us leading the others to the green room.

"To teaming up with Cristy!" Dakota shouted.

We saluted her and everyone shot their Jameson.

"Another round for the band," Cristy said to the bartender. "Barbie shots this time," she added with a twinkle in her eyes.

The bartender nodded and served up a round of fruity pink shots. Taking that dare showed me the lady liked a little vodka and rum. Obviously, we were in for another messy night. I slammed my glass down on the bar with a grin.

Though several groupies approached me, I only had eyes for Cristy, who tore up the bar after Dakota challenged her to a line of vodka shots.

She wore a hot pink halter top with some kind of draping neckline that hinted at the bounty of her breasts. The tight black leather skirt barely covered her ass, but her thigh-high boots took care of covering most of the creamy skin the skirt revealed. As she danced on the bar, I know every guy in the place tried to steal a look up that skirt. But from the way she moved, this wasn't her first rodeo, and we all ended the night disappointed.

Strike that. I wasn't disappointed at all. If I couldn't see anything, neither could anyone else. For some reason, the thought comforted me.

The sweat dripping down her back turned me on though. Visions of her sweating like that as she rode me clouded my brain.

In my drunken state, I probably would have gone all caveman on her and dragged her off that bar and over my shoulder for a trip to somewhere more private. Not that I had the chance with everyone gathered around to enjoy the show and me having no standing whatsoever with the woman—yet.

As we partied the night away, I wasn't the only one who didn't come down until the sun gradually glowed at the edges of the sky. By the time our respective representatives gathered up our asses and sent us back to our hotels—why wasn't Cristy staying with us again?—San Francisco Bay was already emerging from the night's darkness in the distance.

♪

Partying till dawn meant the whole band was slow to arrive in the lobby the next afternoon to regroup for sound checks at Levi's Stadium, nasty kale smoothies in hand all around. Jesus, I hated that shit. Couldn't even imagine how someone could ever dream it up. But I had to admit, I really liked how it worked on killing a hangover in under an hour. Better than aspirin. Almost better than sleep. Certainly a lot faster.

As he'd distributed our smoothies to us, Bailey Saunders seemed to be the only one unaffected by last night's shenanigans. Then I remembered he'd probably spent most of last night moving our equipment and setting it up again, which took a helluva lot less out of a guy than shots of Jameson with beer chasers all night long.

"Everything's ready for you guys at the stadium. Annabelle even ordered in a spread for when you're finally up for some sustenance besides shots." The smirk on his face left no doubt about his level of sympathy for our pain.

None of us was in any shape to flip him shit back. Instead, we responded with a collective groan and almost as a unit lifted our smoothies and downed them.

"All right guys, we need to get this show on the road." Bailey clapped his hands together. "The town car is waiting, the sound team is working out the bugs, and Cristy's assistant texted Annabelle to tell her Cristy is on her way to stadium already."

"Where's Garrett?" Dakota growled.

"At the stadium running Annabelle ragged," Bailey responded. A dark look I couldn't understand passed over his features.

"Well then, we'd better head out there."

The way Dakota launched himself out of the leather chair he lounged in reminded me of a bottle rocket with about that much attitude too. His long strides ate up the lobby, and he'd nearly cleared the front doors before the rest of us managed to haul our asses out of our comfy chairs to follow him. Huh. Dakota never moved like that. I had to wonder what was up.

Cristy

Following the show at the Fillmore, I dragged myself out of bed at the ungodly hour of noon. As I stood in the shower and willed my stomach to stop roiling, Gretchen strolled in. Honestly, why did I allow myself to give in to that woman's demands for a key card to my room again?

"Get out of the shower and drink the smoothie," she commanded without so much as a hello.

"Unnhhh," was all I could manage.

"Your masseur is waiting in the other room."

There it was, the reason I always let her have access to my suite when we went out on tour.

It took every ounce of energy I had to towel off. Mainly because I spent the whole time talking myself into ingesting that vile tasting cocktail mocking me from where she'd set it on the vanity top. Wrapping myself in my towel, I held my nose and chugged as much of the green slime as I could.

From somewhere in the suite, she called, "Don't chase that with water, Cristy. Let it do its job."

How does she do *that?* Stealthily, I returned the water glass to its place on the vanity. With a sigh, I forced myself to finish the smoothie, but I had to brush the taste out of my mouth afterward. Staring at myself in the mirror as I cleaned my teeth, I couldn't help but notice the mocking dark circles under my eyes. *Really, Cristy-girl? What were you thinking last night?* On the heels of that thought came another. *At least I'm not playing every show with the boys on this tour.* I didn't think I could keep up.

An hour and a half later, I felt like I could run the Balefire boys into the *ground.* Funny what a glassful of their secret hangover cure and a good massage could do for a girl. As we sped along the freeway to Levi's Stadium, I grinned in anticipation of seeing the band again—check that—of seeing Adam Tron again.

Something about that man called to me. Not only the part where he was the last Balefire member not currently seeing someone or engaged or married. No, I would have been attracted to Adam whether or not he was single. Him being single made things easier. That guy's hotness nearly melted my panties every time I set eyes on him.

It wasn't only his dark good looks, though. His quiet steadiness gave him authority with the rest of the band and the crew, authority he didn't flaunt or abuse. For some weird reason, he made me feel safe enough to be myself around him. That alone should have scared the heck out of me, but it didn't.

There was something in the way he looked at me sometimes, like he could see inside me—and liked what he saw—that drew me to him like a magnet to a solid iron beam. Like he was my lodestone. Even when I played Balefire's music in the privacy of my home or listened to them on my earbuds or sang along to them in my studio, I found myself seeking the bass, listening for Adam's rhythms. His bass lines rumbled and echoed through me, energizing me long before he got me off during the live show I'd watched him play. Like he got me off during every show since that one. If he had any idea of the effort it took me not to climb him like a tree when we played together onstage, he'd probably laugh at me.

Then again, there *had* been his antics at dinner the other night. Maybe he kind of did want to start something? After the way he carried on with the groupies after the LA concert, I thought I'd have to work pretty hard for his attention. When I smoothed my palm over his thigh and he choked on his beer, I discovered to my delight maybe the attraction wasn't one-sided. Thinking about that dinner gave me all kinds of ideas for having some fun during our show tonight—and at the after-party.

As we arrived at the stadium for sound checks, the smile on my face had a whole lot less to do with playing the show than with playing with Adam Tron. Too bad his manager was such a jerk.

When Gretchen and I spotted Garrett as we walked into the green room, he didn't bother with hello. "Finally, you're here. I know you're the star when you play your own shows, but on this tour, you're not the headliner. Maybe you could arrange it so you don't keep people waiting on you, hmm?"

"*Excuse* me?"

"Let me handle this, Cristy," Gretchen hissed in my ear before she stepped right into Garrett's space.

"Mr. Phillips, do I need to remind you that Cristy's presence on this tour is at the request of your band? Do I need to remind you of the stratospheric responses her appearances with the band have generated with the fans?" She poked one bloodred manicured index finger into his chest to emphasize her next words. "Tell me, do you have a teeny tiny clue what is happening with this tour on social media?"

I didn't bother to stick around to hear his response. Frankly, I didn't need some old guy reprimanding me—in front of other people, no less. I'd endured enough of that crap during the first eighteen years of my life. Annabelle Stewart shot me a helpless look. When I strutted by her toward the door, the bright red apples masquerading as her cheeks told me she didn't share her boss's attitude. Her response was something to remember as we continued the tour—if we did.

In that moment, the prospect of hooking up with Adam Tron invaded my head again, which made it easier to walk away and leave Gretchen to deal with the band's surly manager. Still, the five-minute walk to the stage from the green room wasn't enough to simmer down my attitude.

Chapter Seven

Adam

THE MOMENT CRISTY stomped out onto the stage, I could tell something was off. We were standing around shooting the shit, trying to give those wretched-tasting smoothies time to work their magic when she showed up. I had to smile. For such a tiny thing, she sure could take up a lot of space.

Without so much as a hihowareya, she launched into full-on diva. "Your manager is a jerk. Did you all know that? He's a total tool. I don't get how you put up with him." She pounded more than paced back and forth across the front of the stage, her arms waving around her head for emphasis. "Everyone on this tour is an adult, and we don't need a dad. Perhaps one of you could remind him?" She quit pacing for a second to give us all "the look" every woman on the planet has perfected for calling out a man.

Not waiting for a response, she resumed her attempt to wear a path in the stage floor with her stiletto heels. "Furthermore, someone needs to talk to him about his fashion choices. There is no one in the *universe* who will ever follow whatever trend he thinks he's setting with those cut-off shirts tucked in—tucked in for crying out loud."

She threw her hands up. When I glanced at my brothers, I saw each of us trying to hold it in. Dakota's lips twitched, Jack's cheeks puffed out, and Blu had turned an interesting shade of purple.

Oblivious to our response, Cristy plowed on. "Tucked into five-hundred-dollar custom-tailored dress pants. He looks utterly ridiculous. The man is just a, just a—" She seemed to struggle to say the word, but finally she sucked in a deep breath and whispered, "prick."

We erupted in guffaws we couldn't hold back anymore. As she stood there all indignant, one foot in front of the other, hands planted on her hips, Jack, Blu, Dakota, and I laughed ourselves stupid. We probably should have tried harder to hold it in after the way she ranted about Garrett, but something about that sexy little pixie strutting attitude like a boss—who couldn't bring herself to curse even when she clearly wanted to—struck all of us as hilarious.

At last when I sort of tried to pull myself together, I looked at her and noticed the hint of a smile making her dimples twitch. Then I caught her watching me, a sparkle of mischief in her eyes. Apparently, even she saw the humor in her little tantrum.

Dakota was the last of us to get it together, but as usual, the first to speak. "So Cristy, how 'bout you tell us how you really feel, huh? It's okay if you want to call Garrett an asshole in front of us. We won't tattle to him."

She rolled her gorgeous sapphire eyes. "Screw you, Dakota." But she was grinning.

"Now that we have the preliminaries over, let's put the sound guys to work," he suggested.

Blu turned to me. "Whoa. Tron. You're the usual captain of this boat. Are you going to kick back and let Dakota make all the decisions without a comment?"

Jerking my eyes from Cristy's gorgeous ones, I stammered, "Wh-what?"

Blu laughed. "I see how you're rollin'."

"Whatthefuckever." Strolling over to the guitar rack, I grabbed my bass, flipping him the bird over my head as I settled the strap over my shoulder.

Dakota and Blu didn't stop laughing as they pulled their axes from the guitar cart at the edge of the stage. I might have succeeded in ignoring them if Jack hadn't whispered in my ear as he passed me on his way to his drums. "Don't blame you, man. She's definitely hot."

"*Fuuuuck*," I hissed under my breath. Usually, I'm the cool one. Not that Cristy would know that.

So I ignored her for the entirety of sound checks. Afterward as we enjoyed the eclectic spread in the green room, I concentrated on food rather than on Cristy. Local seafood, our favorite Mexican fare—every flavor of tacos and burritos—and prime rib carved by Jeff Scott, our private chef. Chef Jeff's usual array of workout-challenging desserts—I ate three—kept my eyes off of our sexy-hot guest. My mind was another story.

Visions of all the ways I could have her long legs wrapped around my waist scrolled through my head, each scenario hotter than the last. All of them involved her wearing a pair of her stilettos. Judging from the variety she'd worn so far on the tour, the woman had an infinite wardrobe of the things. I liked them all. The bright purple-and-pink-sequined pair she wore today were kind of hard to miss as they reflected into my eyes from beyond the edge of my plate of cinnamon flan, fudge mousse, and raspberry tart.

I let my eyes take a slow tour up the creamy skin of her toned legs and over her tight ripped denim cutoffs. I lingered at the place where her form-fitting green T-shirt left space for the diamond piercing her belly button to sparkle. How had I missed that piercing in all the times I'd checked her out?

"Tron. My eyes are up here."

"I know where your eyes are."

My lips curved into a grin as I let my eyes continue their

thorough tour of the purple and pink sequins creating a single rose in the middle of her rack and on to the sapphire necklace I'd never seen her without. In my peripheral vision, I noticed her wicked smile when my gaze settled on her cleavage, and I couldn't help my answering smile at the mischief in her eyes when I stopped my tour.

"You have the sexiest smile, Tron."

"Just enjoying the scenery."

"You like what you see?" she sassed.

"Every single thing."

"Even though you're the quiet one in the band, you're used to the ladies giving you exactly what you want, aren't you?"

The tone of her voice suggested a land mine lurked somewhere nearby, but I ignored the warning. "It's a nice perk."

"Yes, it is. I have no trouble getting anything—or anyone—I want either."

Rather than answer, I raised a brow and waited. And tried not to think of Cristy Valor with any other man. The visual flashing through my head made the taste of all that delicious dessert turn to ash in my mouth.

Something of my thoughts must have shown on my face. "You're okay with the change we made in the show for tonight?" she asked.

The abrupt change of topic jerked my mind back into the moment. Trying to recover myself, I said, "Sure. Why not? Like Dakota said, you're our guest."

"Uh-huh."

Grinning, I added, "It's good to shake things up sometimes. Keeps us honest."

"Honest? Yeah, I'm all kinds of interested in honest, Tron."

Before I could ask her what, exactly, she meant by that, her manager interrupted.

"Since you haven't made up your mind about tonight's costume changes Cristy, makeup and wardrobe need you."

When she continued to stare at me with an enigmatic smile lurking on her mouth, her manager prompted, "Now, actually."

Though my eyes were locked with Cristy's, even I heard the eye roll in her manager's tone. With a raised brow, I asked the question.

Instead of answering me, she turned to the other woman. "Gretchen, I don't think I've formally introduced you to Tron yet. Gretchen Hoff, Adam Tron."

"A pleasure, Gretchen," I said. Rather than shake her outstretched hand, I turned it and brushed a kiss over her knuckles. "You must be the Wonder Woman who keeps Cristy Valor under control."

Gretchen smirked at my joke of chivalry. "Controlling Cristy? That's rich. Yeah, I sure as fuck am Wonder Woman."

Without one scintilla of apology, Cristy grinned. "You know you love me, Gretch."

"Only if you're in wardrobe five minutes ago."

Gretchen grabbed Cristy's hand and pulled her toward the door then stopped abruptly and turned back to me. "Your bass lines are fucking fantastic, Tron. They get to girls. Trust me."

She slanted a side-eye at Cristy, winked at me, and returned to her mission. I think Gretchen was trying to tell me something, but I already knew how much the ladies loved my rhythms. After all, they'd been raining sexy lingerie on me for the last ten years.

♪

The low rumble of fans filling the stadium rolled through me. The sound echoed the effect of my bass when I welcomed the notes that flowed out of me and through it and back into me in a perfect loop every time I played. After downing the last of my beer, I tossed the empty bottle at the trash and rolled my shoulders. Next, I did some squats and fifteen or twenty rapid upright push-ups against the wall of the green room and loosened up my torso with a series of twists and bends—my usual warm-up before a show.

The rest of the band stayed busy with their own rituals. Jack sat on the edge of a chair, eyes closed, tapping out rhythms on his thighs. Blu ran several vocal scales, something I'm sure would surprise the casual fan. Dakota took up an entire couch with his man-spread, legs stretched wide in front of him, arms resting along the entire back of it. A beer dangled from the fingers of his right hand before he casually turned his head and lifted it to his lips. Dakota always projected cool, the most laid-back member of the band. But we'd known him almost our whole lives. His casual stance was an act.

After he downed his beer, he bounced up off the couch in one quick movement and strolled over to the door. Obviously, he thought we'd been alone long enough. Time to invite the girls in.

In the past, the girls allowed to enter the inner sanctum of Balefire before a show were of the one-night stand variety. On this tour so far, the girls were Clio and Ashleigh—a wife and a fiancée—and now Annabelle. The way Dakota looked at that woman sometimes made me wonder. Then my thoughts circled round to Cristy Valor.

"You girls come alone, or did you bring along some friends?" I asked hopefully.

"Who did you have in mind, Tron?" Annabelle asked with a little grin.

"Couldn't be Cristy and her entourage. Not after the way he ignored her during sound checks this afternoon."

I shot Jack the bird. From his perch on his platform, the guy maybe saw more than he needed to see. I turned back to the girls.

"There aren't any groupies hanging around outside, anyone who wants to get to know the band—or at least the bassist a little better?"

"There's a whole house full of groupies out there, Tron," Ashleigh said. "But Garrett is busy vetting them for inclusion in the VIP section." She accompanied that last bit of info with a grimace.

It didn't take a genius to know what prompted her sardonic response. Not after the way Garrett tried to break up Blu and her during our last tour. Maybe the guy needed reminding that we liked groupies—or at least I still did. The jury seemed to be out on Dakota, who at the moment had Annabelle gathered up in an intimate tête-à-tête.

A minute later, Bailey blew through the door. "Do you guys hear what's going on out there? This crowd is even wilder than your shows in LA." As usual, Bailey's smile tonight nearly blinded us in its wattage, a contagious light that reflected from all of us. "Guess your teaser at the Fillmore last night created a buzz."

"Well then, we'd better go give the people what they came for," I said.

I didn't wait till the end of all the PDA I knew my friends were enjoying before I stepped through the door of the green room. A wall of screams from the groupies Garrett tried to entertain by himself met me as I rounded a corner, heading toward the tunnel to the stage. I blew kisses at the ladies and treated them to the sexy grin Cristy had complimented. In midstep, I stopped to look around for where she waited.

"Hey, man, no time for that," Bailey shouted over the screams of the groupies he thought had all my attention.

He hustled me past the girls, and before I knew it, I stood in my designated spot, bass in hand, my remote mic in place. Seconds later, Dakota and Blu joined me as Jack situated himself in the center of his massive drum kit. Jack grinned and flashed us the finger—our cue for the show to begin.

♪

After Dakota finished his solo from the dizzying height of his take-no-prisoners platform, I stepped back onstage and smiled at Jack. Even with our earbuds in so we could hear ourselves play, the roar of the crowd was deafening. Dakota's solo marked the segue into the second third of the show. Previously, this part had been my favorite because it was my turn to step out of the background and show off a little. Soloing was such a rush, especially with the way the ladies *always* responded. Anyone with a heartbeat, would feel the rhythms of my bass, especially when I played my own licks.

This time, I couldn't help but anticipate Cristy's arrival onstage. So my solo passed by me in a bit of blur. Then the lights dropped, and my belly tightened waiting for her. The fans, now having a clue what was coming, quieted enough for her opening vocals to "Wonder Woman" to soar over them. As her voice carried through the crowd, the whole place went batshit crazy.

The flash pots illuminated her standing like an Amazon on Dakota's platform a story and half above the floor of the stage. Her outfit mimicked Gal Godot's from the latest *Wonder Woman* movie right up to the long dark wig she wore. If not for her stunning voice, I might not have recognized her as she played her role for the song and the fans. I was glad my bass shielded me from the fans' eyes 'cause seeing her in that outfit left me hard as a rock.

After Bailey lowered her back down to the stage, the lights dropped, and we played the opening sequence for her next song. In the space of eight bars, she left the stage, executed a complete costume change, and like magic, reappeared on the exact right note. Unbelievable.

This time she strutted her stuff in a sexy biker-chick outfit—a tight leather jacket that showed off her considerable cleavage, leather shorts that barely covered her perfectly rounded ass, and clunky calf-high boots.

"Are you having fun?" she asked the crowd as she skipped and danced the entire width of the stage.

The fans roared their response.

Bounding up the stairs to join Jack behind his drums, she shouted, "I'm having a great time." She blew Jack a kiss as she danced to the rhythms of his tom-toms. The crowd loved her, and I couldn't blame them. I didn't even try to look away from her. The woman radiated energy like an atomic bomb. But instead of flattening all of us, she revved up every person in the entire stadium.

She stepped and stomped her way down the steps of Jack's lifted stage and back to the middle of the floor between Dakota and Blu. By the time she finished her second song, the guys and I were playing out of our minds, and the screams of the fans could probably be heard on the moon.

Unlike our first show, Cristy didn't change her costume again before the end of our last set. When we stepped backstage to catch our breaths before the encore, I expected to see her, maybe tell her how fucking awesome she'd been out there. But she didn't join us. The crowd's demands for more didn't leave me time to ponder the situation as I downed a bottle of water and joined my guys back out in front of the frenzied fans.

As we played the first few notes of "Something's Gotta Give," Cristy skipped onstage to join us. I had to work hard to maintain my concentration on the song as she danced for the audience in an outfit that reminded me of Dorothy from the *Wizard of Oz*. That is, if Dorothy only wore the blue plaid apron part of her dress over some kind of frilly underskirt that barely covered her ass. And those shoes? Red-sequined stilettos fitted with enormous bows? So fucking hot.

She sashayed her way from Dakota to Blu, drawing everyone into the party she was having with us. Right as we came to the pause before the bridge, she deliberately stepped in my direction, the look in her eyes a dare—pure trouble. I didn't even try to stop the grin spreading over my face as I watched her come for me.

"We're not in Kansas anymore, are we boys?" she purred during the bridge as she ran a bright blue manicured nail down the middle of my chest.

My breath caught in my throat. My fingers stilled on my bass for one note. And Cristy Valor laughed. I swear she gave her ass an extra shake just for me as she strutted toward the front of the stage.

I finished playing the show in a daze. As the last notes of the final encore reverberated off the back of the stadium, the five of us stepped to the front of the stage, made our final bow, and ran backstage together. Cristy fist-bumped and high-fived each of us as we laughed in pure joy. What a fucking rush.

Before we split to go to our respective dressing rooms, she leaned up and whispered in my ear, "See *you* in a few minutes."

Like an idiot, I stood there grinning my face off. Jack rescued me from looking like a total moron when he dropped his arm over my shoulder. "Come on, Tron. Let's hit the showers. Then we can play with the ladies."

Chapter Eight

Adam

LIKE THE REST of the band, I exited the stage on an adrenaline high that left me euphoric—and horny. Unlike my bandmates, I didn't have someone ready and waiting to take care of that second thing. I knew who I'd like to help me with that, and I didn't think the chemistry I sensed with her whenever we were together was one-sided. Maybe that was why I did without after the show at the Fillmore. Any one of about twenty groupies would have taken care of me after that show, but Cristy distracted me. The shots of Jameson took the edge off. Next thing I knew, it was nearly time for breakfast, and I needed to sleep off the after-party.

Not how I wanted things to go this time.

Too bad we don't always get what we want.

When I tried the door to Cristy's dressing room, I found it unlocked. *Score!*

Or not.

To my surprise, the only person in the room was some dude gathering up Cristy's clothes from the show. "Hey, man. I'm Tron."

I'd seen the guy around every time Cristy joined us, but we'd yet to be introduced.

He shifted some dresses in his arms so he could shake my outstretched hand. "Steve Pullman, Cristy's costumer. Nice to meet you officially."

"Yeah. Hey, you know where she is?"

"Hitting the after-party would be my guess."

The look on my face must have given me away.

"Damn, man." He blew out a breath. "She does tend to have that effect on people. Let me guess. She told you to meet her here."

"Not exactly…"

"Listen, Tron. Cristy's my boss, and I think she's the bomb. You're a rock god, so you probably have a better than average chance." He shifted her clothes a little higher in his arms. "Just be careful."

I raised a brow.

"She's got a lot going on, you know?"

I tilted my head.

"She's not as tough as she tries to appear. That's all." He started hanging clothes on a rack that took up one whole wall of the dressing room.

"You got a thing for her?"

He shot me a look over his shoulder. "I've got a thing for my wife." There was no mistaking the warning in his tone. "But I happen to like my job. A lot."

"So you don't want some asshat to fuck it up for you."

"Got it in one."

I nodded. A guy loyal to his boss in this business deserved my respect. "You joining the party?"

"Soon as I pack these for cleaning and shipping."

"Catch me there. I'll buy you a drink." I stepped over to him and shook his hand again.

"I'll do that," he said with a grin. We both knew the promoter paid for the party, a shared joke that made us equals. Plus, I felt like I'd gained an ally in my pursuit of our sexy, troublemaking guest.

With a salute, I headed to the after-party.

♪

Huh. Cristy had some skeletons. Didn't we all? She'd taken a bit of a beating in the tabs before our tour. Something about some feud with that other pop diva. Usually, I tuned that shit out, but maybe this time, I needed to pay some attention.

A thought flashed through my head, and I stopped dead in my tracks. Was she coming on to me as a publicity stunt? Fuck that shit. I'd done my turn cleaning up other people's messes every time I covered for my older brother Aaron or my younger sister Adele. Nearly cost me this rock 'n' roll life I'd dreamed of having when my brother landed in some trouble that could have stopped him from taking over our dad's shop. In our family, it was expected that I step up if he stepped out. Most of my first check from our label went to bailing Aaron out of a jam to keep me with the band.

I kept walking. Cristy intrigued me. Scratch that. She turned me on like no one I'd ever met—and I hadn't even touched her yet. Still, Steve's words gave me something other than my dick to think about.

Turns out, I didn't have much of a chance to discover Cristy's motives. When I finally caught up to her at the after-party, she was doing shots with the girls. Clio and Ashleigh egged Annabelle and her on in some kind of contest while my brothers chanted behind them. Annabelle finished first, calling out a cheer from Clio, Dakota, and Jack and a groan from Ashleigh and Blu. Looked like Cristy and Ashleigh were one cheerleader short.

"'Bout time you showed up, man. We need some help here," Blu said. For a second there, he even looked and sounded distressed before his face broke out in a grin.

"We're having relays. We're short a drinker on my team. Welcome to the party." Blu handed me a shot. "Step on up. You're taking on Jack, and we all know what a lightweight *he* is," he taunted.

"It's a shot, Blu. How does this not end in a tie?"

Blu stepped back and showed me a line of three more shots, each a different color.

"It's going to be one of *those* nights." I pretended to scowl, but inside I couldn't help but grin. "Before I kick Jack's ass, I need something."

Turning to Cristy, I leaned down and whispered, "You gonna make good on that promise you made out there?"

"Drink up, Tron. We're counting on you for the win." She winked at me, which could have meant anything. Damn it.

"On three, boys," Ashleigh said. "One, two, three!"

I bolted out to two shots ahead before Jack even set down his first glass. When I finished the fourth shot and turned to the group with my hands in the air, Cristy launched herself at me, wrapping her arms around my waist.

"You're my hero! We won!"

Blu clapped me on the shoulder. "Way to go, Tron, my man. You never let us down."

I wrapped my arms around Cristy and held her tight against me. Her soft curves complemented my hard planes like she'd been made for me. For a second, I closed my eyes and gave in to the moment.

Dakota, the dick, interrupted with his whining. "Tell me again why we had Jack on our team? He always has trouble with the tequila shot. Every fuckin' time. Everyone knows that."

"You're such a baby. Every fuckin' time," Blu mimicked.

Dakota flipped him the bird and turned his attention to me. "You can let go of Cristy now, Tron. You won." He saluted her with his beer. "I gotta hand it to you, girl. Not only can you keep up with us musically, but you damn sure can keep up with us at the party. Good idea you had to invite her along, babe." He planted a fat kiss on Annabelle's mouth.

I had no intention of letting Cristy go now that I finally had her in my arms. Too bad her manager had other ideas.

"There you are. Come on. I need you to meet some people."

Much to my satisfaction, Cristy turned her head in Gretchen's direction, but she tightened her arms around me.

"Sorry, Tron. But I need to borrow Cristy. I promise to bring her back in a while," Gretchen said. Something in her tone left me wondering about her sincerity.

Huffing out a sigh, Cristy stepped away from me, but she gifted me with an impish grin. Ghosting the pad of her index finger from my collarbone, over my pecs, and down to my belt, she said, "Go easy on the shots until I come back."

That little move set my body on fire. Damn if the woman didn't know exactly what she did to me. The way she shook her pretty ass in my direction as she walked away left no doubt.

"Got something going there, buddy?" Blu teased as he handed me a beer.

"Might have a minute ago. The way Gretchen leads Cristy around is kinda like the tail waggin' the dog," I grumbled, slugging back a long drink.

Blu busted out laughing, and I caught Ashleigh smirking in my direction from beneath his arm.

"Whatthefuckever," I said as Garrett interrupted to introduce us to some football players from the 49ers.

Somewhere during the rest of the night, I drank too many shots with guys who outweighed me by sixty pounds and made my abs sore laughing at all their jokes. Somehow, I ended up back at the hotel in bed. Alone. Not sure what Gretchen meant by a while, but it sure as fuck didn't mean before the end of the night. Or maybe she was Cristy's out. Maybe Cristy was one of those people who made promises they never intended to keep.

Chapter Nine

Cristy

LYING IN BED, I stared up at the ceiling and sighed. Gretchen was my best friend and the best manager I could have ever asked for. But she needed to work on her timing. I'd made a promise to Adam, a promise I had every intention of keeping until she dragged me away. Without consulting me, she'd agreed on my behalf to auction show tickets, backstage passes, and a private dinner with me for an LGBTQ charity. I was totally on board with all of it—except the part where she blind-sided me as I was making plans with Adam.

I'd had an absolute blast with fans who loved my music, my style, and my attitude. Gretchen never missed a chance to find ways to show me how much people appreciated me—exactly the way I am. Last night, though, I wish she'd given me a heads-up before I made that promise and drank all those shots.

As I dragged myself out of bed, my phone pinged an incoming message. Thinking it was from Gretchen, I almost ignored it for a trip through the shower, but then I saw Adam's name on the screen.

MH: I drank the shots, Cristy. All of them.

I smiled. Of *course* he had. After all, he was Adam Tron, bassist for Balefire, the hottest—and wildest—band on the planet. Mr. Hotness himself, which was how I'd put him in my contacts.

CV: So you're one of those guys, huh?

MH: What guys?

CV: The ones who have trouble following directions. ;)

MH: I did wait—but you disappeared and didn't come back.

CV: I don't have any plans for today. Yet.

MH: I'll be at your hotel in an hour.

Questions raced through my head. He wasn't mad that I didn't come back after Gretchen kidnapped me? He didn't hold it against me that I hadn't kept my promise? He wanted to take me somewhere? Like a date? In an hour? Crap. That didn't give me much time.

CV: What should I wear?

MH: Something that doesn't make you stand out so much—if that's possible. =) And you'll need a jacket. It might be a little nips up on the boat.

CV: Boat? What boat?

MH: You'll see.

A boat ride? For real? What could Adam possibly be up to? I smiled to myself. I always knew to watch out for the quiet ones. They had a way of surprising a person, which was probably part of the reason the man drew me to him like the tides to the moon. That and his arresting good looks. So many times on the tour, I'd seen the banked heat in his fathomless eyes when he watched me. Like covering me in warm melted chocolate and spending all day licking it off me. Catching him sneaking glances at me meant I made sure to give him plenty of opportunities to look his fill.

Yet today he wanted me to dress down, go incognito. But I wanted him to see only me.

Adam

As I texted Cristy from the lobby of her hotel, I wondered not for the first time why she couldn't stay at the same place we were staying. It made no sense. Seriously. We could combine security.

We could sneak into each other's rooms.

Staying in separate hotels was a giant pain in the ass.

While I waited for her to meet me, I found a lounge chair near the elevators and played a round of *Angry Birds* on my phone. The game might have run its course with the rest of the world, but I still got a kick out of it. I'd just launched the last pig on my current level when she stepped off the elevator.

As usual, the woman radiated sunshine and sex. Da-amn.

A floppy straw hat with a big-ass pink flower attached to the bright orange hat band covered her blond hair. A pair of huge tortoiseshell shades hung from the deep cleavage of her floral halter top. Maybe she'd painted on the pair of ripped skinny jeans that made her legs look a mile long. I wanted to explore those legs with my hands and my lips and my tongue before she wrapped them around me. Blowing out a sigh, I discreetly adjusted myself, stood, and walked over to her.

"This is dressing down for you, babe?"

"You were very mysterious about the plan for today, so I had to wing it."

Pure unapologetic trouble. After growing up with all the trouble I did with my siblings, you'd think I'd avoid it rather than ask it out on a date. Apparently, I couldn't resist trouble when it came packaged as Cristy Valor. Especially when she smiled up at me, those sapphire eyes sparkling with delight.

"What are we doing today, Superstar?"

Even though she wore six-inch wedge heels, I towered over her. She made me feel like a man—and more than a little protective of her. Grinning down into those gorgeous eyes, I said, "Superstud, huh? I like the sound of that."

"Yet, you call me trouble." She laughed and shook her head. "Where are we going again?"

"To jail."

♪

Tiny droplets of salt water misted over the bow of the private harbor charter as we motored out to the island known as Alcatraz in the middle of San Francisco Bay. Cristy stood at the front of the boat, her hat forgotten on a bench in the cockpit. Her white denim jacket acted as a sail as she held her arms out from her sides.

"Look, Tron! I'm flying over the water!" she called over her shoulder. The megawatt smile on her face made my whole day.

I'd just exited the cockpit after telling the captain we wouldn't be landing on the island after all. Seems Cristy wasn't much of a history buff—not that I'd taken her for one. But the old prison did have a sordid past I'd thought she might find interesting.

"You like to fly, Cristy?" I asked as I stepped behind her.

"Hold onto me. We can be Rose and Jack from *Titanic*."

"Why is it girls always like the tragic stories where the guy dies saving the girl?"

She laughed like the question was rhetorical. "Because it's romantic, silly."

I could hear the eye roll in her voice, which meant I had to mess with her. "How 'bout a story where the hero only *appears* to die—and then gets the girl in the end?"

"That's been done already. They called it *Superman*. Catch up, Tron." But she was laughing.

"Sure it wasn't Superstud?"

"We're back to that, are we? Yet I haven't felt your hands on me once the entire afternoon. Hmm. I wonder how that fits the narrative."

My hands flexed at my sides as I stood behind her. Even after she'd explained what happened after the show, I still wasn't convinced about her keeping a promise. As much as I wanted to start something with her, I didn't want to make a mess. After all, we had more tour dates in front of us than behind us. Besides, I'd been waiting for an invitation.

Slipping my arms around her, I pulled her back against me. She kept her arms spread wide and laughed that throaty laugh that gave me a semi every time I heard it. Shifting my weight, I spread my legs wide, balancing both of us as we watched Alcatraz grow larger in front of the boat. Her halter top left a gorgeous strip of exposed skin on her belly, soft skin that rippled beneath my palms, leaving me no choice but to pull her back flush with my front.

"From what the pilot said, it's not very likely we'd survive the currents if we shipwrecked here," I said, pretending she didn't get to me either. "Jack and Rose would suffer the same fate together. The end. No romance there, I'm afraid."

"Spoilsport." The pout in her voice made me laugh.

"Not that I wouldn't make heroic efforts to save you, of course. Oomph!"

She dropped an elbow right into my ribs.

"What was that for?"

"Stop laughing at me. I'm trying to have a moment here."

I couldn't help my grin despite the smarting in the spot where her sharp little jab marked me. "Okay, Rose. Have your moment."

While I held her close during her "moment," I had my own experience. Cristy Valor's tight little body rested pliant and warm along the front of me, my hands spread wide across her taut belly. Every now and then, one of my fingers would "slip" and rub over her sexy piercing, and she'd lightly roll her hips against my groin. Like it was an accident or something. Citrus and spice mingled with salty sea air in my nostrils when I leaned down to rest my chin on the top of her shoulder. I couldn't help but enjoy the shudder that tumbled through her as I rubbed the two-day-old stubble of my jaw along the velvety softness of hers. For a little space of time, she and I were the only two people in the world. Damn if I didn't enjoy that moment, which probably should have alarmed me. Instead, it left me strangely happy.

The scree of gulls flying overhead interrupted as we neared the island. Alcatraz loomed like the fortress it was, intimidating in the way it overwhelmed its island. As we'd agreed, the pilot started her slow circle of the old prison. Since we were making the trip, it seemed we should at least take a look at the old pile from the sea.

"Sure you don't want to stop and take a tour? Our pilot is also a tour guide, so we could see the best parts and nothing we don't want to see," I said.

Cristy stiffened in my arms. "I've had enough experience with confinement. I don't need to see anyone else's personal hell. Thanks anyway."

What the fuck?

Before I could pursue her comment, she stepped away from me. "'Scuse me. I need to use the head."

By the time she came out of the bathroom, we'd rounded the island, the pilot pointing us toward Golden Gate Bridge.

"You all right?"

"Sure. Why wouldn't I be?" She pasted a bright smile on her face, but it didn't quite calm the storm in those wild-colored eyes.

"You'll tell me if you're feeling seasick."

"I love the ocean. All this water, even salty, beats the desert any day. Where are we going next?"

"Straight ahead. The gateway to America."

Her mouth formed an O as she stared at the bridge. "Wow! Stunning, isn't it?"

I stared at her. Whatever had happened to her in the past simmered right below her surface. If I looked closely enough, I might even be able to see it. She sucked in a lungful of salty sea air, and I watched in rapt fascination as she dropped whatever memories threatened her moment like someone shrugging out of a heavy winter coat.

"Next time I play San Francisco, I'm going to play from Golden Gate Bridge. Can't you see it, Tron? The bridge supporting thousands of screaming fans. Boats queuing up for miles to watch the light show. It'll be epic." Her whole body vibrated with excitement for her big idea, and I couldn't help but smile.

Somehow, I'd done or said something that had sent her back into a past she didn't want to remember. For the moment, I let Cristy's enthusiasm for her goofy idea draw my mind away from pursuing the cause of her pain.

Chapter Ten

Cristy

ADAM PULLED HIS baseball cap low over his brow and adjusted his aviators over his eyes. He tilted his head expectantly at me. I puffed out a sigh and pulled my floppy sunhat a little lower over my forehead. The pilot had dropped us off at Pier 39. With it being late September and a weekday, the place only teemed with people rather than seethed.

Like he knew exactly what I was thinking, he grinned and grabbed my hand to lead me down the pier. Those long legs of his ate up ground like a racehorse, forcing me to double-step to keep up.

"Hey Superstar. Where are we going in such a hurry?"

His grin faded when he noticed me nearly running to keep up with him. "Sorry. Didn't mean to make this a workout." His lip quirked mischievously. "It's Superstud. How many times do I have to remind you?"

"Uh-huh," I teased. Though I couldn't see it behind his shades, I'm pretty sure he hiked his brow at my feigned skepticism. After all, the size and definition of his shoulders, chest, and biceps said body builder, his loose-limbed stride said athlete, but his deep brown eyes vowed temptation. With a breath, I slowed my heart rate before I started on the sculpted beauty of his lips and where and how I wanted to feel them. Superstud pretty much covered it where Adam Tron was concerned.

Though he slowed down to what he probably considered a stroll, the twelve-inch difference in our heights still meant I had to stride it out beside him. I think he walked his speed deliberately so I had to concentrate on my footing rather than on asking where we were going. The way we moved told me he had a destination in mind, one he had no intention of sharing with the class.

Stopping suddenly in front of a building, he said, "You up for a little fun?"

"Always."

He smirked. "Right answer."

I looked at the marquis and gasped. "7D Experience? Adam, you are such a guy."

Even the bad boy aviators he wore couldn't mask the sheepish look on his face. "It's pretty fun, but if you'd rather do something else…"

"I'm messing with you." I gave his shoulder a playful punch. "Come on. Let's go shoot some virtual bad guys. But I'm warning you. There will be no whining when I kick your butt."

"I knew the first time I saw you that you were nothing but trouble. So far, you haven't disappointed."

Those words stung for a second. Until I saw the grin on his face telling me he maybe liked my kind of trouble.

He tugged me inside the attraction and picked up our tickets without removing his hat or his shades. I followed his lead, keeping my disguise in place until we found our seats and traded our shades for 3D glasses.

After the attendant's pregame pep talk, Adam turned to me. "All right, hotshot," he said. "Let's see what you got."

♪

I worked at catching my breath as we exited the Experience, both of us laughing.

"All I can say, Cristy, is your dance moves paid off in that laser maze. How you can limbo beneath a one-foot-high laser beam in those shoes will be the stuff of legends." He blew out a breath. "Damn girl. That was *impressive*."

Adam's compliment gave me warm fuzzies I'm sure he could see in the blush heating my cheeks. "I had to do something to save face after the way you creamed me in the 3D video game." I stopped moving and smiled at him, resting my hands on my hips and taking a few cleansing breaths to slow down my speeding heart.

"After all that excitement, I'm starving." He patted his taut abs. "You up for some dinner?"

"Definitely."

He tilted his head, waiting.

"Sorry bucko. I'm so onto you. I'm not even bothering to ask."

"Ah, come on, Valorous. You're taking the fun out of it," he said, the whine in his tone so at odds with his size and bad boy sexiness.

Valorous. Hearing that name on Adam's lips left a warm glow in my chest.

"Oh, I think you can do 'tall, dark, and mysterious' fine without me playing your straight man." I tipped my glasses down to wink at him.

One wink and the atmosphere changed, heat shimmering between us. "No one could ever mistake you for a straight man, not with those curves."

Goose bumps rippled over my skin at the low timbre of his voice. My nipples tightened to high alert. Suddenly, my center was slick and wet, my inner muscles pulsing in anticipation of his touch. Adam leaned toward me, and I held my breath, my whole body desperate for the release I instinctively knew his kiss would give me.

"That was freakin' awesome!"

"Best game ever!"

"Let's do it again, right now! Can we Dad? Can we?"

At first, I thought a tsunami dumped cold water on our almost moment. Then I realized it was only a ripple of three dark-haired brothers and their dad, high-fiving and screaming their enthusiasm as they crashed out onto the boardwalk. Like waves against rocks, I doubt they even noticed us as they ebbed and flowed around us.

"Sorry about that," the dad called as he hustled after his sons who raced back toward the entrance.

Adam removed his cap, ran his fingers through his hair, and resituated it on his head. With a rueful grin he said, "Where were we?"

"Dinner?"

"Yeah. Let's go."

His wide bass player's palm spanned my back as he guided me up the boardwalk. Though his touch remained light, it seared like a brand on my skin. True to form, he didn't reveal our destination as we walked at a leisurely pace.

"This is it." He held the door for me as we entered Players Sports Grill and Arcade. When I looked around inside, I burst out laughing. "I sense a theme, here. But I bet there's a game in this place that I can win."

"Slow down, trouble. Let's eat first."

Our hostess, who looked about sixteen, seated us at a quiet table in the luau lounge overlooking the bay. I slid my glasses off to look at the menu and she gasped.

"Cristy Valor? Is it really you? Omigosh! I saw you play last night with Balefire. That was the best show I've ever seen," she gushed.

"Thanks. That's really nice of you—"

Adam interrupted by sliding off his aviators. "That *is* really nice of you. Tell you what, we'll autograph anything you want if you keep us on the down low."

"Tron? Balefire's Tron? Holy crap!" she squealed.

"Not really the down low, darlin,'" Adam crooned.

Immediately, the hostess dropped her voice to a stage whisper. "Of course. You want some privacy. Sure. Omigosh. Adam Tron and Cristy Valor. I can't believe it. Are you two, like, together?"

"We planned to eat dinner together, yes."

Dang, Adam played it cool. So of course I had to mess with him. "You're the first to see us together. Something to show off for your friends, hey?" I said. "Tell you what, you send over the server, and you can have a photo with us to prove your story."

Adam raised his thick perfectly shaped brows and blinked at me. The man was a master at expressing himself with his eyes. *Together?* he asked, which netted him one of my biggest smiles.

The hostess blinked between us like she couldn't believe her reality.

"A server?" I reminded her politely, my eyes never leaving Adam's.

"Oh yes! Yes, right away. Wow! Cristy Valor and Tron. Wow-oh-wow-oh-wow!"

She hustled off, hopefully to find a server.

"Gotta love the fans."

The sober stare he gave me popped my happy bubble. "Wanted to keep our date a little quiet. Maybe have a chance to get to know each other without an audience."

"Have you seen yourself, Adam Tron? Even if you weren't the best bassist in the world, you'd attract an audience."

His lips quirked into half a grin. "Same could be said of you, Cristy Valor." He rested his forearms on the table. "Valor. Is that really your name or is it your stage name?"

"Are you telling me you haven't Googled me?" Setting my elbow on the table, I rested my chin in my palm and pouted my lips. "I think I'm hurt."

Adam huffed out a laugh. "I listen to your music."

"You do? That makes my whole day." Mollified, I answered the question. "It's my stage name."

"What's your real name?"

I gave him a hard stare. "Something I don't share."

He frowned. "Why not?"

Sitting back in my chair, I crossed my arms over my chest. "Because I don't need the press digging around in my past."

"What could you possibly have to hide?" His eyes flickered like he just thought of something. "Out on the boat today, you said something about confinement." He swallowed. "Have you spent time in jail?"

The pained furrow of his brow was so sincere I had to ball my fists to stop myself from reaching across the table to smooth it away.

"Might as well have been. Turning eighteen gave me the keys to unlock my own kind of prison. One I don't intend to revisit. Ever. Especially not in the tabloids."

He relaxed back into his chair. Crossing his big arms over the massive depth of his chest, he said, "So you're not going to trust me with your name, huh?"

"My first name really is Cristy. My middle name is Valorie, so—Cristy Valor." I shrugged with something I hoped looked like nonchalance. "It took everything I had to walk away from my situation with everything I owned in two duffel bags." I stopped. No matter how much I liked Adam's undivided attention on me, there were some places I never wanted to visit again. Even in the private space in my head.

He stared at me with that enigmatic expression I'd seen on his face several times since I'd joined the tour. It simultaneously soothed and disconcerted me. For whatever reason, I found it easy to talk to him. Maybe too easy considering that in the space of two minutes, I'd told him more about myself than I'd told anyone since I left Phoenix nearly ten years ago.

No matter how much I enjoyed being with him, no matter how

much fun we'd had together—not only during our date but also in rehearsals and playing together—I couldn't give him everything. I had too much to lose.

As if he sensed the thoughts tumbling around in my head, he nodded. "Someday Cristy, you're going to trust me enough to tell me your whole story." The sincerity of his expression almost undid me. "And know I won't exploit it."

A flash from somewhere across the room interrupted our tête-à-tête, reminding me of another reason I kept my secrets to myself.

Adam sighed. "Guess the hostess couldn't keep our presence quiet."

"You still gonna give her an autograph and a photo?" I grinned.

"Don't see how to get out of that one." A rueful nod accompanied his words.

A waiter appeared at our table, blocking the view of the amateur paparazzi across the restaurant from us.

"Wh-what can I get started for you today, Mr. Tron, Miss Valor?"

The cute way the guy tried to pretend we were a regular couple having dinner together made me laugh.

"I'll have the turkey club with a sweet pickle on the side. Hold the fries."

"Bring her fries. I'll eat 'em. I'll have the double luau burger and a green salad with blue cheese dressing. Add some blue cheese dressing on the side."

At the look I gave him, Adam said, "Duh. To dip the fries in." The grin he gave me tripped up my heart. For a second, he let me see the carefree boyishness I'd only ever witnessed between him and his guys at rehearsals before I made my presence known. "And a beer."

"I'll have a strawberry margarita on the rocks, thanks."

"You're really, really welcome. I'll get your order in right away."

The poor kid looked as if he might pass out, and I had to laugh again. Adam rolled his eyes, but I caught the tiny grin playing at the corner of his lips. When a flash went off in our peripheral vision, he angled his hat down and scowled.

His response to the fans puzzled me. After all, without them, we'd both be doing something that likely didn't involve music. The thought made me shudder.

"I wanted to have a good time with you today. Hopefully without a scene."

"So you brought me to the pier? A place teeming with tourists?" I didn't even try to hide my incredulous expression.

"I thought we'd blend in."

His dejection was so cute that I sighed and reached across the table to touch him. A massive mistake. The second my fingertips grazed the skin on the back of his hand, heat sizzled up my arm. My scalp tightened simultaneously with my nipples, and I couldn't stop my involuntary gasp.

Adam's eyes snapped to mine, and the answering heat I saw in those dark chocolate depths nearly welded my panties to the chair. Before I could pull my hand away, he turned his over, capturing mine as he twined our fingers together.

"Have you always been singing?"

The abrupt change of subject threw me. "All my life, I think."

"Yeah? What did you sing when you were a kid?"

His fingers playing along mine drew the truth from me. "Hymns."

He shot me a look. "I'm serious, Cristy."

"So am I."

A slow grin spread over his face. "I never pegged you as a 'good girl.'"

I don't know if his words or the air quotes irritated me more. Tugging my hand from his, I glared at him. "What's that supposed to mean?"

"Admit it, Cristy. You're sassy. The way you play a show is flat-ass naughty."

Before I could answer the challenge in his eyes, the server appeared with our drinks. I licked the salt off the rim of my glass and swallowed a cooling drink of strawberry-infused tequila goodness. All the while, I studied him over the rim of my glass. His eyes roamed the length of me as he took a long pull of his beer. He shifted slightly in his chair, and I thought maybe I got to him as much as he was getting to me. Maybe my not being a "good girl" attracted him, which thrilled me and ticked me off in equal measure.

"Which is it for you, Tron. Good girl or naughty?"

"Whichever one you feel like being in the moment."

His answer literally sat me back in my seat. "Are you for real?"

A man who was willing to let me be me? He'd been reeling me in all day. Now I was afraid he might have caught me.

CHAPTER ELEVEN

Adam

CRISTY TEASED THE hell out of me the whole damn date. Sometimes it wasn't even on purpose. First there was the spice and citrus of her perfume. Whenever she leaned back into me as we worked our controllers on the *Super Mario* game we were currently playing, I couldn't stop myself from inhaling her scent like it was my last breath. She'd laugh her throaty laugh, usually at herself for making a silly move that allowed me to pass her, and I'd lose my concentration.

Her megawatt smiles shining from a secret place behind her eyes lit me up. Even though I'd seen her gift those smiles to the crowds of fans in the stadiums we played, she always held something back. With me, she shared a private part of herself. Her responses to me made me even more eager to discover her mysteries. Apparently, she planned to make me wait—or maybe beg for a chance to learn those secrets.

"Okay, Superstar. You own *Super Mario*. But I bet I'll own you on *Ms. Pac-Man*."

I sighed in mock resignation. "Valorous. How many times do I have to tell you? It's Superstud. Guess I'll have to show you."

Taking her hand, I led the way over to the *Ms. Pac-Man* game. As we walked, I took advantage and skimmed the pad of my thumb over the silky skin on the back of her hand. She met me halfway when she gave my hand a tiny squeeze. That subtle move nearly had me tripping over my feet, something that hadn't happened to me with a girl since I was sixteen years old. Probably my reaction to her should have worried me. Instead, she made me want to pull her in close.

The practical side of my brain reminded me more physical contact wouldn't be a good idea in a public place. If the tabs hadn't already caught wind of where we were, it wasn't for lack of opportunity with the fans sneaking photos of us as soon as they recognized us. No doubt those pics flashed all over social media less than two seconds after they were snapped.

I bent down to whisper in her ear. "It's hot the way you like to play video games."

"It's even hotter when I win." Her flirty, nose-wrinkling grin had me tugging her a little closer.

A waiter appeared at our side. "Here you go, Mr. Tron. Miss Valor." He offered a beer to me and another margarita to Cristy.

"We didn't order these," I said at the same time Cristy grabbed her drink and took a sip.

"The guy over there"—he nodded over his shoulder at a fan waving at us with a big-ass grin on his face—"said he wanted to thank you for the great show you put on last night."

An uneasy feeling rolled through me even as I saluted the guy with my beer.

Cristy didn't seem to mind our growing entourage as we played our way through the arcade. In fact, at times she played to it, flirting with the fans with finger waves or asking them to cheer for her. Her sweet little body was made for showing off, and the way she could twirl and sashay and strike a pose said she enjoyed showing off for the crowd. That part I could have done without, but a scolding voice in my head reminded me this whole arcade thing had been my idea in the first place.

After we played to a tie in *Ms. Pac-Man*, I decided this part of our date was over. The crowd growing around us threatened to become something neither of us could handle without security. Catching sight of the arcade manager, I motioned her over to me.

"Do you have a back door to this place? Something off-limits to the general clientele?" I whispered to her.

This one wasn't much older than most of the serving staff, and she gave me a deer-in-the-headlights look that didn't bode well for my nerves.

"A way for us to leave without causing a riot?"

Seeming to shake herself out of her trance, she nodded. "Come with me."

I grabbed Cristy's hand and didn't give her time to protest as I pulled her behind me through the crowd. Since we'd been moving from game to game, people naturally assumed we were headed to the next game and gave us some space.

"Hey, where are you guys going?"

"Tron! Cristy! Can we have a picture?"

"They can't be leaving already. We just got here!"

The shouts and groans followed us as the manager led us through a door marked "Employees Only." Wisely, she flipped the lock when we passed through. Judging from all the pounding on the other side, people had figured out their evening entertainment was over.

"Thanks." Glancing around at the staff room I asked, "How do we get out of here?"

"Go out through that door." She pointed toward the back.

"Thanks again."

"Um, before you go, would it be—" She fidgeted with her hands, drew in a breath, and started again. "Would you let me take a selfie with you? Otherwise, none of my friends are going to believe this happened."

"Sure," Cristy said. "Where's your phone?"

The girl handed it to Cristy, and Cristy whipped off her ridiculous hat, wrapped her arm around the girl's shoulders, and said, "Grin!" She snapped the pic and turned to me. "Now your turn. I'll take a shot of the two of you."

The pounding outside the door intensified, and I worried about how much time we had before the fans made their way around the back of the restaurant. Still, the girl had helped us so far. I looped my arm around her shoulder and smiled.

"Now one with all of us." Cristy handed me the phone. "Your arms are longer, so you do the honors."

With a sigh, I did what she wanted.

"Now can we leave?"

"I suppose. It's just that I was really enjoying our date."

The hot look she shot me went straight to my groin, and more than anything, I wanted to spirit her out of there.

"Me too, but the natives had other plans."

I fished my phone from the pocket of my jeans and made a quick call.

"Where does that door lead?" I asked the manager.

"To a hallway behind the arcade then out to the boardwalk in the direction of the parking lot."

She was staring at the photos on her phone. No doubt they'd be all over social media about five seconds after we walked out. Not much time for making our getaway, especially with Cristy wearing those crazy heels of hers.

"Listen, can you give us about five minutes before you post those and open that other door?"

The expression on her face told me I was already too late for the first request. Never mind. With Cristy's hand in mine, we headed for the outside. "Thanks for your help," I called over my shoulder.

The corridor behind the restaurant seemed to stretch forever. We didn't have much time before those fans would show up again. This time, no doubt the scene could get ugly. Without asking permission, I scooped Cristy high in my arms and started moving down the hallway like we were late for a show.

"What the heck, Tron? Put me down. I can walk," she said, her tone all huffy.

"Not fast enough." I grinned at her. "Besides, I'm still trying to impress you. Is it working?"

"Oh, yeah. Your caveman skills are all kinds of impressive."

I think she was going for sardonic, but the breathy way the words came out told me she liked our current closeness as much as I did. The woman didn't weigh a thing, but she felt damn fine in my arms. The neon exit sign on the door at the end of the corridor was the main source of light, but it was enough to see the sparkle in her eyes. If I played this right, I'd be spending the night in a different hotel.

After shouldering my way through the door, I stopped to put Cristy down. Not wanting her to roll an ankle or something in her hot shoes, I let her go slowly, her body sliding down the length of mine. The feel of her curves as they traced their way from my chest to my thighs left me no choice but to hold her close when at last her feet touched the ground. Over the years, I'd held lots of women even closer to my body, but none of them lit me up the way she did. More than anything, I wanted to kiss her lush pouty lips, make her as hot and bothered as I was, but a camera flashed in front of me, tossing a bucket of ice water over the flames licking between us.

"Damn it," I hissed.

I dragged her behind me, desperate to escape to somewhere a helluva lot more private. Cristy squeaked, telling me I moved too fast for her—again. Knowing my next move would generate atomic fallout in the press, I stopped and scooped her up high in my arms anyway and all but ran down the boardwalk. The sound of camera shutters going off like firecrackers around us didn't quite drown out the shouts of people racing after us in my wake.

Somewhere along the line, Cristy's hat flew off, and she lunged to catch it, nearly tumbling us to the ground. The hours I spent in the weight rooms of every hotel where we stayed paid off as I used our momentum to right us, but her breathy voice in my ear came damn close to tripping me up.

"Isn't this fun, Tron? It's like a scene out of a movie."

"Let me get back to you on that," I said, panting.

Ahead of us I could see the tall gates leading out to the parking lot. If we were lucky, a town car would be idling by the curb when we burst through them.

There was no bursting through the gates. A busload of tourists surged onto the boardwalk right as we arrived. Someone in that crowd recognized Cristy, and in two seconds flat, we were surrounded. Reluctantly, I put her down, knowing I needed to be able to see in every direction, a difficulty when I held her. Still, I wrapped my arm tight around her, molding her to my side.

"Tron! Tron! Over here!"

"It's Cristy Valor. Oh my God, it's Cristy Valor!"

"Hey man, can we have a selfie with you?"

"Move out of the way. We want to see!"

"Balefire? Balefire is here?"

"Cristy! Cristy! Cristy!"

I tried to push our way through the throng of fans, but with it being only the two of us without security, we moved inches at a time as the crowd surged around us. Beside me, Cristy's rigid body told me the fun of teasing the crowds back at the arcade had worn off. We were in serious trouble, and I didn't have a clue how to get us out of it.

When someone wrenched her hat from her hands and someone else stole mine from the top of my head, my heart raced into triple time while the scene around me seemed to wind down into slow motion. On the periphery of the crowd, I saw a security guard on a radio. I raised my hand to him, motioning for help. A flash of a camera momentarily blinded me, and from somewhere nearby, a muffled scream echoed in my ears. Pandemonium broke out as a small army of police officers appeared as if by magic, and the crowd around us closed ranks.

Hands were all over me, and somehow, I lost hold of Cristy. I yelled for her when a pair of police officers yanked me forward and propelled me through the screeching fans. A lifetime later, I found myself hustled into the town car I'd called for. On the seat beside me, Cristy hugged her knees to her chest. The panic in her beautiful sapphire eyes undid me, and I reached for her. With a tiny cry, she shrank back into the corner of her seat, and I died a little inside.

Our date had started so well. She'd been as into me as I was into her. Then I'd fucked it all up by bringing her to Pier 39. Now her playful words reverberated through me like an accusation. She'd warned me. She'd also enjoyed playing to the fans in the arcade. Yet I should have foreseen how things could turn ugly. My band was the biggest rock 'n' roll show in the world. Cristy was a superstar in her own right. How I thought we could spend a day like a normal couple enjoying a cruise on San Francisco Bay and dinner at a regular restaurant proved how absurd and naïve I was. Now Cristy wanted nothing to do with me.

The time the driver spent navigating through the fans who insisted on seeing us dragged like hours. I didn't take a full breath until we were clipping along at a sedate seventy-five miles an hour on the freeway back to our hotels. So much for spending the night in a bed other than my own.

"I'm sorry, Cristy. I didn't think—" I ran my hands through my hair and sucked in a breath. "I didn't think." Of its own volition, my hand smoothed itself over her shin. When she didn't try to tug herself into a tighter little ball at the contact, I continued. "You were right. It was stupid to think we could enjoy the pier like everyone else. I'm so sorry."

For several long minutes, she stared out the window of the speeding car. A tiny shudder shook her body, and she huffed out a breath. At last, she looked at me. "It's not your fault, Tron. You couldn't know the fans would react that way." In a whisper, she added, "Or that I'd have a meltdown."

I slid across the seat until our bodies were as close to touching without touching as I dared. "It is my fault. I should have known a baseball cap and a sunhat and glasses wouldn't be enough of a disguise for going out in public without a security detail." Taking a chance, I slid my arm across back of the seat behind her. "I'm truly sorry, Valorous. I only wanted to show you a good time." I ducked my head down to catch her eyes. "Some of our date was fun, wasn't it?"

Though weak, at least she smiled. "Everything right up to the part when we came so close to making our getaway." A sigh escaped her. "That last part with the fans pushing and pulling at us, crowding us in until I couldn't breathe? Not so much."

"Does this mean"—I cleared my throat—"does this mean you'd be up for another date if I planned better, kept the craziness of the fans in mind and showed you a more private good time?"

"I'll think about it."

Her response might have panicked me except she let go of her legs and leaned her head on my chest as we finished the ride to her hotel in silence. She might not have outright agreed to another date, but her implicit trust was the next best thing.

Chapter Twelve

Cristy

"CRISTY, WHERE HAVE you been? Steve's in a total meltdown over your costume choices for tonight."

"Nice to see you too, Gretch. Did you have a good day?" The words were pretty. The edge in my voice? Not so much.

Tron had insisted on accompanying me to my hotel suite. At the door, he grinned sheepishly. "I hope the day's events didn't scar you for life." Like me, somewhere along the line he'd lost his hat too. He stood in front of me running his hands through his hair like he had more to say but didn't know how to say it. At last, he said, "I should let you get ready for the show tonight." But the heat in his eyes said something else.

I left him hanging as I let myself into my suite.

Gretchen's haranguing the second I walked through door had me seriously rethinking that choice.

"You said you'd be back an hour ago. Cutting it this close to the show doesn't give your team enough time to take care of you right. Did you think of that?"

"I left my mom behind ten years ago for a reason, Gretchen.

Did *you* think of that?" I tossed my jacket over a nearby chair on my way to the bathroom.

Her expression mirrored a slap to the face, not that I cared at the moment. I could have told her about the crowds, the claustrophobia, the panic attack that always came whenever I found myself in a situation similar to all those times my parents and their church friends pressed themselves around me, against me, trying to squeeze the demons out of me. I could have told her about it, and she would have understood. But her bossiness on this tour irritated me in a way it never had before. Never mind that I paid her. At the moment, I needed my friend, not my manager. There had been a time when she would have intuited that from my demeanor alone.

After I slammed the door to the bathroom, I shot the lock and rested my palms on the vanity. For several long minutes, I let myself breathe. Closing my eyes, I thought back on the afternoon. Adam put some real thought and effort into our date. After a decade of hookups and one-night stands, interrupted by the occasional brief publicity affair with another celebrity, it was nice to feel cherished for once. Our date wasn't the same as dates I'd had with other stars. My date with Adam was more like two people whose interest in each other meant learning about each other—outside the sack. I shuddered.

It felt real.

If I wasn't careful, Adam could obliterate all my carefully constructed walls. Those walls protected me, kept my secrets safe. No way could I let him in to see the real me, Cristy Rains not Cristy Valor. What would he think of the girl whose parents beat her with a switch while reciting Bible verses? He'd think I was a fruitcake, a certifiable nutcase, that's what. Nobody in this day and age grew up the way I did. When I was a kid, one glance around my classroom at school confirmed that. Honestly, it was a wonder I had any friends at all when I was growing up. If he ever found out about my past, he'd walk away too—like everyone else in my life.

Except for Gretchen.

Guilt swept through me. Blowing out a breath, I unlocked the bathroom door and stepped back into my suite.

She and Steve, my dresser, were standing in the middle of the room in heated conversation. Standing beside the door connecting our suites, Gretchen's partner, Kelsey watched with her arms crossed over her chest, concern on her face.

"I'm sorry. She does this sometimes. I'm sure you had one or two similar experiences when you worked for Mali, right?" I overheard Gretchen say, her tone placating.

"It's my ass here. I have a wife and a kid at home who expect me to keep my job. I don't need her firing me because she doesn't like the outfits I picked out for her when she didn't show up to vet the damn things when she said she would," Steve hissed.

"No one's getting fired. Not today anyway."

Steve's eyes skittered away from me while Gretchen regarded me with an are-you-done-now? expression.

Smoothing my hand down her arm, I laced my fingers with hers. "I'm sorry for snapping at you, Gretch."

Steve gasped. "Oh my God. What have you done to that T-shirt? There is absolutely nothing artistic about the way it's ripped." He fingered my shirt where a few overzealous fans had helped themselves to some of its fabric.

"Not my doing." I gave his shoulder a little pat. "Listen, I'm sorry I didn't make the meeting today. Tron and I might have accidentally caused a bit of a scene down on the pier." Gretchen's hand squeezed mine like a vise, but I kept going. "Whatever you've chosen for tonight will be fine I'm sure, Steve. In the few shows we've done so far, you've had excellent ideas. I'll wear whatever you prepared."

The comical expression on his face tugged a smile from me. "Are you for real? You're leaving your show in my hands?" He sounded like he'd won the lottery or something.

His response gave me the giggles. Or maybe I was coming down from the adrenaline rush of nearly being crushed to death by hyper-excited fans. When I finally could speak coherently, the affronted look on his face almost set me off again. With a superhuman effort, I controlled myself and said, "Sorry. I had a wild afternoon." I swiped at the last of the tears streaming down my face and smiled at him. "You're not in charge of the show, Steve. Just my outfits."

"What you wear grabs about as much attention as what you sing, Cristy-girl. You know that," Gretchen said.

Her expression told me I might have grown another head, but she should have known by now how much I enjoyed shaking things up.

"Tonight you're in charge of whatever impression I make, Steve. I'm trusting you to do something awesome, and by awesome, I mean outrageous." I winked. "Cut loose. Have some fun. I'm game to give you a shot at being in charge of half the show."

Steve raced to the door of my suite.

"Who set your pants on fire?" Gretchen called after him.

"I'm headed to the stadium to prep everything before she changes her mind." He wrenched the door open and ran down the hall.

Gretchen blinked at the closed door. "What just happened?" Rounding on me, she said, "Steve's only been with us for this tour. How do you know you can trust him not to make you look ridiculous? What if he's still in touch with Mali and takes his cues from her?"

"Gretchen," Kelsey warned as she folded my jacket and seated herself in the chair.

I smiled at Kelsey and turned back to my friend now in full-on manager mode. "Have faith, Gretch. We both interviewed him. We both signed off on his designs. Making me look ridiculous won't advance his career, especially when I'm wearing my costumes on the biggest rock 'n' roll stage on the planet right now." I downed the shot of vodka I'd poured myself at the minibar and set up another. "I need a shower."

"I need a shot."

Without a word, I splashed vodka in two more glasses, handing one to Kelsey and raising mine to Gretchen who snagged the other. Her eyes never left mine as we shot the alcohol. She swiped the back of her hand over her mouth and thumped her glass on the counter.

"What happened today?" The concern in her eyes nearly undid me. Even when I acted like a bitch diva, Gretchen always had my back.

I blew a breath at the ceiling and faced the music. "Tron took me on a date."

"I'm aware." Something in her tone shot my eyes to hers.

"He showed me a great time. A cruise out in the bay, a trip to the pier, dinner, arcade games. It was a perfect afternoon." I made my way over to the couch and sank into its welcoming cushions.

"What did you do, Cristy?"

Did I mention how much I really hate the way Gretchen knows me so well?

Dropping my head to the back of the couch, I closed my eyes against her all-seeing ones.

"Cristy." The way she drew out my name told me her patience danced on the edge of nonexistent.

"The fans in the restaurant and the arcade were such fun."

"So you flirted with them."

Opening one eye, I caught the censure in hers. "Tron was being so discreet. I should have followed his lead. But he's so damn hot, and we were on a date, and I maybe wanted to show that off a little bit."

She joined me on the couch, angling herself toward me, her hand on my knee. "Let me guess. The fans decided you'd given them an invitation to join your date."

"Something like that." Shivering, I crossed my arms over my chest, holding onto myself. "Tron tried to spirit us out of there, and he probably would have been successful if the manager of the restaurant had been a little older or a little less of a fan." The memory of being held close to his chest washed over me, and I shivered again for a different reason. My core clenched as I remembered the heat and strength of his big body cradling and shielding me. Even now when his touch remained nothing but a wisp of sensation in my mind, my body swelled and tightened for him.

My friend's steady presence beside me dragged out the rest. "We could see the gates to the pier, and we almost made it to them when a busload of foreign tourists flowed in, and we had to try to weave our way through them. Some of them recognized us and tried to stop us to take photos." I swallowed down the bile rising in my throat. Beside me, Gretchen kept a steady pressure with her palm on my knee, reassuring me.

"They crowded you, didn't they?" she asked quietly.

I affirmed her question with a shaky nod. Nothing else needed saying. She pulled me into her arms and held me close while I let go of the emotions roiling through me. From somewhere behind me, Kelsey ghosted a reassuring hand over my shoulder.

A knock on the door reminded us I had a job to do.

"Cristy? Gretchen?" My makeup artist Jillian Barlow's voice sounded muffled outside my suite. "Time to do your face. And I brought snacks."

After one last hug, Gretchen stood and offered me a hand up. "Showtime, Cristy-girl. Are you up for it?"

"You know me, Gretch. I'm always up for the show."

The expression on her face questioned my sincerity, but she didn't need to worry. Two shots of vodka, a few minutes of understanding with my best friend, and the promise of seeing Adam again soon were enough to motivate me into the bathroom.

"Out in five minutes. Ten tops."

Jillian rapped on the door again.

"You want to get that while I shower, please?"

Without waiting for a response, I stepped into the bathroom

and made short work of cleaning the afternoon from my body. As I washed, I couldn't help but wonder what would have happened at the end of my date with Tron if the world hadn't decided to crash it. I could almost taste his manly breath when a vision of that near kiss outside the arcade flashed through my thoughts. Phantom heat warmed my side where it had nestled against his body as we made our escape. No doubt I would have missed wardrobe today no matter what, but I'd have preferred ticking off my team because of an afternoon in Adam's bed than for the reason I was late.

While I sat in the chair with a cloth draped over me, Jillian worked her magic on my face. In the mirror's reflection, I could easily see my manager and her lady engaging in some playful PDA. Kelsey popped a grape into her mouth then pushed another one between Gretchen's waiting lips as Gretchen fingered Kelsey's hair. From past observation, I knew Gretch's next move would be to slide her hand behind Kelsey's nape to haul her in for a kiss.

Yep, right on cue. This time they were gentle, easy with each other, and I let out a tiny sigh. They didn't look like they were going to get carried away, maybe sneak next door for a quickie before Jillian finished with me. Normally, I was never jealous of Gretchen and Kelsey's relationship. After Kelsey figured out I had zero romantic interest in Gretchen—or in her—she relaxed. Usually, it was a good thing when she took time off to join us on tour. Today, I secretly wished she needed to be back at the office. Watching the two of them enjoying each other while I endured the frustration of a truncated afternoon ticked me off.

In front of me, Jillian cleared her throat. "I need you to relax, Cristy. You're creasing the foundational layer, which will mess up everything that comes after." She sounded apologetic, like she was the one who'd screwed up.

"Sorry, Jill."

I closed my eyes to the scene of relationship bliss playing out on the couch, but it wasn't enough.

"Hang on a second."

Leaving my gaping makeup artist at her station, I strolled into my bedroom and grabbed my earbuds from the nightstand. As I walked back into the suite, I scrolled through my playlists on my phone, settling on a medley of Balefire deep cuts from some of their early albums. I sat back down, arranging myself for Jillian's best light, closed my eyes, and zeroed in on Tron's bass lines. Within seconds, my entire body hummed, and I crossed my legs to hold onto the way his music always made me react.

Too soon, Jillian pronounced me perfect, and I blinked open my eyes. Checking her work in the mirror never got old. The woman was a certified genius with a handful of brushes and a tackle-box of face paints and powders. I let the song finish before I removed my earbuds and set them on the table beside my phone. It took me a second to catch on that Jillian and I were the only ones in the room. I shot her a look, and she smiled sheepishly back at me.

"They left right after you closed your eyes."

I pressed a number on my phone. After five rings, the call went to voicemail. My message was short and to the point. "Ten min-utes. Tops."

Ignoring the pink tinging Jillian's cheeks as she busied herself with the tools of her trade, I pulled the cape off and tossed it over the back of the chair. Not knowing what Steve planned for tonight's wardrobe left me in a bit of a dilemma about my underwear. Adam's face flashed uninvited into my mind, and I grinned. There would be more than one show tonight, I decided. The first show for the fans could take care of itself. I needed to take special care of the way I dressed for the second, private one.

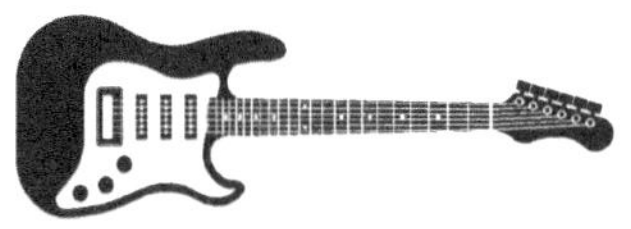

Chapter Thirteen

Cristy

GRETCHEN WORRIED ABOUT Steve for nothing. The way the man put together my costume changes for our second stadium show in San Francisco had me entertaining thoughts of giving him a raise. He gave my outfits a rock 'n' roll edge that let me be me but also allowed me to fit in with a bunch of rock gods who started their shows in leather or jean jackets before eventually stripping down to T-shirts with their jeans. Except for Dakota. That guy gave me a run for biggest showoff. By the end of the show, sweat poured off his sculpted body, highlighting his ink and elevating him to something sublime. I couldn't blame the fans for loving him.

Still, I spent most of my set playing to Tron. The plain white T-shirt he wore to start the show accentuated the gorgeous golden-brown tones of his skin and made his hair look even blacker than usual. As the show continued, his sweat molded the cotton shirt to the strong muscles of his chest, shoulders, and arms. The man could win any wet T-shirt contest ever. From the shower of lingerie puddled on the stage in front of him, it was obvious I wasn't the only fan who thought that way. When he changed into a black

T-shirt before the encore, I wanted to tear it to shreds for hiding his drool-worthy body.

When I joined the band onstage, Adam's eyes followed me every-where. Even when I didn't sing or dance around or directly in front of him, when I was flirting with Jack or Dakota or singing harmonies with Blu, I could sense his eyes on me. After I sang my second song, he managed to ask how I was. I knew what he meant. I flashed him my most brilliant smile and winked. There was no way I'd ever let him know what had really happened to me in that crowd at the end of our date.

He cocked his head, so I blew him a kiss. That coaxed a smile from him, and we both relaxed and enjoyed the rest of the show. My favorite part was when I lured him away from his preferred spot back by Jack's massive drum kit to join me at the front of the stage as I sang "Hot For Me." I may or may not have teased the heck out of him as I danced and sassed and smiled through the song, directing all of it at him. During the little performance I put on for Adam, I caught Blu and Dakota exchanging glances, but the crowd ate it up.

After that song, I backed it off. For the rest of my part of the concert, I divided my time equally among the guys and reserved my biggest flirts for the audience. Though I hadn't tuned in to social media or the tabs since our afternoon date, I had no doubt specula-tion about us ran rampant among the fans and in the media already. It was a scenario in which I'd played a starring role in the past, so I already knew the drill. But this thing with Adam was different, and I wasn't ready to deal with the rest of the world over it.

When the final notes of the show floated away over the stadium and we took our last bows, I headed straight for my dressing room. Our afternoon together promised some things it didn't deliver. I intended to remedy that.

Adam

Like she'd read my thoughts, Cristy stepped out of her dressing room right as I lifted my hand to knock on her door. She'd spent our entire show teasing me, flirting with me, and now I wanted her to make good on those promises.

"Every show is even more of a rush than the last one," she said, a wicked grin playing over her mouth. "Makes me so hot. What about you? Are you wound as tight as I am?"

She slid her hands over my chest, and I sucked in a breath. Before I could reply, she said, "Yeah, you're right there too."

She didn't give me a chance to ask what she meant as she pushed into me enough that I staggered and maybe had to grab hold of her hips to steady myself. Laughing that throaty laugh of hers, the one that stirred my cock every damn time, she crowded me until she had my back against the wall of the dimly lit hallway outside her dressing room. Running her tongue over her gorgeous plump lips, she warned me, but I was slow to catch on. When I tried to lean in to taste that mouth, she winked and in one smooth motion dropped to her knees in front of me.

Before I could even react, she had my fly open, my jeans and boxers pushed down my thighs, her hands busy stroking my everready cock.

Covering her hands with my own, I hissed, "Cristy! Jesus! What are you doing?"

"Taking care of all that post-concert adrenaline." Giving my package an appreciative once-over, she added, "Because clearly, you need someone to do that for you."

"You don't have to—aaahh!"

That beautiful sassy mouth of hers shut off any coherent thought I might have entertained as she went to town on me. Helpless to do anything but let her have her way, I placed my hands on her silky blond cap of hair like I was giving her a benediction. But that woman was the one taking me to heaven. The way she worked me over with her lips and tongue was probably illegal in several states. Her fingers stroking and rolling my balls left me powerless to do anything but thrust into her even though I tried to hold back.

Hollowing her cheeks, she stroked up hard, my cock leaving her mouth on a pop. The sapphire jewels of her eyes glittered up at me as she stared into my eyes. "Holding back is *not* an option here, Tron. I want everything, and you're going to give it to me. I warned you. I *always* get what I want."

For good measure, she warned me a second time with her hand squeezing and jacking my cock. Without taking her eyes from mine, she took me deep into her mouth, her tongue doing nasty beautiful things to the underside of my cock, and I lost it. I nearly knocked myself out as I threw my head back against the wall, my hips pistoning forward. As I thrust into her, the back of her throat spasmed around me, skyrocketing my pleasure as she swallowed me down.

A long time later as she continued to lick and kiss my still half-hard dick, I dropped my head forward. She stared up at me with something like wonder in her eyes, and I blew out a breath. "Jesus H., Cristy. Where the fuck did you learn to do that?"

She tugged my boxers and jeans back up as she stood in front of me. "Glad you enjoyed yourself," she said with an impish little grin.

Grabbing me by my shoulders, she pulled me from the wall and reversed our positions. "My turn."

Oh, yeah. I definitely wanted to fulfill that particular demand. Dropping to my knees in front of her, I saw she still had on the Dorothy stilettos she'd worn onstage, the glittery red ones each with a big bow across the top. "Love these shoes, Cristy. They give me all kinds of ideas."

"I have ideas too. Beginning with what it's going to feel like to have your mouth on me."

Chuckling, I said, "You really do expect to get your way."

"Always."

Grinning at her bravado, I palmed my way from her ankles to her hips, my hands savoring the silk of her skin. She let out a breathy little sigh, as I reached up beneath the neon orange spandex miniskirt shielding her from my view. Sliding my hands around behind her, I squeezed the perfect globes of her ass then hooked my fingers in the waistband of her panties and slowly dragged them off her.

She stepped out of one side, leaving the scrap of white lace clinging to the bright red bow of her shoe. I wanted to take a second to enjoy that view—white lace on bright red sequins—but she had other ideas, plunging her hands into my hair, silently urging me back to business.

"Wider, Cristy. I need some room," I demanded, my voice sounding hoarse in my ears.

She obliged, her skirt riding up to the crease where her thighs met her hips. My dick, the greedy bastard, twitched as I breathed in the musky scent of sex and woman. My eyes cruised over her landing strip, a dark brown totally at odds with the golden blond on her head.

"You're a brunette."

"I can dye that part of me too if you prefer blondes."

"Pretty damn happy with what I'm lookin' at here, doll."

Before she could say anything else, I planted my face in her gorgeous pussy. The hard nub of her clit jumped at the flick of my tongue before I starting sucking her like I could pull every sweet drop of sunshine from her body. She moaned from the first taste, her hips circling, and I clamped one hand on her ass to hold her right where I wanted her. Parting her folds to add one finger then two, I worked her, smiling in delight against her skin as she burrowed her fingers into my hair and tugged.

Going down on a woman always turned me on, but there was something special about Cristy. Something that had the blood roaring in my ears as I lapped and kissed and sucked her. When she sagged against the wall, I held her up with my shoulders. Her knees wobbled at the attention I gave her pussy as I enjoyed her, making me feel like a superhero pleasuring Wonder Woman.

At last a sound penetrated the roar of blood, adrenaline, and sex in my ears.

"Adam! Adam! Adam!" Cristy chanted in her sexy alto voice.

Something inside my chest loosened, shifted, rearranged itself, came together, and locked. I drew a long breath in through my nose and noticed for the first time in my life, I felt free.

No other woman had ever called my name during sex. Always the last name—the stage persona I created when I was sixteen. Cristy called me out, exposed me, but I couldn't stop working her until she screamed my name loud enough to bring down the house.

And then she did.

I licked my lips in satisfaction and didn't even try to suppress the grin spreading over my mouth at the expression of pure bliss on her beautiful face when I looked up at her. Slowly, she blinked her eyes open, coming to from the orgasm I'd given her. When she looked down and locked eyes with me, I could see shock and something else there for a second before she pulled in a deep breath and looked somewhere behind me.

She pasted on her stage smile and said, "Well, that little mystery is solved."

"Which one?"

"The one about the incredible rhythm one can expect from a bassist."

I stood up, towering over her despite her sexy stiletto shoes. "You have a *passing* idea about a bassist's incredible rhythm, but I'm game to show you all of it." I stuck my fingers in my mouth and sucked off her come. Those colors in her eyes darkened as she watched me savor every last drop for both of our pleasure.

She blinked, and I couldn't resist the temptation of her soft skin. Skimming my knuckles along the contours of her cheek, I enjoyed her momentary loss of composure as she closed her eyes and relaxed into my touch.

When I leaned down to kiss her, another voice I didn't enjoy so much interrupted.

"Cristy! Cristy, where are you? People are waiting," her manager called from somewhere down the hall.

The noise of her manager ruined the spell we'd woven over each other. Cristy's eyes widened, and she pushed me away from her and stepped out of her panties completely. Her eyes never leaving mine, she squatted down and retrieved them, stood, and stuffed them into the front pocket of my jeans.

"Another concert souvenir," she whispered then she shimmied her skirt down over her hips, sucked in a deep breath, squared her shoulders, and walked away from me toward the sound of her manager.

"Lighten up, Gretch. Can't a girl take a few minutes to herself after a show?"

Dumbfounded, I stared after her. She'd rocked my world completely off its axis and walked away like all we'd done was discuss the weather.

Oh *fuck* that.

She looked back at me one last time, stared pointedly at my crotch with a little zipping gesture, and shot me a saucy grin as she strutted away.

"Damn it. Cristy, hang on a sec," I insisted as I jerked my jeans back up and zipped the fly.

Like she didn't hear me at all, she kept moving. For such a tiny thing, the woman could eat up ground when she put her mind to it. I hustled after her, but she stepped through the green room door into the party and out of sight before I could catch her.

CHAPTER FOURTEEN

Cristy

GRETCHEN DRAGGED ME into the party and off to the side out of the way.

"The press is everywhere at this little gathering. Not sure whose idea that was, but I thought I should warn you." She looked like she had something else to say before she narrowed her eyes at me. "You're a bit flushed, Cristy-girl. Something happen I should know about?"

"Such as?"

Staring past my shoulder toward the door behind us, she smiled like the Cheshire cat. "Such as you and Tron being the last of us to the party. Both of you looking a bit flushed."

"I think I need a drink. Or maybe an entire line of shots. Think you can arrange that for me, world's greatest manager?"

"Cristy-go-to-church! You did Tron, didn't you?"

"Not so loud," I hissed. "Didn't you tell me there's press everywhere in here?"

"Is he as 'rhythmic' at sex as he is with his bass?"

"Gretchen, you're not into men, remember?"

"Yeah, but you're my friend and my job, and I like it best for my job when my friend is happy." Her eyes narrowed. "He did make you happy, didn't he?"

She smoothed her hand up and down my arm, reminding me of a time long ago when she wanted to be the one to make me happy—so we experimented and figured out she couldn't, at least not in that way. Instead of letting our differences divide us, she became my champion and my protector. Most of the time, I liked her best in those roles. Yet for some reason, this felt different, like an intrusion into my personal space.

"There she is!" someone with a camera called.

For once I welcomed the interruption of the press since it meant I didn't have to hurt my best friend's feelings by asking her to back off. My reaction threw me. I never thought this situation would happen between us. Ever.

"That was some show you put on out there, Cristy. What's it like playing with the wildest rock band in the world?"

"What's it like for you to watch the show?" I couldn't help it. I loved to mess with the press.

"Over the top."

This guy with his band T-shirt, skinny jeans, and Chucks looked and sounded more like a groupie than a journalist.

"My thoughts exactly."

"You and Tron. Are you a thing?"

I batted my eyes and simpered. "I never kiss and tell." Deliberately, I turned my attention to the reporter standing next to him. "Bad form," I said, sotto voice, like the guy was in on my secrets.

"You two seemed pretty chummy out on Pier 39 this afternoon. Any truth to the rumors?"

The avid way the guy asked the question sent alarm bells clanging in my head. But I smiled serenely at him. "I wouldn't know. I haven't heard the rumors."

I tried not to react as Adam sauntered up behind the paparazzi and saluted me with a beer. "Want one?" he mouthed.

"Excuse me, fellas. My date's here. Enjoy the party."

Because their press passes were privileged, the reporters didn't dare try to impede me as I stepped between them. It didn't stop their incessant and intrusive questions or their cameras flashing like a bad night at a car wreck. Gretchen materialized beside me and herded the reporters to their designated area for the post-concert press conference Balefire's jerk of a manager had thought would be a good idea.

Adam handed me a beer and whispered for my ears only, "That escapade you initiated in the hallway a few minutes ago? Consider that the opening act."

I sputtered on a sip of beer, and he rubbed his hand "helpfully" over my back, sizzling my blood with white-hot heat. My mind screamed. *Step away from the rock god*, but my body pushed back, seeking more contact with his big bass player's hand.

When Gretchen grabbed my arm and dragged me to the make-shift dais set up in the green room, I couldn't decide if I wanted to kick or kiss her. One look back at the banked fires smoldering in the dark brown depths of Adam's eyes decided for me. Kiss her. Definitely kiss her. That "escapade" as he called it still reverberated between my legs.

I'd initiated that little party as a way of saying thank you for the date and to assure Adam I was fine. Everything was good. In a million years I could never have predicted my response to him—or his to me. The man called me trouble, but he was danger like a ten-alarm fire. If I wasn't careful, he could burn down all my carefully constructed walls, and that wouldn't do at all.

Adam

Cristy spent the entire after-party running from me. Every time I moved close to her, she found a reason to move away from me. Yet her eyes followed me, teased me, enticed me to keep up the chase.

Several of the pro athletes in attendance worked hard for her attention too, but she deftly gave them the slip without offending any of them. Watching her give a master class on tease and retreat added to the night's entertainment. The woman was a pro at flirting without crossing the line into making a promise.

Except with me.

She'd made a promise to me when she initiated that mind-blowing encounter after the concert—and when she responded to me with more honesty than I'd ever experienced with a woman. Thinking about it forced me to adjust the fly of my jeans. The few beers I'd drunk had done nothing to dull the desire throbbing through my veins every time my eyes wandered over her perfect curves or my ear caught the honeyed rasp of her voice.

Finally, I had enough of the chase. Sidling up behind her as she laughed at some joke the 49ers quarterback told her, I slid my hand over her belly and drew her back against my chest. "Are you ready to finish our date?" I whispered in her ear.

The full-body shiver she gifted me left me rock-hard, something I discreetly let her know when I rubbed my dick along the cleft of her ass as I held her close.

"Tron, have you met Drew Chambers?" Her breathy voice had me tugging her tighter against me.

Setting my beer on the bar, I reached past Cristy to shake the man's hand. "Nice to meet you, man. You enjoy the show?"

Drew glanced from Cristy to my outstretched hand before taking my offer. "It was a rush, Tron. For a minute there at the end, I was afraid the fans might stomp down the stadium."

"A little bit like the way they reacted when you guys won the Super Bowl last year, huh?" I smiled, retrieved my beer, and took a drink, but my other hand never let go of Cristy.

"You a fan?"

I laughed. "I was born and raised in Denver. That answer your question?"

The man grinned good-naturedly. "Fair enough." Returning his attention to Cristy, he said, "So—"

The guy had some nerve ignoring my claim on her. I cut him off before he could embarrass himself. "Babe, the car is waiting," I said, rubbing my cheek over the silk of her hair, but my eyes were on the quarterback.

"Um, Tron—"

"Nice to meet you," Drew said. "I'm a big fan"—he flicked his eyes from me to Cristy—"of both of you." The hot look he gave her left nothing to the imagination. "If you're ever back in San Francisco, Cristy, look me up."

Yeah, no.

I wrapped my other arm around her and held her close to me. "Time to go, Valorous."

"It was fun talking to you, Drew. I'm a big fan of yours too." She gave him a megawatt smile, but that was a consolation prize.

I took her hand and dragged her away from her conquest. We made it out the door of the green room when she balked. "Okay, Caveman. You mind telling me what your problem is?"

Those sapphire eyes spit blue fire, telling me she'd taken it easy on the shots tonight. Good.

"I don't have one single problem, babe." I stepped into her, my hands going to her waist. "What I have is a promise, one you gave me the first time we locked eyes at our first rehearsal." Her body softened a fraction beneath my hands as she stared at my chest. "One you've continued to make at each of our shows when you spend most of your set playing with me." With one finger, I lifted her chin, demanding she look me in the eyes. "One you made tonight when you dropped to your knees for me."

A tiny gasp was all she spared me, so I went for broke, all the cards on the table. "And I made a promise to you when I willingly—and quite pleasurably—dropped to my knees and gave in to your demands."

Desire flared in her eyes.

"Now the only question is"—I smirked—"your place or mine? We need to tell the driver who's waiting with the motor running right outside."

"What are you starting here, Tron?" Her bitchy tone didn't fool me for one second.

"Nothing, babe." Bending down, I whispered in her ear, "I'm finishing what you started." When I traced the shell of her ear with my tongue, she rewarded me with a full-body shiver. I fished her lacy white panties from the front pocket of my jeans and dangled them from one finger in front of her. "These are the sweetest invitation I've ever received." Stuffing my prize back into my pocket, I continued. "You did mean them as invitation, didn't you?" Wrapping my hand around the nape of her neck, I rubbed my thumb along the column of her throat and waited. For all her bravado, the lady struggled with hiding her true feelings when I had my hands on her. I'd figured that out damn fast during our too-brief encounter in this same hallway after the show.

"My place." The words came out on a sigh.

For good measure, I kissed her on the sweet spot behind her ear and led her out to the town car idling at the curb outside. After I helped her into our ride, I slid in behind her, careful to give her space. Our first time may have happened in a hallway, but I damn sure wasn't interested in the groupie experience in the back of the limo. Cristy deserved much better than that.

So did I.

Tapping the driver on the shoulder, I told him which hotel and pushed the button to activate the partition between us. With a sigh, I closed my eyes, leaned my head back on the cushion, and let the quiet wash over me. It was a risk not pushing her, not heating her up in the car. But the ride to the hotel was thirty minutes, and I had no doubt if I touched her before we arrived, the driver would get an eyeful when we reached our destination. He might even have to take a turn or two around the block. Usually with a groupie, that wouldn't bother me. But for some reason, I wanted to be alone with Cristy in a place where there wasn't a chance we'd be disturbed.

Beside me, I heard a bunch of squirming and sighing, but she didn't say a word. I cracked open one eye and watched her uncross and recross her legs then tug her short skirt a millimeter farther down her creamy thigh. She huffed out another sigh and stared out at the light show masquerading as San Francisco at night. All that activity drew my attention to her long legs and barely there skirt. As I stared at the neon orange of the spandex hugging her close, I remembered where her panties were.

Damn it.

Now I was the one trying to suppress a sigh while I adjusted myself behind the fly of my jeans. "The leather of these seats is butter soft. Can't imagine why you're having so much trouble finding a comfy spot."

"Hitting the sheets was your big idea. Now it appears you've lost interest."

Those pouty lips nearly undid me. "Trust me, Valorous. I'm plenty interested."

"Then why—"

"We're headliners, not groupies. I'm not above a quickie in the limo with a willing woman looking for a good time. But that's not who you are." I slid my arm along the back of the seat behind her. "I intend to take my time with you, savor you, make you come so hard you'll know you've seen heaven." Because I couldn't help it, I traced my fingers up and down the smooth column of her neck and smiled at the way she white-knuckled her hands clasped together in her lap.

"You're pretty impressed with your skills," she said, but the way she forced her words through gritted teeth told me how much I affected her.

"As I recall, my skills impressed the hell out of you after the show." Angling myself more toward her, I made sure she saw me adjust myself in my jeans. "I'm looking forward to experiencing more of your skills too."

"Tron!" she squeaked, and squeezed her legs together tight, like she held a row of dimes between them. "If you're not going to take care of business in this car"—she swallowed hard—"then you should probably sit on the other seat." She nodded in the direction of the bench seat across from us.

"What would be the fun in that?"

She considered that for a second then lifted her eyes to mine. Warning bells clanged in my head, and it was my turn to back up. Cristy challenged me with her palm slowly gliding from my knee to a spot barely south of my groin. Mischief sparkled in those sapphire eyes I wanted to lose myself in every time I looked into them. "You're right. What would be the fun in that?" She increased the pressure on my thigh, her index finger brushing ever-so-lightly over the fly of my jeans, daring me.

There was no doubt who would win this game of chicken. I lifted one side of my mouth in half a grin and traced my index finger over the silky skin of her exposed thigh. Teasing her, I drew lazy patterns over her skin and delighted in the way her breath hitched at my touch. Unlike her, I didn't stop playing until I'd made my way under her skirt, the pad of my finger zeroing in on her swollen clit.

"Adam!" She clamped her hand on my wrist but made no other move to stop me.

"Uh-huh?"

Her eyes narrowed at my nonchalant response, and I deliberately relaxed my body. No way in hell would I let her know how close I'd been to going off in my jeans at the whisper touch of her finger gliding over my package.

"I thought you said we weren't doing this in the car."

"Doing what? Having a conversation? Why wouldn't we have a conversation?" I asked as I petted her swollen clit with the pad of my finger.

She narrowed her eyes, and I grinned. Playing chicken with Cristy ranked as my new favorite fun activity to do on tour. The way she squirmed at my touch, like she couldn't decide if she wanted to run toward or away from me excited me almost as much as discovering how wet she was. I slid my finger lower, teasingly tracing the full folds of her pussy, and she squeezed her eyes shut, sucked in a breath, and held it. Fearing the stubborn woman might turn blue, I slipped inside her and pumped my finger in and out, in and out until my name exploded from her lips.

"Adam! Oh, Adam. Don't stop."

The raw desire in her eyes would have dropped me if I hadn't already been sitting down.

"Please. Don't. Stop."

Somewhere along the line, Cristy had relaxed her thighs, allowing me better access to her hot center. She was so tight, but still I added another finger and changed the angle, finding her G-spot easily, judging from the way she surged up off the seat. It was my name on her lips that did it. I could have held out, teased her the whole drive to the hotel, if she hadn't said my name. Did I mention what a turn-on that was for me? How the woman figured that out, I'll never know. Didn't much care, to tell the truth. But damn, if it didn't work for me.

When she surged off the seat, I shifted my arm behind her back so I could wrap my hand around her breast as I continued to pleasure her pussy. For such a tiny thing, she had enough up top to spill out of my hand as I squeezed and tested her curves, paying special attention to her nipple pebbled beneath the silk of her shirt and the lace of her bra.

The breathy way she panted my name wound me up as I watched her beautiful expression change from surprised to desperate as she chased her orgasm. Without warning, she clamped down on my fingers and screamed my name so loud, I'm sure passing cars heard her. Her baby backbend off the seat pushed her pretty breast into the palm of my hand, and I squeezed hard. I didn't let her up either, pumping my fingers inside her until at last, she sighed and relaxed like she was melting into the leather of the seat.

She tasted like peaches and woman as I licked her come from my fingers. When she watched my tongue caress my fingers, her eyes darkened almost to black before a spark of mischief flared in them. Anticipating her next move, I pinned her hands on her lap. A slow grin curved her lips.

"That was some conversation, Tron."

So we're back to being acquaintances, huh? Fuck that.

"I liked it better when you called me by my name." I brushed my finger over her pouty lower lip, and she took the hint, opening for me and finishing off the last of her sweet come.

Her eyes rounded innocently when I tugged my fingers out of her mouth on a sucking pop. "I thought everyone called you Tron. That is your name, right?"

"That's not what I meant."

Confusion furrowed her brow as I watched the wheels turning in her mind. Then something like panic crossed her features. "You know we're just having fun here. It's nothing serious."

"I'm all about fun, Cristy." I ghosted my finger over the smooth skin of her cheek. "But it's more fun when you use my name."

The car slowed as the driver wheeled it around the half-circle entrance to the hotel. Directing her gaze to her skirt as she tugged it down again, she said, "I'll keep that in mind."

It was a start.

A start? Wait. What the hell was I thinking?

Chapter Fifteen

Cristy

"FAIR WARNING," I said as I slid the key card over the sensor. "Gretchen may invite herself into my room at some point tonight."

"You two like to share?" Adam stuffed his hands in his pockets. "I thought she was into women."

I snorted as I pushed the door open and flipped on a lamp. "She's happily hooked up with her girlfriend Kelsey." I tossed the key card onto a nearby table as I walked over to the minibar. "But she thinks everything I do is her business."

We hadn't spoken again until we'd stood in front of the door to my suite, which was fine by me. Something happened between us in that town car, something I didn't want to think about right now.

Adam stepped up behind me, his hands heavy on my shoulders. The subtle pressure stopped me from reaching for the partially full bottle of Jameson beckoning me. "Is everything you do her business?"

His warm breath on my neck sent hot shivers over my skin. "Um—"

"We're here because we want to be alone. No paparazzi. No fans." He breathed a kiss on my nape. "No friends."

Right as I swayed back into him, he stepped away from me, and I nearly landed on my butt. The snick of the deadbolt sliding home told me he meant to have me all to himself. But Gretchen didn't always use the front door to let herself in. He winked at me and sauntered into my bedroom. Out of curiosity, I followed him and stared wide-eyed as he locked the deadbolt to the adjoining room.

"Did I say that out loud?"

He stalked toward me, the desire swirling in the depths of his dark brown eyes lighting fires deep inside me. "You didn't have to." He stopped in front of me, close enough so I could feel his body heat wash over me, but he didn't touch. "I watch you Cristy. You know that."

I didn't even try to hold back the little smile tugging at my lips. I loved it that the man's eyes always followed me when I was onstage during rehearsals and shows. In fact, I might have encouraged his attentions on more than one occasion. Then he leveled me.

"Gretchen isn't only your manager, is she? The two of you go back a ways."

Though I tried not to react, the gasp escaped my lips without my permission.

"I bet the two of you are as tight as I am with Blu and Dakota. Did you know the three of us went to high school together?" He traced one finger down the side of my cheek, down my neck to the hollow of my throat, and lower over my breast, stopping at my nipple long enough to worry it into responding to him. His lips curved in satisfaction and he dropped his hand to my waist. "Is that how it is with you and Gretchen?"

His lazy tour of my body did nothing to slow the racing of my heart. The man wanted my secrets. And the way I reacted to him scared the heck out of me. Of all the people I'd ever met, Adam Tron had somehow figured out how to reach inside me and pull out the real me, the me I only ever showed to Gretchen who'd known me through everything and still loved me. I'd done my homework on him. I knew he came from a stable middle-class family in Denver, people who couldn't even dream of the depravities some parents could inflict on their children in the name of religion. If I let my guard down, if I let him in, no doubt I'd shock his perfect, normal-family, middle-class world, and he'd run away like Frankenstein's monster was bearing down on him.

Yet I wanted him.

I wanted him so darn much.

His long fingers spanned my waist as he closed the small distance between us, his eyes never leaving mine. I braced myself with my hands on his rock-hard biceps, holding on tight. "She's my best friend," I heard myself whisper.

"You need that."

The kiss he brushed over my lips stilled my surprise at his words. Somehow, he knew exactly how far to push. More than anything, that should have scared me witless, but he didn't give me a chance to process. He tasted my mouth, his tongue gently asking to come inside, and defenseless against my own need, I opened for him.

Adam tangled his tongue with mine, sliding and gliding, touching and tasting. With his soft sculpted lips, he increased the pressure, and I melted into him, my arms twining around his neck, the heel of my foot rubbing up and down the calf of his leg. The heat of his mouth drove me wild. He tasted of beer, man, and sin, a heady combination I adored in spite of myself.

I ground myself into his body while we nipped and nibbled at each other's lips then our tongues wanted back into the party. The intimate glide and retreat, thrust and chase mimicked what our bodies longed to do together. He slipped his hand beneath my thigh, pulling me up until my foot rested on his hip. The slow grind of his covered fly against my exposed center revved me up, and I whimpered into his mouth. Still, the hot kiss went on and on, like he wanted to steal my every last breath and give me his in return.

He put his hands on my butt and pulled my cheeks apart,

squeezing and kneading me, and I wrapped my other leg around his waist. A long groan escaped him as he kissed me along my jaw and down my neck, tonguing the hollow of my throat. I tightened my legs around him and held on as he continued to grind himself into me.

"Tron." I swallowed. "Adam. I want you so much."

Hearing his name on my lips did something to him. In two strides, he stood beside my bed. Letting go of me slowly, like he didn't want to, he held my back as I slid down his body. He slipped his fingers beneath the waistband of my skirt and pushed it down over my hips. With a shimmy, I finished what he started, my skirt pooling on the floor at my feet. His eyes never leaving mine, he tugged my T-shirt over my head and tossed it on the floor.

With something like reverence, he stared at my body, lifting a hand to stroke lightly over my lace-covered breast. "Jesus, Cristy. You are so damn gorgeous."

I reached behind myself and unclasped my favorite magenta bra, letting it drop to the floor to join the skirt at my feet. Then I palmed my way up Adam's taut belly, taking his T-shirt with me.

He took the hint and pulled it over his head while I busied myself with the fly of his jeans. The way his length filled them gave me trouble at first, the button and zipper straining to contain him, but finally, I managed to ease his jeans open. I slipped my fingers beneath the waistbands of both his jeans and boxers, sliding the whole works down to his knees before he took over and unlaced his boots and toed off all his clothes at once.

"Leave those on," he said when I bent to unclasp the strap of my shoe.

"You're that kind of guy, huh?"

"You have the most beautiful long legs, Valorous. Those shoes set them off. Honestly, I've been dreaming for a while of seeing a pair of your sexy shoes draped over my shoulders as I get you off."

Butterflies took flight inside me. Adam Tron the rock god had been dreaming of me? Before I could wrap my head around the idea, he stroked his knuckles over my belly, coming to rest above my belly button where a full carat diamond winked in the dim lamplight. "You're full of surprises, aren't you, gorgeous?"

My skin rippled beneath his touch as waves of desire washed over me. I needed to grab my self-control with both hands before he swept it out on the sea of desire threatening to overwhelm me. Grasping for a sanity preserver, I ran my hands over the tribal tattoo decorating his right arm from his wrist to his shoulder. The black ink on his smooth brown skin delighted me, and I traced the designs until I could even out my breathing.

Adam's hands on my hips tugged me into his hard body. When my skin contacted his from my chest to my thighs, electric fire licked over me, sending shock waves of need rippling through me. I swear if I'd seen us in a mirror, we would have been sparking. He must have felt it too because he banded his arms around me and plundered my mouth with his. There was no teasing, no testing, no advance and retreat—only out-of-control want.

His groans met my whimpers as I tried to climb him. He tore his mouth from mine, scooped me high into his arms, and tossed me unceremoniously onto the middle of the bed. Retrieving a condom from the pocket of his jeans, he ripped open the packet and sheathed himself. His jerky movements somehow calmed me. He wanted me as desperately as I wanted him.

When he climbed over me, he rested on his elbows and stared deep into my eyes. "I promised you heaven, Cristy Valor. Believe me when I tell you I'm absolutely going to deliver."

Boy, did he ever. His hot lips on my skin left me writhing with need as he kissed the swells of my breasts but not my nipples even when I tried to move them into the path of his mouth. He toured my belly with his fingertips, lips, and tongue, featherlight touches, nips, and licks. I begged and pleaded for him to touch me for real, but the terrible man laughed deep in his throat and went to work using his tongue to trace the place where my thighs met my hips then meandered down my thighs, behind my knees, and down my calves. Before Adam Tron, I had no idea the space behind my ankle bone was an erogenous zone. In a few minutes—or maybe a light-year—he taught me more about myself with only his lips and tongue than I'd learned in ten years of one-night stands and fleeting relationships.

When he finally made his way back up my body, he zeroed in on my nipples. Finally. He sucked one into his mouth hard, and with a scream, I headed straight for outer space. Transferring his attention to the other hard peak, he continued his exquisite torture with his thumb and forefinger, pinching and rubbing as I arched up into his touch. On a groan, he let me go with a soft pop, his eyes glittering in the diffused light of the bedside lamp.

"I had plans for eating your sweet pussy again, but they'll have to wait till later 'cause I can't hold back anymore. I need to be inside you *now*."

He didn't give me a chance to do anything but nod as he yanked my legs over his shoulders. The expression of pure wild desire on his face as he gazed at my most private place had me squeezing my inner muscles tight in anticipation of his impressive phallus entering me. Yet his movements contradicted his words as he traced over my folds, testing me.

He pushed his finger inside me, pumping in and out a couple of times. "You're so fucking wet, Cristy."

"Adam! You said now. No fair teasing me like this." I meant to scold, but my words came out all needy.

He sucked my wetness from his finger and grinned, wretched man. Then he reached down and positioned himself at my entrance and leaned forward, bracing himself on his hands on either side of my head. With one long, slow thrust, he entered me, and I clamped down on him hard. He was big and hard and delicious, and I never wanted him to leave my body.

"Jesus, Cristy. You're so wet. So fucking tight," he ground out through clenched teeth, the tendons in his neck sexy in taut relief beneath his skin. "Are you okay?" Sweat beaded on his forehead and his arms shook as he waited for me to adjust to him.

With a smile, I said, "So much more than okay."

I feathered my fingers up and down his sides. Huffing out a breath, he started moving inside me. He set a rhythm at something like four/four time, and I lifted my hips to encourage him. When his hips pistoned up to half time, the metronome inside my body lost control. With my head lolling from side to side on the pillow, I chanted his name in time to his rhythm. Then he changed his angle slightly, and the head of his cock hit my G-spot exactly, rocketing me into space, a symphony of sound filling my head as I lost control and gave Adam everything, my body spasming around him in the most exquisite pleasure I'd ever experienced.

A couple of heartbeats later, he shouted, a guttural sound that resonated through me, and I couldn't help but squeeze him tight with my inner muscles as his body went rigid. Jerky movements inside me followed like mini-orgasms trailing the big one. I understood that as the aftershocks rolled through me too.

Words failed us both, and for a long moment, we stared into each other's eyes. At last, he let my legs drop before he collapsed on top of me, his big body squishing me into the mattress in the loveliest way. I wrapped my arms and legs around him, holding him close as I smoothed my hands over the sweaty skin of his back, reveling in the feel of him on top of and inside me. As I breathed in the scents of sweat, sex, and something woodsy that was all Adam, I vaguely thought I'd like to hold onto this moment forever. When it finally registered where my thoughts had gone, I panicked.

This was just sex. We were only having fun. This wasn't real. Adam wasn't real. Adam was Tron, a rock star who gave this to a different woman every night on tour. I was Cristy Valor, devil-may-care pop diva, who never let herself get close to anyone.

Inside me, something shifted. This with Adam? This was

different. He'd made me a promise, and he'd more than delivered. I wanted more, so much more with him. The alarm bells clanged like a disaster warning inside my head.

"Stop thinking so hard," he whispered, his breath warm on my ear.

How did he do *that?*

"I'm inside you. I can feel you." He brushed a kiss over my jaw.

"I said that out loud?"

He chuckled. "We're good together." Lifting up, he looked me in the eyes. "We're exceptional together. Which means"—he gave my mouth a quick kiss—"that we're going to do this again while we're on this tour. In fact, we're going to do this often." He buried his face in my neck and gifted me a long openmouthed kiss.

He'd made good on his promise. He'd most definitely taken me to heaven. So why did I feel like I might be on a one-way path to hell?

CHAPTER SIXTEEN

Adam

"WHAT DO YOU mean Cristy won't be with us when we play Portland?" I demanded as Garrett discussed our upcoming shows on the bus ride north from San Francisco.

The man glared at me, something I was more used to seeing whenever he looked at Dakota these days. His surly attitude toward me made no sense.

"It's in her contract," he said like I should have known that. "She's filming a music video, something she had lined up before she agreed to join this tour."

Why hadn't I heard this from Cristy herself? It's not like she didn't have a chance to say something about it when we were together all night long. Pictures of the two of us in her bed last night and in her shower this morning before I returned to our hotel flashed in my head. That woman fired me up in ways I didn't know were possible. Her tight, hot little body hid all kinds of secrets, and I was a hell of a long way from being done discovering them.

Discreetly, I adjusted myself behind the fly of my jeans. Maybe

I hadn't given her a chance to tell me about her schedule. Still, it bugged me she didn't at least mention it when I kissed her see-ya-later at her door this morning.

"When's she coming back?"

Annabelle glanced up from her laptop. "She'll be playing with you guys again for the two shows in Seattle."

I noticed how she maintained a determined distance from Garrett even as they sat on the same couch behind the table on one side of the bus. Our manager's animosity toward Annabelle made no sense either. As far as I could tell, the woman was an ace marketer, her ideas driving up sales on everything from sold-out shows to music downloads to T-shirts. Yes, I'd checked. I carried a laptop along with me on tour too.

My job, whenever I felt like messing with it, was to track band sales. Dakota understood business, and Blu and I had enough accounting between us to keep an eye on the books. Jack was the only one of us without some college, but he was enrolled in an online program and working toward a degree in music engineering. Sure we were a rock 'n' roll outfit, but we were also a business, one we wanted to keep going. Garrett had managed us almost from the beginning, and it was always in his best interests to make sure he took care of us, but we didn't think it hurt to have a clue about taking care of ourselves. With each of us keeping an eye on managing the business, we kept everyone honest—especially those who worked for us.

From where I sat, Annabelle's obvious interest in Dakota—and apparently his ongoing interest in her so far—meant she worked her ass off for us. The fact she'd need a stellar recommendation at the end of the tour to move on in this business no doubt motivated her to do her best. All of which meant we could trust her. Garrett's behavior, on the other hand, had me watching him a little closer. The man had a problem, but hell if I could figure out what it was.

"Cristy has certainly made this tour fun," Blu said from his captain's chair beside mine. "I didn't know how I'd feel about sharing the stage with her, but I like singing with her." The surprise on his face was almost comical.

"She does put Tron through his paces," Jack said with a smirk as he joined us in the front of the bus.

"What the fuck does that mean?"

"It means you dropped a beat again last night when she shimmied around you as she sang 'Tigers,'" he said as he flopped down in a chair on the other side of Blu.

"You caught that too?" Blu asked with a chuckle.

"You didn't sleep in your suite at the hotel last night," Dakota chimed in, his eyes dancing.

"Excuse me?" I sputtered.

"You were seen sneaking in early this morning," Garrett said with a snarl. "When you boys play with the groupies, they come to you, not the other way 'round, which can only mean one thing."

I cocked a brow and kept my mouth shut.

"I don't blame you, Tron. She's hot," Dakota said.

Annabelle's head shot up, and I noticed a flush climb up her cheeks, but she said nothing. Dakota winked at her as he unlocked his chair, slid it forward toward the table, and locked it down again. She ignored him and returned her attention to whatever was on her screen. Something was definitely going on between those two.

"Balefire has a reputation, one some of you should at least attempt to uphold," Garrett said, glaring at Jack and Blu.

"Jesus, Garrett, lighten up." I leaned back in my chair and rested my hands on the back of my head. "We won't stop being the bad boys of rock 'n' roll because some of us decide to stop entertaining the groupies after our shows."

He snorted. "*Some* of you?"

A look passed between Jack and Blu, and the two of them slid their chairs toward the table. Annabelle pulled her shoulders in and ducked her head lower behind her computer screen. Dakota leaned his elbows on the table, his eyes never leaving Garrett. I remained where I was and waited. If Garrett couldn't take my hint, he was on his own.

"Even before we started this tour, you've been a surly pain in the ass, Garrett," Blu said. "What the fuck is your problem?"

Annabelle peeked over the top of her computer. "Maybe I should go."

Her pleading expression wasn't lost on Dakota who slid back enough to let her exit the banquette, though not without making her slide her ass over the top of his thighs. The little grin on his face proclaimed how much he enjoyed teasing her even when shit between the band and our manager was about to get real.

Once Annabelle had made her way past the rest of us, Blu repeated his question.

"I don't have a problem," Garrett ground out as he stared down the hallway after her.

"The hell you don't. If your eyes were laser beams, my girl would have a gaping hole drilled through the middle of her back," Dakota said, all the playfulness gone from his voice, his hands flat on the table as he leaned forward like he was about to get right up in Garrett's face.

Garrett didn't back down. "Your girl?"

"I've been seeing Annie all summer, so yeah. My. Girl."

Jack shrugged when I silently questioned him. Meanwhile, a tiny grin played around Blu's mouth as he directed his attention to Dakota. Their responses confirmed what I'd suspected ever since I saw Dakota usher Annabelle into his room the first day of the tour.

"Why is it a problem for you that I'm with Annabelle?"

Garrett shrugged. "It's not a good idea for any of you to date the help. It could cause all sorts of legal issues when you move on from her."

"Is that all?"

A sane man would have been shaking in his shoes at the raw anger simmering in Dakota's voice. But apparently, Garrett wasn't firing on all eight cylinders today. "It's not smart for any of you boys to be mothered up." He leaned back and crossed his arms over his chest. "This life chews up and spits out relationships—and marriages." He directed that last shot at Jack—"Kind of like an all-you-can-eat buffet. You know that."

Wrong answer.

Blu stood, his hands planted on the table directly in front of Garrett. "Both of our ladies offered—*offered*—to sign pre-nups. Jack said no way to Clio, and I said the same thing to Ashleigh. We've signed on for the long haul."

Blu blocked my line of sight, so the only way I knew how Garrett reacted was when both Jack and Dakota stood beside Blu in confronting our manager. "You do your job well, but you're not the only manager out there who can do the job."

"Your job is to work with promoters, book our shows and our publicity, and make sure the tour runs smoothly." The edge to Dakota's tone matched Blu's attitude. "But there's absolutely nothing in your contract that says you can weigh in on our personal lives."

"If we want to date someone—or marry her—it's none of your goddamn business," Jack added.

Sitting forward, my elbows resting on my knees, I caught Garrett's attention. "We aren't eighteen anymore, man. After over a decade on the road, we have a clue about this life. From the looks of things, so do the women these guys have invited to join our party."

Garrett directed his gaze out at the passing scenery before returning his eyes to us. "Don't come crying to me when shit hits the fan with your 'understanding'" he air quoted, "women."

Good thing Jack was standing when Blu lunged across the table. In a flash, I jumped up to help Jack restrain him. "If you're planning to pull another stunt, Garrett, I'll kick your ass from here to Denver."

Finally Garrett had the good sense to cool his jets. Holding his hands up in front of himself, he said, "I'm not planning on doing anything. Jesus. But I've got a decade of experience with women on you guys, and I'm just saying they're not always as understanding as maybe a rock star might need them to be."

Even as the bus whooshed up the road at seventy miles an hour, the air inside it didn't move. Then beneath my grasp, I sensed Blu relax, and I let him go along with the breath I was holding. My friends and I sat back down in our chairs, but we all continued to watch our manager.

"I'm always on your side. I'm always looking out for you guys. You know that."

"Yeah, but you do have a problem with us being in serious relationships," Blu said.

Seeing Blu's fisted hands on his lap kept my guard up.

The way Garrett's tongue pushed against his cheek said he was choosing his next words carefully. Took him long enough. "This band has a reputation that draws the ladies."

We all had to smile at that.

"Those ladies come to your shows with a fantasy—and an expectation. If you're all mothered up, you ruin that fantasy, take away that expectation."

"We have no trouble entertaining the ladies. At one time we enjoyed entertaining more than one at a time." Dakota waggled his brows at Blu. Then he turned serious. "But even sex gods like us can't take care of a stadium of screaming fans. They know that. Hasn't stopped us from selling out a show in two years."

"Yeah, but this whole girlfriend and wife thing is recent. You don't know how it's going to affect ticket sales to your shows."

If I didn't know better, I'd think Garrett was almost pouting. This shit had to stop.

"We're in the first third of a sold-out tour, buddy," I said. "Who we bring along with us on this bus or on our plane isn't going to affect jack shit, and you know it."

Garrett glared at me. "Well, rumors of a certain pop diva breaking up the band might slow your roll."

"What the ever-loving fuck are you talking about?" My gut clenched, and Blu braced his forearm across my chest before I registered I'd lunged at our manager.

"I didn't see you sneaking into the hotel this morning. The paps did, and after the clusterfuck with your little outing to the pier, speculation raced across social media like an Indy car. Since it's my *job* to keep track of that stuff, I caught the rumor—and squelched it—before I boarded the bus this morning." I wanted to punch the smug expression off his face, but he wasn't done. "That kind of publicity isn't good for the band, Tron."

Blu kept his arm where it was, restraining me from taking that punch I so dearly wanted to throw. "There were breakup rumors when I left our last tour to chase after Ashleigh following that stunt you pulled, Garrett."

A ruddy hue tinged his face, but he crossed his arms back over his chest, leaned against the bench seat, and said nothing.

"The band is solid. We don't give a shit about rumors, do we, boys?" Blu glanced at the rest of us. "So back the fuck off. What—or who—Tron does in his downtime is his own goddamn business." The mischievous twinkle in his eyes warned me. "Unless the three of us decide to make it our business."

"It's the boots, isn't it, Tron?" Dakota asked, the smirk on his face daring me.

"I think it's the baby doll dresses with the sexy lacy tutu skirts that show off her legs," Blu said, patting my knee. He hopped up and strode to the minibar before I could react.

"You're both wrong," Jack chimed in, and I gave my ally a tight grin. "It's the way she looks at him as she runs her hands over his shoulders and arms as she does her little dance during 'Tigers.'"

I flipped him the bird, and he busted out laughing.

Yeah, Cristy's outfits radiated sexy, no doubt. You'd have to be clueless—or maybe on Mars—not to appreciate the way she wore her clothes, the way she walked in those sky-high heels everyone couldn't help checking out. But what the fuck? These guys were involved with other women, even Dakota apparently. So why were they checking out my girl like that?

Wait. *What?*

We went on one date. We had sex on a couple of occasions. No big deal. She wasn't the first woman I'd done those things with. Hell, I'd lost track of the number of women I'd enjoyed since I lost my virginity sophomore year of high school. So why did it bug me so much that my boys noticed Cristy's incredible sexiness?

"Tron has a thing for Cristy," Dakota singsonged, his eyes dancing.

I glared at him and crossed my arms over my chest so they couldn't see my fists flexing.

Blu tapped an open beer against my bicep. I reached up and took it, thinking he might be on my side after all.

"It's all right, buddy. It was bound to happen." His joking expression mocked his serious tone. "Although I'm kinda surprised you go for the wild ones." He saluted me with his beer and took a long pull.

"Maybe it's true what they say about opposites attract," Jack said as he stretched his legs out in front of him, taking up most of the front of the bus.

"Fuck you." I bared my teeth at him. "I thought the rhythm section was a team."

"Oh, we're a team, Tron," Jack said with a sly grin before he pulled the bill of his trucker hat low over his eyes.

"See? This is the problem when you let women in." Garrett slid out from behind the table to make his way to the front seat. "You start out bickering about them, then the jealousy starts, and next thing you know, John Lennon is showing off his bare ass with Yoko Ono in a hotel room and the greatest band in history is splintered into four solo artists who never toured together again."

The old man disgust in his voice as he worked his way around us to the shotgun seat beside our driver struck us as funny. We laughed until San Francisco was nothing but a speck in the rear-view mirror. Yet even as I screwed around and drank beers with my friends, the road traveling by in a blur, visions of Cristy Valor, and Garrett's weird warnings about her, haunted my thoughts all the way to Portland.

CHAPTER SEVENTEEN

Cristy

EST FRIEND OR not, manager or not, today, Gretchen was on my last nerve.

Focusing my thoughts was a struggle as Steve fussed over yet another costume change and Jilly hovered around me like a powdery hummingbird. The video shoot for my latest single, "Hot For Me," was going as well as every music video I'd made in the last five years, mainly because I used the same director and producer team. We understood each other, which meant we worked well together. I trusted them to make me look good, and they expected me to follow the script and then were not surprised when I deviated from it. My own team, though relatively new to my personal little freak show, functioned like a machine. Gretchen deserved all the credit for that second part. No detail escaped her, which was usually a point in her favor.

Not today.

"This outfit needs different shoes, Steve. Everything in Cristy's repertoire today has to be in a shade of red, orange, or blue."

Steve sighed.

"I chose these boots. They're the perfect contrast to the frills on this dress."

The black thigh-high stiletto boots that laced up the backs of my legs also caught Tron's attention every time I wore them during our shows. Wearing them in my latest music video was my private shout-out to him, but that was none of Gretchen's business.

"You signed off on the costumes, Cristy." The warning in her voice had nothing to do with costumes or contracts, as we both darn well knew.

"Last I checked, this is my video. So I guess I can change my mind." I glanced at Jillian whose eyes moved between Gretch and me like someone watching a professional ping-pong match. "Am I good, Jilly?"

"Um, uh—" She cleared her throat. "Yeah, Cristy, you're all set."

I didn't exactly shoulder my way past my best friend, but I came close enough to make my point. Gretchen didn't give an inch.

"We don't have time to reshoot this when the dailies come in and you don't like the outfit after all," she called after me.

I waved her off over my head and kept walking to the set.

Last night was one of the few times I'd ever locked her out. She pouted about it for the entire plane ride back to LA when she wasn't reminding me about all the times in the past when I'd invited her to watch. Not that she'd ever taken me up on the offer.

It was different with Tron. Because she knew me better than anyone, no doubt she'd figured that out. But I wasn't ready to admit it. Heck, I might never be ready to admit it. I had too much to lose. The thought stopped me dead in my tracks, and I glanced over my shoulder at the one person in the world who kept all my secrets and loved me anyway. The eloquent quirk of her brow said it all.

The woman never missed a darn thing. Dang it.

I tossed an extra swing into my step and rejoined the director on set. Tron had promised me spectacular sex, and he'd delivered. But that's all it was. Sex. Nothing more. No feelings, no secrets, no entanglements. We were professional musicians who toured the world. Trying out new experiences—and people—came with the territory. Sharing more than bodies and pleasure was asking for trouble, pure and simple. Though I often asked for trouble, there were some lines even I wouldn't cross. Attaching feelings to sex was one of them.

The director flicked her eyes at my boots and back to my face, drawing my attention to my latest off-script rebellion. As off-script mutinies went, my wardrobe change was tame. Yet it reminded me about my intentions, and I almost turned around and let the director and Gretchen have their way. What was I thinking when I made this change purely for Tron?

The director broke into my reverie. "Play up the boots in this shot, Bill. I want you to start at the heels and slowly pan up the backs of Cristy's legs. Zoom in on the laces from her calves to the hem of her skirt before zooming back out to catch her winking over her shoulder as she sings the opening line of the chorus." Her attention back on me, she said, "You good with that? Channel every sexy atom in the universe. Make all the boys hot for you."

Lainey James didn't reach the pinnacle of music video direction by not paying attention. Or maybe Gretchen mentioned something when a costume change occupied me. Or maybe I had too much Adam Tron on the brain because even though I know she had to have said something else, all I heard was Adam. A picture of his big body pushing into mine as he held me against the wall in the shower this morning flashed through my head, and every atom inside me responded as Lainey cued my band.

We shot that first chorus scene in one take.

Afterward, I joined Gretchen and Lainey as they screened that part of the video. Even my panties dampened a bit at what I watched with them.

"Damn, girl. Wish I'd thought to tell you to channel all the sex in the universe earlier. That look you're giving the camera here could set the Playboy Mansion on fire." Lainey fanned herself, something so out of character for her I burst out laughing.

One glance at the scowl on my best friend's face sobered me right up. "Guess I won't be changing my mind about that costume deviation, eh Gretch?"

Oblivious to the drama playing out between Gretchen and me, Lainey said, "I want you wearing those boots for the second chorus too. I have an idea."

While she walked over to exchange some words with the script-writer, I waited for the explosion. It came on a hiss. "You need to be more fucking careful, Cristy-girl. Tron isn't just any celebrity rock star. He's the bassist for the biggest band on the planet. If this thing blows up, the fallout could damage your career irreparably." She flicked her eyes back to the monitor where the crew was watching the chorus again. "The rumors about you breaking up Balefire started making their way through social media about the same time I imagine Tron walked through the doors of his hotel this morning."

My heart lurched into my throat then dropped down to my stomach. "It's sex, Gretchen. That's all," I whispered. "Nothing serious."

How the hell *did she know?*

"You might need to make that more obvious when we hit Seattle in a few days."

Behind my shoulder, something caught her eye, and I turned to see Steve hovering with my next outfit in his hands. Without acknowledging Gretchen's remark, I followed him back to the dressing room.

Freaking social media. Yes, I liked the attention. Every performer I'd ever met liked the attention. The problem was, with sites like TMZ and the ease of uploading a photo without any context, no performer could control the narrative completely. So someone saw Adam sneak back into his hotel this morning. So what? That could mean anything. Still, my hotel reservations for the rest of the tour needed tweaking, that was for sure.

"Gretchen, I think a press release is in order," I said as Steve adjusted the skintight red lace dress over my body. Equal parts awe and pique warred inside me as the man treated my body like a mannequin. "Something to the effect of what is social media on about since I left town for a scheduled video shoot, and break-a-leg to the boys for their sold-out shows in Portland."

The eye roll could have won an Academy Award. "I took care of it while we were in the air." She crossed her arms over her chest. "That's not the point."

"What is the point?" I tipped my face up and closed my eyes while Jillian worked her magic.

"I pay attention, Cristy-girl."

It was my turn for an epic eye roll. "Oh, I know."

"Your other celebrity flings were blowing off steam, nothing that could become anything." She ticked off my recent conquests on her fingers. "Accompanying Casey Hurley to a movie premiere followed by a romantic date on the beach, or treating Dante Xavier to backstage evenings at your shows for one short tour after he won a Golden Globe, or hanging out in Europe for a month with Lenny Brown while his band was on hiatus improved your social standing."

"Those guys did all right too, you know."

"Exactly." Gretchen kept talking as she followed me back to the set. "But I've seen the way you flirt with Tron—and the way he looks at you even when you aren't flirting with him. Then there's that date he took you on in San Francisco. Rumor has it, the reason you're even on this tour is because Tron wanted you on it."

I stopped stock-still, and Gretchen slammed right into me. "Come again?"

"So you might want to back off on the guy if you don't want to cause a media storm we can't manage." Pointedly, she stared at my boots.

Sucking a calming breath in through my nose, I let it out slowly, my eyes never leaving hers. "I'll keep that in mind."

At the end of the day, the only shots we had to redo were the early ones when I didn't have my hot boots on. Lainey declared this video was the best one I'd ever done and invited us all out to a celebratory dinner. Even with Kelsey there to whisper sweet nothings in her ear all night, Gretchen spent the entire meal glaring at me. Good thing I'd have a couple of days off before flying up to Seattle to rejoin Balefire, days I'd spend on my own, taking a break from my best friend.

Adam

We played Portland like a boss. Our shows kicked so much ass that the media had to back off on their stupid breakup rumors. Cristy's absence meant we played more of our older hits, much to the fans' delight. Still, when that point in the show came where she usually made her entrance, I had to check myself not to look for her.

Afterward, the number of groupies Garrett allowed backstage nearly overwhelmed us. It was like the guy was trying to make a statement or something. From the looks of things, his ploy just pissed off Jack and Blu who left the parties early. Dakota and Annabelle seemed to enjoy themselves—read that, Dakota didn't pay one damn bit of attention to any other girl in the room while he and Annabelle partied their asses off. All of which meant the groupies figured out I was the last man standing.

Normally, having all the girls to myself would please me immensely. But every time some hot woman would walk her fingers across my shoulders or down my chest, my heart would drop to my belly. The feeling reminded me of my mom catching me doing something I shouldn't have been doing. Never mind those girls who planted their asses on my lap if I sat down. Though I tried to play along, that move left me as tense as guitar strings. So I spent most of the parties on my feet.

I caught Garrett watching me, a speculative gleam in his eye that had me flexing my fists. Whatever game he was playing, I didn't much like being the object of it. On the second night in Portland, I followed Blu and Ashleigh to the town car. "Mind if I join you guys?" I asked and didn't give a shit about interrupting any cozy plans for the ride back to the hotel.

"What's up, Tron?" Blu asked as I slid onto the seat opposite him and Ashleigh.

"If Garrett wants to party with all the groupies, he can do it by himself."

I raided the minibar, popping the top of a beer, and pointedly ignored Blu's smirk.

Probably, I should have had more to drink at the party though. Visions of Cristy Valor kept me up all night after our first Portland show. The breathy, needy sounds she made as I explored her creamy skin with my hands and lips echoed in my brain. Her unerring discovery of the ways I liked to be touched left me harder than I ever remembered being. The way she writhed and undulated beneath me, begging for as much as I wanted to give her fired me up. So I gave her everything. I'd promised her heaven, but she'd sent me to the outer reaches of the stratosphere.

I tossed the empty into the corner of the car and covered my need to adjust my hard-on by grabbing another beer. The alcohol did nothing to slow my swirling thoughts. Over ten years on the road, I'd met some pretty sweet ladies who'd given me some great sex. After the music, the opportunity to experience all sorts of women had been a big draw of the rock 'n' roll life. When Blu, Dakota, our old drummer Dave Brubaker, and I were kids, we often joked about how much pussy we were going to score once we hit the big time. Blu and Dakota used to share with each other or share themselves with multiple women at the same time. I had less exotic tastes. Still, I'd tried a few things over the years.

Nothing like Cristy Valor though.

Damn. One night with that woman would never be enough. Good thing she was joining the tour again in Seattle and staying with us to the end in Houston. I'd checked that with Annabelle yesterday when Garrett was busy haranguing Bailey Saunders about some ridiculous shit. Maybe by the end of the tour, I'd have her out of my system.

CHAPTER EIGHTEEN

Cristy

WITHOUT KELSEY ALONG to temper her mood on the flight to Seattle, Gretchen's pout reached epic proportions. I mean, if huffing out sighs and alternating between glares and eye rolls were an Olympic sport, she'd win all the gold medals for the next century. A couple of days away from me hadn't done a darn thing to help her get over herself about Tron and me having a little fun together.

It was safer to call him Tron instead of Adam in my head. If I could compartmentalize the man as only the best sex I'd ever had, I could still walk away from him unscathed when the tour ended. Whether Gretchen liked it or not, I'd be enjoying him as we traveled together. Not doing so would be a huge waste of all that gorgeous manliness without any payoff for my sacrifice. Besides, between them, she and Balefire's toady of a manager would be able to figure out how to shut down the rumors about me breaking up the band. After all, that was one of the reasons we paid them the big bucks.

Thinking about Tron brought a smile to my lips, one I didn't even try to suppress given Gretchen's current mood. The man was sex on a stick. Over six feet of walking, talking hotness. Despite our differences in stature, we fit together perfectly. His size probably should have intimidated me. Instead, he made me feel safe, like a superhero taking on all the monsters in my world and leaving a trail of monster goo in his wake.

That thought wiped the smile right off my face. Tron could never find out about my monsters, the ones that sometimes still managed to sneak into my life in the cold dark hours of the night. Knowing Gretchen was in the adjoining room to take care of me if the monsters paid a visit—and would keep a lid on it around whoever I was with—gave me peace of mind. This thing with Tron had disaster written all over it if I deviated from protocol again. No wonder she was mad at me.

"I'm sorry, Gretch. I know you're always looking out for me."

She blinked in surprise.

"This thing with Tron is nothing more than a pleasurable diversion. That's it. You don't have to worry that I'll do something stupid and make a big deal out of it."

"That's not what I'm worried about, Cristy-girl."

I bared my teeth at her. "I'm not going to break up Balefire."

"I'm not worried about that either."

It was my turn to pout. Slumping back into the comfy cushions of the white leather couch on our charter plane, I crossed my arms over my chest to wait her out.

"You're not the same with him."

I gifted her a look. "What the heck does that mean?"

Gretchen sighed. "You like him."

"Of course I like him," I said. "I like all the guys in Balefire. Honestly, playing with them is the most fun I've ever had on tour."

With a stretch, she stood and joined me on my couch, not giving me any opening for escape. She'd used this tactic so many times over the years, you'd think I'd wise up to it by now. Instead, I sat still and stared at her like a mouse waiting for the snake to strike.

Sliding her arm across the cushions behind me, she leaned forward and dared me to look away from her eyes. "Tron is not arm candy. Nor is he a boy toy. He doesn't need you to boost his career." She squeezed my knee. "You can't play games with him."

I tightened my arms over my chest and huffed. "I'm aware of that." *Dang it.*

Gretchen settled back into the couch, but her eyes never left mine. "Whatever you've started with him isn't going to end the way your other 'relationships' have ended."

The air quotes reminded both of us that I'd never had a real relationship with a man in my life. In fact, the only real *relationship* I'd ever had sat beside me as we zipped across the sky toward Seattle.

"Indulging in a little sexy time isn't having a relationship, Gretch. Stop worrying."

"I'm not worried about the sex, Cristy. It's the way you watch him." For a second, it seemed she debated with herself before she added, "and the way he watches you."

Adam

"Jesus, Tron. What bug crawled up your ass?"

"The fuck, Dakota?"

"If you keep pacing like that, you're gonna wear a goddamn hole in the floor." The way Dakota sprawled over the couch, so relaxed he barely lifted his eyes, could only mean one thing—he'd been getting laid regularly by the same woman. I'd seen the same expression first on Jack, then on Blu. One tour it was all about the prime pussy we were going to score after the shows. The next tour it was all relaxed satisfied smiles and no conversation whatsoever about their sex lives. "She'll be here. It's in her contract."

I flipped him the bird. "We should have practiced during sound checks today."

"We did practice during sound checks today."

"Not with her."

"Relax, Tron. We've done five shows with the woman so far, and Cristy's been nothing but professional at every one. Can't imagine anything's changed," Blu said before he went back to warming up his voice.

Something was off. There was no explanation for why I knew, but I knew. Cristy liked the grand entrance too much, the shock. Not showing up to sound checks while we were at the stadium didn't fit with her MO. It couldn't be the media rumors. Our managers had shut that shit down pronto. Running my hands through my hair, I hoped like hell I hadn't pushed her too far when I woke her up for some epic shower sex before I returned to our hotel to catch the tour bus to Portland.

Annabelle interrupted my thoughts when she peeked around the door to the green room. "Showtime, boys."

As I ran up the tunnel toward the stage, I deliberately glanced at the door to the room set aside for Cristy. A light seamed the space between the door and the floor, telling me someone was in there. Jack tossed his arm over my shoulder and half dragged me up the hallway.

"She's here, buddy. And she's going to be amazing as usual. Now let's go kick some rock 'n' roll ass!"

His enthusiasm infected me, but a small voice in the back of my lizard brain warned me to pay attention.

When Jack's massive drum kit rose out of the floor, his thundering beats echoing through the stadium, the crowd caught its breath for a second before erupting into a sound-barrier-breaking roar. Like always, the reaction of the fans pumped adrenaline through me, a high more powerful than any drug ever created. For as long as I lived, I was sure this shit would never get old. Strolling out from the wings, I took my place onstage, my bass rhythms complementing Jack's pounding drums. The spotlight lit me up, and the crowd's response soared with the light. I couldn't help but smile. Yep, I could do this every night till my one hundredth birthday, probably longer.

Dakota's wicked guitar licks joined the party, the two of us sharing a grin as the crowd worked itself into a frenzy. He flipped a couple of guitar picks out to the front row fans, and it started raining lingerie. In seconds, the entire front of the stage was carpeted in lacy bras, bikini panties, and thongs of every color. One fan with precise aim sent a black thong high over the stage to land on a peg of one of Jack's bass drums. The underwear bouncing with his pounding rhythms mimicked an activity we all enjoyed. I laughed. I'd have to avert my eyes from that little scene for the rest of the show.

A primal scream ripped from Blu's throat, announcing his entrance to the show. I never understood how he could maintain his smooth baritone and yet unleash that hair-raising sound to open our concerts. The pyrotechnics launched on the next bar with their accompanying strobes and lasers, and we settled in to wow the crowd.

By the moment in the show when it was time for Cristy's entrance, I'd relaxed into the set. My rhythms rolled through me like I channeled the muse of music or some shit. Still, when her voice rang over the stadium like an angel sent from heaven, I clenched my jaw, gripped my axe a little tighter, and concentrated on maintaining the beat. Now was not the time to admit, even to myself, how much the woman got to me.

I glanced up, searching for the spotlight on that hot woman, but it wasn't where it should have been. What the fuck? Were we doing her part of the show with a recording of her? A whiff of her spicy, flowery perfume wafted over me and then I sensed her heat beside me. Damn good thing my bass was made of hardwood because as hard as I gripped it, I could have cracked the fuckin' thing in two.

"Did you miss me?" she asked in a tone meant for my ears only.

Before I could answer, she sashayed to the front of the stage where the spotlight picked her up, and the crowd lost its mind. It was all I could do to keep my hands steady, to concentrate on the notes and maintain my rhythm as my eyes traveled over the red lace dress that barely covered Cristy's ass and hugged her body like a second skin. She sang directly in front of me, so I couldn't miss the peekaboo of creamy skin her black lace-up boots revealed. I loved all her shoes, but for some reason, those boots just did it for me.

Between her perfume, her sultry voice teasing my ear when she showed up onstage, and that outfit, my dick was so hard people could probably see it from the nosebleed seats. Damn good thing I liked to hold my bass low over my body as I played. Still, I squared up and faced the fans. Didn't need anyone noticing the way I responded to her. After the shit the guys gave me for missing a beat in the last two shows we played with her, I damn sure didn't need them to notice how she drove me absolutely fuckin' wild seeing her again after a couple of shows without her.

For the rest of her part of the set, she didn't flirt with me though. She danced for Dakota and Blu and hammed it up with Jack, but me she left alone. I had no idea what game she played, but I damn sure hoped I hadn't scared her off. The way she acted in her hotel room after our last gig together made me think she was as into me as I was into her. Yet the woman had a reputation as a wild card, so who the fuck knew?

After she exited the stage and we launched into our final set, one thing I did know for damn sure—I wasn't letting her off easy. She'd made me too fucking hot to allow her to walk away and leave me hanging.

Right as I'd made up my mind about what would happen after the show, Cristy materialized beside me again. We were several songs away from the encore when she was supposed to rejoin us, and I nearly dropped a beat at this unscripted appearance. Though she stood near me, she gave me enough space to be able to look her over, which of course I did. The red leather halter she wore barely contained her girls, something I appreciated, and the matching leather skirt accentuated her sweetly rounded ass. Then there were those damn boots. That was new. In the past, every time she changed outfits, she changed the shoes too. The deviation from her usual practice told me she was up to something. I quirked a brow, and she grinned and started backing Blu as he sang "My Beauty."

Adding her voice to his signature song wasn't part of the show either. Yet, once he heard her harmonies, he backed away from his microphone a bit and let her in. The song was one he'd written for Ashleigh and also one of our biggest hits. Yet when Cristy added her soft alto to the chorus, she lifted it into another dimension. All the while, she stayed near me, like she was singing to me. The fans' reaction told us they approved of her addition, not that they had a clue we were ad-libbing the whole tune.

When the last notes faded away into the raucous applause of the audience, I turned to her only to discover she'd disappeared. I glanced back at Jack who shrugged and launched into the opening rhythms of "The Limit," one of the oldies the crowd always wanted to hear. This woman was seriously fucking with my head—something else I decided she'd pay for once I got her alone after the concert.

Upon returning to the stage for the rehearsed part of the encore, she wore a bright red tube top and wide-legged pants that rippled and flowed around her legs. The light caught the sequins on her sandals, making her look like she was about to go up in flames. Her fingers taking a walk over my shoulders as she sang her own encore nearly sent me up in flames too. The naughty grin on her lips told me she knew exactly what she did to me. As she started to move away from me, I thought *fuck it* and reached out and gave her ass a love tap. A breathy "Oh" into her microphone alerted the audience to what I'd done, and they cheered their approval. Cristy kicked up a foot and blew me a kiss to tell me she'd taken back the upper hand, but we both knew who was now in charge of our little game.

She stood in her place between Dakota and Blu for our final bow. Strobes bounced over the stage and stadium, camouflaging our exit, and the show ended. The thunderous applause of the audience echoed in my ears as we whooped our way down the tunnel to our dressing rooms. Sweat flew in every direction when I whipped off my T-shirt and swung it around my head. Jack made fun of me, and Dakota goosed me when he ran past me. As I danced in a circle, I caught sight of Blu bringing up the rear with Cristy, his arm slung a bit too comfortably across her shoulders as she smiled up at something he said to her. I stopped in my tracks and waited for them.

Blu winked at me. "I was telling Cristy I think we should consider writing a duet together, something we could play with on tour and release on each of our next albums."

Quirking a brow, I fell into step beside them.

"Everyone's high on adrenaline after that show. We can talk about it later, yeah?" Cristy said to Blu, but her eyes never left mine.

"Sure thing, doll." Finally, Blu dropped his arm from her shoulders and picked up his pace. "Don't be long, Tron. Dakota's head start gives him way too much time to fuck with your stuff." His laugh rang down the hallway as he jogged away.

"You had some fun out there tonight, didn't you, Valorous?"

"Playing with you guys is a bigger rush than I anticipated it would be when I signed on to the tour."

I crowded her against the wall. "That's not what I meant, and you know it." I traced the pad of my finger along the edge of her jaw and didn't miss the tiny shiver that ghosted over her. "From the second you stepped onstage, you were playing a game."

A mischievous grin tugged at her lips, but that's all she gave me.

"You're not the only one who can play games, wild thing." Leaning down, I whispered, "Make sure to leave your door unlocked. And you should probably encourage your people to hit the green room early." My tongue traced the shell of her ear. "I think I hear the party starting."

Without giving her a chance to respond, I stepped away and jogged to our dressing room. Originally, I'd planned for us to ditch the after-party early so we could be alone at the hotel. That all changed when she started our playtime during the show by deviating from our set tonight. For the past two hours, I'd been trying to control my hard-on. Now it was time to take that wild girl up on all the promises she'd been making. I could hardly wait.

Chapter Nineteen

Cristy

WITHOUT KNOCKING, TRON stepped through the door to my dressing room. He carried a duffel bag in his hand and radiated attitude when his eyes landed on Steve, Jillian, and Gretchen.

"Cristy."

The low growl of his voice said everything. Normally, I'd want to fight it, fight him, stay in control. But the man wasn't wearing his shirt. Sweat from the concert shone on his skin like he'd been oiled for a photo shoot, all his gorgeous muscles defined in drool-worthy relief. I knew exactly what he wanted, and I hoped my shower would accommodate his plans.

"Do we need to pack up tonight?" I asked Steve. "You know, since we have another show tomorrow night."

"Not really. I thought I'd take the costumes you wore tonight to have them cleaned is all."

"How 'bout we don't worry about that, and you guys go enjoy the party. We're not traveling tomorrow, so tonight is the perfect chance to twist off, have some fun, and sleep in in the morning."

My voice sounded high and weird to my own ears. Judging from the scowl on Gretchen's face, she wasn't buying anything I was trying to sell. Of course, it didn't help to have tall, dark, and too-hot-for-my-own-good giving everyone the stink eye either.

Steve and Jillian exchanged a grin.

"The wife and kids wore me out for the few minutes we were home for the video shoot. I could use a beer—or six. What do you say, Jillybean? Join me in the green room?"

"You good to do your party makeup yourself, Cristy?"

I nodded.

Her eyes danced as she glanced over at Tron and back to me. "All right then. Steve, the first round is on you." She laughed as she linked her arm through Steve's and the two of them walked out the door.

Gretchen stood statue still but managed to radiate attitude all over the room like a thousand-watt bulb.

Seriously, Gretch?

Apparently, my expression said it all. Without a word, she spun on her heel and followed Steve and Jillian. The slamming of the door, however, proclaimed her feelings rather eloquently.

The corner of Tron's mouth tugged up. He dropped his duffel bag and flipped the lock on my friend's dramatic exit. "About those promises you made out there on the stage, Valorous—" He closed the distance between us in two long strides, stopping inches from me. "I've come to collect."

Though he had yet to touch me, the heat from his big body rolled over me, drawing me to him like I stood in front of a fire after years in the Arctic. Trying to control the shivers of anticipation raising goose bumps on my skin, I said nothing. Instead, I let my eyes roam the brown-skinned perfection of his sculpted body. The definition of his shoulders, pecs, and biceps told me all about the time he must spend in a gym. The six-pack masquerading as his abs tempted my fingers to take a tour. Yet I remained still, waiting for him to make the first move.

Tron surprised me when he reached for my hand, tracing my bones then sliding his long fingers between mine. He lifted my palm to his mouth and gently bit down on the base of my thumb, his eyes black fire as they burned into mine. A tiny, involuntary cry squeaked out of my throat, and he took advantage, setting an open-mouthed kiss in the middle of my palm. In an instant, my panties were soaked, and all he'd done so far was hold and kiss my hand. Boy, was I in so much trouble.

Seeming to sense my thoughts, he tugged me into him, wrapping his arms around me and holding me tight to his sweaty body. Answering the question I'd asked him onstage, he said, "I did miss you. Did you miss me?" His voice rumbled through me, and I closed my eyes and relaxed into him.

The deep breath I drew in filled my nostrils with the scent of sweat and some undertone of his woodsy cologne. Then I let my other senses take over, imprinting Adam: the resiliency of his skin beneath my fingertips, the even rhythm of his breath, the salty taste of him as I teased his nipple with my tongue. He hissed in a breath but otherwise didn't move, letting me have my turn. His willingness to share control when it would be so easy for him to overpower me turned me on more than anything else he could have done.

When I told Gretchen it was all a game with Adam, I think I might have lied.

"We need a shower." I pulled back and looked down at my tube top, now stained with his sweat.

He barked out a laugh and his expression turned serious. "Something you should know about me, Valorous. I am a patient man. Very patient." He cupped my face, his calloused thumb sending a riot of sensations over the skin of my jaw. "You'll tell me when you're ready."

How the heck did he do that? How did he look inside me and see everything, even the parts *I* wasn't ready to look at yet?

I stepped away from him and sat on a nearby chair, busying

myself with the straps on my sandals. He took the hint and bent to unlace his boots. When he stood up, devilry danced in his eyes as he reached for the fly of his jeans. "First one into the shower gets to decide whose room we use tonight."

My tube top hit the floor seconds before he dropped his jeans and boxers. I ripped my thong as I jerked it over my hips to follow my pants lying in a pool of red chiffon at my feet. The crashing sound of my chair hitting the floor echoed behind me as I ran to the bathroom adjoining my dressing room. Adam's laughter warned me before he scooped me up from behind and carried me to the shower stall. Instead of setting me down inside it, thereby proclaiming me the winner of our little race, he spun around and set me down, his big body blocking the entrance. With a wink, he stepped back into the stall.

"Winner, winner, chicken dinner."

Panic washed over me at the idea I'd have no backup in Adam's hotel room. I'd had no choice but to play his silly little game, but the consequences of losing hadn't factored in.

His big hands covered my shoulders, and he ducked his head, insisting on my attention. "Hey, hey, gorgeous. You know I don't care whose bed we spend the night in as long as we're sharing it."

There he was, doing it again. Slaying my monsters without even knowing it.

Summoning a cheeky grin, I said, "Something you should know about me, Tron. I really, really, *really* hate to lose."

In a blink, I slipped under his arm and entered the shower.

"What's with the name? We're alone now."

I knew what he asked. But it was too much considering how butterflies danced in my belly when I'd changed the rules and stepped out onstage beside him tonight. It was too much considering how much I'd wanted him the second he'd walked through my dressing room door. It was too much considering how wet I still was even after the confrontation with Gretchen and the panic of spending the night with a man where she couldn't run interference if I needed it. I did the only thing I could do to repair the chinks in my carefully constructed armor. If I called him by his name, I gave him an opening to see the real me, the person who could never be enough. I couldn't risk that.

Flipping on the water, I stepped under the spray. Deliberately, I ran my hands over my body, palming my breasts and sliding them down my belly and raising them back up to run through my hair. My heart raced faster as I watched Tron's eyes follow my movements. The hunger in his gaze backed my breath right up in my throat.

They were so warm, his hands following the same path over my body. Anticipation shivered through me, my skin rippling beneath his touch, reveling in it. Never in my life could I remember wanting a man as much as I wanted Adam Tron. Like he knew that too somehow, he cradled my head in his hands, his eyes seeking mine. Willing him to play by my rules, I settled my gaze on the perfect curve of his full lower lip. In case he needed more of a hint, I slicked my tongue along my own lower lip.

Guess he was bad at taking hints.

"Say it, Cristy."

By itself, the command in his low tone wouldn't have been enough. What did it was the reverent kiss on my forehead that he lingered over, waiting for me.

"Please."

"Like I said, babe, I'm a patient man. But whatever your ghosts are, I'm not one of them." He pulled me into his chest and let the water and his words wash over me. "I'm your present, not your past. And for as long as it works, I want to be your future. Let me in, Valorous."

The insistence of his hard-on pushing into my belly was not what he meant, and I knew it. The reverent way he held me told me exactly how patient a man he was. Though he could overpower me in a second, he chose to give me control. The other time we'd been together, it had been this way too. My whole life experience told me not to trust him, but right now, in this moment, I wanted to stop refusing, stop resisting, stop rebelling. I wanted to rest. The safety of his arms promised that rest, and I sagged into him.

"It scares the heck out of me how much I want you, Adam."

A self-deprecating laugh chuffed out of him. "I want you that bad, too, Cristy." For emphasis, he rubbed his impressive phallus along my skin, and my knees turned to water.

It didn't feel like I'd given in when he took control, lifting me up to wrap my legs around him while he took my mouth in a devouring kiss. Tightening my arms around his neck, I clung to him, digging my heels into the thick muscles of his backside as I slicked my wetness up and down his hard shaft and kissed him back with everything I had. For long minutes, we traded breath, our tongues mimicking what our bodies longed to do. He traced my lower lip, nipped it, and plunged his tongue back inside my mouth. I pressed my lips hard into his and explored his teeth and every luscious slick surface of his mouth with my tongue. He tasted of beer and sin and something mysteriously him, and I couldn't get enough.

At last he tore his mouth from me, his breath sawing in and out of his lungs as he rested his forehead on mine. "How the fuck do you do that, Cristy?"

Too dazed to give him a coherent response, all I could do was sigh.

A growl reverberated in his chest as he pushed my back into the wall of the shower. "Condoms are in my duffel. Fuck."

"Look on the shelf behind you." I smiled at him. "Problem solved."

For a second, he hesitated, but I flexed my hips, my core more wet than the water sluicing over his back and shoulders, trickling between our bodies. While he held my hips in his hands, I rolled the condom over his length. He shifted, positioning my opening over him. Before he let me slide down to join our bodies together, he captured my eyes with his again. "Watch us Cristy. Watch how incredibly fucking hot we are together."

Every nerve ending crackled and buzzed as I watched him drive into and pull out of me. His slow rhythm ensured I'd experience every deliciously hard inch of his impressive length. The kisses and touches we'd shared to this point had wound me up so tight that it didn't take much for him to have me teetering on the edge of release. Watching us together turned me on even more. He shifted again, changing the angle slightly, and found my G-spot like I was magnetized. Somehow, his thumb was on my clit, and my inner muscles spasmed hard. A scream tore from my throat as I spiraled out of control. I came and came until the whole world burned away to nothing but Adam Tron pounding deep inside me.

When I returned to some semblance of coherence, the gorgeous sight of his corded neck and powerful shoulder muscles rigid beneath my fingertips alerted me to his coming release. A guttural sound tore out of his lips to echo through the shower stall. He thrust into me again, once, twice, three times, and the aftershocks rolled through me like a second earthquake. Before Adam Tron, I thought that old saying that the earth moved was an exaggeration. After Adam Tron, I knew an earthquake could only approximate what being with him did to me.

When we finished, he gently let me go to slide slowly down his form until I stood in front of him. As though he knew my legs were jelly, he pressed me to the wall with his body, holding me upright until I could find the strength to stand on my own. All the while, he murmured to me, my name like a song. At last, I squeezed my arms tight around him and planted a kiss over his heart that still thundered in his chest beneath my lips.

Leaning down, he found my mouth with his. The kiss he gave me held all sorts of promises of dark delights, and I flattened my chest to his and promised back. After what we'd shared, how could I do anything else?

He smiled against my lips. "It's so fucking hot when you sing my name while you come. I could listen to that refrain all night long."

I blinked up at him. "What do I do?"

"AdamAdamAdamAdam!" he said as he rubbed his body along mine. "When you start chanting my name, all I want to do is make you come for days. It's the sweetest song I've ever heard you sing."

Yeah, I had no idea what to do with that. "We should probably actually shower and head to the party before the rumors start up again."

He confused me and rattled me and sneaked under my skin. I should have raced away, outrunning the hurricane of feelings he unleashed inside me. Yet I clung to him, my words and actions in direct opposition—as usual. Gretchen understood how to deal with me when I was like this. But I'd sent her away. Now I was alone with Adam Tron and all the flotsam of my thoughts churning through me.

Beneath my fingertips, I sensed him stiffen for a second then relax, a quiet laugh rumbling under my cheek where it rested on his chest. "I'll wash your back, and you'll wash mine?"

My eyes squeezed shut as he did it to me again. For some reason, this man had tuned into me, reading me perfectly like notes on a staff. I had no idea how he could do that, and even less of an idea of what I was going to do about it. Though I'd deliberately shaken things up as I rejoined the tour, you know, like skipping the ensemble rehearsal and varying my entrance to the concert and messing with his head as I left him alone before showing up again beside him during the show, it seemed nothing rattled Adam. No matter what, he remained even, steady, unwavering. No wonder *Rolling Stone* magazine named him to the top ten bassists of all time. It seemed nothing could throw him off-balance or interrupt his rhythm. In every way, he was diametrically the opposite of me.

Yet he wanted me.

And he was willing to play the game by my rules.

What the heck was I supposed to do with that?

Warm hands slid up and down my back, the fresh scent of cucumbers wafting up around me. I leaned back and said, "Hand me the soap, please."

He smirked and dropped the bar into my hand. For a couple of pleasurable minutes, we washed each other's backs before he demanded the soap back. Kneeling in front of me, he took his time lathering my legs and my belly, slowly making his way to my breasts. Concentration tightened the muscles in his face as he took special care in soaping my hypersensitized nipples. A moan escaped my lips as my body undulated beneath his touch without my permission. A feral grin curved his mouth.

"Adam." Though I tried, I couldn't keep the breathiness out of my tone. "I think I'm clean now."

"Just making sure, Valorous. Playing a show is sweaty business." The laughter in his voice relaxed me.

I plucked the soap from his hand. "Your turn."

A sun-blinding smile lit up his face as he stood in front of me again. "Did you see how my T-shirt stuck to me out there? It's going to take a lot of soap to clean me up."

Narrowing my eyes, I lathered the bar between my hands and went to work. Exploring his shoulders, chest, and arms delighted me. His long legs were as sculpted as the rest of him, smooth muscles that told a tale of strength honed by hard use. Such a turn-on. When I came to the apex of his thighs, his member jutted up full and proud. I sneaked a peek at his face and saw the desire—and the curiosity there. Good. He should wonder what I'd do next.

Batting sassy eyes at him, I tongued him from base to tip and reveled at the shudder that rippled through him. His hands smacked the wall of the shower, and his deep groan echoed around the stall while I went to work with my hands and my mouth. Adam's pleasure fed my own. He acted like no one ever went down on him, like he was the one who always had to give. Enjoying him like this gave me back a little of what I'd given away to him. Somehow, he knew that too and let me have my way with him.

He palmed the back of my head but left me in charge as I hollowed my cheeks on the upstroke, sucking hard then tonguing and kissing the head. I plunged back down, taking as much of him as I could, my hand stroking the base below my lips. His hips jerked, and I set my rhythm to his, humming in the back of my throat because it was so good.

"Cristy." His fingers tangled in my hair. "Fuck."

I dropped one hand between my legs, pleasuring myself as I pumped him with the other, my head bobbing, his hips pistoning, my hands moving on both of our bodies, our rhythms accelerating from four/four to double time.

"Jesus, Cristy! Fuuuuck!"

My body convulsed in my hand as I swallowed him down.

For several seconds, I held him inside my mouth then pulled away with a tiny kiss. Bowing my head, I blew out a breath and tried to collect myself. Always before, giving a guy head gave me power over him. I was the arbiter of pleasure, and afterward, I'd smile and walk away, leaving him breathless and begging. It wasn't the same with Adam. Each time was better than the last. Each time left me craving more. Each time invited him that much deeper inside me. What the hell was I doing?

Before I could spend any more time with those thoughts, Adam slipped his hands beneath my arms and lifted me to stand in front of him.

"You took care of yourself that time too, didn't you, babe?"

I nodded.

"Just when I think you can't be any hotter, you change the rules and blow my mind."

The intensity of those deep brown eyes intrigued and terrified me in equal parts.

"Men. Always thinking with your little heads." I winked.

Adam cupped my face in his hands, the pressure light but firm. "You're special, you know that? A shining fucking star, and I don't mean out on the stage."

The steady strength of him as he held me, the intensity of his expression, the low rumble of his voice as he spoke those words unlocked something inside me. When I pulled in a deep breath, pieces rearranged and came together. For a second, I almost thought I belonged to this man.

Someone pounding on the door to my dressing room interrupted whatever else his expression promised. Praise the Lord. Playful Adam, sexy Adam, bassist Adam I could handle. Serious Adam, my private monster-slayer? Not so much.

"Cristy!"

Though the sound was muffled, I'd know that voice always.

"Sounds like playtime's over, big guy."

Chapter Twenty

Adam

CRISTY'S COSTUMES, HER entourage, her mercurial nature all screamed high-maintenance diva. But ten minutes after Gretchen interrupted us, Valorous was dressed in a bright orange minidress, something that resembled a sack when she'd pulled it out of her impressive wardrobe, but it bared her shoulders and clung to her curves in a way that made my mouth water. The pair of hand-tooled cowboy boots she pulled on lacked the sexiness of her thigh-high lace-up boots, but they complemented her dress in such a flirty way I couldn't help but grin. In seconds it seemed, she transformed her face from scrubbed clean and beautiful girl-next-door to glamorous pop star. Watching her apply makeup fascinated and distracted me. Before I caught up, Cristy was ready to hit the party while I stood around in my jeans and bare feet.

"Are you coming?"

"I was." I smirked. "And I'd like come again—soon."

She rolled her eyes, but I caught the tiny upturn of her lips as she turned toward the door. "It might be better if we didn't walk into the party together."

"Not so fast, Valorous." I put my hands on her hips and dragged her against me, holding her close. "I like what we're starting here"—I ghosted a kiss beneath her ear—"and I don't give a flying fuck about any rumors social media or TMZ or whoever wants to spread. Give me five seconds."

With my hands splayed over her hips, I waited her out until she nodded. Then I jerked a T-shirt over my head, shoved my feet into my socks and boots, and hitched my duffel over my shoulder. Five seconds flat, no doubt.

Since I didn't completely trust her not to try to have her way on this, I took her hand. Lacing my fingers through hers, I held on as I led her down the hallway to Balefire's dressing room. I dropped off my duffel bag, nodded to a roadie who gathered up our gear to secure for the night, and headed for the green room, Cristy in tow. Before I opened the door to the chaos of a Balefire after-party, I leaned in close and whispered, "Do all the shots you want tonight, babe. I'm still spending the night with you. You know I'm—"

"—a patient man," we finished in unison.

I didn't even try to stifle the laugh that barked out of me. Tightening my hand on hers when she tried to tug away from me, I turned the knob on the door and braced for the blast of laughter, music, and shouted conversations awaiting us on the other side.

A kaleidoscope of light and sound washed over us as we stepped into the party.

"Follow me," I said into her ear as I wove us through the crowd of groupies, roadies, and celebrities enjoying our promoter's generosity tonight.

We almost made it to the bar where I'd spied Dakota standing beside Annabelle, a row of shots lined up in front of them when Garrett intercepted us. "Nice of you to grace us with your presence, Tron. Finally," he sneered. One of his arms draped the shoulders of a spectacularly endowed blonde, a flashback to *Baywatch* Pamela Anderson, her tits barely contained in the lacy tank top she wore.

His other arm held a dark-skinned beauty who looked like a young Alfre Woodard, her full kissable lips begging for a taste, her smooth brown skin infinitely lickable. On another tour in the not-so-distant past, I might have taken him up on his unmistakable offer of such delectable ladies. But I hadn't had nearly enough of Cristy Valor yet. After what she revealed to me in the shower earlier, revelations I'm sure she didn't intend, I wasn't sure when I'd have enough of her.

With a nod to his companions, I said, "Looks like you haven't had time to miss me."

"Janie"—he nudged the Alfre look-alike—"and Betsy here"—he nodded at the Pamela look-alike—"are quite keen to meet you, if you know what I mean."

Ignoring his innuendo, I inclined my head. "Ladies. Hope you enjoy the party. If you'll excuse us, Cristy is thirsty." Giving her a wink, I took a step toward Dakota and the bar.

"Seriously, Tron?" There was an edge to Garrett's voice.

I bared my teeth. "How long have you been managing us? Ten years? And you haven't figured out that after playing a show, we need to hydrate? Preferably with Jameson."

"I knew from the start this was a bad idea," he muttered, but I ignored him.

Without another word, I headed for the bar, my arm wrapped tight around Cristy's waist.

"What did he mean? What is a bad idea? Throwing those women at you when I was standing right there?"

Over her shoulder, she threw our manager the filthiest look I'd ever seen. I had to admit, I liked the way she bristled up at Garrett's ham-handed attempt to keep me from hooking up with her. Her display of jealousy told me we were on the same page. I liked that. A lot.

"He's been pissy since our last tour. Ignore him." I signaled the bartender and ordered a couple of shots as we joined Dakota and Annabelle at the bar.

"Welcome back, Cristy." Dakota grinned. "You fuckin' rocked it out there tonight—again." He saluted her with a shot of what smelled like tequila and tossed it back. Nodding at Annabelle, he said, "Damn good idea you had inviting her to join us on this tour, Annie."

A smile ghosted Annabelle's lips as she gave me a secret wink.

I nodded. "Agreed, Dakota. Damn good idea."

Dakota wrapped his arm around her and pulled her in for a smacking kiss. "My lady here is full of good ideas." The way he waggled his eyebrows at her left no one in the dark about what he meant. Annabelle warned him with narrowed eyes, but I noticed she snuggled in closer to him.

The bartender set our shots in front of us, and I raised mine for a toast. "To good ideas."

The four of us tossed back our drinks, and the bartender replaced them with full ones almost as fast as we set the empty glasses on the bar. Dakota and I exchanged a grin and tossed back another. Apparently not to be left out, the girls clinked glasses and shot theirs right after us.

"Have you noticed, Tron, how well our ladies can keep up?"

With a smirk, I gave Cristy's ass a discreet squeeze. "You don't say."

It hadn't escaped my attention that in some ways, Cristy was a little bit of a prude. Her sexy outfits and even sexier dancing onstage aside, she blushed at innuendo sometimes, and I'd never heard the woman use a swear word. Always, she used some PG variation instead—heck, freakin', dang. It was kinda cute. So when I grabbed her ass so blatantly in public, I half expected her to try to wiggle away from me or bat at my hand. Then again, Cristy never did the expected. She pushed herself farther into my touch and undulated her hips in invitation for more contact, all while she conversed with Annabelle.

"I think these boys underestimate us. What do you think, Annabelle?"

"If there's something I do exceptionally well, it's holding my liquor. Ask Jack's wife. In college, she led our sorority to the top in grades while I made sure no one touched us when it came to winning drinking games."

I couldn't decide if the smirk she gave Dakota was a warning or a challenge.

"I'd never underestimate you, Annie. I'm all about the things you do exceptionally well." The leer on his face left little to the imagination.

Because her thin dress didn't offer much of a barrier between my palm and her perfect round ass, the brief second of tension at Dakota's words drew my attention to Cristy's face. Yeah, there it was. A hint of a blush climbed up her neck to color her cheeks at my bandmate's blatant sexual flirtation with our intern. Yeah, a bit of a prude. Yet there was nothing prudish about that little party she gave me in her dressing room after the show. This woman was an enigma. Giving her ass another squeeze, I smiled at her. I'd always enjoyed solving puzzles.

"This is my fourth show so far with the boys. I guess they must be slow learners." Some sort of understanding passed between the girls. "I believe I was still standing in San Francisco when your roadies—and Annabelle—dragged your backside to your room," Cristy patted Dakota's shoulder in such a patronizing way I had to cough into my hand to cover my laughter.

He groaned. "That was an off night." Annabelle patted his other shoulder with teasing concern, and he brightened. "But I'm feeling damn good tonight. Let's see what you got, Cristy Valor." He handed her another shot.

With Dakota's pronouncement, the drinking games began in earnest. Before I realized it, we were surrounded by our friends with Clio and Ashleigh cheering Cristy and Annabelle while Jack and Blu had Dakota's and my backs. Their interest drew fans with backstage passes, roadies, and the assorted promotions people who always ended up at our parties. The media labeled me the quiet member of Balefire, but the guys knew better. Still, Cristy matched me shot for shot.

At some point, I noticed Gretchen moving in close to Cristy who was laughing at something Dakota said, her hand resting on his chest after she'd slammed her glass on the bar. Her other hand remained buried in the back pocket of my jeans where she deliberately messed with me. I'd spent the better part of the evening half hard, and I had no doubt she knew it. From somewhere on the periphery of our circle, a camera flashed. The sour expression on Gretchen's face told me I had about a minute before she tried to steal Cristy away from me.

Not.

The.

Plan.

"Hey, babe. If I concede now, can we head back to your hotel?" I said into her ear. For emphasis, I slid my tongue along the shell of it and puffed a gentle gust of air over it.

With her tucked tight against my side, I felt the full-body shiver ripple over her, and she squeezed my ass hard. A single nod gave me my answer.

"Well, boys and girls, this has been fun. But it's time to call it."

"Are you giving in, Tron?" The incredulous expression on Dakota's face tugged a grin out of me.

"We're both still standing, D. Might be a good idea to let the ladies win this round." I pulled Cristy in front of me and wrapped both arms around her. "If you know what I'm sayin'."

A slow smile slid over Dakota's mouth. "Good idea, Tron."

"Yeah, I'm full of good ideas."

Annabelle started to protest when Dakota kissed her cheek and whispered something in her ear.

"Dakota Perri! You are a naughty man."

"Lucky for me, Annie, you like naughty men."

Because I couldn't help myself, I ducked my head to check for Cristy's blush. Huh. She must have had enough to drink to lower her inhibitions. Maybe that's what Gretchen noticed too. Didn't matter what her manager thought. I had plans for enjoying an incredible night with the hottest woman I'd ever met. Lowered inhibitions were a bonus for both of us.

Making sure to angle us in the opposite direction from Gretchen, I stepped back out of the circle. Since my arms remained around Cristy, she had no choice but to back up with me. Once we cleared the circle, which took some doing with people wanting to talk to us and try to encourage us to keep entertaining them with our drinking antics, I ushered her toward the door.

"Cristy." Gretchen intercepted us. "We need to talk."

"Can it wait till morning?" Cristy sounded wary.

"No."

"You're wrong, there, Gretchen," I said, tugging Cristy closer into my side. "Whatever it is absolutely can wait until morning." I brushed a kiss over Cristy's temple. "We have a date, one I've been waiting for since we played in San Francisco."

Gretchen caressed Cristy's arm, her tone soft but with an edge to it neither of us missed. "Think about what you're doing here, Cristy-girl."

Along my side, Cristy's body tensed. Fearing I was about to lose her to whatever nonsense her manager had dreamed up, I slid behind her and wrapped both arms around her, resting my chin on the top of her head. After all the shots we'd downed, I certainly wasn't feeling any pain, but Gretchen's interference was harshing my buzz, something I communicated when I caught the woman's eye.

"I'm a big girl, Gretch. Big enough to handle this guy." She covered my hands at her waist and laced her fingers through mine.

It took me a second to relax. Then I gifted Gretchen with a triumphant grin. "I like it when Cristy handles me." My little prude gasped at my innuendo, and I set my lips by her ear. "I like it a lot."

"Enjoy the rest of the party, Gretchen. We'll see you back at the hotel." I maneuvered Cristy around her friend to the open door and hoped they both heard what I'd said. For some reason, Cristy didn't want to spend the night in my room. It didn't matter much to me in whose bed we ended up, but it did matter that she was comfortable. For some reason, she brought out the protector in me, and I needed for her to feel safe.

"Where are you staying, Valorous?" I asked as we settled into the deep leather back seat of the town car waiting to drive us away from Lumen Field.

"At your place."

CHAPTER TWENTY-ONE

Cristy

THE LOOK ON Adam's face when I told him where I wanted to go sent me into fits of giggles. He gaped sort of like a guppy then snapped his mouth shut. The wicked gleam in his dark chocolate eyes told me I might be the one in trouble though. I tried not to let the nerves in, tried to channel my sexy stage persona. But a flash of sensation jerked through me, my body telling me something my mind wasn't ready to hear.

My tongue slipped along my lower lip as I clamped my legs tight together, which only seemed to draw him to me. My heart pulsed in my core. I knew the second he discovered the soaked state of my panties, I'd be a goner. For reasons I'd never understand, this one man's touch did things to me, deep things, things that I feared I'd never experience with anyone else—a terrifying thought.

"My place, huh?" He slid his arm along the back of my seat, the heat of his jeans-clad thigh along mine tingling my skin.

I shrugged. "Yes—and no."

He quirked a brow. "Come again?"

"That's the plan."

I melted a little at the way his eyes danced when I delivered my innuendo.

The touch of his calloused fingertips as he stroked my cheek sent tiny tremors through me, and I couldn't help but snuggle into his side. He'd used my soap in the shower, but on him, the cucumber scent smelled hot and dangerous. That scent was the reason I sucked in air, certainly not the way he was touching me. The way his eyes caressed my mouth fascinated me, so I wasn't prepared for his words.

"You're such a badass onstage, all swagger and sass. But I've noticed you color up almost every time someone implies something about sex." He continued to stroke my cheek. "You even blush when you're the one making the innuendo."

I huffed out an exasperated sigh, and he chuckled softly.

"I like it." He smiled his perfect, straight-white-teeth smile. "It's another part of the Cristy Valor puzzle I want to figure out."

Giving him what I hoped was my sassiest grin—I couldn't be sure I pulled it off with my heart hammering at the walls of my chest the way it did—I distracted him the best way I knew how. Turning my head, I filled his palm with my lips and slipped my tongue out to taste him. The shudder that rippled through him satisfied me that my diversion had worked.

Desire flared in his eyes, and I crossed my legs at the answering sensations flooding my center. With a slight shake of his head, he dropped his hand to my thigh, giving it a squeeze. He pushed my leg back down and feathered his fingers up to the apex, taking the hem of my dress up with them.

"Open for me, Valorous."

I couldn't have denied him if the entirety of the tabloid press had their cameras pointed in the limousine's windows.

"Jesus. How long have you been in this state?"

His fingers rubbed over the soaking wet silk of my thin bikini panties.

The way he played over me, I could barely find the air to answer him. "Since you conceded our drinking game."

When he palmed my mound, he left me no choice but to open more for him as he lit little fires under my skin. For a long minute, he held my eyes captive then lowered his head and took my mouth. I couldn't help myself. I reveled in the welcome pressure of his lips, the heady taste of tequila combined with the unique flavor that was only Adam Tron on his tongue. Desperate to deepen the kiss, I grabbed two fistfuls of his T-shirt and hauled myself up to straddle his lap, our greedy mouths never breaking our hot connection.

His big hands completely covered my backside as he kneaded me and pulled me closer to the delicious hard-on behind the fly of his jeans. Needing the friction, I rocked my wet center along his length, and he groaned deep in his chest. That groan set me off, and I sealed my lips to his, my tongue gliding over his before I explored those perfect teeth, the roof of his mouth, the whole length of that tongue that could do such wild and wicked things to my body.

I have no idea how long the kiss went on, but by the time Adam tore his mouth from mine, I'd already had a mini-orgasm that only whet my appetite for more—much more.

"Valorous." The flames burning in his deep brown eyes fired me up, and I couldn't keep from rocking harder against him. "Slow down, baby. You're too special for me to do you in the backseat of car." Punctuating his words, he clamped his hands on my hips, holding me still in his lap.

Narrowing my gaze at him, I said, "Don't tell me you've never had sex in the back of a limo."

"I'm not telling you that." He squeezed my hips, his hands covering half my body. "I'm telling you that *we* are going to wait to finish this in the privacy of a hotel room."

"The windows are blacked out. No one will see, not even the driver."

"Not the issue, babe."

Gently, he set me on the seat beside him.

"But I'm so wet and ready for you." I kinda hated the whine in my voice. Then again, I wanted this man inside me, like ten minutes ago. "You're as hard as stone." With blatant intent, I palmed his impressive length through his jeans.

His hand swallowed my wrist and half my forearm, stopping me on the downstroke with a groan. "Makes the anticipation all that much sweeter." The expression he gifted me was pure sin. "Besides, it's bad manners to make the driver wait in front of the hotel while we finish."

I glanced out the window at the passing lights of the city and figured out we must be close to where we were staying. "If you're worried about what the press swarming the hotel will report—"

"Not even a little bit. But that also doesn't mean we have to share what's happening between us with a world of strangers either."

Those four words washed over me like a cold rain. *What's happening between us.* Nothing was happening between us. We were fooling around, sharing some epic sex. That's all. That's all it could ever be. If Adam ever found out about my past, he'd scream away from me like escaping a monster in a horror flick. Was that Gretchen's concern back at the party? Maybe tonight, I'd ask him not to lock the door between my room and hers. Or I'd double back and unlock it behind him if he insisted.

"Hey, where'd you go?"

"What?"

"You want the paps to see us all disheveled and smelling of sex when we exit this car?"

"Huh?"

"I'm not in this with you for the publicity. I don't need it." It seemed he tried to penetrate my brain with his eyes. "*We* don't need it. We both sell millions of records without needing to be on the cover of the tabs."

I shot him a side-eye. Better to give him that than let him know what was actually going on in my head. The limo slowing down to make the turn toward the front door of our hotel interrupted our conversation, praise the Lord.

"Apparently, our drinking game outlasted the paparazzi. I only see one guy with a camera lounging outside the door." Years of alternately courting and dodging the press gave me a second sense for when and where they were in my vicinity. The exception was that little mess on Pier 39 in San Francisco, but then again, I might have contributed to that fiasco. "That puts us in the clear, I'd say."

The expression in that one quirked eyebrow spoke volumes before he grabbed the handle of the door. He stepped out first and reached down for me. It took the photographer a minute to figure out who was leaving the limo, then he all but shoved his long lens between the two of us.

"That's enough. Let these people get out the car at least," the driver said as he came around to stand between the cameraman and us. It was only then that I noticed the driver's size and fitness, his pecs bulging under his tight black T-shirt, and was that a shoulder holster under his suit jacket? As big-time as I'd become, I'd never even considered a body guard. After all, I had Gretchen. But after the way the photographer shoved himself at us, maybe having one would be a good idea.

Adam didn't give me time to ponder it further. His hand at the small of my back ushered me in front of him, taking care of me—protecting me. The only person who'd ever protected me was Gretchen. At the after-party, he'd glared her away, and now he'd taken over her role.

Oh, this man. What was I doing with him?

When we stepped into the elevator, I hit the button for my floor.

"You missed." Adam reached over me to hit the button for his floor.

"I said I'd go back to your hotel with you. I didn't say we were spending the night in your room."

"Excuse me?" The confusion on his face would have been adorable if it didn't teeter on the edge teed off.

"I thought it would be more convenient if I stayed in the same hotel, so I asked Gretch to change our reservations"—I winked at him—"for the remainder of the tour."

In half a heartbeat, he pinned me to the wall of the car, his wicked grin doing all sorts of naughty things to my insides. "I never know what you're going to do next. But I know I'm probably going to like it."

In point two seconds, the hard and urgent kiss he laid on me revved both of us right back up to where we were in the limo before he lifted me off his lap. He pushed his thigh between mine, and shamelessly, I rubbed myself along its length while I met his tongue stroke for stroke. When he covered my breasts with his hands, I surged up into his touch and moaned as he kneaded and squeezed. We were well on our way to all-out elevator sex when the car slowed for my floor. The chimes warned us right before the doors opened.

I grinned saucily up at him as I pushed my dress back down.

He grabbed my hand and started moving. "Which room?" The gravel in his voice left me no doubt round one was going to rock my world.

With a little skip, I slipped ahead of him, leading the way to my suite. After all the foreplay, first in the limo then in the elevator, it took me a second to find the key card I'd tucked into my bra. Adam's eyes widened as he watched me fish around inside my dress before I waved the card triumphantly in the air. I'd barely turned the handle when he shoved the door open, using his body to urge me inside the room.

Before the door clicked closed, he had me up against the wall, his hands everywhere as he ravaged my mouth with his lips and teeth and tongue. My foot seemed to have a mind of its own as it slid up the back of his calf and along his thigh to hook over his hip. My dress conveniently slid up too, and he took advantage. He tore his mouth from mine for the millisecond it took him to rip my dress over my head and was back to kissing me with a desperation I felt in my bones.

I nearly wrecked my manicure as I worked the fly of his jeans. He nipped at my lower lip and took a tour of my jaw with his lips on his way to my ear, and I whimpered with need.

"Not here, Valorous."

When he scooped me up high into his arms, he chuckled at my squeak of surprise. He carried me as though I weighed nothing as he strode to the bedroom in my suite and deposited me in the middle of the king-size bed. After flipping on the nightstand lamp, he headed over to lock the door to Gretchen's adjoining room.

"You don't have to do that." I hated how small my voice sounded, but I kind of didn't want to lock my best friend out.

"It's just the two of us, Cristy. No friends. No audience. I told you that in the car."

With a flash of insight I didn't normally possess, I understood that Adam was asking—no, demanding—that I trust him. I had no doubt if I asked, he'd unlock that door. But how would that affect was happening between us? Did I want to pursue what was happening between us? Adam made my decision for me.

Reaching behind his head, he grabbed a handful of his T-shirt and pulled it over in that sexy way guys have of taking off their shirts. Next went his jeans, which I'd so helpfully already undone for him, his boxers joining them at his ankles. He wrenched his eyes from mine only long enough to unlace his boots and kick the whole works somewhere behind him. Standing beside the bed in all his magnificent nakedness, he stole my will, my self-control, my—nope, not going there.

I squeezed my eyes shut for a second before letting them roam over his beautiful body. His broad shoulders and massive chest drew my attention as always. The sleeve of tattoos down his right arm begged me to explore them, cataloging each one with my fingers and tongue. Those six-pack abs proclaimed the time he spent in a gym, framed with the perfect vee that ended at the most impressive erection I'd ever seen. My mouth watered at the thought of what he could do to me with that amazing part of his anatomy. From this angle, I couldn't see the entire length of his long sculpted legs, but I already knew their power.

"What are you thinking behind that naughty grin?"

"How lucky I am to be the woman who's sharing a bed with you tonight."

His warm palm on my calf shot tingles through me as he tugged off first one boot, then the other. "I would have enjoyed you wearing these as you ride me, Cowgirl, but then I'd have to rip those pretty panties off, and I kind of like this pair." He rubbed his finger up and down my center, his touch through the thin silk driving me wild. "So wet. So gorgeously wet," he murmured as he watched his finger play over me.

"Adam. Please."

His expression turned positively wicked as he continued his exquisite torture. Unable to help myself, I writhed beneath his touch. "That's it Valorous. I love it when you beg."

I pulled my knee up, giving him even more access to my center, and palmed my breasts through the pink lace of my bra. His name escaped my lips on a moan, and I closed my eyes at the intensity of my need for this man.

He shifted, the sexy stubble on his face lightly abrading my skin as his voice rumbled in my ear. "Don't hide from me, babe."

When he sat up, he pushed my knee down, slid his fingers under my panties, and pulled them down my legs. His eyes captured mine as he took my feet in his hands and kissed and nipped at each of my toes and ravaged the center of my left arch then my right with his lips and tongue. Sensation overwhelmed me, and I would have catapulted off the bed if he hadn't held me.

The grin he shot me promised all sorts of wild delights as he retrieved his jeans and extracted a handful of condoms from a pocket. Leaning over me, he tossed them on the nightstand except for the one he tore open with his teeth.

Glancing over at the pile of condoms on the nightstand, I asked, "You have some big plans for tonight, mister?" Though I tried to sound sexy, like a vamp in one of the old movies Gretch and I used to like to watch, my words came out breathy and maybe a little needy instead.

As he rolled the condom on, he glanced down at himself. "Very big"—he smirked —"plans. All for you, babe."

"Oh," was all I could manage as he slowly pushed himself inside me.

I couldn't help it. His body was incredible, and I wanted him so much, I surged my hips up to meet him. His eyes widened and he shook his head, stilling me with his hands. "You're going to have your turn, babe. But round one is mine. After what you did for me in the shower after the show, I owe you one."

I'd been on the edge of orgasm from his lips and his hands on me alone. The slow thrusts of his beautiful erection only ratcheted up my need to come. When I tried to move, tried to urge him to increase his rhythm, Adam merely flashed that wicked grin and shook his head, his hands holding my hips where he wanted them. My back arched, my head thrashed from side to side on the pillow, and I couldn't stop the whimpers and moans leaving my throat like a song.

"Adam, please. I can't—oh!"

His thumb on my clit added a new layer of intensity to the sensations rippling through my body. Involuntarily, I clenched my inner muscles around him, the orgasm I chased right at the edge of my grasp.

"Look at me, Cristy."

I squeezed my eyes shut tight.

"Cristy. Give me your eyes."

I might have withstood a demand, but he whispered it, a sweet ask I couldn't deny. The desire flaring in the rich chocolate depths of his gorgeous eyes overshadowed something else flickering behind it, something I couldn't quite name. He drove into me at last, his powerful rhythms building a wild heat inside me.

"Adam! Yeesss!"

"There it is, sweet woman. Don't look away."

Subtly, he changed the angle, and I shot into the stratosphere, my eyes never leaving his until he thrust into me again.

"Fuuuuck! Cristy!" The cords of his neck stood in stark relief in the low lamplight as he shouted his release to the ceiling.

A storm of green and blue stars danced behind my eyes, the orgasm rolling over and through me like thunder. I might have screamed like the wind rushing down a mountain canyon as I dug my nails into the tops of his thighs. Until that moment, I wouldn't have thought it possible to dent steel with acrylic, but the half-moons I left behind on his skin said otherwise.

The gentle touch of his calloused fingertip along my cheek returned me to earth. When I opened my eyes, the expression I saw in his sent my stomach into free fall.

"Fuck, Cristy. That was the most intense experience I've ever had." The wonder in his voice as he whispered those words added a rock chaser to my dropping stomach.

Yet I couldn't stop the words.

"Me too."

CHAPTER TWENTY-TWO

Adam

"WHAT DO YOU mean, you're not riding with us?" The mutinous pout on Dakota's face would have looked feminine on anyone else. On him, it was comical.

"Leave it alone, Dakota," Jack said as he wrapped his arm over Dakota's shoulders and attempted to haul him toward the steps and into our tour bus.

"But we're a band. We play together because we stay together," Dakota said, his pout morphing into a glare.

I scrubbed my hand over my head. "It's a three-hour ride, for fuck's sake. I'm not abandoning you." Quirking a brow at Jack, I said, "Garrett thought Cristy was the diva." I gestured with my thumb. "Guess he forgot about our buddy here."

Jack snorted a laugh, and Dakota elbowed him in the ribs. Still, Jack held onto him and dragged him to our bus. "See you at the stadium, Tron. Enjoy your ride." His parting shot came with waggling eyebrows and a smirk.

A strobe of flashes went off somewhere to my left, and all three of us groaned.

"Our 'fight' is going to be all over social media in about a minute flat," Jack said, air quoting with his free hand. "Time to load up, Dakota."

As Jack spoke, Annabelle joined us, and Dakota's eyes went all soft.

Huh.

I smiled. "You're not going to miss me. Admit it."

"Sure he is, Tron. Just like he misses me when we're on hiatus." Jack slanted Dakota a look and winked at me. "He needs our rhythms to perform."

Dakota swung at Jack, but Jack danced out of the way and up the steps. "See you in Vancouver, Tron," he called over his shoulder as he laughed his way on board.

Annabelle flashed a quizzical expression between us before she too headed into the bus. "You coming, Dakota?"

"I wish," he said to her with a leer.

She huffed out a sigh, but I caught the subtle curve of her lips before she disappeared inside.

"Don't be late, Tron. That's all I gotta say."

"Don't worry about me, old friend. I'm always on time."

He rolled his eyes, turned on his heel, and boarded our bus. But I heard him chuckling as he said "on time" under his breath and I knew we were all right.

♪

Though girly in its color scheme, Cristy's bus was as tricked out as ours. Where our banquette and captain's chairs were black leather, hers were white. The interior walls were painted in some sort of sixties style geometric pattern in shades of pink from pale to hot but toned down with the occasional shot of turquoise or forest green or lemon yellow. It should have set my teeth on edge, but it was so her that I got used to it in about ten seconds. Or maybe the black carpet on the floor toned it down a notch. Whatever. A Bruno Mars tune danced right out of the state-of-the-art sound system, and I grinned.

Gretchen emerged from behind the door at the back of the bus and wrinkled her nose in my direction like I'd passed gas or something.

"Good morning to you too," I said. "Cristy back there?"

She glared at me. "You know she is."

I took a step, but Gretchen didn't budge.

"What's the deal? You the gatekeeper?"

"She only does flings, nothing serious. You know that, right? Publicity for her brand."

Last night didn't feel like a fling. And I'd made sure the paps weren't around. Declan, our driver, texted to tell me the lone photographer who got up in our faces when we arrived at the hotel "lost" the photos he took. So everything that happened between Cristy and me had been only about us and only between us. Not the show, not her brand, not publicity. When we spent the night rocking each other's worlds, our focus had been on us—mine on her, hers on me. For the space of last night, I had everything I'd ever wanted and didn't know I needed right there in her bed.

It wasn't enough.

Then the rest of the world butted in. I hadn't seen Cristy since we'd fed each other bacon and pancakes in bed before Gretchen started banging on the connecting door I'd so thoughtfully locked the night before. Dragging my mind back to the moment, I rubbed my palm over the burning sensation in my chest and gazed past her at that firmly shut door at the back of the bus. The feeling should have scared the shit out of me, but for some reason, I was more afraid of Gretchen barring the door to Cristy than what heartburn might mean.

"She invited me to ride with her. I assumed I'd spend the time *with her.*" I motioned with my hand. "So if you don't mind—"

For several seconds she seemed to mull something over in her mind. With one last glare, she shouldered her way past me into the public cabin of the bus, leaving the hallway open. It wasn't until I reached Cristy's door that I heard Gretchen talking to the other members of Cristy's entourage who must have boarded the bus behind me when my attention was on my little standoff with her.

With a soft knock, I called through the door. "Hey, babe. You gonna let me in?"

Some rustling answered my knock and the door swung open to reveal Cristy wearing nothing but a fluffy white towel. I grinned at her, my cock thickening behind the fly of my jeans in approval of her outfit. A gruff throat-clearing from behind the door alerted me to the other person in the room. What. The. Fuck?

"Thank you, Ben." She directed her words to the faceless voice behind the door. Quirking a sassy brow at me she added, "Unless you want a turn, Tron."

We were back to Tron again? And who the fuck was Ben?

"Excuse me?"

She pushed the door open wider, and a man about my own size came into view. His upper body stretched the hell out of his white T-shirt, and I noticed his white pants strained to cover his impressive thighs. Either the guy was a linebacker or a bodybuilder, neither of which mattered to me. The only thing I cared about was what the hell he was doing alone with Cristy in her private bedroom in the back of her bus.

As I stared the guy down, from the corner of my eye, I thought I saw the front of those tight pants start to swell. Cristy chuckled as she reached out to trace her finger down my chest. "I've never watched two guys. You're both so hot, it might be a fun show."

"What the hell? After last night, you want us to share?"

"You misunderstood, Tron." Her eyes toured my body. "Ben and I would be sharing."

That action in the guy's pants was about me? Huh.

I reached out and shook his hand. "I'm flattered, man. Truly. But my soldier prefers to land in a soft bed."

"Worth a shot, yeah?" he said, giving my hand an extra squeeze. "If you ever change your mind—or you just want a massage—let me know." His card appeared as if by magic, and I nodded as I stuffed it into my back pocket.

When he brushed past me, I caught Cristy's mouth curve into a half grin as she stepped farther back into the room. I closed the door behind her masseur and waited.

"What?"

"You tell me."

An expression of pure confusion flitted over her features, and she hitched the towel higher over her pretty rack, crossing her arms to keep it there.

I mirrored her stance. "What happened between breakfast in bed and your massage that put me back in the Tron zone?"

Her eyes skittered to the bed then back to my face, specifically my mouth, not my eyes. As hot as that little move was, it didn't change the fact she was avoiding answering my question.

Right then, the bus lurched into gear. My knees hit the bed, and Cristy fell backward toward the nightstand beside it, her towel dropping to the floor as she put her hands out to stop herself. The sight of her gorgeous curves, her skin all flushed from her recent massage, made me forget what my problem was. I crawled across the bed and snagged her with one arm, pulling her down on top of me. The laughter bubbling up out of her sounded a bit like relief, but I ignored what that might mean because she was touching me.

Tracing her finger along the collar of my T-shirt, she turned on the flirt. "It's three whole hours to Vancouver. However will we fill the time, do you suppose?"

Her light touch on my skin arrowed sensation directly to my half-hard cock. Bending my knee, I pushed between her legs, spreading her over my thigh. When I started tapping a slow rhythm on the bed with my foot, she gasped as I tickled her clit with the denim covering the muscle of my thigh.

"Adam!"

"That's correct, Valorous. Adam. Always Adam to you."

As she trailed her lips along the stubble covering my jaw, she seemed not to have heard me. Instead, she kissed and tasted and nibbled her way to my ear obe. When she closed her teeth over it and gently tugged, I groaned. My hands found their way to her beautiful round breasts where I smoothed the rough pads of my thumbs over her impossibly tight nipples that begged me to roll and pinch, which I was only too delighted to do.

Her moans and whimpers as I played her naked body fired me up. Between the rocking motion of the bus, the rhythms I built with my thigh on her hot pussy, and Cristy's insistence on more as she moved over me, I had a real fear of going off in my jeans, and that most definitely was not the plan.

"Babe."

She moaned again, and my hips did their own thing, surging up to rub the length of my cock along her hip bone. Her tongue in my ear, the vibrations of her body in my hands, the rocking of the bed beneath us as the bus accelerated pulled me ever closer to launching my load long before I wanted to. I grasped her hips and squeezed and lifted her off me. In two seconds, I stripped out of my clothes, snagging a condom from the pocket of my jeans right before they hit the floor beside the bed.

The way her eyes glittered as she watched me slide the condom on flipped a switch inside me. I wanted to ruin this bed for any other man she might want to invite into it. I wanted to ruin *her* for any other man, period. "Sit on me, Cristy. Let me give you a ride."

That sweet pink tongue of hers sneaked out to glide over her lips as she eyed me like I was her favorite treat and she couldn't wait for a taste. Taking myself in hand, I squeezed the base of my cock, desperately trying to hold onto some control. Had it only been a few hours since I was last inside her? It felt like weeks.

"Fuck, babe. What are you waiting for?"

The kaleidoscope of blues coalesced into deep sapphire before the irises disappeared into the dilated pools of her pupils while she took her time climbing over me. Nudging my hand away from my dick, she took over touching me, holding me where she wanted me as she pleasured her clit with the head of my erection. I loved that she used me to warm herself up or get herself off—whatever. It didn't matter when that dreamy expression flowed over her face, her cheeks flushed, her smile unguarded. *Fuck*. Cristy was gorgeous all the time, but especially like this when she was open to me in every way.

She blinked her eyes and stared into mine as she sheathed me in the wet hot paradise of her pussy. I took over then, holding her hips exactly where I wanted them as I surged up deep inside her. No doubt her fingernails would leave marks on my wrists where she gripped them, not that I gave a shit. Snapping my hips, I thrust up hard enough to make her pretty tits jiggle, and I licked my lips in anticipation.

"Lean down here, sweetheart. Let me taste some of that sugar."

Instead, she moaned and gyrated her hips over me, her inner muscles working me over and driving me wild. Selfish bastard that I was, I wanted more of that, and I knew exactly how to get it. With one hand holding her body where I wanted her, I played her nipples with the other, teasing one then the other until she whimpered and leaned forward, her hands grasping my shoulders. Still, I kept driving into her, even as she offered me her ripe peaks for our mutual pleasure. I flicked my tongue over her and tugged a tight bud into my mouth, nipping and sucking and loving the sounds she made as I worked her. The chorus of whimpers and moans and tiny gasps was the prelude to the main verse I loved to hear her sing. The rhythmic pulses of her pussy on my cock told me all about how much she was enjoying herself.

Then her rhythms changed from steady four/four to a staccato two/two to something syncopated and out of control, signaling she was close. I tried to hold back, tease her a little, but the bus bumped hard over something, driving me deeper inside her, and she screamed my name. Her whole body convulsed around me, electrifying me as she sang my favorite song over and over. "Adam! Please, Adam!" A white-hot bolt of pleasure shot down my spine, and with another deep thrust, I came so hard I rocketed from seeing stars to seeing whole galaxies.

When my heartbeat at last slowed down to something like a sprint, I tried to remember what day it was and where we were. Neither mattered when I stared into the swirling chaos of blue that was Cristy's eyes. Raw vulnerability warred with the desire the aftershocks generated where we remained joined together. She blinked several times, but whatever she saw in my eyes didn't let her look away. What I saw looked too much like longing, and more than anything, I wanted to hold her close, watch over her, slay all her monsters.

My gaze never left hers as I traced a path over her temple, down the satin contours of her cheeks, and along the sculpted edge of her jaw until I reached the lush fullness of her mouth. Sensing she was on the verge of pulling away from me, I held her chin with my finger and thumb and pulled up to her. Though I remained gentle, I insisted she join me as I brushed a kiss over her lips. We hadn't known each other long, but already I knew her tells. After what had just happened between us, no way was I letting her run.

Wrapping my arms around her, I pulled her down with me as I relaxed back into the pillows. Beneath my hands, her body vibrated, and I had a bad feeling it wasn't all from the pleasurable connection we still shared. Somehow, I needed to convince my girl to open up, tell me what put that sad expression in her eyes after we'd experienced the most epic sex of my life.

"It's complicated, Adam."

Huh. Guess Cristy had some things figured out about me too.

"Talk to me."

For long moments, she remained silent as she smoothed her fingers over and through the hair on my chest. Right as I was about to prompt her, she said, "I'm not ready to stop playing with you yet."

"We're another month on the road, Valorous. I plan to spend as much of that time as I can with you."

"Then we can wait to talk."

Wrong answer. But when I lifted my head to look into her face and call her out, I saw a bleakness that scraped my insides raw. Whatever she saw in her unfocused gaze, it was tearing her up. I tightened my arms around her, letting her know with my touch that I wasn't going anywhere. After ten years on the road, ten years of one-night stands and short flings, I knew a keeper when I held her.

CHAPTER TWENTY-THREE

Cristy

THE MEDIA LOST its ever-lovin' mind when Adam rode my bus with me to our gig in Vancouver. Instead of the positive attention Balefire's management assured me would come of our joint venture, the tabloids blew up with rumors I was breaking up the band. It had been a three-hour drive, for crying out loud. We didn't run off and elope or something.

Yet as I prepared to go onstage for our second show, I couldn't help but wonder what the rest of the guys—and Adam—thought about the negative publicity. Of course, it didn't help that my former friend and now nemesis Mali Tatum was shooting her mouth off on social media, publicly speculating all sorts of nefarious things I was doing to undermine the biggest rock band in the world. She went so far as to warn Dakota, Blu, and Jack that I was in the final stages of my plan to steal Adam from them to replace the bassist in my band.

Ridiculous.

Her dancers left her because she couldn't stop at dipping her toes in the diva pool. She took a swan dive right in and didn't bother coming up for air. I couldn't help it if her people liked working with me more. What can I say? I'm fun and I'm open to other people's opinions, especially when they make me look better. Playing a diva is one thing. Being one is something else. It wasn't my fault Mali never learned the difference.

But the way she weighed in on social media dredged up our old feud and added fuel to that particular fire. None of my dancers were participating in this tour. I stripped down my set because the hottest rock band in the world backed me. Sharing the stage with Balefire meant I didn't need all my usual trappings to keep the audience engaged. The novelty of a pop star teaming up with a hard rock band was enough. Anyone with half a brain could see Mali's "opinions" were all and only about her trying to tarnish my reputation in a vain effort to steal some of my popularity. Or maybe that was her way of trying to lure back the part of her team that had defected to me. Like I wouldn't have taken care of them when I went out on tour without them. Geez.

Still, the new fans I'd attracted on this tour were turning on me, and it didn't take a genius to see the ugly written on the wall. Somehow, I needed to flip the script—fast. I was contemplating my entrance as I waited in the wings for the crowd to finish cheering Balefire's last song when I heard Blu change up from what we'd rehearsed.

"Tron, my man. Step on up here."

If Adam was surprised at Blu's command, he didn't show it. Instead, he sauntered to the front of the stage with that loose sexy stride that always made my mouth water.

"There's been some chatter out in cyberspace. You got anything to say about that?"

I couldn't tell if the crowd was jeering or cheering, but someone launched a lacy black thong at Adam who caught it one-handed and grinned.

"Thanks, darlin'." He made a show of tying it to Blu's mic stand then leaned in to speak. "My momma taught me to be nice to guests.

So I'm being extra nice to Balefire's guest. With a voice like hers, being anything but nice to Cristy Valor would be fucking stupid. Have you heard the woman sing?"

The crowd definitely cheered this time, and they clearly loved his grin. "I take it that's a yes."

More cheering, and I started to feel better about where this was going.

"Yeah, so in the interest of being extra nice to our guest, I took a little ride on her tour bus the other day. Seems some people thought they had to share opinions about that. These boys here"—he threw an arm across Blu's shoulders and nodded at Dakota—"we've been together since we were virgins."

A roar rocked the stadium.

Adam laughed and said, "Jack's married. Blu's engaged." A collective groan reverberated into the sky above the stadium. "And we're still playing music together. So if I carpool to work with another musician, I guess our rock 'n' roll world will keep spinning, yeah?"

Carpool? That was one way to describe the ride we gave each other all the way to Vancouver.

Judging from their applause, I was back in the audience's good graces. Maybe. With a huge grin, Blu clapped Adam on the shoulder, and Adam stepped back to his usual place by Jack's massive drum kit. The lights dimmed, cuing me to step out onstage. Jack's tom-toms drummed me in with a jungle rhythm for my hit song "Fever." When the spotlights flashed red in time to his rhythms, the crowd screamed, and I had to let him play a couple of extra bars before my voice could be heard over the screaming fans.

A new shower of lingerie and more than a few pairs of boxers and briefs rained down on me and covered the front of the stage. With a laugh, I strutted across the stage and encouraged the crowd's antics. One pair of boxers caught my attention, and during the instrumental bridge in the song, I picked them up and inspected them, a pair of black ones with bright red lettering: "Cristy Valor sucks ass."

"Harsh, man," I said as I held them up for the front row to read. Then I stuffed them into the backside of the waistband of my micro-mini and turned my back to the stadium, wiggling my butt and those boxers.

The way I handled that met with approval, and I left the boxers right where they were until my costume change after my third song. As I strolled offstage, Adam reached out and snagged those undies from the back of my skirt. In the twenty seconds it took me to change, I heard him say, "Hey, now. I thought we talked about this. Is this any way to treat a guest?"

As I danced my way back onstage, I saw Adam shoot the boxers back at the crowd. For some reason, that one chivalrous gesture threw me. No one but Gretchen had ever stood up for me before. But Adam didn't think twice about it, in front of fifty thousand screaming fans, no less. I didn't know what to do with that, which must have shown on my face because Blu sang the opening bars of my signature song, saving me from a certain freak-out. Taking a deep breath, I sauntered over to him and harmonized with him as he sang my song. With a secret wink, he kept going, and I realized the whole band was on my side.

After we finished the song, Blu asked the crowd if they'd like us to release a new version of it as a duet. The raucous applause affirmed the fans' opinion, and I let out a breath. The rest of the show mirrored our previous gigs on the tour, but I'd be lying if I didn't admit tonight's show threw me. Because there were fans in attendance, I made an appearance at the after-party. I signed some shirts and CDs and one guy's decidedly not toned abs, but I only participated in one round of shots with Balefire before calling it a night.

Gretchen met me at the door to the green room. Before she could open her mouth to tell me where to meet the town car, a wave of heat washed over me. I didn't need to turn around to know who stood behind me. Those long-fingered hands that played me even better than he played his bass cupped my shoulders, his thumbs massaging along either side of my spine, his fingers working right below my collarbones.

His warm breath sent shivers over my skin as he whispered in my ear. "Do I get your spare key?"

I sighed. "Adam."

"It's expected I stay for a while longer, but I don't want to sleep alone."

One glance around the room at the groupies eyeing him like he was water in the desert told me sleeping alone was a problem he wouldn't have.

He nibbled at the sweet spot behind my ear. "Not interested in the local talent, Cristy." Gently, he pulled me around to face him.

"Cristy, the car is waiting." Gretchen's tone conveyed a world of impatience.

Adam held up one finger in her direction while his eyes captured mine. "Your spare key card, babe."

"Gretchen, I need the spare key to my room."

"Cristy—" The warning was unmistakable, but I ignored it, reaching my hand back for the key card instead.

Adam leaned down and kissed the side of my mouth as I slid the card into the back pocket of his tight jeans. "See you soon."

The smoldering promise in his dark chocolate eyes did funny things to my insides, making me want to climb him like a tree and simultaneously run away until the end of the tour.

Like he knew how off-balance he'd rendered me, he spun me back to Gretchen. "Make sure she's safe tonight."

Until the band addressed it during the show, I'd thought Adam and his boys had blown off the breakup rumors. But the way he treated me now and during my set told me he understood what those rumors could do to my career. Even more, he worried about me. It was almost more than I could deal with.

Gretchen gave me no time to process. Grabbing me by the elbow, she tugged me through the door and away from Adam Tron. Though she waited until we were securely inside the town car and speeding back to our hotel, she didn't hold back.

"Will you kindly tell me what the *fuck* you think you're doing? You're not playing with matches here, Cristy-girl. You're flirting with a full-blown burning-down-the-house fire, a fire I might not be able to put out for you." She slumped back into the plush leather cushions, crossed her arms over her chest and glared at me.

I could take quite a bit, but I was never very good at Gretchen being truly mad at me. Her tone and the daggers shooting out of her eyes made it clear she'd passed go, skipped collecting two hundred dollars, and parked herself at the corner of fuming and furious with no intention of moving on.

With a sigh, I stared at the blur of lights and traffic passing outside the windows of the town car and wondered about my choices as well.

"Gretch, it's a novelty. It'll wear off once we finish the tour."

"You know, Cristy, I think you believe that."

I whipped my head around to stare at her. "Exactly what's that supposed to mean?"

"I see how you look at him when you think no one's paying attention."

I crossed my arms over the flutter in my belly.

"And I see how he looks at you regardless of who is or isn't watching."

"The sex is fantastic. But that's all it is, Gretchen. Don't read something into it that isn't there."

"You've never given anyone your key card, not even the guys you've 'dated,'" she said with air quotes. "Then there's the fact that every time you've been with him, you've locked the connecting door between our suites." Her eyes glittered with something feral. "Tell me. What's been Tron's response to your nightmares?"

It never occurred to me that letting Adam lock that door had hurt Gretchen so deeply that she'd attack me like this. Yet her question gave me pause. The look on my face must have given me away.

"Seriously, Cristy? You haven't had one?"

I couldn't understand the fear in her eyes. I couldn't deny the truth either. Every time I'd been with Adam, I'd worried about what would happen if the monsters invaded my dreams with that connecting door locked. But when I lay in his arms, there hadn't been any monsters. What the heck did that mean?

"Oh fuck. This could be bad," Gretchen said under her breath, but in the close confines of the car, I heard her loud and clear. "This could be very bad."

CHAPTER TWENTY-FOUR

Adam

PLEASANTLY TIPSY, AND more than a little horny, I let myself into Cristy's suite a couple of hours after she left the party. The soft glow emanating from the bedroom told me where to find her. On my way there, I stopped at the connecting door to Gretchen's suite. Finding it unlocked, I remedied that situation and headed into the bedroom. I sure as fuck didn't need her manager's attitude during my private time with my girl.

Cristy lay on her side at the edge of the bed. The lamplight haloed her features, stripping away the hardness she projected when she was awake and leaving a beautiful angel behind. For several long moments, I stared at her; the tiny smile curving her lips, her lashes shadowing her impossibly silky skin, the smooth slope of her bare shoulder rising and falling with her breaths. Her elbow obscured my vision of all but the outer curve of her breast, and lower, the sheet draped her hip, exposing the perfect lines of her back and an enticing strip of smooth skin on her side exactly the width of my hand.

In every other circumstance, she regularly stole my breath. In this moment, she owned me. As much as I wanted her, wanted to see desire darken her sapphire eyes, hear her cries of pleasure, feel her sweet pussy clamped tightly around me, I also had an overwhelming need to protect her, to hold the monsters at bay, to keep her safe.

Where the fuck did that come from?

I waited for the panic to set in, but it didn't come. Instead, a sense of calm stole over me. Peace flowed through me as I watched my gorgeous girl softly recharging while she waited for me. Quietly, I toed off my boots and slid my jeans and boxers to the floor where they joined my T-shirt. Padding around to the other side of the bed, I dropped a string of condoms on the nightstand and slid between the sheets behind her.

Lightly tracing my fingertips along her arm, I whispered, "Hey babe. You wanna wake up?"

A sigh escaped her, and she wriggled back into me. Then her breath evened out again, making me smile. "Come on, Valorous. You can sleep later."

I slipped my hand beneath her arm to cup and knead her breast. Discovering her nipple taut and hard sent an answering response through me, and I rubbed and rolled and played there until she wriggled again, her sweet little ass snuggly pushed against my now very interested cock.

"Adam? What time is it?"

"Playtime, babe. Can't you tell?"

A laugh rumbled out of me at her snort, then I gasped as she reached back between us and palmed me.

"Of course it is," she deadpanned, and I marveled at her quick mind and the speed of her interest.

She rolled over to face me, her creamy hand looking beautiful against my brown chest as she explored the contours of my body. Beneath her questing fingertips, my abs rippled involuntarily, and I sucked in a breath. I might have lost myself in the sensations she called from me but for the look on her face and the controlled nonchalance of her tone.

"Anything exciting happen after I left?"

Knowing a minefield when I heard one, I said, "Define exciting."

"Oh, you know. Somebody got fired or someone else downed too many shots and started a riot or some groupie was giving out lap dances all around."

Was she jealous? The idea held promise. I kinda liked my Cristy being jealous.

I cupped her face and ran my thumb along her jaw, inching her tempting mouth closer to mine. "Lap dances, huh?"

Her hand stilled on my hip. "Or riots. With you guys, there could definitely be riots."

For a second, I thought about teasing her, but the flash of vulnerability I caught in her eyes before she lowered them to my chest slowed my roll. "Dakota tossed Annabelle over his shoulder and carried her out to the car after he'd downed a row of Jameson shots." A laugh escaped me as that scene played in my head. "I'm not sure he's getting lucky tonight if the way she was screaming at him is any indication."

I tugged her closer, my attention on her pouty lips leaving no doubt about my intentions. "I may or may not have been encouraging those shots of Jameson. When their little show was over, I came straight to you."

Taking my time, I brushed my lips over hers. She puffed out a tiny sigh and lifted her chin, intensifying the pressure. That was my cue, and I teased my tongue inside her mouth as I rolled over her and pinned her to the bed. When I explored her mouth, I tasted minty toothpaste and something deep and feminine and all Cristy. Kissing her was pure pleasure as I explored her mouth, nipped at her full lips, and pressed my lips hard enough to hers to feel the outlines of her teeth. When we both needed air, I gentled to sip at the corners and along the upper edge of her perfect mouth. The part I truly liked was how greedy she was, giving back everything I gave her and demanding more.

I sucked on her lower lip and let it go with a pop. She growled and I laughed, making a tour of her face with my kisses, starting with her jaw, up her cheek, along her eyebrows, and down the other side until I landed at the sweet spot behind her ear. Her growl changed to a moan as I kissed and licked the sensitive places on her body. I reveled in the way she turned her head to the side to allow me better access while she arched her gorgeous breasts up against my chest. The sensation of her erect nipples brushing my skin fired me up.

"I love how you waited up for me, Valorous," I murmured into the shell of her ear.

"Thanks for coming to me still smelling of our after-the-show shower rather than like some random lap dance." Though whispered, an edge honed her words.

Yeah, she harbored a jealous streak. Good. Because I didn't want to share her either.

♪

The sun made its appearance along the curtain line in Cristy's hotel room when each of us finally sated the other. In the afterglow of a night filled with the most incredible sex of my life, I traced my fingers over her shoulder as she mimicked my patterns with her fingertips on my chest.

"Do you like to gamble?"

Along my side, her body stiffened for a second then she relaxed. "Depends. Are we wagering for something?"

I lifted my head off the pillow to look at her. "Wasn't thinking like that, but now I might be."

She puffed out a breath. "Ask your question, Adam."

"Our next stop is Vegas." I shrugged. "I wanted to know if you like to gamble."

"Sometimes I play the slots. They're kind of like playing video games without the skill." She laughed.

"Huh. I had a different idea about you."

She pushed up on her elbow to stare me down. "Based on what?"

"Based on your stage show."

That raised eyebrow was even more eloquent than the ones my mom used to use back when I was a kid and she caught me in a lie. Did women teach each other how to do that when they had those annoying sleepovers like my sister used to have? Or were they born with that skill? Either way, Cristy had it perfected.

"Come on, babe. The first time you showed up for practice with us, you wanted to fly on Dakota's hydraulic stage. If that isn't taking a chance—on a shit-ton of levels—I don't know what is."

My answer seemed to satisfy her as a smile ghosted over her lips, and she settled back into my side, resting her head comfortably on my chest again.

"There's gambling and there's taking chances. Gambling is tame. Taking chances is fun."

I took a breath and let it out slowly. This whole scene with Cristy felt like taking the biggest chance of my entire fucking life.

"So you don't gamble much when you play Vegas, I take it. What do you like to do when you're there?"

She warned me when her cheek puffed up against my skin, telling me about the naughty grin spreading over her face. "Gretch and I like to hit the strip shows." From beneath her lashes, she peeked up at me. "All of them."

"Judging from some of your hot dance moves, that's research for you."

Surprise wiped that grin off her face. "Anyone ever tell you that you might be a touch too observant?"

"Are you saying you don't like it that I watch you?" I stroked my hand down her arm to tangle my fingers with hers. "'Cause that does fuck-all for explaining why you put on private shows just for me when we play our concerts."

She huffed out a breath and lay her head back on my chest.

"Mind if I join you when you hit the clubs in Vegas?"

With a giggle, she asked, "Even when we go to Thunder from Down Under? You into watching guys showing off their junk?"

"I'm into watching you enjoying yourself." Her hand slid over my abs to hug me close. "Besides, I might learn some moves I can use onstage too."

Another giggle. "You'd have to play a stand-up bass for anyone to appreciate the full effect."

"Hmm. Gives me something to think about." I stared up at the ceiling, pictures of entertaining Cristy with my awesome dance moves floating on the edge of my thoughts. "Guess I might surprise you when we play Phoenix."

Her body went rigid. "I'm not playing Phoenix."

Shifting to face her, I said, "What do you mean, you're not playing Phoenix? I thought the only shows you had to miss were in Portland."

"Checking up on me, Dad?"

The tone pissed me off way more than her words.

"Jesus. I want to play with you." I pushed my fingers into her short blond hair, cupping the side of her head. "In every way. So when you didn't do the shows in Portland, I asked Garrett about the rest of the tour. He didn't say anything about Phoenix."

"It's in all my contracts. I never play Phoenix."

"What do you mean, you don't play Phoenix? The fans there not worthy or something?"

What the fuck? What musician didn't play shows for seventy thousand people?

"Wait. Aren't you from Arizona?"

"*From* being the operative word. Once I got out of that state, I promised myself I'd never go back." She whispered to my chest, "And I meant it."

"Don't you have family there? Friends?" I ducked my head to catch her eyes, but she stubbornly kept them from me. There was a story here, one I desperately wanted to know. Changing tactics, I said, "When we go home to Denver, we play Red Rocks and Broncos stadium. After our shows, we throw epic parties for our family and friends—the people who supported us before we became rock stars."

"Good for you."

"You don't want to give back like that?"

I'd watched her with her people. Without being showy about it, Cristy was everything generous and kind. So her attitude about her hometown made no sense.

"Not everyone shares your experience, Tron."

No fuckin' way was I going to let her distance herself from me. Not after what we shared all night. Not after I'd fallen for her the way I had. I didn't give myself time to process my feelings before I launched in. "Not judging, Cristy, so you can stop with the Tron bullshit. But, damn. Don't you think your family and friends would want to congratulate you on your success, maybe share a little in it?"

"You don't have a clue about my family and friends. Leave it alone."

The way she said the word "family" set alarm bells ringing in my head. Something was off there, something I needed to know if I was ever going to know her the way I wanted to. Somehow, I had to convince her to let me in.

"Hey, where are you going?"

"To take care of business." She shot me a look. "And I don't need a chaperone."

For a second, I might have panicked before I remembered I lay in her bed. If anyone was going anywhere, it would be me after she kicked me out. Which was not going to happen. Cristy needed a friend, and I knew exactly how to be one.

When at last she emerged from the bathroom, she wore a sheer white baby doll nightie. If that pretense of virginal innocence was meant to put me off, she'd seriously underestimated me. That scrap of fabric and lace only enticed me to explore her beautiful body and the interesting workings of her mind even more.

With a huge grin, I patted the bed beside me.

"We're done playing for tonight, Adam. I need to rest if I'm going to be any good in Vegas."

"You can sleep on the bus, babe."

"Uh-huh. Like I 'slept'"—she air quoted—"on the drive to here from Seattle?"

"We didn't need to sleep on that leg of the tour, babe."

"Whatever." She sighed, but there wasn't any heat in it.

"Come back to bed, Cristy."

"On one condition."

I quirked a brow and waited.

"No more discussions about Phoenix. It's in my contract not to play there. Ask your manager."

"But you'll be with us in Dallas after that?"

"Yes."

I'd find out about Phoenix but not during what was left of tonight. I sat up and swung my legs over the bed. "Good enough. Come here," I said, patting the tops of my thighs.

She dragged her feet a little, but at last she perched on my lap. Wrapping my arms around her, I pulled her in close. Her pixie hair-cut left her neck exposed, making it easy to nuzzle her there until she relaxed into me. "Did I mention how much I've enjoyed touring with you?" I whispered as I traced the shell of her ear with my tongue.

She shrugged, but the shiver that went through her at my touch told me she liked me too.

"I'm looking forward to researching dance moves with you when we get to Vegas."

Her response was to gift me with "the look," which made me laugh.

"After we hit the clubs, we can come back to your room and practice with each other, give each other a private show." I waggled my brows for emphasis and finally dragged a tiny smile out of her.

"Come on, babe. Let's grab some shut-eye."

When I stood with her in my arms, she squeaked and wrapped her arms tight enough around my neck to shut off my air. Still, I puffed out a laugh and lay her gently on the bed, climbing in over her and pulling her in close.

"Adam."

"Close your eyes, Cristy."

♪

"No! No! I won't do it! Pleeease don't make me do this. Please."

The anguish in Cristy's voice jolted me from a sound sleep. Beside me, she thrashed her head from side to side on the pillow while the rigidness of the rest of her body told its own story. Wherever she'd gone in her sleep terrified her. I'd read somewhere that when a person is having a nightmare, it's best not to awaken them until they quiet down, but watching my girl fight her inner demons on her own killed me. Sweat broke out on her forehead, and tears made tracks down the sides of her temples. With the palm of my hand, I traced light, slow circles over the sheet covering her belly, soothing her the best way I knew how until she escaped wherever her dreams had taken her.

"It's wrong! I'm a kid. He's an old man. Don't you see?" Her pleading tone shifted down to all-out begging. Then she started sobbing. "Please, God, no. Noooo!" The sobs ratcheted up to screams, and I couldn't take it anymore.

"Cristy, it's all right. I'm here," I whispered. "I'm right here, and I'll always keep you safe."

She surfaced on a sob and sat straight up, her chest heaving as her eyes darted wildly around the room. Clutching the sheet to her chest, she fought for breath on a hiccup and her eyes landed on me.

"Adam?" She swallowed and dabbed her eyes with the sheet. "What time is it?"

I sat up and slipped my arm around her. "Time for you to tell me what that was all about."

Her eyes skittered away from me. "What are you talking about?"

"You know what I'm talking about. The nightmare you just had. Jesus, babe. You scared the shit out of me."

"I don't really remember." The rigid way she held herself and wouldn't look at me only reinforced her lie.

From the way she was acting, this wasn't the first time she'd had this particular nightmare. Something in her past haunted her to the point of terror, a demon I discovered I desperately wanted to slay for her.

"Tell me, Cristy. Let me help you."

Her laughter was hollow.

"You can't change the past, Adam. No one can."

The handle on the connecting door jiggled and Gretchen started pounding on it. "Cristy! Cristy, are you all right? Open the fucking door, Cristy."

"Better do as she says, or she'll wake the entire floor."

I rolled out of bed and strolled over to the door.

"You might want to put something on before you open that."

I shot her a look over my shoulder before giving my attention to her manager. "Cristy's safe," I said through the closed door. "I'm with her, Gretchen."

"You don't understand." She thumped the door for emphasis. "Let me in, Tron."

"Might as well do as she says, Adam. She won't stop until you let her in." Though she sat exactly where I'd left her, Cristy sounded a million miles away, which terrified me all over again. The demon stalking her controlled the situation, at least for the moment, and it would stay that way until someone let me in on what it was.

I stalked over beside the bed to pull on my boxers. Gretchen nearly slammed me into the wall with the force of opening the door the second she heard me turn the lock. A blur of red satin negligée raced past me and landed beside Cristy on the bed. Gathering Cristy into her arms, she rocked her back and forth and hummed something I couldn't quite catch while I stood there like a useless dick.

"Someone want to clue me in, here?"

"Maybe you should go, Tron," Gretchen said. Though her tone remained soothing, her eyes shot daggers at me.

"I don't think so, Gretchen."

Cristy's glance darted between Gretchen and me, and I could feel her slipping away from me.

"It might be best if you go, Adam."

This subdued Cristy was completely out of character, which only made me desperate to stay with her, take care of her, help her through whatever the nightmare was that had followed her into the daylight. "I'm not leaving you, babe."

"I've got this, Tron. You have no idea what's going on." Gretchen actually made the shooing gesture at me as she said, "Now be a good boy and get the hell out."

My blood boiled at her words and the haughty tone she used to say them. But I understood one thing—Gretchen was afraid of me. Not physically, because even as angry as she'd made me, I hadn't even twitched. No, she was worried about my influence over Cristy. Even as my girl played along with her manager, she told me something important every time she used my given name. I wasn't another celebrity fling for her. Gretchen must have sensed that too.

"Cristy and I need a shower, Gretch." I opened the door to her room wide. "And contrary to what you may have heard about me, I don't like an audience."

She bared her teeth at me and made no move to leave.

On a scale of one to ten, the tension in the room ratcheted up to a fifty as Gretchen and I waged our silent standoff. Then something passed between her and Cristy, and she snorted a very unladylike sigh.

"Remember what I said, Cristy-girl." The ominousness of her tone set my teeth on edge.

What did she say? Was she warning Cristy away from me? What. The. Fuck?

As she passed me, she shot me a glare that could have set the whole building on fire. For good measure, she also sent a sharp elbow into my abs, and involuntarily, a grunt escaped me. Letting the woman have even that second of power grated on me, but I kept my cool and let the door click softly shut behind her then I shot the deadbolt home with a loud thunk.

In three strides, I was beside Cristy's bed. Reaching a hand to her, I said, "Come on, babe. Let's grab that shower."

Normally, she came across as ten feet tall and bulletproof. The shield she wrapped around herself was obviously Teflon, judging from the way nothing ever stuck to her. But after she woke up from that nightmare, she seemed tiny, vulnerable. The king-size bed swallowed her up. More than anything, I wanted to watch over her, defend her from whatever it was that stole her strength from her. I opened my mouth to say as much, but the regret clouding her eyes and the embarrassment cherrying her cheeks shut me up. Something like relief passed over her features as she took my hand and climbed off the bed.

We showered together in silence. Though we took turns washing each other as usual, it wasn't about playtime. I used my hands to soothe her, to let her know through my touch that I wanted to look out for her, help her. The way her hands lingered on my body told me something else—something that eerily felt like goodbye.

Like I was going to let that happen.

Chapter Twenty-Five

Adam

GRETCHEN SCOWLED AND growled, but in the end, Cristy ended up on our bus for the trip to Vegas. If anything, the woman should have been happy. Cristy joining Balefire in front of all the paparazzi waiting around our bus meant less work for her. After all, my girl riding with me and the guys would jack down the rumors about her breaking Balefire up. If anything, Gretchen should have been thanking me for talking Cristy into such a strategic move.

It was selfish, of course. After our shower and all through breakfast, I sensed her distancing herself from me, and I wanted to keep her close, which meant keeping her away from her manager. Whatever telepathic communication she'd shared with Gretchen back in her room before I ushered the woman out had definitely messed with Cristy's head. No way in hell could there be any other explanation. Ever since that night when she blew me after the concert, something special had been growing between us—and it wasn't only my cock. Damned if I was ready to let whatever was happening with us go before we finished exploring it.

Still, it took a couple of hours on the road before Cristy relaxed enough to snuggle into my side as we sat together on the bench behind the table. She was enjoying a margarita—her third one—and egging Dakota on as he told yet another outrageous story about his four-wheeling adventures in the lime-green behemoth he bought when we signed our first big contract.

"Annie especially likes the way the seats in it recline, don't you?" Dakota waggled his brows at Annabelle who rolled her eyes and glared at him as she walked toward her captain's chair beside him. "Aw, come on, Annababy. You know it's true." The bus hit a bump in the road, causing Annabelle to steady herself on the back of Dakota's chair. Taking advantage of the situation, he pulled her down onto his lap. "No need to be embarrassed. All the ladies on this ride today like to recline with their favorite Balefire player." He placed a smacking kiss on her mouth and sat back with a laugh at her narrow-eyed expression then turned his attention to Cristy. "Ain't that right, pop diva? Even after I shared my hydraulic"—he couldn't stifle his grin—"stage with you, your favorite is still Tron."

"His hydraulics are excellent too."

Dakota barked out a laugh at Cristy's cheekiness, and I hugged her even closer to me.

"Tron's 'hydraulics' are so good, he should probably think about marketing them as a sex toy," she added, and I almost choked on my surprise.

"*What?*"

She went on as though I hadn't reacted at all. "You know, like Marilyn Manson and Buck Cherry."

I gaped at her.

"They each have a line of toys so fans can have them 'in' them. Pretty clever, huh? Bet the sales of sex toys modeled after your 'equipment'"—she air quoted—"could rival your record sales." She batted her eyes at me. "Something to think about."

"You wouldn't mind sharing me that way with the whole world?"

She shrugged but refused eye contact.

"I think our music sales are enough." I might have growled at her, but what the hell? She wanted me to commercialize my dick?

"Speak for yourself, Tron. I kinda like this idea," Dakota said, completely ignoring the way Annabelle stiffened in his lap, her eyes shooting daggers him. "Where did you hear about this, Cristy?"

I cut her off. "Maybe ten years ago, that might have been a good idea. Now?" I slipped a finger beneath her chin and forced her to give me her eyes. "Not so much."

Right as she tried to put a little space between us, Garrett abandoned the copilot seat by our driver and sat in the chair Annabelle had vacated earlier. "What's the plan for marketing the upcoming shows, Annabelle?"

"Sex toys," Dakota answered for her. "Right, babe?"

Annabelle and Dakota struggled over her remaining in his lap, and it would have been hilarious if not for the fearful looks she kept sending Garrett's way. And the scowl he shot her.

"Kidding, Garrett. Lighten up already. Have a beer or something," I said.

"Actually, the sex toys were my idea," Cristy piped up from beside me. "But maybe you're not fun like that, Mr. Manager."

For some reason, Cristy had attitude about Garrett. She'd made it clear at our first rehearsal and not backed down for a second since. After the way the morning went, I had no doubt she made her outrageous suggestion to provoke me. Her response to Garrett made it clear she was spoiling for a fight.

There were ways around that.

I pushed out from behind the table and grabbed Cristy's mostly empty margarita glass. Handing it to Garrett, I said, "Maybe you want to finish this. Mellow you out."

"Hey! I wanted to finish that," she said as she pushed herself around the bench to chase after her drink.

Perfect.

"I have a better idea." With her hand in mine, I tugged her down the aisle of the bus to my bunk and lifted her in.

"Tron! What do you think you're doing?"

She tried to slide back off the bed, but since I climbed in behind her, she had no way to escape. After I secured the curtain, I rolled over on my side and propped my head on my palm, while I easily corralled both her hands against my chest with my free hand, stopping her from pummeling me.

"You wanna tell me what's going on with you?"

She huffed out a sigh and a second one, blew a raspberry, and refused to give me her eyes again.

"It's a long drive to Vegas, Valorous." I rubbed the pad of my thumb over the impossibly silky skin of her hand. "And I'm a patient man."

"Not enough tequila on this bus," she muttered under her breath.

"What was that?"

"Nothing's going on with me, okay? Not one darn thing." Though she lowered her voice to try to sound tough, I caught the quaver in it anyway.

"Try again."

"Listen, Tron. Nothing is going on with me. Except maybe I've been spending too much time with you."

Now she gave me her eyes. Defiance flashed there, which was damn weird. As far as I knew, we weren't fighting. In fact, until she'd had that nightmare, we were 100 percent into each other. When she was ready—and sober—I planned to pry out the demon haunting her dreams. But that would have to wait. Right now, I needed to remind her about why she was going to trust me with that task.

"We're back to Tron again, huh? Looks like I have some work to do." I pulled her hand up to my mouth and kissed her palm, a lingering exploration with my lips and tongue before I gently bit the pad at the base of her thumb.

Her eyes dilated and her body relaxed into me.

"I like spending time with you." Another kiss, another tiny nip. "I had the idea you liked spending time with me too." I tugged her hand up to my neck and slid my hand down her arm and along her body to rest on her hip.

"I do, it's just"—she tightened her hold on my neck—"Gretchen and I go way back. She's the only real friend I have. She knows how to take care of me."

Between her words and the way her voice became so small as she said them, realization, hard and painful, turned over in my chest. I wanted to be her friend. I wanted to take care of her.

A hollow laugh huffed out of her. "You wouldn't if you knew my secrets."

Wait. Did I say my thoughts aloud?

"How do you know?"

Her eyes shuttered, and I scrambled to stop her from shutting me out. "There are things I know about the other guys in the band that could probably ruin them, but I don't share."

"That's different. You have a stake in keeping their secrets."

"I have a stake in keeping yours too." I leaned in and kissed her, a soft declaration of my intent.

A loud banging sounded down the aisle of the bus and Dakota boomed out, "If the rest of you guys could hurry up swappin' spit and other bodily fluids"—he laughed uproariously at his own crudeness—"some of us would like to practice our poker-playing skills. Next stop, Vegas, baby."

With a groan, I pulled back from Cristy. Such incredibly bad timing proved why Dakota wasn't part of the rhythm section.

"If you knew my secrets, Adam. This between us"—she gestured with her hand between our chests—"would be over."

"Give me some credit, Valorous."

For a second, pain flashed over her features yet she marshalled them into a grin. "When I was a kid, I had to sit in the front of the bus. But I always wanted to ride in the back and play poker with the cool kids." She pushed at my shoulder. "Come on, Adam. Let's go have some fun."

"We could have all kinds of fun here."

She pouted up at me from beneath her brows, and I had to admit the spell was broken. Dakota had ruined whatever headway I'd made. Still, I didn't concede. "We're not done, Cristy. With anything."

She blinked and said nothing.

"Come on, you candy-asses. Get out here and put your money on the table," Dakota shouted from the front of the bus.

With an eye roll, I opened my compartment and crawled out, helping Cristy down in front of me. She patted down her sexy short dress—damn, did I love how good she looked in spandex— and strutted her way to the front of the bus. By the time we rolled into Vegas late that night, Cristy had managed to win about three grand from the band, most of it coming out of Garrett's pocket. The delight she took in being "one of the cool kids" and the way Garrett scowled at her for hours kinda made the long ride without her in my bed worth it. She was comfortable with us. She fit in with the guys and their women like she belonged with us. More than anything, I wanted her to stay with us, with me. The thought punched me directly in the solar plexus.

My thoughts must have played across my face, because when I glanced away from Cristy, I caught Annabelle's eyes on me. She gave me a slow wink, and I grinned back at her. She was a great addition to our little party too. I hoped Dakota didn't screw that up. Especially after the way she took the reins when I suggested to her to bring Cristy on board for this tour. I might have said something about how it would give her more street cred if she could manage that as her first assignment. Honestly though, I wanted a chance to get to know the woman whose music grabbed my attention before I ever saw the person behind the voice.

Now that I'd met her, worked with her—made love with her—I

knew Cristy was so much more than her music. If only she'd let me in all the way, I knew I could slay all her monsters. What I didn't have an answer for—yet—was how to convince her to trust me. But I had a couple of ideas.

CHAPTER TWENTY-SIX

Cristy

WHEN WE ARRIVED at our hotel in Vegas, Gretchen wasted no time in whisking me away from the guys and hauling me up to my suite. She stomped around the living room like she wanted to punch holes in the floor with the heels of her six-inch Louboutins. As she paced in front of me, their red bottoms flashed in the low light coming from the wall sconces and the lamp she'd flicked on beside the couch.

"Do you even hear what you're saying, Cristy-girl?" The rage in her voice gave way to fear as she stopped to gaze at my face.

"Geez, you're acting like I'm replacing you with Adam." I grabbed a throw pillow and hugged it to my chest. "You're my manager—"

She rolled her eyes.

"—and my best friend. My oldest friend." I patted the cushion beside me. "But this thing with Adam is…"

Pictures of the man flashed in my mind. Adam playing his bass, the beautiful muscles of his torso flexing while his fingers flew up and down the neck, his other hand plucking the strings in rhythms that left those who listened no choice but to dance with him. Adam smiling down at me from his six-foot-four-inch height, his broad shoulders and chest and massive arms straining the fabric of his T-shirt in the most delicious way. Adam throwing his head back and shouting my name at the sky as I swallowed him down, his pleasure giving way to awe that left me feeling like I ruled the world. Adam's concerned expression as he ran his hands over my skin while I surfaced from the nightmare our conversation about playing Phoenix dredged out of me.

I blinked, and Gretchen came back into focus.

"You figured it out, I see," she said, her voice and demeanor suddenly calm as she sat next to me. "If you keep this party going with Tron, at some point you're going to have to tell him why you don't ever step a toe in Arizona." She squeezed my hand. "When you tell him, he's going to run."

No doubt, the hurt her words caused me flashed across my face as she hurried to add, "Worse, he'll know the one thing about you that could ruin your whole career, everything we've built for the last decade."

"Adam's not like that," I whispered.

She slid her arm around me and hugged me to her side. "Stop thinking with your pussy, Cristy." I glared at her, but she ignored me. "He's a strong, proud man. He's not going to take it well when he discovers what your parents forced you to do. When he discovers you're still married."

For several seconds, I think my heart stop beating, then it kicked into high gear to compensate for the lapse as Gretchen's words penetrated my lizard brain. "You told me my annulment went through. You swore it."

I leaped up, pacing frantically between the door and the couch.

"It did, but that's not what your old man thinks. It's not what your parents think."

"But, but, what does that mean? Can he still come after me? Take half my money? Ruin my career?"

Now it was Gretchen's turn to pat the cushion beside her.

"He can't take your money, Cristy-girl. But he can damn sure ruin your career."

"And Adam?" I hated how small my voice sounded as I sat back down on the couch. Yet I couldn't help it. Somehow when I wasn't looking, he'd sneaked under my skin and made himself at home. It made sense for me to curb this relationship before it had any real chance of going somewhere, but—and here was the big one—I wanted a relationship with Adam Tron.

Gretchen played her fingers through my hair, a soothing gesture that always dragged me away from the edge of whatever cliff appeared in front of me. "I don't want to see you hurt, Cristy-girl." Her eyes remained on her fingers. "Adam Tron has the potential to wreck you."

I tipped my head to rest on the back of the couch and blew a long, jagged breath at the ceiling. Gretchen had had my back since we were sixteen years old. My mind told me my only course of action was to do as she suggested, cool things off with Adam. My heart had other ideas. For a long time, we sat together, me lost in thought as Gretchen petted me. At last, I rose from my semireclining position and headed to my bedroom.

"It's been a long day, and I may have drunk more than my share of tequila. I need to sleep."

Gretchen made to follow me, but I put up a hand. "Alone." With a quiet snick of the catch, I closed the door on my best friend's intentions, even though I understood she only acted with my best interests at heart.

Adam

Vamping the role of a sixties sex-kitten, Cristy slinked and purred her way into everyone's hearts during our first Vegas concert. It was a perfect set for Vegas, simultaneously saluting old-timey entertainers like Ann-Margret and Eartha Kitt while putting her own spin on Vegas glamour. I'd wanted to kiss her through the whole damn concert.

Afterward, though, she'd been distant. Gretchen met me at her dressing room door and told me Cristy needed some downtime, whatever the fuck that meant. At first, I pushed until I gazed past Gretchen's shoulder and saw how Cristy retreated further into herself even as she appeared ready to give me what I wanted. So I cleaned up in the band's locker room, and because I was so amped up, jacked off in the shower to visions of Cristy in a leopard-skin catsuit going down on me.

When I arrived at the after-party, I discovered that B-list douchebag Rip Slater draped over my girl like a baggy dress. A line of shots waited in front of her, and she downed them like she was on a mission—or she'd made a monumentally bad bet. Either way, I was determined to have some time with her after going without since we left the bus the night before.

Again, Gretchen cockblocked me. "Cristy's moving on. Even you can see that."

I glared at her.

"Do you want to make a scene, or do you want to take a hint?" The look she shot me was equal parts bossy and pleading.

"I play for Balefire. Making scenes comes with the territory."

But when I interrupted Cristy's crazy, she blew me off.

"I need a break, Tron. Can you give me some space?" The snotty tone of her words made no sense with the way she wouldn't meet my eyes.

The shocked expression on Slater's face gave way to a sly grin, and I cocked my arm to punch some character into his pretty boy face when Dakota intercepted me. He pulled me into another line of shots, and the next thing I remember, I woke up slumped on the floor beside my bed in my suite by myself. I'd texted and called her several times this morning, but she didn't return either. Something was dangerously off.

That afternoon, when I caught sight of Cristy strolling through the casino on the arm of Rip Slater, I nearly blew a gasket. Yeah, that same B-list moron whose only path to the A-list was through a woman like Cristy Valor. Guys like him always tried to hang around with us too, be our "friends," like that would ever happen. I could see the draw for Slater, but he made absolutely no fucking sense for Cristy. We all had a past, but hers was littered with A-listers, not some wannabe like Slater.

An elbow to my side jolted my attention from the bullshit I watched walking toward a craps table. "You shouldn't be surprised. It's always like this with Cristy, Tron. Believe me," Gretchen said, her eyes on the scene playing out in front of us. "I've been her manager for almost ten years, but we were best friends in school before that." She blinked up at me. "Kinda like you and the other guys in Balefire. That kind of history tells you what to expect." Jamming her hands into the pockets of her wide-legged pants, she gazed around the casino. "I've seen this coming since Seattle." She patted my arm. "But you're a big boy. You'll get over it."

With that parting shot, she sidled away from me toward where Cristy laughed at something Slater said as she reached for the dice. Gretchen stood behind them, blocking my view of my girl. After a couple minutes, she must have felt my eyes trying to bore holes through her because Gretchen glanced over her shoulder and shot me such a filthy sucker punch of a look that I nearly doubled over.

Shock gave way to rage, but now was not the time or the place to vent it. I spun on my heel and headed for the hotel gym.

♪

My arms were on fire when I racked a set of dumbbells. After four sets on the incline bench, you would have thought I'd worn off some of my rage. You would have thought wrong. I was slamming plates on a bar when Dakota blew through the door to the gym like he wanted to tear a hole in the world. I was right there with him.

He caught sight of me and stomped over to the rack, grabbing a forty-five and shoving it onto the other end of the bar. We didn't need words as together, we loaded it with two hundred and sixty-five pounds before I slid onto the bench beneath it and went to work, Dakota spotting me. After I racked it, he slid in and took a turn. We went on like that for six sets before either of us spoke.

"What the fuck is it with women?" Dakota asked as we stripped the bar.

"Fuck if I know."

"They get their panties in a twist if we so much as glance at some cute ass"—he glared at me—"with no intention of doing anything but looking, mind you." Like me, he stretched his arms over his head to release some lactic acid. "Then they're hiding out behind a stack of speakers making plans for later with some other guy." He retrieved the dumbbells I'd racked earlier and went at his sets of flat bench flies like his triceps and shoulders had pissed him the hell off and required serious punishment.

Made perfect sense.

On another bench, I mimicked his movements. For a time, the only sound in the room was grunted air and curse words as each of us worked through our private turmoil. Whatever Cristy thought she was doing, it needed to end. Today. That dipshit Slater meant nothing to her, and all three of us knew it. Then the image of Gretchen's dirty look floated across my mind, and I had another target for my anger.

By silent agreement, Dakota and I switched over to triceps dips, each spotting the other. Sweat poured off me as intense as any show under the lights, yet I refused to surrender until my arms literally wouldn't hold my weight anymore.

Dakota looked me over. "She left the party with Gretchen, not Slater."

"Which totally explains why she's in the casino playing craps—with Slater." I forced his name through gritted teeth.

"She's playing some kind of game, Tron. She came with a reputation. You knew that." Dakota swigged water from a bottle and poured the rest over his head. "What are you going to do about the huge hard-on you have for her?"

I nearly choked on a slug of water. When I finally got my body back under control, I shot back. "Yeah? What's eatin' at you? Didn't your girl come with a similar reputation?"

Dakota bared his teeth.

I shoved the peg into the hole, grabbed the handles on the cable fly machine, and went to work, forcing myself to breathe properly through the exercise rather than blowing up instead. The exercise gave me the added benefit of not being able to talk. Cristy's reputation had nothing to do with it. We weren't playing games, and she damn well knew it. Which begged Dakota's question. What the fuck *was* I going to do about my feelings for her?

Apparently, Dakota didn't want to think about his own woman problems. While he waited his turn, he talked plenty. "She's a wild one, your girl."

"And yours isn't?" I panted.

His face darkened, and I'm pretty sure I heard him growl. "You about done?"

Even after I'd lifted myself into exhaustion, sweat running off me like I'd showered in it, I couldn't get the picture of Cristy laughing with Slater out of my mind. I stepped away from the machine with a broad gesture for him to take his turn and blew out a breath. Again, we finished our sets in silence, but by the time I counted my final twelve reps, I'd calmed down some from when I'd entered the gym. I hadn't decided how to fix the situation with Cristy, but after taking it out on the weights with Dakota, I felt strangely better about it.

One constant remained in my life—no matter what happened, no matter that neither of us had resolved our woman problems, I never doubted I always had my band brothers backing me.

CHAPTER TWENTY-SEVEN

Adam

AFTER THE SECOND show in Vegas, I determined not to let Gretchen shut me away from Cristy again. When she'd flirted with the band during her set, she didn't leave me out. Before we went out onstage, I worried she might. In the end, she was a professional—always. I appreciated that about her, but it didn't give her a free pass to walk away from what we both knew was something special, not without a conversation at least.

I turned the knob on Cristy's dressing room door instead of knocking, but Gretchen stood in my way like she'd been expecting me. "Cristy will catch up with you at the after-party, Tron." She put her hand on the door and held it only half open, positioning herself so I couldn't walk straight in unless I walked her over first.

"Cristy will 'catch up' with me now, Gretchen." With one hand still on the doorknob and the other gripping the handle of my duffel bag, I couldn't have intimidated her physically, yet she flinched as though I'd raised a hand to slap her. Maybe I didn't sing lead, but that didn't mean I had no clue about how to use my voice.

"You can let him in, Gretch," Cristy called from the showers.

Gretchen hesitated, and I jacked a brow. With a look that made me think she wanted to stick her tongue out at me, she let go of the door, and I brushed past her into the room.

"Cristy and I need to talk."

Gretchen crossed her arms over her chest, her stance telling me she meant to stick around.

"Alone."

"It's okay, Gretch. Tron's not going to upset me."

Upset her? What the fuck did that mean?

Whatever their secret code was, Gretchen must have decided to believe Cristy, because with one last fiery glare at me, she turned on her heel and left the dressing room.

The door barely clicked behind her before I locked it. Then I gave Cristy my full attention. "You put on one hell of a show out there tonight, Valorous."

Her eyes rounded. Obviously, she wasn't expecting a compliment.

"I mean it. From the second you stepped onstage in that sexy Vegas showgirl outfit, your voice soaring even higher than it usually does, you blew the doors right off our show."

"Thank you," she whispered. Seated on a chair, she started unclipping her glittery stockings from the garter belt that held them up.

"Hey." I knelt in front of her and covered her hands with mine. "I've been dying to do this since you stepped into the spotlight tonight. You mind?"

For a charged second, I thought she'd deny me. Then she nodded and pulled her hands away. Beneath my fingertips, I sensed the tension in her muscles, and though I wanted it to be anticipation of where we were going, I had a bad feeling it was more about what we needed to discuss.

Taking my time and keeping my touch gentle, I unhooked the tapes and slowly slid those sexy stockings down her legs. Lightly, I palmed my way back up the outsides until I reached her hips where I squeezed and held her.

"Look at me, Cristy." She'd been staring at my T-shirt still plastered to my chest with the sweat of the night's work, and I needed her eyes. "Please."

Pain flickered over her face for a second. She sucked a breath in through her nose, let it out slowly, and straightened in her chair, her eyes coming to mine at last.

"You're not with Rip Slater."

For long seconds, she left me hanging. "No. I'm not with him."

"You going to tell me what's going on?"

"I'm not touring with you in Arizona."

I arched a brow and waited.

"It's not—" She swallowed. "I can't. It's not a good place for me."

Puffing out a laugh, I said, "Why? Someone got a warrant out for your arrest?"

She pulled in her lips, and her eyes slid away from mine. "Something like that."

Giving her hips another little squeeze, I ducked my face down right in front of hers. "Can't your people fix it? You're a star. You're one of the biggest stars in the world."

"Don't you get it, Tron? There are just some things that need to remain buried." She pushed my hands away, stood, and started pacing. "You ask too much of me. You've been asking too much of me since the beginning, since before we even met."

Her voice trailed off on that last part, but I was so tuned into her I heard it anyway.

"Because I want to be with you?"

She stilled, the sorrow in her eyes gutting me.

"I can't do this, Adam. I've worked too hard for too long to give it all up now." She stepped behind a screen and came back out dressed in a silky robe that covered everything from her neck to her ankles. Not a good sign. "I'm not playing Phoenix. I'm not playing Tempe. I may or may not meet back up with you guys in Houston."

"What are you saying?"

She went on like I'd remained silent. "Gretchen is working on the details of ending the contract early."

"Cristy—"

I took a step toward her. She stepped back.

Definitely not the dance I'd anticipated when I walked into her dressing room.

"You have to understand, Adam." The rasp in her voice told me about the lump in her throat.

"Whatever your demons are, I can fight them." I offered my hand to her. "I want to fight them." She crossed her arms over her chest. "Why won't you trust me?"

"The only person I can trust is Gretchen." If anything, her voice became smaller. "She's always looked out for me."

Blowing a frustrated breath at the ceiling, I stuffed my hands in my jeans pockets and leveled my gaze at her. "Don't you think there are other people in the world who can care about you too?"

The way she hunched her shoulders and tightened her arms around herself, like she was trying to roll up into a tiny ball, ripped at my insides. She truly believed no one else could ever care about her. Love her.

Shit. Where did that come from? Yet as I let the thought settle in the recesses of my mind, I knew it was exactly right.

"Give me a chance, Cristy. Give us a chance."

Swallowing a couple of times, she cleared her throat. "I can't Adam. Don't ask this of me."

"Ask what? To let me care about you?"

My voice cracked on the words, but I didn't give a shit. The woman was killing me. All I wanted to do was hold her, love her, and she kept backing away.

"You want so much more than that, and we both know it." She

pulled her plump lips in, closed her eyes, and let out a long slow breath. "But if you knew what you think you want to know, you'd run to the other side of the world to put enough distance between us. Trust me."

I'd been on the road with Balefire for ten years, but with the exception of Jack, we'd all been friends since we were kids. We'd done things together and on our own that we weren't proud of, that we'd rather not have splashed all over TMZ. We all had demons. I got that. Cristy's couldn't be any worse than any of ours. Yet the way she was withdrawing into herself—I couldn't understand what she might have done to ever make me want to distance myself from her. Had it only been two days since we shared a bed? It seemed like an eon.

"Babe, we've all done things. None of us is perfect." I was pleading now. "Don't you get that none of that matters?" But I could see I was losing her.

"Adam, I need"—she stopped, drew in a breath—"I need some space. Can you just give me a little space?"

Her haunted expression terrified me. Fuck. I knew what "give me space" meant. But somewhere along the line, I'd gone all in, fallen for her, and I wasn't ready to give her up.

A knock at the door followed by the rattling of the knob told me Gretchen had returned before she shouted through the door. "You two need to be done in there. People are waiting for you."

"You should go, Adam." Cristy's whispered words said one thing. Her eyes said something completely different.

"Cristy."

"Please."

It was the wrong fucking move. I knew that even as I picked up my duffel and headed for the door. But I couldn't force myself on her. Even if I didn't love her like I did, I could never do that. Yet I couldn't leave it there. I unlocked the door, but before I stepped through it, I looked back at her. "You know where to find me. I'll be waiting, Cristy. Take your time. I'm a patient man."

She said nothing. Merely gazed back at me with those eyes I'd see in my dreams every night for eternity.

♪

When I arrived at the after-party a little while later, Cristy was nowhere to be found. In fact, none of her entourage seemed to be in the room, which was odd. The woman who did her makeup, Jill or Jilly or something, was a quiet little thing, but the girl could throw down after a show. I'd seen her slamming shots with the roadies on more than one occasion, yet tonight, I didn't see her with them.

Cristy loved the trappings of playing music, especially the parties. With the exception of the monk—AKA Jack Whitehorse—we all did. So where the fuck was she? Exactly how much space did she need? My chest had started burning before I walked out of Cristy's dressing room. Now it was on fire.

I stuck my face between them and shouted. "Blu? Ash? Either of you seen Cristy?"

Blu glanced away from his fiancée to take in the party. A kaleidoscope of lights pulsed around the room. Some local band played loud enough to fill a stadium. People danced and drank like the night was all they had. When his eyes returned to me, he leaned in and shouted "No. Haven't seen her."

The heartburn that accompanied me into the party flashed white hot, and I rubbed at my chest with the heel of my hand, which did nothing for it. With a nod at my friends, I went in search of Garrett.

Chapter Twenty-Eight

Adam

IT TOOK ME at least an hour to weave my way through the gyrating and jostling bodies to find Garrett in a corner banquette. He'd snagged a couple of groupies, one of whom was giving him a lap dance while the other fed him hors d'oeuvres from a communal plate in front of them. He downed a long drink of beer and pretended not to notice me standing in front of him.

When he started on the second pull of his beer, I leaned over the table and snagged the bottle out of his hand.

"What the fuck, Tron?"

His glare didn't faze me.

"You know where Cristy is?"

Fear flashed in his eyes for a second before they skittered away from me. He mumbled something I couldn't hear over the pounding of the music coming from the band across the room.

I pushed the plate of food to the side and leaned right over the lap-dancing groupie's shoulder. The woman smiled at me, but Garrett didn't.

"What was that, Garrett?"

"She left town."

"Come again?" How I managed to keep my voice even when my heart threatened to explode in my chest was one mystery I'd probably never solve.

"She was a bad idea from the start. I told you guys that, but you wouldn't listen." He motioned to the girl on his lap to get back to work since she'd stopped moving to listen to our conversation. "I say, good riddance to her and to that pain-in-my-ass Annabelle who spooled up and flew out today too."

"She's gone?" If I'd ever wanted a mutant ability, in that moment, I wanted to be able to shoot fire out of my eyes like Cyclops. From the way Garrett tried to melt back into the cushion of the booth, he knew it too. "What the ever-lovin' *fuck*, Garrett? Don't we have a contract or something?"

Straightening, I jammed my hands in my hair and blew a breath at the ceiling.

Right then, the band took a break, so everyone in the vicinity of his table heard him. "Forget her, Tron. You're better off without her. This whole tour is better off without all that Cristy Valor drama."

The gasps from the groupies milling around us alerted me the rumor mill had cranked on full blast. Murmurings rumbled to whispers, crescendoed to shouts. In seconds, the room reverberated with Garrett's words: *Cristy left the tour*. The words buffeted against me like a raging storm, and I had to escape.

People were calling out to me, tugging at me, getting in my way. I didn't want to be rude, but some of them left me no choice. I thought I heard Blu shout my name, but I didn't care. When I finally broke through the doors and into the hallway, I raced to the elevators and nearly punched the call button through the wall in my desperation to reach her suite.

The hallway on the top floor of the Bellagio echoed with emptiness. I could feel her absence like a throbbing bruise. Still, I marched up to the door to her room and pounded on it. "Cristy! Cristy! It's Adam. Open up!"

I didn't stop pounding and shouting until at last, Jack emerged from his room down the hall. Another time, I might have flipped him some shit for how ridiculous he looked in a hotel bathrobe, but the sadness in his eyes told me what I didn't want to know.

"She's gone, Tron."

"How do you know? Maybe she's down in the casino again. I haven't checked there yet."

As I stepped past him, his hand shot out and grabbed my arm. "She's not in the casino, Adam."

The use of my name in that gentle but firm tone told me that as usual, Jack had my back. Crossing my arms over my chest, I stared him down and waited.

"To keep Garrett off my back, I drank a beer, posed for a couple pictures, and left the party. When I stepped off the elevator up here, Cristy and Gretchen were standing in front of it with all their gear. Gretchen nodded at me but wouldn't answer my questions. Cristy slid past me and wouldn't meet my eyes." He sucked a breath in through his nose and let it out. "She's gone, buddy."

What the fuck?

I couldn't process with that pitying expression on Jack's face. Spinning on my heel, I headed back to the elevator. Somewhere on the ride down to the lobby, autopilot kicked in. When I tuned back into my surroundings, Mandalay Bay loomed in front of me, and I had no idea how I'd arrived there. Not that I cared.

The opulent lobby of the place left me numb. Gambling was no longer on my agenda. I'd placed the biggest bet of my life on Cristy Valor and went bust. But I wandered through the casino anyway, stopping at a bar where some guy pounded the keys on a gorgeous baby grand piano with about as much attitude as I felt. Straddling a barstool, I tossed two hundreds down and told the bartender to keep the shots of Jameson coming.

"You should go, Adam," played on a loop in my head. No, I damn sure should *not* have gone. Now she was gone from my life. Whatever demons drove her, they were stronger than any feelings she had for me. I knew she had a thing for me. Her eyes never softened for the other guys, even that asshole Slater, the way they always did when she looked at me. The way she touched me, with fire and wonder, told me how special I was to her. But it was the way she always used my name when we were alone that did it for me. The woman reached inside me and took my heart in her two hands, and I let her because I'd wanted to hold hers so bad. What a dumbass move. Two words tore that sucker right out of my chest. *"She's gone."*

After a while, the thumping notes on the piano or the Jameson kicked in. Either way, I finally stopped hearing Cristy's voice in my head. I came to when a bright light pierced my eyelids with Jack on one side of me and Bailey Saunders on the other.

"Time for you to wake up, Tron," Bailey said as the two of them hauled me up off the bar.

"What the fu—?" My other hand swung on its own as I struggled to make sense of where I was.

Jack snagged my bicep, and they dragged my ass to a limo waiting in front of the hotel. The sun faded the lights of the Strip as it topped the buildings along the street and seared my brain. The headache began immediately, the pounding between my ears threatening to dredge up whatever I had in my stomach to spew onto the street.

"Hold it together for five minutes, will ya, Tron?" Jack hissed in my ear.

Somewhere at the edge of my vision, a flash went off and I groaned.

"I've got a whole pitcher of my hangover cure waiting in the car, Tron. All for you," Bailey said in my other ear.

The promise of our road engineer's special concoction gave me the strength to walk the last couple of steps to the car more or less under my own power. Almost as soon as my ass hit the seat, Bailey shoved a glass of green elixir into my hand, and I chugged the whole thing down in one breath. He leaned across the car from his seat opposite me and poured me another, tipping up his chin to encourage me to drink that one down too. None of us had ever been able to pry the recipe out of him, but the whole band swore by whatever Bailey put in that drink. Today of all days, I needed it.

"How did you guys find me?" I asked as I sipped at my third glass of green hangover shake and glanced out the window as the Vegas Strip sped by.

"In a lot of ways, Garrett can be an asshole, but he's always looking out for us," Jack said.

"Garrett told you where to find me?" I asked, confused. Last I remembered, I'd had no destination in mind when I'd walked away from our hotel. I damn sure hadn't told our manager.

"He's got tracking on all our phones. Didn't you know that?"

"Son of a bitch! Isn't that illegal or something?"

"He manages a rock band of musicians who don't always make good choices," Jack said, sounding like some prissy-ass school teacher.

Bailey snorted out a laugh. "Seems like it worked out well for you, Tron," he said. "Otherwise, you probably would have missed the bus."

I closed my eyes and rested my head against the seat. Maybe it had been my intention to miss the bus when I walked out last night. Not my intentional intention, but something subconscious. I honestly didn't know. What I did know was playing the rest of the tour without Cristy didn't sound like a helluva a lot of fun anymore.

"FYI, Tron, since the tour has sold out so far, Garrett added more dates. Looks like we're headed to Florida after we play Dallas and Houston."

I cracked one eye open and shot Jack a side-eye. Of all people, I didn't expect him to be the one to stab me first.

"Fan-fucking-tastic," I mumbled and shut my eye again. If I concentrated hard enough, maybe I could make the last forty-eight hours disappear, and when I reentered it later, the world would be right again.

Like he knew exactly what I was thinking, Jack said, "We're the biggest band in the world, Tron. Everyone wants a part of us. If they get it, they don't like to give it up."

Whatever. I wasn't in the mood for Jack's platitudes. Cristy had given up on us without even giving me a chance to talk her out of it. If she truly wanted to keep the piece of me I'd given her, I'd have spent last night in her bed rather than alone on a barstool in a casino. The woman didn't want what I had to give, but it hadn't stopped me from giving it to her anyway. Now I had to figure out how to keep the beat without my heart.

Cristy

"I owed him that much, Gretchen, and you know it."

Though we'd been home in LA for the past two days, the argument hadn't stopped. My manager packing me up and putting me on my bus without letting me say goodbye to Adam tore me up. It wasn't the right way to end things. It wasn't respectful of him or of what had been building between us. Yes, I could admit something was happening there, something I wasn't sure I wanted to walk away from yet. When I did, I certainly wanted it to be on my terms, not my manager's. The fact that she'd been in such a big hurry to put distance between us nagged at me too. She'd never acted this way with any of the other guys I'd had flings with.

"Do you think he says goodbye to the loads of groupies he leaves behind?"

"Neither of us is a groupie and you know it." I gathered bubbles in my bath and pulled them up around my shoulders like a blanket.

"Do I? Annabelle told me bringing you on board the tour was Tron's idea, not hers. He hid behind her to keep it quiet from the rest of the band, but he's been a big fan of yours for a long time."

Averting her eyes, she arranged and rearranged my moisturizers on the vanity beside the sink, one of her nervous tells.

I sat up so fast, water splashed on the floor beside the tub. "Adam wanted me on the tour? He's the reason I joined them?"

Gretchen shrugged.

"Why didn't you tell me?"

She repositioned the pots and bottles again and said nothing.

"What's really going on, Gretch?"

Her head jerked up, and I caught a flash of fear in her eyes as they reflected to mine in the mirror. She glanced down, took a breath, and gathered herself. "I'm trying to protect you, Cristy-girl. It's what I've done since we were sixteen years old."

Leaning forward, I wrapped my arms around my knees and hugged myself hard. "I'm still married, aren't I, Gretchen?"

Giving herself a minute to compose her answer, she seated herself on the edge of my Jacuzzi tub. "You signed the papers. I made sure your lawyer served your ex. But I was young too." She traced a pattern in the water on the side of the tub. "His lawyer was making noise about you not being of legal age to even get a divorce or an annulment or whatever." Glancing up at me she whispered, "I was angry. I didn't follow up like I should have."

"Angry?"

"Yeah. What the fuck kind of country do we live in where a sixteen-year-old girl is considered old enough to get married but she's not considered old enough to divorce until she's a legal adult? I mean, how fucked up is that?"

I could see Gretchen was warming up to one of her favorite rants about female injustice, and while I generally shared her opinions, they weren't going to do anything for my current problems. "Are you saying I'm not divorced? And if I divorce him now, he's entitled to half of what I've worked my butt off to make for the last decade?"

"I'm saying we need to follow up, get your lawyers on it."

I slid under the water, blocking out the world for a minute.

When I slowly surfaced again, I stared deep into her eyes. "Is that why you keep me far away from Phoenix? Because you're afraid he'll come after me there?"

She slanted me a look.

"Not that I have any interest in revisiting the worst years of my life either, but I'm curious."

"You're an international superstar, Cristy-girl. Your ex can't touch you no matter where you go. I keep you away from Phoenix because it's toxic to your mental health."

I popped a few bubbles with my fingers. "Do you think Adam is toxic to my mental health? Is that why you don't want me to be with him?"

Her eyes couldn't hold mine as she answered. "Yes."

In the silence, I could hear the bubbles floating on the surface of my bath evanescing, tiny puffs of air escaping their confines. At that moment, I wanted to be air too, escape this bubble of a life I'd allowed Gretchen to create for me when I wasn't strong enough to stand up for myself.

"I need a couple minutes." When she didn't move, I added, "Now. Alone."

Her whole body stiffened like she wanted to say something she knew I wouldn't want to hear. Without looking at me, she stood and left the bathroom without another word.

I rested my head on the little pillow attached to my tub and stared at the ceiling as the water cooled around me. Nothing made sense anymore. For years, I'd lived as I pleased, wrote and sang the songs of my heart, some of them pretty darn revealing if anyone took the time to look. I'd taken care of my people as much as they'd taken care of me. Heck, the whole feud with Mali Tatum happened because I took better care of her dancers than she did. The whole time, though, something was missing. Watching the way the guys in Balefire had each other's backs because they were friends first and musicians together second drove home how isolated I'd become.

Or maybe I'd always been isolated, but Gretchen kept me so busy, I didn't have time to notice—or to feel alone.

Then Adam Tron used his rhythms to pound into my life before we'd even met. Gretchen knew me well enough to expect I'd go after one of the guys in the band, either Adam or Dakota since they were the single ones when I joined the tour. When I discovered Dakota's obvious interest in Annabelle, the band's intern, that left Adam. But the truth was, I'd had a secret thing for Adam from the first time I listened to a Balefire song. When I heard his driving rhythms on "Helluva Ride," one of their early hits, I couldn't sit still. His dark sound spoke to me of sensuality, desire, and freedom—experiences I had yet to have.

Being forcibly married to a man twenty years older than me because he was a big deal in my parents' religious community meant I had none of the experiences of a normal teen. Like meeting a boy, exploring our physical and emotional lives together, maybe falling in love. Instead, my parents had commanded that I submit to my husband in all ways, and though he was mostly patient with me, I was never allowed to say no. If not for Gretchen's friendship, I'd probably still be married to Joren, lost in my misery, and practicing petty combat as I struggled to retain even a whisper of myself.

Yet for everything Gretchen had done for me over the years as my friend and as my manager, I was starting to see that she controlled my life as much as first my parents then my husband had. Her management of my career meant endless rehearsals for tours or television specials or events like Coachella. If there was downtime, I was writing new material, spending months nonstop in the studio, or shooting a music video somewhere.

As the bubbles disappeared in my bath and I started to shiver, I tried to remember the last time I'd had a vacation. Hawaii five years ago maybe? Gretchen met some girl in a bar, and for three or four blessed days, I'd been left on my own to wander the beach, get a tan, take a snorkeling excursion. A laugh escaped me as I thought about the surfing lesson I'd had. For someone who dances as much as I do, I certainly had no grace or balance on a surfboard. Another memory sobered me. Gretchen's fling ended badly, and she cut *my* vacation short.

Now she was cutting my tour with Balefire short. The combination of her evasiveness and her ham-handed way of ending my tour with the band told me something else was going on. Then she dropped the bomb about my ex-husband. All the fear and self-loathing and dread of life within my parents' effed-up religion descended on me, stripping away years of rebellious self-empowerment and making me feel like a helpless sixteen-year-old again. My heart dropped into my stomach as another thought surfaced.

Shivering, I dragged myself out of the tub and wrapped up in a fluffy towel warmed on the rack between my Jacuzzi and my walk-in shower. I stared at my reflection in the mirror over the vanity. My bleached hair ,cut in a stylish cap, exposed the delicate features of my face rather than hiding them behind the thick fall of mahogany-colored strands I'd been born with. Always my best feature, the deep sapphires of my eyes glittered in their own way. I'd heard from more than one man, including Adam, how much they loved the natural pout of my lips. I sighed. Without makeup, I still looked like that scared sixteen-year-old, someone others could manipulate to their will.

But that's not who I was anymore. I left Cristine Valorie Rains Smith in Phoenix, Arizona when I was eighteen, and I'd be darned if I'd ever go back to her. Squaring my shoulders, I marched out of my bathroom and into my bedroom. Without sparing a second glance at Gretchen where she sat on the edge of my bed, I dropped the towel on the floor in front of the door to my massive walk-in closet and headed straight to the rack of power clothes. Three minutes later, I walked out of my bedroom wearing a fitted red pencil skirt and matching blazer over a lacy black camisole. The leopard-print stiletto pumps on my feet added four inches to my height.

The clutch matching my shoes tucked firmly under my arm held my cellphone, a slim wallet with my credit card and ID, and a tube of my favorite red lipstick.

"Where are you going?" Gretchen demanded as she trailed me out of the room.

"To take care of my own business. Finally."

CHAPTER TWENTY-NINE

Adam

IT SEEMED I was the only one who missed Cristy's set during our show, and it pissed me the hell off. But when we rolled into Dallas two days after playing a second sold-out concert in Phoenix, the guys finally figured out to leave me the fuck alone. All except for Garrett, that is. He kept saying stupid shit like how much better we sounded when we played for two hours without frivolous interruptions and the fans loved it. Did the dumbass pay any attention to the crowds when Cristy joined us onstage? The fans almost blew the fucking roof off the sky when we backed her songs with our signature sound or when she added her exquisite harmonies to Blu's vocals on our songs.

It had been nearly two weeks since she'd abruptly left the tour, and I was discovering there might not be enough Jameson in the world to numb the marrow-deep ache her absence inflicted on my life. When I'd approached Annabelle with the idea of bringing Cristy onto the tour, I knew what I wanted. I wanted to play some kick-ass shows with the reigning queen of the pop charts, a woman whose voice transcended her genre. I knew about her fondness for celebrity hookups and thought maybe I'd like to have one with her. What I didn't sign up for was feelings. Caring about her, worrying about her, falling in love with her? Damn sure not on the set list.

Ignoring Garrett's insistent invitation to hit the bars on a rare night off, I headed to my room. Alone. But it only took me a couple of minutes to figure out what a bad idea that was. So I shot Bailey a text, and half an hour later, a knock at my door announced the arrival of my request. The messenger girl's eyes offered me another kind of delivery, one I probably would have considered before Cristy upended my life. Now there was only one woman I wanted to spend that kind of time with, and she'd walked away from me without a backward glance.

After tipping the messenger girl and gently closing the door on her invitation, I ambled over to the couch, settled the mini-keyboard on my lap, and went to work. Ever since that morning in Vegas when Jack and Bailey rescued my sorry ass from the bar, a song had been scratching at the corners of my mind. Jack and Blu wrote most of our music, but occasionally I had something to say too. The texts I'd sent Cristy went unanswered. Same with the messages I left when I called her and her phone went straight to voicemail. At least she hadn't blocked me—yet. But I wasn't giving up. Not without a fight. I couldn't. The woman had walked away with my heart. I needed her to know that.

I noodled around with the notes for a bit, tried out the lyrics, fiddled with some rhythms. Time disappeared as I worked to tell Cristy what I needed her to know using the only medium I had left. Writing music was always work for me, which is why I usually left it to Jack and Blu, only suggesting ways my bass could enhance or balance or layer their ideas. I was content to let them be our John and Paul while I remained quiet like George. But there were times when the only way I could express my feelings was through a song. By the time soft morning light made its quiet way into my suite, I had something to run by the rest of the band.

In the writing, I found a little peace, and for the first time in weeks, I could breathe. Laying my head back against the cushions of the couch, I closed my eyes—just for a minute—and startled awake to the noise of someone pounding the hell out of my door.

"Tron, open the fuck up already." Even through the heavy door, I could hear Dakota's bad mood, a situation I understood only too well. After all, I wasn't the only one whose girl had left him behind in Vegas.

As I stumbled around the coffee table, I whacked my shin against a corner, jerking a curse out of me. Mirthless laughter greeted me when I opened the door.

Dakota looked me over from top to bottom, obviously drawing his own conclusions from the fact I hadn't changed my clothes from the day before. "Spent another night alone with your new best friend, Tron?"

"Thought about it." I opened the door wider, inviting him in.

"I'm the messenger boy. We needed to be in the lobby to catch our ride about fifteen minutes ago."

Shoving a hand through my hair, I said, "Shit. Why didn't someone call me?"

He leveled me with a glare. "Someone did."

Crossing my arms over my chest, I said, "Is that so?"

"Blu, Jack, Garrett, Bailey," he ticked off on his fingers. "Me. Our calls went straight to voicemail."

I fished my phone out of my pocket and discovered five missed calls. Huh. After finally releasing all those feelings into a song, it seemed I'd finally slept for the first time in years. Standing in the doorway to my suite and facing a pissed-off Dakota, I also tuned into the fact that I wasn't fogged in for once. Guess I'd needed a few hours of unmedicated sleep.

"Sorry man. Didn't hear my phone." I shoved it back into the pocket of my jeans. "Give me a second to put on a clean shirt and we're outta here."

♪

"Still can't believe you spent the night writing a song, Tron," Blu teased as we tuned our axes for Bailey's sound checks.

Though they called it AT&T Stadium now, it would always be Cowboys Stadium to me. Growing up in Denver, it was expected I'd be a die-hard Broncos fan, and like all my friends, I conformed to that expectation. So after Denver's biggest rival, the Kansas City Chiefs, I despised the Dallas Cowboys like a true Denver native. Still, playing a show in their massive stadium was always a rush. Over the years, we'd played here three or four times, including a Thanksgiving show back before Jack figured out the band was Garrett's boss, not the other way around. Of all my bandmates, he truly understood my attitude these days.

"Yeah, miracles sometimes still happen, Blu." I rolled my eyes. It hadn't been *that* long since I'd written a song, or at least since I'd helped the rest of the band to write one.

He snorted out a laugh and Jack joined him. "Beats spending the night cuddled up to a bottle of Jameson."

"Asshole."

It hadn't been all that long ago that none of us had a woman, but you wouldn't know it from the way those two acted. Though I tried to shove my attitude deep, I couldn't help but envy them their relationships with Ashleigh and Clio, neither of whom played an instrument or sang a note, at least not that I'd ever heard. Maybe that was the secret; find a woman who didn't share your passion for playing music so she wouldn't be famous and want to love and leave men in her wake.

An image flashed in my head. Cristy's beautiful eyes catching mine over Slater's shoulder as he leaned down to say something in her ear at the craps table in Vegas. She'd let me see longing and vulnerability and—sorrow. Then she'd lowered her head, hiding everything from me. Maybe with the other guys, it had been an act.

But I believed to the marrow of my bones she hadn't been acting with me. Those nights after our shows when we were alone together, she'd let me in whether she meant to or not. She let me see her vulnerability, her playfulness, the passion she held in check out in public. Walking away from us…Fuck, it didn't make sense.

The guys and I ran the set, giving Bailey a chance to adjust the sound. Video played on the big screens behind our stage and on the jumbotrons on either end of the stadium. More than once I thought about how hot Cristy would look in giant living color doing her thing in my favorite fuck-me lace-up boots. Thinking about her distracted me, and I dropped a beat. From across the stage, Dakota shot me a scowl, and Blu actually turned around and leveled me with a look then returned his attention to his mic.

"You're going to have it back together for the show tonight, right Tron?" Dakota asked with a sneer as we took a break to down some water.

His comment didn't deserve a response.

"How 'bout you run your song by us?" Blu asked.

Pictures of Cristy, the sound of Dakota's angry hurt, the risk of baring my soul tumbled around in my head. For a second, I worried I might heave up the breakfast sandwich I'd downed in the limo on the ride to the stadium. A heavy hand on my shoulder brought my head up to stare into the reassurance of Jack's calm face, and I nodded.

Stepping over to Blu's keyboards, I asked one of the roadies for a chair. I took my time to settle my racing heart, ran some scales to test the keys, stretched, and generally tried to gather myself. Dakota called me out for stalling. With a glare in his direction, I started to play.

CHAPTER THIRTY

Cristy

I WAS NEVER LEGALLY married.

After I'd lit a fire under my lawyers, it seemed it took them hours rather than years to determine my sham of a marriage wasn't legal. I was certain I'd signed some papers at the time, a marriage certificate and some others. My parents had stood over me, my mom looking fearful, my dad the picture of determination while Joren waited with his hands wrapped around a Bible, the picture of piety.

The week before my marriage, my parents had caught me sneaking out of my room wearing makeup, a Papa Roach T-shirt, and a pair of tight jeans. The next day while I was at school, my dad sealed my bedroom window shut and placed a padlock on the outside of my door. My mom cleaned out my room of everything except a framed photo of a cross, a Bible, and the hideous clothes they'd insisted I had to wear to maintain my modesty. My things, which admittedly hadn't been much, were gone. The poetry books and regular panties instead of the ugly granny-panties my mother demaded I wear were things I'd paid for with babysitting money I'd earned. The makeup and the collection of band T-shirts I'd hidden in a panel in the back of my closet I'd paid for as well. When I had the audacity to ask about them, my parents informed me I wouldn't need such frivolous things when I was busy taking care of my husband.

Thinking about that conversation made me throw up in my mouth—a far cry from losing my lunch on my mother's immaculate linoleum floor, but every bit as vile. As long as I lived, I'd never understand how the people who professed to be devout Christians could do such a terrible thing to their only child, a sixteen-year-old girl. All I'd wanted was to be normal. Turns out, normal was never an option for me.

The memories washed over me in thick viscous waves that threatened to suffocate me. Especially the subsequent conversations with Gretchen over the years, the ones where she commiserated with me, consoled me, assured me she was working on it and would protect me always. We were best friends forever, she'd told me, and she'd always have my back. Yet now it seemed she was my biggest threat. At that thought, my stomach threatened to send up more than bile.

Though they searched every database and archived record in the state of Arizona, my lawyers could find no evidence of a marriage certificate with my name on it filed anywhere. More importantly, the information they discovered about my supposed ex-husband indicated Joren Smith was an alias for a known pedophile who worked the map of religious communities extending from Alberta, Canada to Arizona. Currently, his whereabouts were unknown, but it would be highly unlikely he'd out himself to out me. Though I hadn't spoken to them in years, in all likelihood, my parents wanted nothing to do with me or with revealing secrets about me that might put them in jail.

The news should have lifted the ten-ton cloak of fear I'd been wrapped in for nearly half my life. Maybe it would have if not for Gretchen. After the lawyers informed me of my single status, I'd driven straight over to her place to tell her the good news. It couldn't erase the two years and the loss of innocence my "marriage" had cost me, but at least I could put it behind me now without the fear that somehow my family could trap me again like they had during that nightmare week leading up to my "wedding."

The shouting coming through her open windows as I strolled up the sidewalk to the front door of her bungalow sent shivers through me. Though I'd spent my whole life rebelling against what society demanded of me, I'd never tolerated open confrontation well. My finger hovered over the doorbell when I caught my name.

"This past year with you has been nothing but a lie. You've always loved Cristy!" The tears in Kelsey's voice dropped my hand to my side like a lead weight.

"She needs me, Kels. It's not the same."

"I need you, but you're never here. Even when you are here, even when you're in my bed, you're with her." Kelsey was screaming now. "I see how you look at her when you think no one's watching."

"She's my client. You know that." Gretchen sounded tired. "It's my job to look out for her."

"Is that why you deliberately forced her to break things off with the band? Because you're looking out for her?" Sarcasm dripped from Kelsey's tear-roughened voice. "Is that why you sabotaged her relationship with Tron?"

I flinched at the slap that cracked through the open window. Spinning around, I raced down the sidewalk, jumped into my car, and tore away from Gretchen's house. Hours later when she called with the news that she and Kelsey had broken up, I couldn't find it in me to give her the sympathy I knew she needed.

"Gretch, one of us needs a happy love life. Go beg Kelsey for forgiveness and make things right with her."

The line went quiet.

"I mean it, Gretchen. Since you ended my tour early, you can take some time off, take your lady on a vacation or something."

"But"—there was a hitch in her voice—"you need me."

"Right now, I need you to make sure you haven't screwed up the best thing that ever happened to you." *Like I screwed up the best thing that ever happened to me.*

Alone in the gathering dark of my living room, I replayed my life so far. Singing in dive bars for tips, signing my first recording contract, going on my first tour as the opening act for Mali Tatum, the empty affairs with celebrities—all of it orchestrated by my best friend. I'd trusted Gretchen with my whole life because I thought she loved me like a sister. I'd made it clear from the start we'd never be lovers. All this time, I thought she'd accepted that. I thought everything she did for me was because she was my family.

Now what did I do, knowing she'd always had a different agenda? Knowing she'd served her own interests over mine? Before I could go very far with that thought, a tiny voice in the back of my head wondered if I wasn't guilty of doing the same to her. If I hadn't lied to her as much as she'd lied to me.

When I started out in this career, I couldn't have been more naïve—about everything. I didn't have a clue how to handle money, people, contracts. Heck, basic travel stymied me since I didn't even learn how to drive until I was twenty-one. Gretchen took me in, taught me the little things in the beginning and took over the big ones as my career took off. There'd never been a formal agreement between us. Falling into our relationship just happened, and so far, it had worked out well because I never asked questions I didn't want to hear the answer to. Until I'd met alone with my lawyers. Until I heard that conversation between Gretchen and her girlfriend.

I dropped a single large ice cube into a tumbler and poured the glass mostly full of Jameson. As I took the first sip, my mind immediately conjured images of Adam. On autopilot, I sat back on my couch and pulled up Balefire's tour on my laptop. There were several videos from the shows we did together in LA, San Francisco, Seattle, Vancouver. Nothing from Vegas, which was odd. Even weirder, there was no video featuring songs we'd played together. All the clips were only of the band. Guess I deserved that with the way I'd run out not only on Adam, but on all of them. Then I saw the ones from Phoenix. Just seeing the inside of State Farm Stadium in a photo made my stomach cramp. Even with knowing as much of the truth as I did, I couldn't stop a visceral response to anything associated with my home state. Quickly, I scrolled past those shots and landed on a video produced sometime in the last two days from Balefire's show in Houston.

Unable to help myself, I played it.

Shock rippled through me, and I played it again.

I downed most of my whiskey, the liquor scorching my throat already on fire, and played the video again.

By the time I registered someone pounding on my door, the whiskey was gone but not the tears.

"What the fuck, Cristy? Why aren't you answering your phone?" Gretchen blew past me into my living room. "I've been calling you for the last two hours."

She flipped on a lamp like she owned the place, and I put up my hand to shield my eyes from the glare. From my laptop sitting on the coffee table, Blu's voice filled the silent space where my answer should have gone. She stared at me for a long moment then gently wiped my tears with the pad of her finger, not that she did much good at stemming their flow.

"Judging from your silence and that voice I'm hearing in the background, these aren't for me." The sorrow on her face told me she knew everything. We'd been best friends since our teens. We could read each other better than anyone.

Except for Adam. Somehow in the short time since meeting him, I'd let him see parts of me I'd kept hidden, even from Gretchen. Yet he still wanted me. And I'd run away. I could lie and say it was all Gretchen's fault, but then I'd be perpetuating the lies we'd been telling ourselves and each other for the past ten years. Lies Adam had seen right through. Gretchen had convinced me that once Adam knew about my past, he'd run away from me so fast, he'd be nothing but a speck in the distance. It was a convenient fiction—for both of us. It kept me closer to her, which I now saw was her goal. And it allowed me to keep hiding from my past, which is all I'd wanted to do my whole adult life.

It was time to crawl out of the shadows.

"He wrote a song, Gretch. About me."

Tugging her by the hand to sit beside me on the couch, I refreshed the video of the song I'd memorized the third time I'd listened to it. During the rest of the however-many listens I'd done, I'd internalized it. Like Adam, his song was a part of me now.

Blu's gorgeous baritone voice echoed around us. "Usually, Tron's a lazy bastard."

A *what-the-fuck* bass riff shot back at Blu's words, and he laughed.

"But when he decides to sit his ass down and write a song, it's pure gold. Anyone remember 'Back Seat?'"

The crowd roared in anticipation of Adam's homage to first love, a rip-roaring rock tune that melted panties every time the band played it. A smile tugged at my lips as I remembered my surprise at the second lingerie shower that fell halfway through that first show we did together when the band played that song.

"Yeah, yeah," Blu said with a laugh. "That one is Tron's. But he's been busy on this tour, and he's written a new one. Wanna hear it?"

Beside me, Gretchen tensed.

Deafening screams signaled the audience's desire for Adam's new song, and Blu laughed again. "See, Tron? They're telling you to write more songs."

The camera panned to Adam who flipped Blu the bird, but he was smiling.

And I wanted to die.

"This one is a little different from 'Back Seat,'" Blu warned the crowd, "but we hope you love it as much as we do. This one's called 'Run Away (Runaway).'"

Adam's rhythms introduced the song, a heartbeat that made my heart stop every time I listened to it. Jack's tom-toms joined him and accelerated the rhythm with his snares, working up to a massive cymbal crash that fell simultaneously with Dakota's lead guitar riff screaming into the tune. Three bars later, Blu's vocals laid me bare.

You fight the truth
But it's too big for you,
Too much for the lies
You try to sell.
I wanted to hold you,
Ring the bell.

Run away (runaway)
What are you running from?
Where are you running to?
Run to me baby, I'm standing here
Waiting for you.

Everyone wants a slice of your sweet
They leave you bleeding
Cut you so deep.
You leave me pleading
Baby, Baby
Don't run away.

Run away (runaway)
What are you running from?
Where are you running to?
Run to me baby,
I'm standing here
Waiting for you.

We all hide our scars
Lines of shots in forgettable bars
Bashing our thoughts with screaming guitars
Yet I'm standing here
Waiting for you.

Run away (runaway)
What are you running from?
Where are you running to?
Run to me, baby
I'm standing here
Waiting for you.
I'll always be
Waiting for you.

Blu's voice took on a melancholy tone on the last lines and the song ended on a bass riff. When the camera panned to Adam, his head down, his long fingers plucking a melody rather than setting a rhythm, I couldn't stop myself from reaching out. My fingertips skimmed the screen on my laptop, desperate to feel the heat of his skin beneath them. A tear slid down my face and plopped on my keyboard.

"I need to see him, Gretch," I whispered over the tears in my throat.

For the first time in my life, I wanted to run to something—someone—rather than run away.

She stood and walked to the window facing the ocean and stared out at the darkness. I'd pressed pause on the video, and Adam stood onstage before me, the gorgeous contours of his arms and shoulders revealed by the black tank top he wore. He'd let his dark hair grow since I'd left the tour, and my fingers itched to smooth away the lock that fell over his forehead as he closed his eyes. The spotlight looked good on him, and I wondered why I'd never paid attention to that before.

I was so lost in Adam that it took me a minute to figure out Gretchen was speaking.

"…the past. I guess—" She swallowed. "I guess I kept hoping you'd see how good we could be together and give us a chance—give me a chance." Though she turned away from the window, half her face remained in shadow. "But in the end, we can't change who we are. I'm not straight. You're not gay." She blew out a breath. "No matter how much I've longed for you ever since I embraced my sexuality sophomore year, you were never going to see me the same way."

Crossing the room, she poured herself a generous portion of Jameson and downed half of it in one go. Leaning back against the bar, she continued as though we'd been having a conversation rather than Gretchen carrying on a monologue. "You're right. I've been selfish." She sipped and covered her mouth on a little cough. "And dishonest. I didn't know the first thing about how to get your marriage annulled or whatever. All I knew was that I had to protect you. Even from you."

"Gretch—"

Her hand in the air stopped me. "You were on the edge of imploding every time someone brought up your past. So I made sure we stayed as far away from your past as possible. But I couldn't stop the nightmares."

I wrapped my arms around myself at the images that one word conjured.

"When you let Tron lock me out, I knew something was different." She sipped her drink, thoughtful. "He was different." After adding more whiskey to her glass, she wandered back over to the couch. Instead of sitting beside me like she usually did, she settled into the corner, and tucked her feet beneath her. "The way you watched him was different." Over the top of her glass, she leveled me a look. "You started keeping secrets from me. In all the years we've known each other, you never kept anything secret from me, but you didn't want to share anything about Tron."

"I couldn't."

Her eyebrow shot up, but she said nothing.

Pulling my knees up to my chest, I wrapped my arms around them and hugged them to me, a shield against Gretchen's hurt. "Talking about what happened between Adam and me felt like a betrayal. Like it was cheap or something. When it's nothing like anything I've ever experienced before."

She closed her eyes, sucked a long breath in through her nose, and let it out slowly. When she looked at me, the sadness I saw in her expression gutted me, but it didn't change anything.

"You're in love with him."

"Yes."

More whiskey before she rested her head on the back of the couch and stared up at the ceiling. In the silence, a chasm opened between us, one I had no idea how to bridge, one that terrified me on every level—except one. As much as her friendship meant to me, had always meant to me, if she made me choose between Adam and her, I already knew I was taking the chance on Adam.

"I suppose you want to rejoin the tour."

"The other night in Houston was their last night." The enormity of what I'd done when I breached my contract and didn't play those last shows sat in my stomach like a stone. Not only had I run out on Adam—I'd abandoned the whole band and the tour a lot of people had worked hard to promote.

"I heard from that toad Garrett that Balefire is extending the tour into Florida and Georgia. Three weeks. Maybe a month." Finally, she looked at me. "If you're interested."

My feet hit the floor with a thud. "Seriously? They'll take me back?" My heart threatened to leap out of my chest.

"Face it, Cristy. You elevated their brand every bit as much as they elevated yours." She leaned forward, cradling her drink in her hands. "And there's that other thing."

"Adam?"

With a sigh, she said, "Yeah, that one too." She downed the rest of the whiskey, set the glass on the table, and pulled my laptop into her lap. "Mali Tatum has made a run at the band."

"*What?*"

"After I saw this on TMZ"—Gretchen turned the computer so I could watch the clip of Mali running her mouth about how flaky I am and how Balefire would be so much better off touring with a true professional—like her—"I gave Garrett a call. From what Garrett said, the guys might be interested in playing with Mali."

Chills raced over me, and nausea threatened to upend my stomach.

"But they did like playing with you."

I slumped into the back of the couch. As much as I knew I wanted to return to the tour, I had to wonder what kind of reception I could justifiably expect. Especially from the man I hurt so badly he'd written a song about it. If I returned, would he really be waiting for me?

Chapter Thirty-One

Adam

"HEY, TRON. ABOUT time you stopped being a hermit," Blu called from the lounger where he rubbed sunscreen on his fiancée's back.

Ashleigh glanced over her shoulder at me. "Join us."

With a nod, I tossed a towel down on the lounge chair beside them and settled back into it. Tugging the bill of my hat lower, I tried to send a message.

Blu deliberately chose not to pay attention to it. "This a permanent return to the living or just a vacation?" He laughed at his own joke. "Ouch! What the fuck, Ash?" He rubbed his thigh where she'd pinched him.

Good girl.

Ignoring him, I crossed my arms over my chest and stared out at the waves rolling in and gently kissing the shore. Thinking about kissing inevitably led to visions of Cristy's plump pink lips and the ways she liked to use them, and I had to stifle a groan. It was coming up on a month since I'd seen her, and still, pictures of her played in my head like it had only been last night. Over the past few weeks, I'd learned that hell wasn't some nebulous place full of fire and brimstone. Hell was falling for a woman who had no idea how to trust—not herself and certainly not me.

"Hey, sad sack. We're at the beach. The day is gorgeous. We have a night off from playing. Drink a beer already."

Icy water flicked over me as Blu pulled a beer from a cooler between us with a flourish meant for maximum effect.

"Asshole," I muttered as I jerked the bottle from his hand. Twisting the top off, I shot it at him from between my index finger and thumb, a direct hit in the middle of his chest.

"Hey! Is that any way to treat your best friend?" But he was laughing as he dropped the metal cap back into the cooler.

I'd just taken a long pull when he dropped the bomb that had me spraying beer all over my feet and the sand beyond the end of my chair.

"Awesome, ain't it, how Cristy's joining back up with us on tour?"

Trying to regain my composure, I scrubbed the back of my hand over my mouth and turned to look him fully in the face. "What did you say?"

He dropped his sunglasses so I could see his eyes. "If you'd bother to hang with us sometimes, you'd know shit. Garrett told us last night."

Ashleigh stifled a giggle, but Blu didn't bother to hide his laughter.

"Close your mouth or you're gonna catch flies."

When Blu made that elementary school comment, Ashleigh cracked up, the two of them having one hell of a good time at my expense. No doubt I was doing a pretty good fish-out-of-water imitation. But damn. How did I not know this?

I rubbed my hand over my chest as reality smacked me like a brick. Cristy hadn't returned a phone call or responded to any of my texts. After a couple of weeks, I got the message and quit bothering her. Instead, I tortured myself by watching videos of her shows, our shows together, her social media feed—anything to hear that pretty voice, see that beautiful face, watch her move with the power and grace that gave everyone the idea she owned the world.

There were shadows there. Now that I knew to look for them, I could see them, especially in the interviews Gretchen kept so tightly scripted. In fact, everything about Cristy in public was a fine-tuned orchestration, not the real her. After spending time with her away from the stage and the trappings of the life, I had a good idea of who she was—a smart, sassy, talented woman whose scars left her crying and shaking in the middle of the night when no one was around to hear.

"Yeah, I gotta go."

Blu and Ashleigh sobered up on a breath.

"Hey, I didn't tell you to piss you off," Blu said.

"I'm not pissed." As I rolled off the chair, I jerked hard on my towel to free it and nearly jerked the chair on top of myself. "Thanks for the beer."

Back in my room, I stomped and paced and threw some shit around and generally made an ass of myself. At least I kept it private. But it wasn't enough. I dragged on a pair of shorts, slid into my tennis shoes, and headed for the hotel gym where I spent the next hour trying to sweat out all the anger and hurt thundering through me after Blu's little announcement.

The guys didn't have a clue about my feelings for Cristy. Dakota only thought he knew what was going on inside my head, but I'd kept the truth buttoned up tight. When they'd asked about that song I wrote, I shrugged it off as inspired by Dakota and Annabelle's antics. Which might have gotten me decked if the two of them hadn't worked some things out after Vegas.

I racked the bar with a clang and pulled off the plates, returning them to their place with a thud. Since no one else was stupid enough to lift in the heat of the day, it didn't matter how loud I was. No doubt I should have found someone to spot me, but I didn't give a shit about that either. It wasn't lost on me that I'd always been the steady one growing up and later on in the band, the one who always thought first—about consequences, about risk and reward, about other people. That part of me attracted Dakota and Blu in the first place. Then they discovered the stability of my parents' home, and they liked that too. Our mutual interest in music led to the band, and my insistence that Dave get some help led to Jack joining us. I knew my role. I was the fucking glue that held the whole damn thing together.

Cristy's return to the tour without *one fucking word* to me? That threatened to rip me to pieces.

After I downed some water, I poured the rest over my head and chest, cooling off from my workout. Exercise always made me feel better, all those endorphins doing their thing after I'd spent an hour revving them up. Not today. With images of Cristy dancing through my brain with every rep, if anything, my body pulsed like one big bruise, like I'd gone fifteen rounds with a heavyweight champ. For such a tiny thing, she'd managed to punch the shit out of my heart, and I had no idea how to make the pain go away.

When I saw her again, since I had no way to avoid that, what was I supposed to say to her? How was I supposed to act around her? Was I supposed to pretend she meant nothing to me? That I didn't want to drop-kick into the next millennium whichever douche-of-the-day she chose to hang out with?

The empty water bottle bounced off the mirror with a smack right as the driver for Cristy's bus walked into the gym.

He glanced back and forth between the plastic bottle ricocheting across the floor and me. "Was it something I said?"

The sight of him shocked my pulse up to the speed of sound. She was back. She really was back with the tour. "No." Looking to calm myself the fuck down, I grabbed a towel off the bench and rubbed it over my still-dripping head and chest. "I take it you're all here?" I asked when I thought I could sound halfway unaffected.

"Rolled in a couple hours ago." He pulled his T-shirt over his head and dropped it over the rail of a treadmill as he stepped onto it. "Drove most of the last three days, and man, I'm beat. Thought I'd work the kinks out before I hit the sack for the rest of the day."

"Sounds like a plan." With a nod, I walked over to my discarded water bottle, picked it up, and shot it into a recycling container as I headed out the door.

It was probably rude to walk out on him like that. Scratch that. It was rude, but I couldn't worry about it. Cristy was somewhere inside this hotel, and I didn't want to stink like a gym when I ran into her. I tugged my T-shirt on as I waited for the elevator and gave myself a pep talk about how cool I was going to be when I saw her again.

♪

"Shit! Sorry! I didn't see you there," I said as I righted the woman I nearly ran over when exiting the elevator. Seconds before she spoke, a spicy, flowery scent filled my nostrils and I froze.

"Hello, Adam."

For an eternity, I stared into the eyes that haunted my dreams every night before my brain woke up. I dropped my hands from her upper arms like she was fire. Running one hand through my sweaty hair, I stepped back from her and tried to project something resembling control.

"Cristy. Hey. Heard you were rejoining the tour."

It was all I could do not to shout at her.

But why the fuck did you leave it in the first place?

She smoothed her hands down the front of her skin-hugging, hot pink dress and nodded. "Yeah. After you guys extended it, I thought I'd hop back on board." She cleared her throat and wrung her hands in front of her, caught herself, and hid them behind her back. "I owed it to you for bailing out on the Texas dates," she finished quietly, her eyes zeroing in on my chest.

I crossed my arms, shielding my heart from her view. "Who's

your latest conquest?" I nodded to the guy sort of dancing from foot to foot about ten feet down the hall from us.

Cristy blinked at me. Might have been something in my tone, not that I gave a flying fuck. It was the first time I'd seen her in a month, and she was with some scaredy-cat pussy who wouldn't even stand beside her as she waited for an elevator.

"That's Steve's new assistant." For a second, she shifted her attention to the guy. "Hey, Max. Come meet Adam Tron." Turning back to me, she whispered, "He's a huge Balefire fan. So be nice. I don't need him messing up my costume changes tomorrow night because he's afraid of you."

Aaaand now I'd made a complete ass of myself. Extending my hand, I said, "Nice to meet you. Welcome aboard the crazy train. Hope you enjoy the ride."

"Thank you. Thank you so much. You have no idea how excited I am to be part of this show." He kept shaking my hand. "Thank you. Damn, it's so cool to meet you."

I stared down at our joined hands, and he finally got the hint.

"S-sorry." His face did its best to imitate a beet.

Up close, I could see he was younger than us by a few years.

"This is my first big show. Balefire is my favorite band in the world."

Beside him, Cristy cleared her throat. The guy's face turned purple. "No offense, Cristy, 'cause you're great too." He glanced back at me. "But I've been listening to Balefire for half my life."

Now I felt ancient. If he'd been listening to us for half his life, he must be what—eighteen? Did I act like that ten years ago? Scratch that. I acted like that ten minutes ago. In the gym with Cristy's driver. Jesus.

I huffed out a laugh. "Hope that pedestal you've set us on isn't too high, 'cause I bet we all fall off it before the end of tomorrow night."

When he started to gush again, I had no choice but to cut him off. Zeroing in on Cristy, I said, "Where you off to?"

She furrowed her brow and I nodded toward the elevator.

With a nervous laugh, she said, "Max and I were going out to the arena. I've played the Amalie before, but Steve wanted to get a sense of it for planning my costume changes. Max unpacked my day wear for me so he knows what I brought along since he wasn't involved in the selections. Now we're headed out to meet Steve."

Cristy's gushing sounded a lot like her assistant. Her hands had gone back to smoothing her dress, which naturally drew my eyes to her pretty curves, curves I itched to put my hands on. So I shoved my hands in the pockets of my shorts. Fuck, if the two of us weren't a pair.

With a nod, I moved to step around her.

She crossed her arm over her chest, smoothing her palm up and down her other arm. "Maybe we can talk after rehearsals?"

I arched a brow and waited.

"Without an audience." Discreetly, she side-eyed her assistant.

Glancing past her new assistant, I asked, "Where's Gretchen? I didn't think you went anywhere without her."

Cristy crossed both arms over herself. "She's finalizing some things with your manager, I think." After clearing her throat again, she added, "I haven't seen her since I got off the bus a couple hours ago."

Her whole entourage must have arrived while I was out on the beach with Blu and Ashleigh. Wonder if those two knew that too. It didn't matter. Cristy said she wanted to talk—after rehearsals. Which weren't until tomorrow. Guess it was time I figured out how to kill way more time than was good for me to be alone.

"Guess you two should go do your thing. See you later."

It took everything I had to walk away from her when all I wanted was to scoop her into my arms and kiss the living hell out of her. As I shoved my key card into the slot in the door to my suite, I heard the elevator ding, but I didn't give in and glance back at her. I'd made it clear the whole tour I wanted her. Hell, I even chased her down in Vegas and made an absolute ass of myself. And she left. If she wanted me now, she'd have to make the next move.

CHAPTER THIRTY-TWO

Cristy

IF I COULD have suspended time, I would have stood there with Adam's hands on me all day holding on to the happiness I saw in his eyes for a split second before it disappeared. His T-shirt read, "Here I am. What are your other two wishes?" I nearly told him, "Please forgive me, and can you work up another sweat—in my bed?"

Instead, I'd stammered like my starry-eyed new assistant. I didn't see him again for the rest of the day. That was probably a good thing since I hadn't figured out how to ask him about that song. Or if he'd take another chance on me.

From my suite down the hall from Adam's room, I stared out at the lights playing over the water of the Gulf. A dancing kaleidoscope of color on the dark surface of the sea, its beauty didn't touch me the way it usually did. Instead, all I could see was the look on Adam's face when I told him I'd moved on. No warning. No explanations. No chance at changing my mind.

It had all been Gretchen's idea. She'd said hanging out with

Rip Slater and ignoring Adam would build intrigue and give me an excuse to avoid the Phoenix shows. Maybe roil the tabs a little.

Now I knew better. It had all been done to split me up with Adam because she could see what no one else could—my feelings for him were real and growing with every minute we spent together. Somehow, the man figured out my tells, saw my scars, and still wanted to be with me. He wanted to slay all my monsters and take care of me. The only other person who'd ever offered me that kind of safety was Gretchen, but in the end, her friendship came with strings as thick as ropes. The way Adam treated me professionally then walked away from me today without a parting glance told me exactly what I needed to know.

I'd hurt him. And I was going to have to earn my way back to him. But how?

Adam

"You okay with this?"

"With what?"

Over the years, I'd learned the best way to avoid an uncomfortable topic was to pretend you didn't have a clue. Jack wasn't buying it.

"Don't be a dick, Tron. You know exactly what I'm talking about."

We were waiting for Cristy to arrive at rehearsals for the Tampa show. I'd spent the night before holed up in my room with a keyboard and a bottle of Jameson. Not that either had done me any good. I'd remained ridiculously aware of how much my heart hurt, and the song I was writing reflected that. I'd never share it. The rock we played tended to be a party. There wasn't any room for all the anger and pain I poured into that song. Maybe I'd sell it to someone like Nine Inch Nails.

Or not.

The idea of outing how much I cared for Cristy, how much I wanted her back even after the way she'd hurt me churned my stomach. Nope. That song had been an exercise in catharsis. I just had to make it to the end of the tour without giving away my feelings.

The woman who never left my thoughts strolled out onto stage right. My eyes toured those sexy boots that climbed up her perfect legs and revealed a flash of soft skin above her knees. My hands flexed with the need to skim the tight red minidress that hugged her body and showed off her luscious curves. For a second, her posture turned in on her, something not at all Cristy-like, and I wanted to race across the stage, gather her up in my arms, and protect her from whatever monsters followed her. Before I could act on my irrational need to take care of her, she blinked several times at something behind me and squared her shoulders like she was headed into the ring for the championship fight.

"You might want to close that before something nasty flies in," Dakota whispered from somewhere to my right.

I shut my mouth so hard, I nearly cracked a tooth. Still, I couldn't get over the change that came over Cristy. Did she think I was going to make a scene over her return?

From somewhere behind me, Garrett's voice interrupted whatever was going on between us. "I wasn't sure you'd actually show."

If anything, Cristy seemed to grow bigger, her attitude expanding like a force field around her.

Turning, I discovered Garrett with his arm around Mali Tatum, and I figured out Cristy's attention hadn't been on me at all. Somewhere in the back of my head, I remembered something about the two of them having a falling out, but since most of that shit is manufactured in the tabs, I hadn't paid much attention. Judging from the way the women eyed each other, like two heavyweights about to go fifteen rounds, maybe the rumors were true.

"The fans seemed to like pairing a pop diva with the biggest rock band in history, so I thought if one was good, two would be better. Boys, this is Mali Tatum. I think you two already know each other." He said that last part to Mali who glared cannons at Cristy.

Which begged the question of what the ever-loving-fuck Garrett thought he was doing.

Dakota was on my same page. "Garrett, how 'bout you join us in the green room?" He started moving toward the back of the stage.

"Look, I invited Mali for Tron since he seems to like pop singers these days." The fake innocence on his face was almost comical. "Now that Cristy's back, you can have a pop singer too, Dakota."

At Garrett's asinine suggestion, Dakota shot him a look that could have singed fire. I was thinking the same thing.

"Or you can trade off, which would probably be fun too." He winked. "Plus, the press will have all kinds of fun if the four of you are having a rock 'n' roll party, which will only ratchet up publicity for the tour."

"Adam?"

The anguish in that one word from Cristy's lips tore my heart.

Before I could react, Mali sidled over to me, slipped her arm through mine, and smiled. "You're so hot, Tron. The word is, you know exactly how to show a girl a good time." As she walked her fingers up my chest, she shot Cristy a filthy look. "You win some, you lose some. Better luck next time, loser."

A split second before she turned on her heel to march away, Cristy's face crumpled. When I started after her, Mali tightened her hold on me, dragging me back.

"What the fuck do you think you're doing?" I growled at Garrett as I peeled Mali off me.

"Taking care of my boys." He crossed his arms over his chest. "Like I always do."

The urge to punch his lights out overwhelmed me, and before I could think about it, I was moving. Dakota wrapped his arms around my chest and dragged me back before my million-dollar fist could connect with Garrett's ten-cent face. "Not worth it, man." He spun me in the direction Cristy had gone. "Go after your girl. The rest of us will take care of Garrett," he said into my ear.

Dakota gave me a not-so-gentle shove, and I stumbled a couple of steps before I righted myself and sprinted after Cristy.

CHAPTER THIRTY-THREE

Adam

"HEY! CRISTY! WAIT!"

She took three more long strides down the hall toward the parking lot before she stopped. With her head down and her shoulders hunched, her demeanor was nothing like my wild, vibrant, take-no-prisoners girl. It killed me. Still, when I caught up to her, I didn't touch, even though touching her was the only thing I wanted to do.

Blowing out a breath, I said, "Are you going to look at me at least?"

An eon might have passed before she finally turned around. Red-rimmed eyes slammed into mine, and that was it. I wrapped her up tight in my arms and held her as hard as I could and said nothing. When she was ready, we'd have it out, but her eyes had already told me everything important I needed to hear.

The sound of loud angry voices echoed down the tunnel from the stage, interrupting our reunion. "Want to take this somewhere more private?"

She nodded into my chest. As we walked back to her dressing

room, I kept my arm wrapped around her, holding her close to my side. Though she didn't return the favor, she didn't try to move away from me either. When she keyed us into the room, I discovered her entourage seated with their heads together, whispering animatedly. Didn't take a genius to know what their conversation was about.

"You guys want to give us a minute, please?" Though I'd tacked on polite, my tone wasn't asking for permission.

Jillian, Steve, and that kid Cristy had introduced me to yesterday scrambled out of their chairs and sidestepped us as they headed for the open door behind us. Gretchen took her time. Standing and walking slowly toward us, she said to Cristy, "He needs to hear it from you."

My heart dropped to my knees. "Hear what?"

When she reached us, she stopped and stared me down hard. "Don't fuck this up, Tron." Emphasizing her point, she shouldered by me and slammed the door behind her.

Beneath my arm, Cristy flinched at the sound of Gretchen's attitude before she sagged into me. Gently, I turned her to face me, holding her with my hands on her hips. "Talk to me, Valorous."

She stared at a spot in the middle of my chest and swallowed hard two, three, four times. At last, she said, "Maybe we could sit down?"

I led her over to a chair, sat, and pulled her down onto my lap. "What happened? Why did you run?"

"You were—" She brushed at her eyes. "We were—"

I thumbed away a tear she missed. "Take your time, sweetheart."

"I thought maybe you meant what you said in that runaway song you wrote." She stared up at the ceiling and pulled in a breath. "But you moved on already."

"We've only played that song publicly once," I ground out.

She squirmed on my lap, and I relaxed my hand where I'd dug my fingers into her hip. But I didn't let her go. "Were you at that show in Houston? Why didn't you let me know? Why didn't you join us?"

"I saw it online." Clearing her throat, she said, "How long have you been with her?"

"How long have I been with who?" I asked, genuinely perplexed.

She'd heard the song, knew I'd written it about her. I was waiting for *her*. There was no one else.

Cristy nodded in the general direction of the stage. "Her."

"Mali Tatum?"

I think she might have growled as she inclined her head at me. It was all I could do not to burst out laughing. She was jealous.

"It was all fine for you to hang out with some B-list nobody to piss me off, but you're not having it from me?"

Her body went rigid. "That was all Gretchen's idea. For all the wrong reasons. I—" She looked me directly in the eyes. "Hanging out with him left me nauseous. I hated every second of it. But you were so angry." Her voice trailed off. "Then you walked away, so I thought I should too."

"I met Mali for the first time right before you ran off that stage just now." I smoothed the pad of my finger over the furrows on her forehead. "I have no idea what the fuck Garrett is up to, but there are one or two things you should know." My eyes followed my finger as I traced it over the delicate shell of her ear, and I smiled as she shivered at my touch. "It was my idea to bring you on board our tour."

Her eyes saucered. "But Annabelle—"

"—went along with it because it helped her too." I smiled at the confusion playing over her features. "I've been listening to you for a long time. Your voice reached inside me, made me want to know the person behind it." I settled her closer to me. "So I hatched a plan and talked Annabelle into executing it. The next thing I know, I've fallen flat on my ass for you." I smoothed my fingers over her hand resting in my lap and lifted it to drape her arm over my shoulders. "Judging from the fact that you returned to the tour and these tears you're killing me with, you feel something for me too."

"So much, Adam. I feel so darn much for you."

A laugh escaped me. "Someday, you're going to tell me the story behind the sexy-as-fuck woman who never utters a single swear word."

She slid me a side-eye, and I laughed again.

"But for now, I'll settle for a kiss."

Her eyes darkened before they slipped to my mouth. "You meant it when you said you'd wait for me?"

"Every word."

A choked sound somewhere between a laugh and a sob erupted from her as she pulled both her hands down to her lap. "I have something I need to tell you." She stared down at her hands clenched so tight her knuckles were white. "If you don't feel the same way when I'm done, I'll understand."

Smoothing my fingertips over her fists, I tried to calm both of us while she gathered her thoughts to say what she needed to say. Intuitively, I knew I had to hold it together, not react to whatever she was going to tell me.

"I was married."

"*What?*"

She flinched, and I worked to jack myself back down.

"My parents are fundamentalists. They call it a religion, but it's more like a cult."

The expression on her face told me she expected judgment. I schooled my features into something I hoped looked neutral and nodded for her to go on.

"When I was sixteen, they caught me sneaking in from a rock concert. I was wearing makeup and modern clothes I'd bought with my babysitting money and kept hidden from my parents."

My brows shot up. "Modern clothes? Doesn't everyone wear 'modern' clothes?"

"The cult my parents belong to sees women as subservient to men. We wore shapeless cotton sack dresses that might have been fashionable on the prairie in 1850." Her pretty mouth turned down. "Kids made fun of me in school."

That explained her racks of clothes, each outfit sexier or more outrageous than the next.

"After they caught me, they decided to marry me off to one of their friends, a man who'd shown up a couple of years before claiming to be a prophet. A man my dad's age."

My hands curled into fists, but I let her keep talking. She'd wandered back into the past and didn't seem to notice my reaction to her words.

"When I was eighteen, Gretchen helped me run away from all of them. She had a friend who introduced me to a lawyer who said he could have the marriage annulled if I paid his fee."

When I tensed up even more, she shook her head. "It was a standard legal fee. I worked doubles bartending to pay it. Then my parents came after me, and I had to leave the state. Gretchen helped me. We moved to LA, I started singing in bars, she became my manager, and you know the rest."

"Did you get the marriage annulled?"

Cristy picked at the hem of her dress. "I never really knew. All I knew was that I couldn't go anywhere near the state of Arizona in case my parents and my ex might drag me back into their mess." Her voice lost its power. "And I never wanted anyone to know where I came from." The bleak desperation in her eyes when she blinked up at me gutted me. "If people knew, they'd judge, make fun of me, not take my music seriously."

I wrapped my arms around her and hugged her tight to my chest. "Oh, Valorous. No one who's ever heard you sing could blow off your music." I let that sink in for a minute, setting my lips against her temple. "What happened with your marriage?"

She cleared her throat. "Turns out, the marriage was never recorded. As far as the law is concerned, I was never married." Her body tightened up again. "Something Gretchen conveniently forgot to tell me all these years."

"That the reason for your nightmares?"

My question took all the fight out of her, and she sagged into me. "Gretchen did everything she could to keep my past out of the press. Then one night when I was on tour with Mali, we got good and drunk together, and I let it out that I was married." She pulled in a deep breath and released it slowly. "That's all I managed to reveal before Gretchen whisked me out of there. Then Mali and I had our fight, I gave her dancers a better deal, and the tabs have loved the heck out of our feud ever since. I think Mali enjoys it too," she said quietly. "It keeps her in the public eye when her music isn't charting so well. But I still worry she's going to ruin everything for me. In fact, I can't understand why she hasn't done it already."

"Probably because she can't find proof of your marriage."

"Now that you know everything, I won't blame you for walking away." The bleakness in her tone undid me.

"Baby-girl, you aren't getting away that easy."

Those gorgeous sapphire eyes of hers blinked up at me, questions and hope playing tag inside them.

"Even if that marriage had been real, I wouldn't care. You're not married now. You weren't married when we hooked up. Or if you had been, you didn't want to be. And you'd taken steps to end the marriage even though you weren't clear on the outcome of those steps. As far as I can tell, you were free to pursue a relationship with me from the moment we met."

I picked up her hand and pressed a kiss into her palm. "I had no choice but to wait for you."

She arched a brow.

"What we have is real, Valorous. I've never felt this way about anyone before." I held her palm to my jaw. "I don't think you have either, or we wouldn't be here with you trusting me with everything you just told me."

"Until you, Adam, I've never had anyone who wanted me only for me. No strings. No control. No music or fame or money. Just me. I didn't know what to do with that. And I panicked." She let out a shaky breath. "Can you forgive me? Give me another chance?"

"You haven't been paying attention, Cristy." My eyes followed my finger as I traced the contours of the face I wanted to wake up to every day for the rest of my life. "I'm in love with you. If you run again, I won't make the same mistake of staying behind, of giving you space or whatever. I'll follow you until you believe that you're worth all the love I have in me to give."

When her lips brushed mine, every second of need I'd kept bottled up inside me since the day she'd walked away from the tour spilled out. Before I knew it, I'd pulled her over to straddle me, my hips working my hard-on against the heat between her legs as I mapped every inch of her with my hands.

Cristy wasn't idle either. In seconds, it seemed, my T-shirt lay on the floor somewhere, the skin on my chest and shoulders, arms and back catching fire as her hands and lips roamed over me. She whimpered into my mouth as our lips ground together, our tongues tangling and teasing, and I worried I might explode in my jeans from her kiss alone.

At last, I pushed her off my lap to stand in front of me on shaky legs. Grinning up at her, I slid to my knees on the floor. The pretty lace thong I discovered when I pushed up her hot dress had to go. With one hard tug, the fabric tore, giving me access to her sweet center. "Open for me, Valorous. It's been way too long since I've had a proper taste of you."

I feathered my fingertips along the insides of her creamy thighs and up to caress her pretty ass. With my forearms, I urged her to widen her stance, leaned in, and kissed her. One long, slow lick along her seam ended at her hard clit. I lapped at her until her fingers tangled in my hair. Licking and kissing and sucking her pussy with a happy hum in the back of my throat, I could have stayed right there all day. To hell with rehearsals. To hell with the band. When I slid two fingers inside her, curling them exactly the way I knew she liked, she started singing my name over and over, and I remembered how much I loved Cristy's harmonies with me when I went down on her.

My name on her sweet lips did it for me. I worked her until her pussy pulsed around my fingers and a scream tore from her throat. Sitting back on my heels, I smiled up at her as I sucked her lovely juices from my sex-slicked digits. Her gorgeous eyes focused on my mouth and darkened even as she labored to catch her breath. If I lived to be a hundred, going down on Cristy Valor would never get old.

"Adam."

"Do you believe me now?"

An impish grin tugged at her mouth. "I'm trying. I really am." She reached a hand down to help me stand. "But I might need a bit more convincing."

Her eyes never left mine as she freed my cock from my jeans. Cool fingers skimmed featherlight along the length of my rock-hard dick, and I didn't even try to stifle the groan that rumbled out of my chest at the feel of her hands on me. It had been weeks since I'd touched her, since she'd touched me. That first taste only showed me how much I'd missed while we'd been apart. I was dying for more of her taste, more of her touch, more of her sounds, more of *her*.

"Cristy."

"You should probably sit down for this next part."

The gentle pressure of her palm in the middle of my chest put my ass back in the chair, and she wasted no time climbing onto my lap to sheath me inside her. She pushed up and sat back down hard, taking more of me as a moan slipped from her lips. When she went to move again, I stayed her with my hands on her hips.

"Babe. We forgot something." It was all I could do to speak, but it was my job to take care of her.

Confusion flitted over her face.

"Condom."

Tilting her pelvis, she clenched me again, a velvet vise that had me gritting my teeth to hold onto her, not let her move on me.

"Valorous, you're going to be the death of me." I shifted her to slide up and lightning fast, slid a condom out of my jeans. In seconds, I protected us before I let her slide back down my cock. "But I'm going to die with a smile on my face."

The sunshine in her grin lit up my universe. Her powerful dancer's legs went to work as she rode me, her pussy clenching my cock like a tight silken glove. Needing more contact with her beautiful skin, I stopped her moving over me only once to tug her dress off her, baring her luscious breasts to my greedy mouth. As she had her sweet way with my cock, I palmed and kissed and sucked her gorgeous full breasts. Teasing her taut nipples with my teeth and tongue elicited the symphony Cristy always sang to me when I fucked her, the one that drove me wild.

When we both needed more friction, I held her hips steady while I thrust hard and fast up into her.

"Adam!" she screamed as her pussy clamped down on my cock.

That's all it took to send me over the edge. With a shout, I let go inside her, the orgasm rippling down my spine and up my legs as I gave her all of me.

Time stopped as we basked in the afterglow of our return to each other. She tucked her face into the space where my shoulder met my neck, her lips brushing soft kisses over my skin with every breath she took. I skimmed my hands down and up the beautiful curve of her spine, holding her close, trying to absorb our homecoming deep inside me. All the while, her inner muscles pulsed around my still mostly hard dick, the aftershocks of our lovemaking reminding me how no one else would ever satisfy me like my Cristy.

For a millisecond after the thought entered my head, my hands stilled on her body. If she noticed, she didn't react. Maybe she wanted to be my Cristy. As I rolled the idea around in my mind, held it up and examined it from every angle, the rightness of it became more and more clear. Cristy was mine. Holding her like this, close to her like this, bared to her like this, I'd never felt so free, so alive. A smile tugged at my lips as I turned my face to catch her mouth with mine.

A loud, unwelcome pounding at the door jerked us out of the paradise our reunion had taken us.

"Tron, Cristy, you two need to hustle your asses out to the stage. Team meeting," Dakota shouted through the door.

I dropped my head against the back of the chair and groaned. "Fuuuuck."

Cristy sighed. "I was hoping for more of that too."

Her comment jerked a laugh out of me. When I tipped my head up, I caught the grin on her face, her eyes dancing with mischief. Reluctantly, it seemed, she slid off my lap, stood, and stretched. She was temptation personified standing there in nothing but her fuck-me boots with all that glorious skin on offer.

This time when Dakota pounded on the door, I feared for the health of his million-dollar hands. "You don't have time to get busy in there. We need you guys on the stage in two minutes."

Cristy threw a sassy grin my way. "Duty calls, Adam."

She killed me dead when she sashayed over to her wardrobe and pulled out another pair of lacy panties. I watched in fascination as she maneuvered them over those boots and shimmied them up her perfectly shaped legs to cover the prize she'd let me enjoy for the past however long. Her beautiful girls filled a matching lace bra, and turquoise blue became my new favorite color before she covered all that beauty with a body-hugging sleeveless dress in a kaleidoscope of iridescent colors that looked like it came straight out of 1965.

Clearing her throat, she nodded at my still mostly naked state. "You're wearing my favorite outfit, Adam, but I don't want to share my view with anyone else."

When I didn't move to pull up my jeans right away, she arched a brow, a hint of a smile playing over her luscious lips. With a long-suffering sigh, I stood and pulled up my boxers and jeans. As I tucked my half-hard dick carefully inside my clothes, my eyes never left hers. "This is a promise for later."

"I'm counting on it, babe."

Snatching up my T-shirt, she gave it to me and hand in hand, we left her dressing room and hurried up the tunnel to the stage.

Chapter Thirty-Four

Adam

A LOW RUMBLE OF conversation greeted us as we neared the stage. My guys were sitting on folding chairs in front of Jack's massive drum kit. Ashleigh stood behind Blu with her arms wrapped around his shoulders while Annabelle sat on Dakota's lap. Jack sat alone. From somewhere off stage right, I heard a baby squeal followed by soft feminine laughter, which told me Clio was entertaining Jack's and her daughter somewhere out of sight. Bailey leaned against the edge of the hydraulic platform that held Jack's drums.

Judging from the way she let a little circulation back into my hand, Cristy figured out Garrett's and Mali's absence at about the same time I did. Cristy's crew, particularly Gretchen, was also conspicuously absent. Weird.

"What's up that had Dakota trying to pound his way into Cristy's dressing room just now?"

"*Just now?*" Dakota's brows shot to his hairline. "I tapped nicely on your door half an hour ago."

I winked at Cristy who gifted me with a sly smirk.

"Whatever. What's going on?"

"Pull up a chair," Blu said. "Team meeting."

Team meeting was our code for the band only—no Garrett, no roadies, no girls, no one but the four of us. Which begged the question why all these people—and Cristy—were invited. I arched a brow first at Blu, then at Dakota and Jack as Bailey hustled over with a couple of chairs for Cristy and me.

"Garrett and Gretchen are working out something with Mali," Blu began.

Beside me, Cristy went completely still.

"The dumbass signed a contract with her in our names—"

Blu didn't have a chance to finish before I stood directly in front of him.

"—without consulting any of us. When you two ran off"—a smirk played over his face—"he tried to push Mali off on Dakota and told her she could have you next."

"*What?*"

Blu nodded at my hands flexing into fists at my sides. "That was Dakota's response too. Only his connected with Garrett's eye."

My attention swung to Dakota where I noticed Annabelle holding a cold pack to his right hand.

At my unspoken question, Dakota laughed. "Damn straight it was worth it."

I eased down in the chair beside Cristy and waited.

"Jack grabbed Dakota before he could ruin his hands and the rest of the tour while Bailey grabbed Garrett." Blu's attention shifted to Cristy. "About that time, your entourage arrived on the stage, and Mali went after Gretchen. The screaming and shouting turned into a pretty entertaining catfight." He chuckled.

Cristy glanced at me, and I shrugged.

Dakota took up the story. "In the course of all the shouting, it came out that Mali thought she was playing with us for the next three shows. The three of us"—he nodded at Blu and Jack—"demanded to know what the fuck she was talking about, and that's when Garrett started talking fast."

"He can't sign us to anything without our John Hancocks on the dotted line. That's in *his* contract," I reminded my buddies.

Dakota rolled his eyes. "We *know* that, Tron. But Mali has a signed contract, and she's threatening to sue."

Cristy snorted. "Of course she is. Why is Gretchen with them?"

"Because we signed a contract with you, a contract that has an addendum about additional shows if we added them at the end of the tour. Which we did," Dakota said, but his eyes were on me.

I shot him a grin that included Annabelle who smiled back at me.

"Now what?" Cristy asked. "Because I have to tell you guys, I'm not playing any shows with that witch." The mutinous expression on her face didn't hide the anguish I saw in her eyes.

"You're our touring partner, babe." I slid my chair closer to hers and draped my arm over her shoulders, pulling her into my side. "If you don't want to perform with Mali, we won't perform with Mali, right?" I asked, eyeing each of my brothers.

"After that clusterfuck that went down with her earlier, I can't say she made a good impression on me," Dakota said.

I noted that he pulled Annabelle even tighter to his body than she already was.

"Which brings us to why we're having a team meeting—with all of us." Blu included the girls and Bailey. "I don't know what Garrett's problem is, but ever since last year when Jack and Clio got back together and Ashleigh and I hooked up"—he wrapped his hands over his fiancée's where she rested them across his chest—"Garrett's been actively pushing for one-nighters like in the old days. It's like he doesn't want us to move on, grow up, or whatever."

"I don't give a shit what his problem is. He nearly cost me my lady." Dakota nuzzled Annabelle's cheek then gifted her with a smacking kiss. She directed a long-suffering glare skyward, but a smile ghosted her lips. "And he deliberately tried to interrupt your return to Tron, Cristy."

At her gasp, Dakota plowed on. "Even though the tabs mostly get it wrong, sometimes they nail it. Like you and Mali Tatum not being friends."

Because I held her next to me, I felt the tremors roll through her at Dakota's words.

"I…um, we're…"

"Together," I said with finality. No way was I letting the best thing in my world get away from me again. In case that declaration wasn't crystal enough, I dragged her onto my lap and kissed her pillow-soft lips.

Right as things started to heat up rather perfectly, Dakota put all his diva skills behind clearing his throat. I cracked open one eye, gave Cristy another promise for later, and let us both up for air.

"Damn good thing. Quiet, steady Tron we can deal with. Moody, boring Tron's a pain in the ass." Blu's eyes danced and he sobered. "We need to decide what we're going to do about Garrett."

Dakota didn't hold back. "I say, fire his ass."

"He's been with us since the beginning, Dakota. Maybe we should give him a chance to explain himself."

The way Cristy blinked at me told me she thought I might be a couple squares short of Bingo. But up until we started meeting people we wanted to keep in our lives, Garrett had done everything right by us. It seemed only fair to let the man talk, at least. Plus, he had a clause in his contract that would cost us plenty if we let him go in the middle of a tour.

"Since you invited me," Bailey said, "I'm assuming you're okay with some input from the crew."

"Go on. Give us your two cents," Blu said.

"I haven't been with you guys as long as Garrett, but I've been engineering your shows for going on seven years. I have a stake here."

We all nodded.

"Up until this tour, working with Garrett was easy." Bailey sucked in a breath. "Now it seems all he wants to do is take care of all the groupies you guys are disappointing these days."

He let that sink in.

"At the risk of pissing you off, I think Garrett's problem is that all of you are in exclusive relationships." Resuming his perch on the edge of Jack's stage, he crossed his arms over his chest and shut his mouth.

Blu nodded. "That explains a lot when you think about it." He pulled Ashleigh's hand to his lips, kissing her palm and settling it back across his chest. "He put a run on Ash, but when she didn't return his interest, he made a mess that broke us up for a while." The kiss distracted him for a second before a laughing Clio packing a squirming toddler walked over to Jack. "He extended a tour so Jack couldn't go home to his girls. And he's been an asshole to Annabelle for this whole tour." As he spoke, he stared at Annabelle seated on Dakota's lap with her arm draped across his shoulders until his eyes landed on me. "Today, he shows up with Mali Tatum, knowing full well we'd be rehearsing with Cristy."

"You might be onto something," I said.

"An even better reason to fire his ass," Dakota chimed in. "He's given Annie enough trouble." His hand roamed dangerously high on Annabelle's thigh, and she batted it away. Not that it stopped Dakota.

"Thought your team meetings were exclusive to the four of you," Garrett said, glaring at our ladies as he strolled onto the stage to join us.

Since she was sitting on my lap, I could feel the tremor shake through Cristy. But Garrett was alone.

"Things change," Blu said.

"Not for the better," Garrett said. His eyes shot fire at Ashleigh.

"Watch your mouth, Garrett," Dakota growled.

Knowing how important it was to Cristy—and why—I asked, "What's the situation with Mali Tatum?"

"That depends on how much of her dirty laundry Cristy wants aired," Garrett said with a sneer.

She'd barely relaxed before Garrett's words turned her body to stone.

"No one's airing anything," I said as all eyes zeroed in on Cristy and me. "Not one damn thing if you want to keep your job, *Garrett*."

"I thought we already agreed to fire his ass," Dakota chimed in.

The color drained from Garrett's face when he spun around to face Dakota. "What did you say?"

"The team"—Dakota scanned the whole group of us—"was talking about how much we don't appreciate the ways you've been trying to sabotage our relationships."

Garrett made a *simmer down* motion with his hands. "Wait, wait, wait. I haven't sabotaged anything."

"Not for lack of trying," Blu said.

The only other time I heard that steel in his voice was when he commandeered the band's jet to go after Ashleigh on our last tour. From the panic on Garrett's face, he remembered that scene too.

"Listen, guys. This is a rock 'n' roll show, not a couples' retreat." He glanced over at Clio holding Jack's daughter. "Or a daycare center. If you're all mothered up, how do I help you maintain your persona, keep the girls coming to shows, sell records? Tell me that, huh?"

"If anything, the fans are even more inventive in the ways they try to launch their panties at Jack, and it's no secret he's married," I said. "We haven't had a dip in sales since Blu quite publicly asked Ashleigh to marry him." Pulling Cristy closer, with one hand, I extended the other. "We had to extend this tour because Cristy brought another dimension to our sound, something the fans are loving." I stared down our manager. "Your arguments are bullshit, Garrett. What's the real problem here?"

With his hands on his hips, he stood in the middle of us staring up at the ceiling. He remained quiet for so long, I didn't think he was going to answer the question. When he did, he shocked the shit out of me. Judging from the looks on my brothers' faces, he shocked them too.

"My whole life is this band and the road. The music, the parties, the girls. I didn't have any of that before." He fixed his eyes on Blu. "When you brought me on board, you gave me a life. Now with all this"—he gestured at Ashleigh and Clio standing near her—"what happens to me when you all decide you don't want to tour anymore, don't want to play and party and be a rock band? What the fuck happens then?"

The emotion in his voice stunned me as much as his words.

"What the fuck, Garrett? You thought sabotaging our relationships with our girlfriends would keep the party going? Was that your dumbass plan?" A sane man would have been backing up fast at the tone of Dakota's voice. Guess Garrett thought he had nothing to lose.

With a shrug, he said, "Yeah."

Probably the only thing that saved our manager from getting his ass kicked was that two of us had our women seated on our laps, the third had his lady wrapped around his shoulders, and the fourth had his arm around his wife who held his baby. As it was, little Chloe screeched right along with the cacophony of voices that started yelling all at once.

"What the fuck is wrong with you, man?"

"You're a fucking moron."

"I knew you didn't like me much, but, wow. Wow."

"We deserved better from you."

"Selfish asshole."

Bailey stepped in the middle of us. "Hey, hey. Slow down. All of you." When he raised his voice, silence rang in the air. "That's better. You all need to think about this. We have three shows left on this tour. If you fire Garrett now, who's going to take care of the logistics for those shows?"

"Annie could do it," Dakota volunteered, his eyes going all soft as he stared at the beauty seated on his lap.

"She could," Bailey said. "But if she does, she won't have much time for you."

Dakota pulled a face, but Blu backed Bailey. "He's right, buddy. You have a clue about pulling off logistics for this traveling circus," he said in reference to the early days when Dakota did most of our booking and negotiated with the managers of the venues we played.

"Emily could do the job from the office." Dakota never could let anything go easily.

"Yeah, but she can't put out fires in Florida from our home base in Denver," I said.

"What about Cristy's manager? She could take care of both of us, couldn't she?" Clearly, Dakota was determined to punish Garrett's betrayal.

Standing in the middle of us, Garrett's shoulders sagged. "Look. You're right. I fucked up." He glanced around the circle. "But you're all still mothered up, so maybe you could rethink firing me?" Shoving his hands in the pockets of the lame dress slacks he always wore, he added, "Like Bailey said, you still have three shows on this tour, shows I've already set up and worked on."

He had a point, but there was one detail I couldn't let go. "What about Mali Tatum? She gonna be around to make life hard on Cristy?"

When I asked the question, Cristy's gorgeous eyes zeroed in on me. I shot her an *of course I'm looking out for you* side-eye and returned my attention to Garrett.

He blew out a breath. "Gretchen's taking care of that right now."

Dakota piped up again. "See, we don't need this asshole anymore. We can let Gretchen manage us to the end of the tour."

"Yeah, I don't think so," the woman in question said as she breezed out onto the stage. I couldn't quite read the look she shot me, but I was pretty sure I'd heeded her warning earlier and hadn't fucked anything up. "I've got my hands full managing the world's biggest pop star."

"Whoa, wait a minute—" Dakota's diva ego made me laugh.

Gretchen's lips twitched too. "Pop star, Dakota. I said, 'the world's biggest *pop* star.' Balefire is the biggest rock band."

Looking only slightly mollified, Dakota sat back in his chair.

"Anyway, Garrett's done good work for you guys. Why would you want to fire him?"

Bailey said, "It seems to me the problem here is groupies, or the potential to have fewer of them following the band."

Color stained Garrett's cheeks, making it clear our head roadie's observation was spot-on.

"I'm not seein' any less groupies on this tour than on some of the others. Although the girls on our last European tour were outrageous. Wouldn't mind at all if you guys wanted to take us back over there." Bailey grinned large. At some other time, I might have wanted to hear the story.

Not today.

Cristy shifted on my lap, and I squeezed her hip where my hand rested on it, reassuring both of us.

At last Jack weighed in. "Garrett's been an A-one moron. But he's taken good care of our music. I vote we give him a second chance."

"With conditions," I added.

Garrett nodded at Jack and me then turned his attention to Blu.

Blu glanced at Ashleigh who leaned down to whisper something in his ear. Arching a brow at me, he said, "Yeah, I vote for a second chance. With conditions."

"Seriously, you guys? You want to keep this asshole on after all the grief he's caused us and our girls?" The pout on Dakota's mouth might have been funny at any other time, but this was serious. "For the record, I vote no." He gave his attention to the leader of our crew. "Bailey? What do you say?"

"I work for Balefire. I'll follow where you lead."

"Guess you're outvoted, Dakota," Jack said. A ghost of a smirk crossed his mouth, but otherwise, he kept his tone neutral, the ongoing competition with Dakota banked for the moment.

Dakota might have growled. "As long as you understand if you hurt Annabelle again, you're out on your ass, Garrett."

"Agreed," Blu seconded. "And you'll go out of your way to be decent to Ashleigh."

"And you make sure nothing about Cristy's past gets leaked—by anyone."

"Clio?" Jack asked.

"We're good as long as you don't tour anymore on Christmas." She blew a raspberry on Chloe's cheek, giving the toddler the giggles.

That sound deflated the tension in the room, and everyone started moving at once.

"Time to go to work, kids." Dakota set Annabelle on her feet, stood, and stretched. "It's been a while since we rocked Miami's world. Guess we better be ready to do it right." The words he spoke might have been meant for the band, but Dakota's eyes never left Annabelle.

I nibbled the soft skin below Cristy's ear. "You heard the guys, woman. Time to get to work." But I didn't let her stand. Instead, I kissed my way along her jaw to the luscious mouth I craved all the damn time and sealed my lips to hers.

Whatever else happened, Cristy was back in my arms where she belonged, and I had no intention of letting her go again.

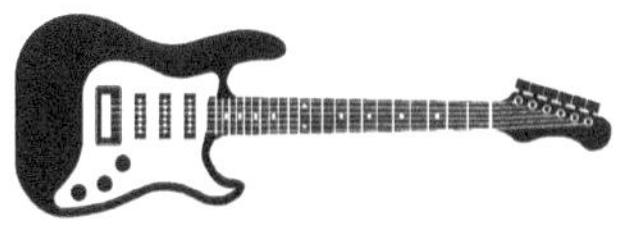

Chapter Thirty-Five

Adam

IT WAS A good thing I hung my bass low on my body for our last raucous show, because I was hard for most of Cristy's set in Jacksonville. Her outfits alone sexed up our concerts to a level none of us could have ever imagined. Especially when she sang to me. The look in her eyes as she sang and danced around me during "Hot For Me" promised all kinds of naughty fun when we had each other alone now that the tour was wrapping up.

When I turned the tables on her and proclaimed she was the inspiration for "Run Away (Runaway)" as I sang my part to her, she surprised me again by singing along with Blu's harmonies. On the last chorus, he dropped out, leaving the song to Cristy and me. I might have taken her hand and walked her off the stage right then if the fans hadn't increased the decibel level of their appreciation to supersonic. Their interruption reminded me we weren't alone, but I made all kinds of promises to her with my eyes before I thought, *fuck it*, and hauled her in for a long kiss.

She melted into me, and the world fell away. With her hand on the nape of my neck, she anchored herself to me. Her pillowy lips parted, her hot, sweet tongue glided over mine, an erotic dance that shivered my entire body in spite of the sweat I'd worked up playing for her. A thought flashed through my mind—I'd been playing for her since the first time I heard her voice long before I met her. I wrapped my arm around her and hauled her in tighter as I deepened our kiss.

Someone poking hard at my shoulder dragged me out of the beautiful world Cristy's kiss pulled me into. "Hey, Tron. Save it till after the show, already." Blu's laughter rang out through the speakers.

Even as my face heated, I couldn't stop the grin spreading my lips as Cristy thumbed her lipstick off them. With an impish smirk, she turned her attention to the crowd. "You heard it here first, folks. Tron and I are a thing."

As she sashayed toward the front of the stage, she nodded to Dakota, who strummed the opening lines of "Fire Me Up," but she'd already heated me to molten lava. Our kiss and her announcement carried the crowd there too, judging from the fact we could barely hear the first five bars of our song over their screaming and stomping. In a fog, I played the rest of the show, my eyes never leaving Cristy even through the encores.

At the end of the concert, we took two steps offstage before I swung her up into my arms. She shrieked out a laugh and clung to my neck.

"You've been teasing me for the last two hours, woman. Time to pay up," I growled into her ear.

"Because those looks you've given me all night haven't promised a darn thing, right?" Her eyes sparkled even in the dim lights of the hallway to the dressing rooms. "Seems like *I* might be owed a promise or two."

Shivers left behind goose bumps on my skin as she sank her teeth into my earlobe and worried it with her lips. Her tongue took a tour of the shell of my ear and slipped to the sensitive spot right behind it. I tightened my hold on her, hugging her closer to my body.

"Careful. We're still in public."

"Mmmhmmm."

I barked out a laugh, my pace doing double time toward the door to her dressing room. A long time later, we joined the rest of the band and crew as we celebrated the end to another successful Balefire tour.

♪

With no tour dates on the horizon, we decided to enjoy a scenic ride back home. Rolling through the Ozarks, the raucous party that was our bus was quiet for once as we stared out at the passing scenery. Except for Cristy who'd been weirdly glued to her phone. A sob escaped her before she clamped a hand over her mouth. The eyes that locked with mine ripped my heart out.

"Valorous, what is it?"

She showed me her phone screen, and my blood boiled over with rage. In two seconds I was out of my banquette seat and hauling Garrett out of his captain's chair by the front of his shirt. "You'd better fuckin' fix this," I roared, "or this is your last tour as Balefire's manager!"

Everyone started talking at once.

"What is it?"

"What the fuck, Tron?"

"Hey, dude, settle down!"

"Whoa! What's going on?"

Garrett's eyes nearly popped out of his head. Not that I gave a fuck. The bus hit a bump in the road, and involuntarily, I loosened my grip on his shirt. Probably saved his ass, not that I gave a shit. He put up his hands and said, "I already texted Gretchen over on Cristy's bus. We're working on it, I swear."

Cristy stared unseeingly at her phone, all the color drained from her beautiful face. Without another word, I hauled her limp body up from her seat and guided her to the private bedroom in the back of our bus. I closed the door firmly behind us and pulled her down onto my lap as I sat on the bed. Gently, I took her phone from her hand without a protest from her and tossed it behind us.

"Babe." With my fingertips, I caressed the silken contours of her perfect face. "It's going to be all right." I cupped her cheek and waited until she finally looked into my eyes. "I promise."

"H-how"—she swallowed hard—"how can you say that? There's a photo of my wedding day in that article." A sob escaped her. "My career is ruined." She buried her face in my neck, and I felt the warm wetness of her tears on my skin. "She threatened to take my secret public if I ever crossed her again." A hiccup, another sob, another crack in my heart. "Taking her spot on those last tour dates crossed that line."

Cristy wrapped her hand around my neck and held on like I was her only lifeline in the shitstorm the tabloids unleashed on her. Though my chest muted her sobs, I heard them—and felt them— all the way to my soul. My woman's hurt was my hurt too. Jesus, I wanted to punch a hole in the side of the world, open it up so it would suck all the assholes causing her this pain right out into space.

Instead, I tightened my arms around her, murmured my love to her, and let her cry it out. At last, she heaved a deep sigh and settled quietly into me. I have no idea how long we sat silently together before she sat up in a rush and stared hard into my eyes.

"What did you say earlier?"

"It's going to be all right."

"No. After that. When I was embarrassing myself by crying all over you."

I thumbed the tracks of her tears off her cheeks. "There's nothing to be embarrassed about. You have a right to cry."

She sniffed back a sob and stared down at my chest. "I don't deserve you. When you read the whole article, you'll see that too."

"Not giving you up, Valorous. Not now. Not ever."

"You meant those words? When I was crying?"

I brushed a kiss over those lush lips I'd never tire of as long as I lived. "You mean when I said I loved you?"

A blink. A nod. "Yes," she whispered, her voice raspy.

"I love you, Cristy Valor. No matter what." Because I couldn't find another way, I said against her lips, "Always," and kissed her again.

Pulling back, she fluttered her hand nervously up and down my bicep. "I ran away from you." Clearing her throat, she stared at her hand as she fingered the collar of my shirt. "I lied by omission, and I hurt you." At last she raised her eyes to mine. "After all that, how the heck can you love me?"

I huffed out a laugh, grabbed her busy hand, and planted a kiss in the middle of her palm. "You were scared. I can see that now. I think I could even see it at the time." Laying her hand on my chest, I covered it with mine. "But I was into you long before I even met you. Your voice, your take-no-prisoners style, your willingness to push the limits—your whole package turns me on. The fact that you're beautiful and generous in the sack is a bonus," I finished with a grin and a waggle of my brows.

Though her eyes remained dark with fear and worry, a tiny smile tugged at the corner of her pretty red lips.

"We get each other, Cristy. From the moment we met, we've had a connection. I've never felt that with any other person, not even my brothers in the band, guys I've known my whole life." Tightening my arm around her waist, I pulled her even closer to me. "You do it for me, Valorous. You just do it for me." I cupped the back of her head and brought her back to my mouth. To my relief, when our lips met, she took over, pushing her tongue inside and relishing me like she was a starved waif and I was Christmas dinner.

When she finally let me up for air, a smile replaced the darkness she'd shown me earlier. "I love you, Adam Tron. I never thought I'd find someone to love who'd love me back. Then you came along with your steady strength and played your way deep inside me. I tried to ignore my feelings for you—"

The low rumble in my throat sounded like a growl in my ears, but I didn't care.

"—but I couldn't. I was already half in love with you when you played the first concert in LA, the one the night before we officially met."

Now it was my turn to smile.

"Gretchen knew it before I did."

At that, my smile flipped upside down. "So why did she try so hard to keep us apart?"

"Because she's in love with me too."

I jacked a brow and waited.

"In the end, I don't think we can help who we fall in love with. She's my best woman friend, but that's all she'll ever be to me." She ran her thumb over my lower lip. "But you're my best friend, my lover, the person I love most in the world. I don't know how that happened so fast, but I can't fight it." Sucking a breath in through her nose, she let it out slowly and added, "But I hope you know what kind of crazy you're signing on for here. This whole thing with my marriage is going to be a huge mess. If we're together, it's going to drag you down with it."

All the sorrow and sadness she'd chased away seemed to descend on her again like dropping a heavy black cloak over her shoulders.

"We'll fix this, Cristy. I promise."

"You keep making promises, but you read what they're saying."

The fear and sadness in her tone killed me. But I meant every word. "Valorous, when this is all over, you're going to be even stronger. *We* are going to be stronger."

She pulled a face.

"We already are stronger." I smoothed the frown on her forehead with my fingertip. "We have each other. We love each other, and nothing 'they' can say is going to change that."

She wrapped her arms around me and settled her cheek on my

chest. "Never in my wildest dreams did I think there was someone like you out there waiting for me," she whispered into my shirt.

"You're the best thing in my world, Cristy. Never doubt that."

As the bus ate up the miles, we clung to each other, letting the silence do the rest of the talking.

CHAPTER THIRTY-SIX

Cristy

GRETCHEN AND GARRETT stepped onto the dais for the Denver press conference. Reporters surged forward, nearly breaking through the line of security guards standing below the podium. Even from where we stood behind a one-way window, the camera flashes were more blinding than the afternoon sun. Don't even get me started on the cacophony of questions they shouted over each other.

We'd arrived in Denver in the middle of the night—on purpose. Adam and I spent that night and most of the next day sleeping at his place. This afternoon, we met our managers and the rest of the band at Balefire's studios to go over the plan. Within the safety of the studio, the plan gave me strength, a small feeling of control. Now that it was time to face the music, my insides turned to jelly.

"Is Cristy married?"

"Are Cristy and Tron together?"

"Is Cristy having an affair? Where is her husband now?"

"Is it true that Cristy split up Balefire?"

Demanding one question at a time, Gretchen stunned me by toning down the snark. Perhaps it was her serious demeanor for once or because Garrett sat beside her too, but at last the reporters reined in their yelling.

"Cristy is not married now, nor has she ever been legally married," Gretchen stated.

"Balefire just came off a monster tour of the western and southern US to promote their latest album. Taking a little downtime to relax and recharge their batteries is necessary," Garrett said in answer to the never-ending questions about a Balefire breakup.

"In a few minutes, Balefire and Cristy Valor will come out to answer questions," Gretchen said. "I know it's hard for some of you to remember that these musicians are people, but try anyway." There was the snark I'd known and loved for most of my life. "Maybe act like human beings with at least a touch of class if you can't find any humanity inside yourselves."

"If you can't contain your more invasive questions, we won't hesitate to cut this news conference short. Fair warning," Garrett added.

That was our cue. Adam squeezed my hand and led me out, followed by the rest of the guys in Balefire. Before he'd had a chance to seat himself beside me behind the bank of microphones on the table, before the other guys had even made it to their chairs, the questions started.

"Cristy! Cristy! Are you and Tron a couple?"

Dakota leaned into his mic. "You must not have caught our last show in Jacksonville." With a smirk, he crossed his arms over his chest and leaned back in his chair.

"Tron, how do you feel about Cristy being married?"

Gretchen took that one. "For the last time, Cristy is not now, nor has she ever been legally married."

Clearing my throat, I leaned toward my mic. Beneath the table, Adam's warm palm on my thigh gave me a reassuring squeeze, and I let out a breath. "I'd like to take this chance to set the record straight. When I was sixteen, my parents married me to a man in their church, a man who was twenty-eight years older than me."

A collective gasp rippled through the gathered reporters.

"Because I was a minor, I had no say in their decision. They gave their permission for the marriage, so it was considered 'legal'"—I air quoted—"even though I was underage and didn't consent. I was forced to marry and couldn't legally obtain a divorce until I was eighteen."

I didn't notice I was shaking until Adam slid his arm around my shoulders and pulled me close to him.

Gretchen took over the narrative. "When I became Cristy's manager, I looked into her 'marriage' and discovered it had never been registered in the state of Arizona. The rite was performed inside her parents' church by church members who didn't file any marriage certificate or any other documentation. Basically, Cristy was tricked into believing she was married as a way for her parents and her 'husband'"—her air quotes were typical aggressive Gretchen—"to control her. Outside of their 'church,' what happened to Cristy would be considered statutory rape."

Hearing those words stated out loud in front a hostile audience made me throw up a little in my mouth, but Adam's steady presence beside me kept me upright in my chair.

"Like many other child bride victims, Cristy kept her mouth shut precisely to avoid what we're doing today—sharing her terrible experience in public. But this is a serious issue facing too many girls all over the world—even in the United States," Gretchen said.

As she spoke, her voice vibrating with barely leashed contempt, she gave me courage. That and Adam's steady presence beside me. "This is why we're here today—all of us"—I stared down the table at the members of Balefire—"to announce that we're starting a foundation to combat this practice in America. I don't want any other girl to share my experience. Balefire wants to help." All the guys in the band nodded, affirming me. "Today, we're announcing the Be Valorous Foundation whose goal is to join with other groups to insist politicians enact legislation to safeguard the well-being of girls throughout the United States and protect them from the predatory practice of child marriage."

The room held its breath for a beat before it erupted in a cacophony of questions, some directed at Gretchen, some at me, most of them at Balefire. The wall of sound threatened to flatten me.

"Tron! Tron! How do you feel about Cristy?"

"How long have you known about Cristy's marriage, Tron?"

"How are things with you and Mali Tatum? Is it true you kicked her off the tour? Is that why she outed you?"

"Are you touring together again?"

Garrett stepped up. "Cristy has answered your questions concerning her experience when she was a teen. Please confine your questions to information about the Be Valorous Foundation, which Balefire has already signed onto and is inviting their fellow musicians and any concerned persons to join."

Adam leaned into his mic. "Actually, I'd like to answer your question. Cristy and I are together." The smile in his eyes warmed all the parts of me that had gone completely cold days before when I opened my phone on the bus and saw the headlines.

Dakota stepped in next. "Not sure where the rumor started." He slanted a look at Garrett who stared straight ahead. "Mali Tatum wasn't kicked off a tour she was never invited to join."

Before Dakota could really get going, Blu interrupted. "We want to tour with Cristy again. Especially now that we're working together for the foundation." He grinned. "Did any of you actually catch our shows together? Because the five of us kicked some serious rock 'n' roll ass. Just sayin'." He rocked back in his chair with a smirk.

At Blu's pronouncement, Adam tugged me tighter into his side, and all I wanted to do was melt into him. Except, we had an audience, and I doubted that many of them were true fans.

"I think that covers it," Gretchen said, her tone ending the news conference as effectively as a slamming door.

Not that the reporters respected that. Still, as one, the guys stood up, Adam gently taking me with him. We filed out of the room behind Gretchen while the reporters continued their barrage of invasive and nonsensical questions. In the past, I'd loved riling them up, planting little morsels here and there to feed their frenzy. Now, for the first time since I felt the rush of an audience's response to my voice nearly a decade ago, I wished I'd remained anonymous.

♪

"Hey, are you okay?" Adam whispered in my ear as we sat on the plush leather couch in his living room.

"I don't know," I replied, puffing out a breath, and with it, a little more of the weight I'd carried around with me for nearly half my life. "I've kept my story a secret for so long, tried to bury what happened to me, that after a while, it felt like maybe it had happened to someone else. I'd become someone else, so that story couldn't possibly be mine."

"Except at night when you were asleep." He tightened his arms around me and spoke softly. "Your nightmares told me you'd experienced something that scared you and never left you alone." With his lips on my temple, he added, "Now that the story is out, maybe you'll sleep better."

For a long minute, I could only stare at him. "You're not creeped out by me? By what my life was like in my parents' house?"

Though he kept it toned down, the warmth of his smile radiated from all of him. "I could never be creeped out by you, Valorous." His gorgeous chocolate-brown eyes turned stormy. "Your parents, on the other hand, have a shit-ton to answer for."

Besides Gretchen, no one had ever defended me like this. No one else had ever cared about me beyond what I could do for them. From the beginning, Adam had been different, and for the first time since I could remember, I relaxed.

"I'm in love with you, you know."

"'Bout fucking time you admitted it, babe."

"Hey, now—"

His rich laughter resonated through me as he pulled me close and brushed a soft kiss over my lips. "I love you, Cristy Valor, my beautiful phoenix. You rose from the ashes of a life you had to burn to the ground to escape. Now, you soar over the world, a gorgeous wild creature. I was half in love with you before we ever met." His eyes zeroed in on my mouth again, and I raised my face for another kiss. "Knowing you, all of you, makes me love you more."

"Thank you."

He arched a brow.

"You never gave up on me. Even when I ran away from you, you never gave up." I traced my fingertip over the strong slant of his dark brows, his prominent cheekbones and the beautiful hollows they created. As we'd traveled across the country, he'd let his beard stubble grow out, a short, soft furring over his carved jaw I held in my palm. "Maybe someday we'll record the song as a duet."

This time his smile lit up the whole room.

Chapter Thirty-Seven

Adam

WHEN WE WOKE up together in my bed the morning after the press conference, I realized two things: one, I wanted to wake up with Cristy beside me every day for the rest of my life, and two, she'd slept peacefully. She hadn't cried out or thrashed the sheets into a tangle or sat straight up with wild eyes that saw monsters. I cuddled her still-sleeping form closer and told my dick to shut the fuck up.

She blinked her eyes open and gifted me a sleepy smile. "Good morning," she murmured.

"Good morning." My hand slid over her short silky hair. "How are you this fine day?"

She stretched her body along mine like she wanted to glide her skin over all of me at once. It was an idea I could wholeheartedly support, but she'd have to grow about a foot to make it work. I grinned and palmed my hand down her side, deliberately lingering for a few extra seconds on the curve of her breast.

"I'm fantastic." A naughty smile flitted across her face as she pushed her hip into my dick. "And you've been awake for a while."

"My delicious warm woman is lying beside me in nothing but the outfit the good Lord gave her. How else would I be?" I rolled her over on top of my chest.

Laughter bubbled out of her as she slid down my body to make room for herself between my thighs. The sassy batting of her eyelashes as she gazed up at me told me all about her intent. While I'd had a different plan for how we'd start our day, I knew instinctively that I had to let her lead. Sliding my hands beneath my head for a better angle to watch, I lay back on the pillows and waited. When she licked her luscious lips in anticipation of putting them on me, it was all I could do to stop myself from surging up to meet them. I was so keyed up I nearly lost my shit when she deep-throated me on the first touch. No kissing, no licking, no teasing foreplay. Just a long slow downstroke. She held me inside her for a second then hollowed out her cheeks on a hard suck as she pulled up.

"Cristy." I gritted out as I desperately grabbed for self-control.

A smile danced in the deep sapphires of her eyes, eyes she locked on me as she took all of me again. I fisted two handfuls of the sheets on either side of my hips. My abs clenched hard as stone as I tried not to take over when she rocked my world with her pretty mouth doing all kinds of naughty things to my cock. With one hand, she got busy with my balls, teasing and massaging while her other hand feathered over my belly. Though I tried to hold on, she dared me with her beautiful eyes. Her name erupted from me, our only warning as white-hot lightning shot down my spine. Involuntarily, I pistoned my hips, and she swallowed me down with each stroke.

When at last I quieted from the orgasm she gave me, she climbed on top of me. Resting her chin on her hands stacked on my chest, she gave me the gift I'll cherish for the rest of my life. "I could get used to this," she said conversationally. "Waking up every day with you." She smiled. "Imagine the adventures we'll have."

"Every minute with you is an adventure, Valorous." I rolled her beneath me. "And I want all those adventures for the rest of my life."

Her hand came up to caress my jaw. "Me too, Adam." She stared deep into my eyes. "I'm so in love with you."

I had to take a second, let her words settle into every cell. "You're it for me, Cristy. There's no one else for me but you." Tracing the contours of her face with the pad of my finger, I said, "The first thing I want to see when I wake up every day is this face. And it's the last thing I want to look at before I close my eyes at night." I brushed a kiss over her mouth. "I love you, all of you, Cristy Valorie Rains."

She gasped at my use of her full real name, but I'd anticipated her and cut her off with my mouth on hers. She tasted of sex and wildness and pure feminine sugar. Knowing I needed to head off her worries, I spent some time plundering as much of her deliciousness as I could before I kissed her smooth skin on my way down her body to paradise.

Spreading her thighs wide, I took a minute to feast my eyes on her perfect treasure. With a wink and a grin, I went to work kissing and tonguing and sucking her pretty clit before my fingers joined the party. Not to brag, but being a bass player means my dexterity is off the charts, and I put that to use pleasuring her. In seconds it seemed, she started harmonizing with the happy humming coming from my throat. Her sounds rose as I increased the pace of my fingers and tongue until at last, my name burst from her lips in one long gorgeous scream.

It took her a bit to quiet down from the loving I gave her, time I spent touring her skin with my hands and, because I couldn't help myself, with my lips. When her breathing approximated normal, she leaned up on her elbows and stared me down.

"Why?"

"I love you. All of you." I climbed up the bed and lay on my side facing her. "What happened to you should never have happened. Ever," I growled. "But you transcended it. Made an international name for yourself with your talent and your sass."

She pulled a face, and I smirked.

"You aren't a scared and powerless sixteen-year-old, Cristy. You're an incredibly strong, brilliant, sexy"—I toured her body with my eyes—"woman. Did I mention how fucking sexy you are?"

That pulled a chuckle out of her, which was far better than the darkness hovering at the edges of her eyes.

"You've rocked my world from the first time I heard you sing. After we got together, you tipped it completely off its axis. Believe me, babe. There's nothing about you that I don't love."

"There's nothing about you, Adam Tron, that I don't love." Her palm in the middle of my chest warmed my heart.

An expression crossed her face, one I couldn't read as she stared at her hand in the middle of my chest.

"What is it?"

"We trust each other."

I covered her hand with my own. "Implicitly." Slipping a finger beneath her chin, I urged her to look at me. "What's going on?"

"I—" She swallowed and started over. "I'm on the pill. And I'm clean."

"I know. So?"

"And you're clean."

A frown pulled at my brows as I tried to figure out where this conversation was headed.

"Well, I thought we could maybe try sex completely naked."

I stared down at all the skin we were both showing. "Huh?"

A nervous-sounding laugh escaped her. "Maybe we could try making love without a condom."

What?

She cleared her throat. "Ooh-kay. The idea weirds you out. No worries." Rolling away from me, she reached for the box of condoms on the nightstand.

Guess I said that out loud. But she misunderstood. Pinning her to the bed, I covered her hand with mine and pulled it away from the condoms before she could grab one.

"Hey," I whispered into her ear. "The idea of going naked with you turns me on." I turned her onto her back and stared into her eyes. "It turns me on so fucking much. I was just surprised you wanted to go there too."

For a long minute she stared back at me then nodded like she'd come to some decision. "I've never done it without a condom. It was never safe." Reaching up, she palmed my jaw. "But I'm safe with you. I wanted you to know that. So I thought—"

"—we could be bare to each other. In every way."

"Yes."

"I've never had bare-naked sex before either, Valorous. But I can't wait to experience it with you." My eyes followed my fingertips as they traced over the satin of her skin.

"You know what this means, Adam."

My eyes met hers and I waited.

"It means we're virgins, having condomless sex for the first time."

A grin split my face as I figured out where our whole conversation had been going. "You want to start fresh."

The shy expression in her eyes as she locked them on me humbled me. This brave, gorgeous dynamo of a woman wanted—no—needed to start over. And she wanted to start over with me.

"I love you, Cristy Valor. I love you so much."

Before she had a chance to respond, I molded my lips to hers. Her tongue slipped out to trace over my mouth, and I accepted her invitation by plunging my tongue inside her lips. For long minutes, we played tongue-tag until we needed air.

Cristy gripped my shoulders, breath sawing in and out of her. "Adam, I want you, I want this. So much."

I nibbled along her jaw to her ear, tugging at the lobe with my teeth, tonguing and teasing along the tiny hoops she'd had pierced along the shell. "Me too," I whispered.

Her hands left my shoulders to explore my chest on their way to testing and teasing the skin over my obliques. The knowing way she zeroed in on my sensitive areas drove me wild. Sliding down her body, I kissed and licked my way down the column of her neck, across her collarbone, and over her chest. A whimper escaped her lips, and I shot her my best wicked grin before I took her busy hands and pinned them above her head.

My attention focused on her nipples, puckered so pretty like ripe strawberries, begging so delightfully for me to devour them. Which meant I had to tease. I kissed all the skin of her gorgeous tits except for the parts that most wanted kissing, and Cristy rewarded me. Arching and shifting beneath me, she offered her luscious breasts up to me with a growl, demanding I take what she wanted to give.

Chuckling, I brushed my lips over the tight bud, but the temptation was more than I wanted to stand. Pulling her deep inside my mouth, I sucked and licked and nipped at her until she writhed and moaned beneath me. The heel of her foot slid up the back of my thigh and over my hip as she opened herself to me. Her hips moved, her slick pussy gliding up and down my naked cock, and a groan escaped me.

"Babe. We have all day."

"Adam," she demanded, "I don't want to wait that long."

She tugged a hand free of my grasp where I still held her with one hand. Slipping her hand between our bodies, she stroked me, her touch leaving me powerless not to give her what she wanted. Transfixed, I watched as she positioned the tip of my cock at her dripping center.

"Adam."

Desire dilated her pupils, the mesmerizing sapphires of her irises a thin ring on the edge. The way my woman wanted me was more intoxicating than the finest whiskey that ever passed my lips.

"Now."

Never in my life had I wanted to give a woman all of me—until this moment in this bed with Cristy. I held her in my eyes as I slowly pushed inside her tight, wet heat. Feeling her, skin on skin, was a paradise I had no idea existed. My breath whooshed out, prompting me to pull out and thrust deep into her again.

"Fuuuuck, Valorous. Oh, fuck, you feel incredible."

I thrust again, and her Adam song started. I might have smiled at how fast we were both moving toward climax except that every nerve ending in my body was tuned in to my cock and how mind-blowing it was to be balls-deep inside my woman with nothing between us. The tempo of my thrusts crescendoed with her cries until with a scream, she clamped down hard on me. Lightning shot down my spine, and a minute later, I joined her. Good thing we were in the privacy of my house because my shouts echoed off the walls of my bedroom when I came.

Long minutes passed before I rolled over on my back, taking Cristy with me. I played my fingertips up and down the smooth curve of her spine as I worked at gathering my scattered thoughts. She wrapped her arms around me and rested her head on my shoulder, her legs splayed over me as we maintained our intimate connection. While we held each other close, what I took as a shiver turned out to be the beginning of giggles. We'd shared the most epic experience ever, and she was giggling.

"What's so funny?"

After a couple of gasps, she pulled herself together. "I have to move in a minute."

Wrapping my arms around her, I held her tight to me, letting her know exactly what I thought of that plan.

"Why is that funny?"

She propped her chin on her hands resting on my chest, a puckish grin tugging at her lips. "Because now you're getting the wet spot."

"We just experienced a morning of off-the-charts sex, and you're thinking about who gets stuck with the wet spot?"

"I've never had to worry about that before." Her eyes sparkled. "Now we get to argue about it."

Joy bubbled through me and I cracked up. This woman. This wild, wonderful woman.

Gently, I pushed her off me, slid out of bed, and padded into the bathroom. A minute later, I returned with a bath towel. With a flourish, I covered the wet spot and climbed back into bed, gathering her in my arms.

"How's that, milady? No one's stuck in the wet spot."

"Hope you have a lot of towels, big guy."

I barked out a laugh and planted a smacking kiss on her lips.

"You're perfect, Cristy Valor. The perfect woman for me." I kissed her again and settled her along my side. "After Blu and Ashleigh got together, I stumbled in on a conversation Blu and Jack were having." Threading my fingers through the soft cap of her hair, I continued. "They were talking about being naked with their women."

Cristy pushed up, digging her elbow in my chest, and glared down at me. "You guys talk about your wives and girlfriends like you talk about groupies?"

Jacking a brow, I shook my head and settled her back into a more comfortable position on my chest. "Of course not. They were talking about how awesome sex is with someone you trust enough to go without a condom." Clearing my throat, I added, "I might have made fun of them for trying to tell me how much better making love is than just getting off."

I sensed her lips stretching into a smile along my skin. "And now?"

"Now I'm addicted to naked sex." I tipped her chin up so I could have her eyes. "With you."

"I love you, Adam. I tried to push you away, but you wouldn't let me. You saw all my scars and still, you stayed." Her voice hitched. "I don't deserve you, but I'm never giving you up." Her eyes held mine as she kissed me over my heart.

That one gesture warmed me to my soul. This stunning phoenix of a woman loving me was a gift I would cherish forever. In fact, I spent the rest of the morning and most of the afternoon showing her exactly how much she meant to me.

CHAPTER THIRTY-EIGHT

Adam

NOT ONCE IN all the years I'd been playing had I ever experienced true stage fright. Jitters maybe. The pure adrenaline rush of hearing the fans' response to our band ripping through my veins—always. But honest-to-God stage fright? Like being afraid of standing in front of the crowd and performing? Nope. Couldn't say I'd ever felt that—until today.

Because Cristy had spent most of the last decade living in hotels, it hadn't taken a whole lot of convincing to talk her into moving in with me. Especially after I gave her the green light to decorate my place however she wanted. Gretchen hadn't been nearly as excited about the prospect since she still harbored some territorial feelings for my girl. But the two of them spent a weekend together at some spa they liked in Hawaii, and when they returned, Gretchen took care of all the logistics for Cristy moving in with me. That had been the easy part.

Living with Cristy was easy. We'd spent the two months since the press conference settling in together. Letting her set up my house the way she wanted had been surprisingly fun. Not that I didn't take some shit—lots of shit—from the rest of the band for enjoying the whole decorating process. Before she came into my life, I had no idea picking out flooring and drapes and paint could be so absorbing. Now, more often than not, my seventy-six-inch television was cued up to HGTV the second someone turned it on.

The thought had me chuckling at myself, something I needed as I watched our friends laughing together, drinking my favorite microbrews, and enjoying Diane Connolly's delicious catered spread. Not that I'd know how any of it tasted since I'd yet to eat a thing, what with my stomach churning like the base of Niagara Falls.

A born hostess, Cristy flitted from person to person. The happiness on her face gave me my heartbeat. The shadows she'd worked so hard to hide when we met were long gone, replaced with a radiance that warmed me from the inside out. Even when she wasn't looking directly at me.

She flicked her eyes up at me from where she sat between Ashleigh Baker and Clio Whitehorse, and a frown suddenly marred her stunning features. Right as Clio leaned in to say something to her, Cristy rose and walked away from our friends without a backward glance.

Placing a cool hand on my heated forearm, she said, "What's wrong? You look like you ate something bad."

"I didn't eat anything. I'm fine." My voice sounded strangled to my own ears.

The look on Cristy's face said she couldn't decide between worry and total exasperation. I needed a different emotion from her entirely.

Without explanation, I took her hand and led her to spot in the middle of the stone patio our guests were sitting around. After loudly clearing my throat, I said, "I have something I want to share with all of you," but my eyes were only on Cristy.

If the situation weren't so important—like the rest of my life important—I might have grinned at the expression of pure terror that crossed her face for a nanosecond. The tiny gasp that escaped her was the last sound I could discern over the roaring in my ears before I dropped to one knee in front of her.

"Valorous, you're my everything. I want the whole world to know it. Will you marry me?"

I held the two carat princess-cut pink diamond out to her. The LED light in the ring box did its job showing off all the sparkles winking out from the ring I'd had custom-designed for the only woman who would ever wear it. Two smaller diamonds framed the large stone where it rested in a thick platinum band. The ring was one-of-a-kind—like her.

Her hand flew to her mouth, and tears shimmered in those sapphire eyes that I loved to look in. Time stopped as I waited for her answer.

Some might say it was a douche move for me to ask her in front of everyone from the band and both of our crews. Maybe it was. But I wanted Cristy to know that there was nothing about the two of us being together that I ever wanted to hide. Her parents rejected her. Some of her fans got ugly on social media for a time after her story initially broke. The tabs stomped on her for supposedly breaking up Balefire. Then came the wash of gossipy speculation about her "marriage" when she was sixteen. She'd experienced enough of people's judgments and scorn. I wanted her to know I was proud of her and proud of being her man. Asking her in such a public way to marry me was my way of showing her that pride.

Her hand shook so much when she reached for the ring that she snatched it back. Wrapping her arms around herself, she broke my heart a little when her words came out in a voice way too small for her. "Do you mean it?"

"Yes. And that's your answer too, right?" I stood and pulled her stiff body into my arms.

A shudder rippled through her, and for a second, she had me

worried. Then her laughter bubbled up between us as she said, "Yes! Yes! Oh my God, yes!"

My hand shook as I slid the rock over her finger. She held her hand out in front of us to admire the ring that sparkled in the rays of the setting sun. With another giggle of pure joy, she threw her arms around my neck, tugged me down to her, and kissed me stupid. When at last she let me up for air, I didn't need the teasing comments of our friends to know that I sported the dopiest of expressions on my face. And I could give a flying fuck.

Cristy loved me. I loved Cristy.

We had everything.

E P I L O G U E

Adam

UPENDING ALL THE rules was natural for us, but the boys and I gave in to Garrett's incessant chatter and wore suits over our T-shirts for the Grammy ceremony. I had to laugh every time I glanced over at Dakota in his lime-green Versace as we walked the red carpet into the Staples Center. Cristy's dresser had insisted I wear the charcoal Armani he'd fussed over. Something about making sure everyone saw my girl when we walked in together.

Like they wouldn't?

Cristy wore a strapless magenta Dior that hugged her curves exactly right and flowed in long pleats to the floor. A subtle pattern of charcoal-colored sequins created a phoenix rising from the ashes, a gorgeous "fuck you" to all the people who'd ever tried to hold her down. Earlier in the day when I walked into her dressing room, uninvited and unannounced, I nearly fell on my ass. I'd commissioned a phoenix necklace of pink topaz and diamonds to give her for this big night, but she didn't need any adornment. I'd likely never get over how stunning Valorous could be exactly as she was.

Steve and Gretchen tried to shoo me out of her space, but Cristy wanted me there. And she wore the necklace, which looked amazing lying in the hollow of her neck. I had some ideas about her wearing that phoenix and nothing else back at the hotel after the ceremony. She must have caught on because the wicked grin she shot me had me adjusting those fancy pants I was wearing.

The paparazzi were obnoxious as always. The cameras flashing in our eyes was expected on this night, but the questions were ridiculous.

"Is this the swan song for Balefire?"

"Are you trying to take over the band, Cristy?"

"When are you two getting married?"

"Will you be joining Cristy's backup band once you're married, Tron?"

I tried to tune them out, but the irritation must have shown on my face.

"Stop taking them personally," Jack hissed into my ear. "They need a story. When we win the Grammy, we'll give 'em one."

We were up for five awards: best rock band, best rock song for "Fire Me Up," best rock album, best cross-over hit for "Run Away (Runaway)," and vocal event for the duet I wrote specifically for Cristy and us. It went without saying that I wanted to win that one the most. I also wanted to cheer like a maniac when Cristy won for best female pop vocalist, one of the three other awards she had been nominated for. Together, Balefire and Cristy Valor were a musical juggernaut. It stood to reason the press would be hyperinterested in us, I guess.

Since we had so many nominations, we were one of the featured acts of the night, prime time with a national audience. Which meant we practiced one thing during rehearsals for the show and planned something else entirely for our actual performance. Nothing that would get us censored, but definitely something to get the press off our backs for a minute.

♪

"That was epic!"

"Fuckin' A!"

"Best damn performance of the night so far."

"Feel better now, Tron?" Jack shouted, a grin splitting his face as the four of us congratulated each other backstage.

I hadn't told Cristy about the new song the four of us wrote together. We only had a couple of those in our entire catalogue, what with Blu and Jack doing most of the writing, usually. "Brothers" came from all of our hearts because it told the story of how no matter what other people thought, we were always going to be true to each other. The song was loud, raucous, and fun—a true Balefire anthem that gave each of us an opportunity to solo. It also ran over our allotted time, but the director didn't shut off our sound. A smart person knows that when history is being made, it's best to let it play out rather than try to redirect it. Besides, we'd just won the Grammy for best rock band, so we had an obligation to show the world why the Academy was right about that.

Afterward when we returned to our seats, properly dressed again in our monkey suits, Cristy all but jumped into my lap. "That was an incredible performance, babe," she said into my ear before she kissed the side of my jaw and sat back in her seat. How the hell she did it, I'd never know, but that kiss tingled on my skin for ten minutes and left me rock hard for longer. Good thing we didn't have to go back up onstage for a bit.

Then we won best vocal event. I stood with Cristy in my arms the second the word *Balefire* left Lady Gaga's lips. I all but carried her onstage as we gathered to accept our award. The other guys in the band included their wives and fiancées as well, so we created quite a party in front of God and everybody.

Alicia Keys handed the Grammy to Blu, which stood to reason, but he passed it off to Cristy, giving her the floor first. I wanted to hug him.

Instead, I wrapped my arm around her and listened to her speak.

"The reason representatives from Balefire called and asked me to tour with them was because Adam asked for me." She grinned up at me, her eyes shining. "If you don't believe me, you can ask him."

Leaning forward, I said into the mic, "Best damn ask I ever made."

"I'm forever grateful to my manager, Gretchen Hoff for convincing me to say yes. My life has changed in so many wonderful ways because I have the opportunity to play with the greatest rock band on the planet. Thanks, guys, for taking a chance."

"Because of you, Cristy, Tron got his lazy ass in gear and wrote a rippin' song for us," Blu said with a laugh. "So thank *you*."

Jack and Dakota stepped up the mic to thank our families and management and all the rest. Before we walked away, Dakota added, "In case you all didn't figure it out from the new song we debuted tonight, Balefire is solid. Our ladies make us better." He hugged Annabelle tight to his side. "So stop with the bullshit about us breaking up. It ain't happenin'. Not now. Not ever. We're gonna be like the Rolling Stones, still making kick-ass rock 'n' roll when we're in our seventies. Count on it."

The roar of the crowd rang in our ears long after we walked off the stage with our little statuettes.

The sun was sneaking in under the drapes in our room when Cristy and I finally made it back to the hotel following the ceremony and all the after-parties. We each carried three Grammy statuettes, which Cristy lined up on the dresser at the foot of the bed. Somewhere in the night, she'd changed into a super-short turquoise sequined dress and those thigh-high boots I loved so much. Sitting there on the edge of the bed staring at our haul, she looked like an angel.

"I suppose I'll need to add a special shelf in our bedroom for those so you can look at them every night before you close your eyes to sleep," I teased.

"Nah." She huffed out a laugh. "The only thing I want to see every night before I close my eyes is your handsome face smiling at me. The rest is details."

I took her in my arms, lost in the sapphires in her eyes. "You're every song in the universe, every color in the rainbow, every dream I never let myself have. I love you Cristy Valor. Wanna run away with me and get married?"

She didn't even hesitate.

"Yes."

Hot For Me **Playlist:**

"It's a Party"—Buckcherry

"I Almost Told You That I Loved You"—Papa Roach

"Shatter Me"—Lindsey Stirling (feat. Lzzy Hale)

"Mystify"—Saving Abel

"Love Falls"—Hellyeah

"Song #3"—Stone Sour

"Scars"—Papa Roach

"Wicked Game"—Theory of a Deadman

"Hymn for the Missing"—Red

"Under Your Scars"—Godsmack

"Every Part of Me"—Godsmack

"Forever"—Papa Roach

"I'm Broken Too"—Killswitch Engage

"Killing Me Slowly"—Bad Wolves

"Can't Sleep"—Blacktop Mojo

"Come Around"—Papa Roach

Thanks so much for reading *Hot For Me.*

Watch for Garrett's redemption in *Stay For Me,*
coming in the fall of 2022.

Turn the page for an unedited excerpt.

CHAPTER ONE

Olivia

SEEING HIM AGAIN was inevitable.

I just didn't expect it to hurt this much.

Ten years ago, Garrett Phillips made a decision. Okay, maybe I helped him make that decision, but that's beside the point. He chose to go with "his boys" and leave me in the dust of a ratty old tour bus. The memory gripped my heart, sharp pain lancing through it, and I gasped in a breath. Curling my hands over the back of my chair, I stared at the man on the screen in front of me. There he was, looking ridiculously hot in an Armani suit that fit him like he owned the company. Unlike "his boys" who showed up on the red carpet—again—wearing cheap T-shirts beneath their five thousand dollar suits, he actually wore a silk dress shirt and a tie. He'd cut his hair since the last time I Googled him. Short looked good on him.

Who was I kidding? I'd liked his hair any way he wore it. Sometimes, like now, I could still feel his thick coarse mane sliding through my fingers. On cue, that thought led to what we'd been doing the last time I'd had my fingers in his hair, and my body flashed fire.

"You okay, boss? You look a little flushed," Jeremy, my assistant said. "Would you like me to grab you a water?"

I blinked, and the world righted itself again. Wrapping my hand around my mic, I nodded. "That would be great. Thanks."

Pulling a long breath in through my nose, I willed myself to let go of the past. Garrett Phillips managed Balefire, the biggest rock band on the planet, but tonight, it was my job to make sure the bad boys of rock 'n' roll behaved on live television. Or at least, I could control the narrative with quick, creative editing if the situation called for it. Judging from what I'd seen when I studied previous Grammy productions in preparation for directing this one, Balefire could, and likely would, cause a ruckus at some point in the show. I needed to be ready.

If life were different, I might have coordinated with Garrett, had his help in making sure his "boys" played nice for national TV. I might have had *him*.

Squeezing my eyes shut, I willed my mind to focus, to stay on point for the task at hand. I was well aware that landing the job of directing the Grammys—a woman at thirty-three—was a monumental deal. I landed the gig because I'm a rock star director and producer in my own right, something I needed to remember. If I wanted to run a studio someday, which had always been the goal, I couldn't blow my first big chance. Especially not for a man who couldn't wait to start his dream, even if it meant leaving love behind.

"Here you go, boss." Jeremy handed me my water and glanced at the screen in front of me. "Wow! Is that Balefire?"

The awe in his voice revealed a true fan.

"All four of them with their ladies."

"No doubt they're going home with hardware tonight. They're legit!"

Arching a brow, I reminded him where we were and what he was supposed to be doing.

"Sorry, Olivia. Sorry." A sheepish smile slipped over his features. "It's just that—it's Balefire."

Like that explained everything.

Which it did. Damn it.

It was difficult to hear my colleague over the screaming fans lining the red carpet. Staring at the screen and listening to the commentary through my headphones told me all about what an incredible job Garrett had done managing Balefire into a household name all over the world. The band sold out stadiums wherever they played. With the exception of the first one, which only hit gold, every one of their albums had gone platinum. No doubt, the players were stunningly talented musicians and song writers, but they never would have come this far without the shrewd management of one man. To my disgust, my eyes strayed to Garrett.

Though each of the members of Balefire escorted a beautiful woman, no one was holding onto Garrett's arm. Somehow, him being on his own made him even more dangerous. Somehow, it would have been easier to see him again in person for the first time in ten years if he'd been with someone. Questions swirled through my head. Was he with someone but choosing to go solo tonight? Was he single? Was he still anything like the excited and exciting young man with stars in his eyes who left me behind to chase a different dream? Google never divulged these details, which left me to speculate.

"Zoom in on Cristy Valor and Adam Tron, please," I directed into my mic. Immediately, all the feeds switched from the entire band to the bass player and the pop diva who'd joined Balefire during their last tour. With Tron's tall, dark good looks and Cristy's blond pixie cut and delicate features, the two made a stunning couple. Add to that the story of how her Be Valorous Foundation to put an end to child marriage came to be, and the two of them would be a massive draw during the ceremonies.

On cue, our red carpet commentator stepped over to them.

"Thank you for asking, Natasha," Cristy said. "It's the goal of the foundation to make it illegal for any girl younger than age eighteen to marry for any reason in any state in the US. Since only adults eighteen and older can divorce, it seems only right that only adults can marry. Anyone can help our cause by joining the Be Valorous Foundation."

Natasha turned her mic to Tron. "I understand Balefire is part of the Foundation?"

"One hundred percent."

He stared into Cristy's eyes with his heart in his.

"Hold the camera on them. We need this," I said into my mic.

When Cristy turned away from Tron's stare, I instructed the camerawoman and Natasha to move on to Parker Malone and Jennifer Hartwell, two major movie stars attending the Grammys as presenters but more to be seen. We gave them three seconds and moved on to Lady Gaga who gave us a show as only she could. The woman was every director's dream.

On it went until all the stars were seated in the cavernous space of the Crypto.com Arena, more widely known as the Staples Center. I hadn't seen Garrett during rehearsals, which wasn't exactly a surprise. The band didn't need their manager with them when they rehearsed, I supposed. Balefire would be playing their song with Cristy Valor, the one currently tearing up the charts, as one of the first songs to open the show. Later on in the production, they'd be playing their number one hit, "Fire Me Up," one of their other songs up for several awards. The band was a musical juggernaut. No doubt they'd win multiple awards tonight.

Another certainty popped into my head. Garrett would be at the after-parties, the ones that, as director of the show, I was expected to attend. Any other time, I'd relish the opportunity to hang out with so many major musicians. But the idea of seeing Garrett again left a knot of gargantuan proportions twisting in my stomach.

Knowing this would be my only moment of calm for the next three hours, I finished off my water in one long swig as we cut to commercial and opening credits. Pulling in a long breath, I held it then pasted on my best smile and spoke into my mic. "Okay, folks, this is where shit gets real. Let's make this one the most memorable event of the season."

Author's Note

Between 2000 and 2018, over 300,000 children were married in the United States. Eighty-six percent of these marriages took place between minor girls and adult men, the marriages superceding statutory rape laws. Some of the girls involved in these marriages were as young as 12. Many of the girls experience violence, abuse, loss of education opportunities, early pregnancies, and psychological trauma. In most states, minors cannot legally divorce or leave their spouse, and domestic violence shelters typically do not accept minors.

Even though the US State Department has declared child marriage a human rights violation, the federal government is silent on the subject, leaving states to enact their own laws. Only six states and two US territories—New Jersey, New York, Minnesota, Delaware, Rhode Island, and Pennsylvania and American Samoa and US Virgin Islands—ban any marriage if either party is under the age of 18 with no exceptions. If you would like to know more about child marriage or want to help end this human rights violation in the United States, please visit *https://unchainedatlast.org*.

♪

While *Hot For Me* was in production, the world lost Charlie Watts, drummer for the Rolling Stones. I had the good fortune to see the Stones live in concert at Empower Field at Mile High (previously, Broncos Stadium) in Denver during the last tour Charlie played with the band. He, Mick Jagger, Keith Richards, and Ronnie Wood performed an outrageous rock 'n' roll show that belied their ages, transporting the entire audience and inspiring Dakota's line in the epilogue. Long live rock 'n' roll.

ACKNOWLEDGEMENTS

Writing this series has been a rush, a true labor of love. I couldn't have done it without the help of some great people. My beta team of Bri Weigel, LindaRae Sande, Jacque Coburn, Sara Vinduska, and KJ Gillenwater gave me valuable input that made the story stronger. I'm so grateful for your time and expertise.

Nikki Busch, you're a rock star editor. You've helped me grow and improve with each book, but your experience as a rock guitarist in a band added an extra dimension to your work with me on this book and the entire Balefire Series. It might have been a happy accident—or fate—that brought us together. Either way, I'm truly grateful.

Connecting with readers is the goal of my writing journey, and I'm thankful for each person who picks up my books and enjoys them. Thank you for reading *Hot For Me*. I also appreciate your feedback in the form of reviews because they help me connect with other readers. So when you have a minute, if you would kindly leave a review on your favorite book seller sites, you will be helping me reach more readers. Thank you. You can also connect with me on Instagram @tamstales32, at Tam DeRudder Jackson reader group on Facebook, and via my website: *https://www.tamderudderjackson. com* where you can sign up for my newsletter.

About the Author

Like the tagline of her first novel, Tam DeRudder Jackson's personal motto is "love is worth the risk." Readers and reviewers have praised her stories for her swoon-worthy characters, movie-quality world building, and strong writing. Though she's a voracious reader of all genres of romance, her favorite genres to write are paranormal and contemporary. When she's not writing or reading, she's probably traveling or skiing or dancing at a rock concert.